Dear Reader,

Welcome to the new millennium! Just as exciting as the year 2000 is the great lineup of books we have throughout the upcoming months.

In Duets #17 Cathie Linz weaves another hilarious BEST OF THE WEST story in *The Cowboy Finds a Bride*. These three Best brothers sure are learning there's something *better* than being single. Then new author Isabel Sharpe makes her debut in Duets with *The Way We Weren't,* a charming and original tale of revenge, mayhem and love. No matter how the heroine tries to ruin the hero's life, it only keeps getting better and better. Maybe fate is trying to tell her something....

In Duets #18 Jennifer Drew is back with *Baby Lessons,* a fun, delightful story about a woman who gives baby lessons to the hero, but learns a lesson about love herself. Then Kate Thomas, well-known to readers of Silhouette Romance, writes an entertaining and quirky story of a hero who has too much good luck, while the heroine is cursed with bad luck. Together, they kind of even out the luck thing...but what about love?

Wishing lots of love and luck,

Malle Vallik

Malle Vallik
Senior Editor

SUPER ROMANCE

Baby Lessons

Nate was another wrong number on her romance hotline.

She'd had it with domineering handsome hunks; Becky didn't want a man who'd take her life and try to mold it to his satisfaction. No, Nate Dalton was wrong, wrong, wrong!

And you'd better remember it, she thought on the way down to his apartment.

He was foaming at the mouth when he opened the door.

"Sorry, I'm still shaving," he said, bare chested and with most of his face masked by white lather. "Lucy just went down for her nap."

"Shaving. That would be my guess," she said, trying to pretend she didn't see the way his biceps bulged even when he wasn't flexing them. Wouldn't it be fun to spray her initials on his chest with shaving cream?

She was losing it! She didn't want to play games as his pretend fiancée, even if it was for baby Lucy's sake. She wanted a warm, loving, funny, sexy, for-real husband.

She wanted someone just like Nate....

For more, turn to page 9

Too Lucky for Love

"Ty? Are you sure you're okay?"

He'd clunked himself really hard on the head with the alarm clock, but he wasn't about to tell Marisa that. Ridiculous, but even now, numb with fatigue, that low, soft voice stirred him.

"I'm so sorry, Ty," Marisa said, biting her lower lip. "Last night *you* suffered the consequences of *my* bad luck."

Ty covered his eyes. Holy macaroni—how could someone so cute be so nuts?

"There is no such thing as luck," he declared. "Or evil eyes. Or curses. Or—"

"You don't need to shout," Marisa said, lifting her adorable little chin. "I get your point."

"I'm not shouting!" Ty...er, shouted.

Marisa leaned close to study his eyes. Hers looked the way he'd first seen them, brandy warm and filled with concern. *For me,* he thought, grinning.

Then he frowned. His life plan did not include involvement with a petite stick of sensual dynamite who believed in...*nonsense.* Even if she kissed like blue blazes...*and believed that her bad luck would counterbalance his extraordinary good luck.*

For more, turn to page 197

HARLEQUIN DUETS

ISBN 0-373-44084-7

BABY LESSONS
Copyright © 1999 by Pamela Hanson & Barbara Andrews

TOO LUCKY FOR LOVE
Copyright © 1999 by Catherine Hudgins

JENNIFER DREW

Baby Lessons

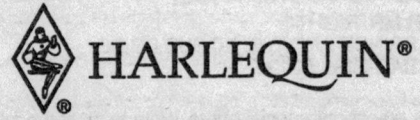

HARLEQUIN®

TORONTO • NEW YORK • LONDON
AMSTERDAM • PARIS • SYDNEY • HAMBURG
STOCKHOLM • ATHENS • TOKYO • MILAN • MADRID
PRAGUE • WARSAW • BUDAPEST • AUCKLAND

Dear Reader,

What will bring a strong man to his knees? With six children between us (Jennifer Drew is the pseudonym of mother and daughter Barbara Andrews and Pam Hanson), the answer was easy: a pint-size dynamo too young to walk but old enough to cause chaos in the life of our hero, Detective Nate Dalton.

Like any mother with a preschooler, we've both pulled our hair wondering how to keep a human hurricane from wreaking havoc in a day that seems thirty-six hours long. Fortunately for Nate, he gets help before *and after* dark!

Enjoy!

Jennifer Drew

Books by Jennifer Drew
SILHOUETTE YOURS TRULY
28—DEAR MR. RIGHT
60—THE PRINCE AND THE BOGUS BRIDE
77—THE BAD-GIRL BRIDE

For Andrew, who can drive when he's sixteen
and not before!

1

Becky Ryan parked her seven-year-old compact, carefully choosing a spot far from the sickly pink glow of the streetlight at the far end of the rutted service alley. She got out and closed the door as quietly as possible, then stood motionless, listening for the Dobermans patrolling inside the chain-link fence of the salvage yard across the way. If they started howling, she'd lose her nerve for sure.

Insects chirped in the weeds, and the wind blew grit in her face. She pulled the bill of her bad-hair-day baseball cap lower on her forehead, gripped the end of the unlit flashlight, and crept toward the rear entrance of Green Thumb Landscaping and Lawn Care, Inc.

Burglars had to have genetically deficient nervous systems to make a career of breaking and entering. Technically speaking, she was only entering, but her jaw was trembling, and her palms were so sweaty she was afraid she'd drop the key.

"I have a right to do this," she whispered aloud for courage, cautiously approaching the solid steel rear door of the building where she'd worked for almost two years.

Kevin thought he was a hotshot owner and manager, but he sure wasn't big on security. A single bare bulb over the door was the only illumination at the back of the building, and the faded alarm-warning label was a phony.

No one told Kevin Stalnaker how to run his business, she thought disgustedly, propelled forward by a burst of anger. Being fired by a boss who was also her boyfriend was bad enough, but he'd actually expected her to continue their relationship in spite of his lame story about needing to downsize.

"It doesn't have anything to do with our personal life," she said, mimicking his parting words to bolster her determination.

It was still hard to believe she'd been stabbed in the back by someone she'd hoped to marry. She'd been crazy to trust him. The man spread manure for a living, and not just the kind hauled in from cattle farms in the Iowa countryside. She vividly remembered the time she'd caught him leaning over his new receptionist's desk, trying to impress her with his witty observations while he eyeballed her cleavage. Courtney, the target of his slobbering, had lots of frizzy blond hair and a little lisp she turned on and off at will. *She* hadn't been downsized!

Becky fumbled with the key but finally succeeded in opening the stubborn old lock. Holding her breath, she pushed open the heavy door, searched with the toe of her sneaker for the wooden wedge that served as a doorstop, and propped the door open for a quick getaway. Otherwise, she'd have to waste time using the key to get out. She should report this death trap to the fire marshal!

"In quick, out quick," she muttered, thinking of Kevin, not the door. "I really know how to pick 'em."

Oh sure, Kevin was handsome—and charming when it suited him. He'd grown up doing hard outdoor work in his father's lawn-care business before he took it over himself, and just thinking about his muscular, tanned shoulders and chest gave her a wholly involuntary shiver.

She really attracted winners, she thought, wondering if she had some psychological defect that made her go for hollow hunks. Before Kevin there had been Jerry, gorgeous Jerry, who looked like a Greek god but who barely managed to tie his own shoelaces. Now she was back in circulation with prospects like Phil, who heard voices—and not via AT&T.

She used the flashlight to find Kevin's office without bumping into anything. It was just beyond the cubicle where she'd done the billing and kept the books, jobs supposedly being taken over by Kevin himself with a little help from bosomy Courtney, who counted on her fingers.

His office door was locked, a setback but not a serious one. She knew where he hid the key. She stretched her five-foot-one-inch frame to the max but couldn't quite reach the ledge above the door.

All the chairs in the office rolled and swiveled; standing on one was an invitation to the emergency room. Using the flashlight, she looked for something else to use as a boost. A nearly full carton of lawn-care brochures would do. She switched off the flashlight and laid it on Courtney's desk, then tugged the heavy box through the darkness to Kevin's office door.

The added three inches were just enough. She ran the tips of her fingers along the ledge until the key clattered to the floor.

"Darn!"

This was taking much longer than she'd hoped. She retrieved the flashlight and futilely searched the floor for the key.

"It's here...be calm...don't panic!" she muttered, crawling on hands and knees trying to locate it.

She needed more light. How risky could it be to turn on one of the overheads at 3:00 a.m.? She found the wall switch and flooded the area near the office with the dead-white glow of a single fluorescent.

Now she could see the key under a cart by the wall. She dropped to her knees and stretched her arm to get it.

"Freeze! Grand Rapids P.D. Don't make any sudden moves."

She shrieked in terror and didn't dare look behind her.

"Get up slowly and put your hands on the wall," a deep voice ordered.

She didn't even think of not obeying. She scrambled to her feet, bumping her elbow on the edge of the metal cart, too frightened to rub it. There had to be a way to explain this, but when she tried to speak, all that came out was a humiliating squeal.

"Do you have a weapon?" the voice demanded to know.

She frantically shook her head and risked a glance over her shoulder. The man looked like a cop on a TV show, but he wasn't faking it like an actor on a testosterone high.

"No gun," she squeaked. "Are you really a cop?"

Did cops like to be called cops, or were criminals supposed to call them policemen, or was she completely unhinged? This was worse than the time her brother Steve caught her stuffing his car full of crumpled newspaper on prom night.

"Yes, ma'am."

Still pointing the gun at her, with his free hand he reached into his jacket pocket. He snapped open a leather holder and thrust a blur of metal two inches from her nose as if she were severely nearsighted. Or mentally impaired. Or both.

"It's a badge, all right. Detective Nate Dalton."

She was trying to joke but felt more like crying. How could she go to jail? Her mother would break out in hives; her father would bail her out but keep her prisoner on the farm for the rest of her life. He hadn't wanted her to go to the big city, even though her three older brothers had pretty much covered the globe in their military service before coming back to Iowa to marry and raise corn and kids. But, according to her father, that was different: they were men. And though she adored the men in her family, she was really tired of their domineering ways and sometimes found herself being confrontational from all the years she'd had to stand up for herself.

"Keep your hands flat on the wall and spread your legs. It's in your best interest to cooperate."

She did.

"Ma'am, do you have any needles on your person?"

"No, of course not! I don't want to get stuck. I'm making an embroidered pillow for my parents' anniversary, but I don't carry the needle in my pocket."

She was babbling and knew it. He was a policeman. He was asking about drug needles. Before she could explain that she wasn't totally stupid, his hands were on her.

Oh, were they on her! Up and down her legs, patting her person, checking pockets, scaring her silly—make that sillier. This was even worse than being fired by Kevin, and she hadn't handled that well, either. Why couldn't she think straight in a crisis?

"If you were my date, you'd have two slaps and a knee to the groin coming," she joked halfheartedly.

She knew it was stupid, trying to be funny when a policeman thought she was a burglar, but what was a girl supposed to say to a strange man who had a legal right to feel her up?

Good grief, if he took her to jail, they'd strip-search her, and she couldn't even remember what underwear she was wearing.

"I'm sorry...I didn't mean it. I'm not thinking straight. Please listen. I only came here to get a check that belongs to me. I'm not a burglar. Please believe me!"

"Calm down, ma'am. Turn around and tell me what you're doing here and why you were doing it by flashlight. I saw the light flickering through the front window."

"I know my way around the place. I didn't need a light until I couldn't find the office key. It was on a ledge, and it fell under the cart, but I didn't know that until I turned on the overhead.''

"Whoa, slow down. Are you an employee here?"

"Yes, well, I was until this morning. The owner is—was—my fiancé, sort of. Not that he'd exactly committed himself, but—"

"Just a minute."

He took out what had to be a handheld radio and talked into it. Now that she was a little calmer, she realized he was canceling backup. She had a horrible vision of the building surrounded by police cars with flashing lights: Bonnie without Clyde, Ma Barker, bullhorns and bullets.

No more police shows for her! From now on she watched nothing on TV but kids' shows and the weather channel.

"What's your name?" he asked, shutting off the metallic voice of a distant dispatcher.

Finally an easy question!

"Rebecca...Rebecca...Rebecca." No sane person forgot her own last name! "Rebecca Ryan," she gasped triumphantly.

"Can you show me some identification?"

She patted her pockets, but if anything had been in them, he would have found it.

"I guess I left my wallet in the car. But I am who I said."

She knew she must sound pathetically eager to be believed, but was he going to accept her word about anything, even about who she was?

"You entered the building with a key provided by the owner?" he asked.

"Yes, definitely yes," she agreed, unable to stop herself from being overly anxious. "With a key from the owner."

"That should be easy to verify. Give me his name."

"Kevin Stalnaker." His name was repellent to her now. "You don't have to wake him up. I can prove I worked here. There's my office, back there, the little windowless cubicle. He calls it a cozy corner. Hah!"

The cop made a low growling sound in his throat and muttered, "I don't need this after an eleven-hour shift."

If she'd been a little more skillful at illegal entry, he wouldn't have seen her light flashing inside the Green Thumb. How could he think she was a criminal when she wasn't even good at it?

And how could she be finding him so good-looking at a time like this?

NATE DOUBTED any criminal intentions on her part, but he had a bad feeling about her anyway. Whatever her reason for being in the building in the middle of the night, she was costing him sleep. The tiny waifs with tales of woe were always the ones who complicated his life, and the last thing he wanted was to make her troubles his. He'd been down that road before and still had the scars on his ego.

"All right, tell me your story, but make it quick."

He wished he hadn't been so impressed by her shapely legs and cute, compact butt stuffed into skin-tight black jeans. He was too tired to have his objectivity tested this way.

The suspect was braless under a white T-shirt that

read Green Thumb has the Right Touch, and the nipples of her perky little breasts provided some eye-catching punctuation for the slogan. He forced himself to look at the baseball cap covering most of her hair and to concentrate on what she was saying.

"You see, I lost my job this morning, and that wouldn't be so bad—the pay was awful, to be honest—but my boyfriend was the one who fired me. He thought I could get a better-paying job and we could still have a relationship. Can you believe that? So he gave me a check for two weeks' severance pay. But I was so upset—you can understand why—I left it on his desk. I didn't want anything from him, but then I accidentally dyed my hair blue, and it's going to cost a lot to have it fixed professionally and—"

"You dyed your hair blue?" He knew he'd regret it, but he lifted off the cap...and laughed.

"You see! You don't even know me, and you're making fun of it!"

"No, it just surprised me. What color is it really?"

"Oh, one of those nondescript colors...dark blond, light brown—it doesn't matter. Now it's blue."

"Only in streaks. You can have it fixed."

His fingers itched to separate the short blue strands. Her hair did look strange, but it was oddly cute.

And he was out of his mind to be giving advice to a suspect with peacock hair! He urgently needed to wrap this up before she got under his skin.

"Please, can I go now?" she asked in a little-girl voice that made his protective juices flow.

"I can't release you just because you dyed your hair blue."

"But I wasn't going to accept the severance check until I ruined my hair. How can I go to job interviews looking like a freak?"

"You could've waited until business hours to get it."

"I never want to see that louse again! And I absolutely don't want him to see my hair. He'll think I was trying to look like Courtney—she's his busty blond receptionist, and you can bet he didn't downsize her! If he hadn't spent so much time ogling her, I wouldn't have decided to be a platinum blonde myself. And without the check, I can't get this mess fixed." She tugged on a short strand hugging her ear.

"Please, Miss Ryan, it will be easy to verify your story. I'll call the owner of this place—"

"Do you really have to?" She didn't whine, but the misery in her voice made him uncomfortable. "I shouldn't have said that, should I? Now you'll be even more suspicious, but Kevin won't deny knowing me. He's too dumb to believe we're really finished. It's Kevin Stalnaker, 555-0815."

"I have to check out your story, then you can go."

He didn't like detaining her. He liked the idea of booking her even less. He found a phone on a front desk and punched in the number, hoping one call would send her on her way. He knew his weaknesses, and petite blondes with heart-shaped, elfin faces were at the top of the list. He didn't want to get involved with helping this one, not after Margo's helpless ways had kept him tied up in knots for nearly two years.

After four rings, an answering machine kicked in. A

man's voice said, "I'm otherwise occupied. Leave a message if you want to."

The guy sounded like a jerk. Him he'd like to throw in a holding cell with a Saturday-night collection of drunks.

"No answer," he told her.

"Try again. Please. Maybe he'll wake up and answer."

Three tries later they both knew this Stalnaker wasn't going to answer.

"Look," Nate said, "you haven't stolen anything. I don't see any damage. Even a public defender would plea bargain down to simple trespass."

"Are you going to arrest me for that?"

He was only thinking out loud, but she'd paled so much he was afraid she would pass out. Irrationally, he felt guilty as hell. The helpless little fluffs had that effect on him, but his instinct told him she was telling the truth in her own jumbled way. All he wanted to do was forget the whole incident.

"Here, sit down."

He kicked an office chair in her direction, feeling like a bully when she lowered herself to the edge and hung her head in misery.

"Hey, it's not the end of the world."

"You *could* let me go." She said it matter-of-factly with the emphasis on "could."

"It's a possibility, but we've had a rash of burglaries in this part of town—small businesses losing expensive equipment. I can't let you go until I verify your story. I have to take you in for questioning unless—"

"Try Kevin again! Please! Or maybe someone else can vouch for me."

"We'll just ride downtown and—"

"No! I mean, isn't there some other way?"

"Are you going to resist?" He struggled not to smile.

"No, but all you have to do is look on Kevin's desk. He's a slob. Even if he noticed that I left the check, he probably wouldn't have bothered to move it. That would prove I'm telling the truth."

"I guess it would." He was losing it. He wanted that check to be there almost as badly as she did. "Show me where you left it."

She used a key to let him into an office decorated like the inside of a Dumpster. She hadn't exaggerated about the guy being a slob. Stalnaker's desk was a jumble of soda cans, loose papers, mail and crumpled fast-food bags.

"I was standing here." She gestured, unintentionally calling attention to her braless state. "He slapped the check down—as if he were giving me a great gift— then we had some words, and I ran out."

He saw it first, a pale-green check with the Green Thumb logo. Picking it up, he read it and said, "It's made out to Becky Ryan."

"That's me! Becky's short for Rebecca. I told you!"

"I guess I have to believe you now." He grinned, unable to believe how relieved he felt. Now there was no reason for him to hang around, but he wasn't about to leave her alone in the deserted building.

"Can I...?" She gave him a pleading look he felt all the way to his groin.

"Leave? Yes." The sooner the better.

"No, can I take my check?"

He couldn't be that liberal. "We'd better leave things as they are. You can come back at a more conventional time or call and ask them to mail it to you."

"Okay." She sounded disappointed but not defiant.

"Hey, the blue streaks aren't as bad as you think. They sort of match your eyes."

"My eyes are hazel. Blue matches yours."

He was oddly flattered that she'd noticed his eye color, then annoyed at himself for caring.

"Is anything here out of place?" he asked.

When she nodded, he helped her to straighten up, first replacing the office key, then the box she'd stood on, and finally the chair he'd moved for her to sit.

"Where's your car?" he asked as she locked the rear door behind them.

She gestured at a vehicle halfway down the alley.

"I'll walk you to it."

"You really don't need to."

"I'm going to."

His shoes crunched on the gravel of the alley, but she walked with soft, almost soundless footfalls. They'd nearly reached her car when a piercing howl startled him.

"The Dobermans in the scrap yard," she said with a nervous laugh. "Thank heavens they're on the other side of a sturdy fence."

BECKY LIKED the way it felt walking beside this tall, broad cop a little too much for her peace of mind. The last thing she wanted was to rebound from Kevin into the well-muscled arms of the law.

After he'd seen her safely into her car, she watched Nate—bad sign, already thinking of him by his first name—sprint back to the rear of the Green Thumb where he'd parked his car, then she reached under the floor mat for her key.

She hadn't brought her purse. She didn't even have her driver's license with her to prove who she was. If Kevin had torn up that check, she'd probably be on her way to the police station right now. She was breaking more laws tonight than she had in her entire life. She'd be lucky to get away before Nate cited her for driving without her license.

He was the most gorgeous man she'd ever seen. He had eyes like deep blue pools, and strong masculine features set off by brilliant white teeth and dark-brown hair cut short without a buzz look. She liked his straight, prominent nose, high, lean cheekbones and square chin. He moved with uncommon grace for such a large man, and she'd swear he had zero body fat except maybe on his nicely rounded backside.

"Forget it, he's too tall," she mumbled, turning the key again, having trouble getting the ignition to catch.

He was at least six-two, and dancing with him would make her feel like a pixie. The last thing she needed was another big, strong he-man to erode her hard-won confidence. Her parents called her the runt of the litter, their little preemie baby who always commanded an extra bit of care and attention. But she was fully grown now and not looking for a superhero to spread his cape over her and make her troubles disappear. She'd come to Grand Rapids to stand on her own feet, but she kept meeting macho men who wanted a smiling, compliant female to bolster their own egos. No more!

"Don't listen to your hormones!" she told herself, starting to worry because all the starter did was rasp.

Unfortunately Detective Dalton reminded her that she was a fully functional female on her own again in the dating jungle.

She could still feel his hands patting her down, an unintentional intimacy she wasn't likely to forget for a while.

She gave the starter a minute to rest, hoping it would do its thing and get her out of there. She reversed the baseball cap and fluffed the strands of blond-and-blue hair hugging her forehead. Maybe she'd overdosed on dye fumes when she'd ruined her hair. She'd sworn off big, macho, handsome hunks, and here she was, thinking about the man who'd wanted to arrest her.

Kevin had taught her a lesson she wouldn't forget in a hurry: a man who thinks he's God's gift to women is never a prize package. She wanted someone her size, someone in her league—short, plain, and reliable.

"Get a grip, girl!"

She tried the starter again, getting a very bad feeling about her car when the engine still didn't turn over. At least she wasn't stranded alone in the middle of the night in this none-too-savory neighborhood. The cop had pulled his car close enough to hear the grinding of her starter.

Of course he'd heard her car grating and had rushed to the scene. She counted to a hundred and tried the starter again, pretending she didn't see her would-be rescuer. She'd be better off in lockup than having him think she was a helpless cream puff.

She refused to give up. The car had gotten her there, and it darn well could get her home. Stupid car! It was mocking her, and here Nate was, getting out of his vehicle and walking up to her.

"I'll give you a ride. You can have your car towed in the morning."

"It should start in a minute." She remembered the driver's license she didn't have with her.

"Yeah, and I'm expecting to sprout wings any time now. Let's go. I can't leave you alone in this neighborhood."

Becky hated having to accept his offer. All she wanted was to go home and sleep for a year—or at least until her blue hair grew out. Now she had a new problem: her car. She didn't know what it would take to max out her credit card, but a big repair bill would probably more than do it. Her pride wouldn't let her borrow money from her father. He'd loan it willingly, but not without putting more pressure on her to return home and forget about making it on her own.

Her police escort had returned to his car and was holding open the front passenger door, assuming she'd hop right in. But she didn't want to be rescued by a man who knew from hands-on experience how well-padded her thighs were.

"I'll go back inside and call a friend," she said as she got out of her car and locked the door.

"No need. I'll drive you home."

It sounded more like an order than an invitation. She bristled but got into his car, knowing how hard it would be to get her best friend moving at this time of morning. Becky could become a missing-person statistic before Zoe assembled an outfit suitable for a late-night rescue mission.

He got behind the wheel, making the interior seem as crowded as a space capsule. His shoulders were as wide as the driver's seat, and his knees were spread so one brushed hers. Making out with him in the back seat of a car would be a tighter fit than the jeans she'd bought a size too small as an incentive to lose weight.

"I have to make one stop," he said. "I have a storage unit in that place on Highway 10. That's why I'm on this side of town."

She knew the place. If her finances got any worse, she might have to rent one—to live in. She shuddered, imagining sink baths in a service station rest room and scavenging for soda cans along the roadside. She'd be better off living in her father's barn—except for that pride thing. She couldn't breeze into her parents' cozy kitchen and say, "Hi, folks. Your hopelessly incompetent daughter is back."

"I'll just be a minute," Nate said a short time later, pulling up to a row of storage units. "I have to take a box back to my motel."

He lived in a motel? It was none of her business! She wouldn't even ask.

True to his word, he quickly found what he wanted and dumped it into his trunk, then got back into the car.

She had to ask. Curiosity got her into trouble every time.

"You live in a motel?"

"Temporarily."

He wasn't forthcoming, which only piqued her interest more.

"Did you lose your lease?"

"They're tearing down the building I used to live in to build something this town really needs—another bank." He sounded like someone who was regularly overdrawn.

"Didn't they give you enough notice to find a new place?" She was enjoying this. The cop had a vulnerable spot.

"I've been working my butt off," he said defensively. "No time to look. Anyway, I'm sick of boxy little rooms with neutral carpeting and too many neighbors."

He didn't say anything else on the ride across town. She'd have to brush up on interrogation techniques if she wanted to have a real conversation with Detective Dalton—but then, she didn't expect to see him again. Breaking and entering wasn't her favorite sport.

"Nice house," he said appreciatively when he stopped in front of the charming late Victorian house where she had one of four apartments.

"Maybe I shouldn't mention this," she said, ignoring the warning voice booming inside her head. "My landlady is picky about her tenants, and she may have someone in mind, but there is a vacancy here. One of the nicest apartments—ground level, high ceilings, hardwood floors. I was tempted to move downstairs myself, but it's $125 more than mine, and Kevin wasn't exactly a generous employer. He was always promising to raise my salary when the business got better, but…'' She shrugged.

"I might think about it," he said cautiously.

"You probably wouldn't like it," she said, immediately sorry she'd mentioned it. "It's a creaky old house—never enough hot water."

"Sounds awful."

"It's a real chamber of horrors. Shrieks in the attic, spooks in the cellar. Lights going on and off for no reason."

Why couldn't she keep her mouth shut? Even in the dark, she was sure he was smirking.

"Oh, there's another drawback," she said when she was standing beside the open car door, ready to go inside. "No loud music after 10:00 p.m."

"Would you mind giving me your landlady's number? It's probably not what I want, but I'm tired of motel living—not to mention being the butt of homeless jokes at work."

She recited the number, watching while he scrawled it in a little notebook. Then she thanked him for the ride and hurried up to the house.

He didn't drive away.

She found the key under the doormat and gave him a halfhearted wave, but still he didn't budge.

Feeling as though she'd lost a game of chicken, she unlocked the door and went inside.

2

BECKY PARKED in her spot at the side of the house, elated because she finally had a job that could lead to better things. The new garden center didn't want her to start in inventory until just before their grand opening, nearly four weeks from now, but what the heck! All she had to do was make half a tank of gas last until her first paycheck and live on the food in her kitchen. Kevin's severance check had paid her monthly bills, and fortunately Ozzie had nearly a case of cat food left, ensuring that her finicky little fuzzball wouldn't starve.

For the first time in eight days she forgot to be wary of crossing paths with her new neighbor, not that she was afraid of him, but what could she say to a man who'd nearly arrested her? A very sexy man. Worse, if they became friends, hanging with him would be more tempting than a gallon of double chocolate fudge ice cream in the freezer. The last thing she wanted was another gorgeous hunk trying to supervise everything she did.

She'd managed to avoid Detective Dalton since he'd snatched up the downstairs apartment the day after she told him about it. The man didn't waste time. He rented it on a Thursday, much to the landlady's delight, and on Saturday half the police force showed up to help him unload a rented truck. Or so Mrs. Vander Polder had told her, gushing like Old Faithful because she was thrilled to have live-in police protection in her apartment house.

He's only a cop, Becky thought. Nothing special about that. But she still made a point of never arriving or leaving when he did. Once she'd driven around the block because she'd spotted him pulling into their mutual drive just ahead of her.

She had the car door open when he pulled in beside her, his somber dark car making her little red job look frivolous.

He saw her, of course, eagle-eyed cop that he was, and waved through his driver's side window. This time there was no escape. She'd look like an idiot if she started the car and backed out when he'd obviously seen her arrive. She was as cornered as she'd been that night at the Green Thumb.

For such a big man, he really moved fast. He was out of his car and standing in front of hers before she could think of some witty remark to slough him off.

"How's my favorite cat burglar?" he asked.

"The only cat I know is my four-legged, mouse-chasing beastie."

"Somehow I knew you'd have a cat."

Why was he grinning? And why was he looking her over from her newly restored pale blond hair to the hem of the tan suit she'd worn for her second interview at the garden center? His gaze felt more intimate than the thorough pat-down he'd given her that night.

"Why would you think I have any pet?" She brushed an imaginary cat hair from her sleeve and felt the involuntary warmth of flushed cheeks. Darn, this man made her uncomfortable! And the worst of it was, he was nice in his own way.

"You're the kind of woman who needs something to cuddle," he said.

"Really!" She was indignant, and it was annoying to have to look up to scowl at him.

She got out of the car, then remembered the thick policy manual the garden center had given her to study after she accepted their offer this morning. Leaning into the car to retrieve it from the passenger seat, she could practically feel his eyes taking in the way her short skirt rode up when she bent over.

Eyeball all you like, she wanted to say, but any more patting and I'll get your badge number!

"Need any help?" he asked.

"No, thank you."

He had a home now. Why didn't he go to it?

"I guess you got your check."

"How would you know that?"

"Your hair. It looks great."

It was hard to be snippy to a guy passing out a compliment, but words were her only weapon against the big hunk. She didn't want him to like her. She might be tempted to like him back.

"Thanks to you, I had to wear a dorky-looking scarf to three job interviews before the new girl in Stalnaker's harem mailed the check to me."

"Did you get a job?"

"Yes, but it doesn't start until next month." She banged her car door shut.

"Congratulations. Aren't you going to lock your door?"

He sounded like her father! Would she never be free of men who wanted to tell her what to do? This one didn't just make a suggestion; he opened the door, pushed down the button and locked it himself.

"What if I'm leaving again in a few minutes?" she asked.

"Are you?"

"No, but you didn't know that."

"It's only common sense to lock car doors," he said complacently. "By the way, what was wrong with your car the other night?"

He was blocking her escape route, standing so close she caught the scent of vanilla in his aftershave and the outdoorsy tang of his skin under the hot sun. He was wearing a white dress shirt with pale gray stripes, the sleeves rolled up on his powerful forearms. A dove-gray jacket was slung over one shoulder, and his pleated cotton slacks were dark charcoal and creased across the front from sitting. He'd probably look sharp when the burgundy paisley tie hanging around his neck was knotted in place, but now he was hot and rumpled—and sexy enough to leave an army of panting women in his wake.

But not her. No way!

"It was only the battery," she said, keeping her eyes averted so he wouldn't pick up on her involuntary interest.

The currents between them were strong enough to recharge an aging battery, she admitted to herself.

Chemistry like this could only lead to another big disappointment.

"Glad it was nothing serious," he said mildly.

How did he manage to make conventional chitchat sound like pillow talk?

He didn't! she scolded herself. It was her overheated imagination.

"Well, see you," she said, feinting to the right then charging past him on the left, a move she'd learned from her brothers when they'd condescended to let her play touch football with them.

She hugged the bulky manual to her chest and race-walked to the front entrance that opened into a small entryway shared by the two front apartments, his and hers.

Mrs. Vander Polder believed in security; it took one key to get into the house and another to open the door to her apartment at the top of the stairs. Becky had the key to the outer door poised to enter the lock when a bronzed arm shot around her, beating her to the keyhole.

"By the way," he said, "I took the spare key from under the mat."

"Well, you can put it back. I don't bother carrying my keys when I go out at night."

"I suppose there's another key under the rug by your door," he said, gesturing toward the top of the stairs. "You might as well put a Burglars Welcome sign on the front lawn."

"You're paranoid. I can't fit a bunch of keys into the clutch purse I use on dates."

"Be creative. Put one key in each bra cup—if you

ever wear one. I'm not living in a place where keys lie around in obvious places.''

She blushed, hating the image that popped into her head: his strong fingers fishing for keys hidden in her bra.

''I almost always wear one, not that it's any of your business. And you wouldn't be living here at all if I hadn't told you about the vacancy.''

''Yeah, thanks a lot. I mean it.''

He crinkled his eyes when he smiled, his blue eyes electrifying even through narrowed slits.

She caught herself shifting from one foot to the other, fidgeting in front of him when she should have been sprinting up the stairs. She couldn't feel more squirmy and off balance if the man had X-ray eyes. He had no right to notice or comment on her undergarments!

''I'm always happy to help an officer of the law,'' she said, hoping he recognized insincerity when he heard it.

This conversation was going nowhere, which suited her just fine. There were a half-dozen things she'd like to know about him, such as how did he keep his waist so slim when his shoulders and chest were so broad? And was the rest of his body as tan as his arms and face? But she'd been down this path before. He seemed a lot nicer than Kevin, but what man wasn't a sweetheart until he had a woman under his thumb?

''See you,'' she said, sauntering over to the stairway to impress him with her casual indifference.

Indifference—ha! She wanted to sit on his lap and let her fingers play peekaboo between his shirt buttons.

She wanted to nuzzle his throat and see what happened from there.

She needed a keeper! Forget about making a dignified exit! She raced up the stairs and didn't look back, retrieving the key from under the braided rug she kept on the hardwood floor in front of her door. She'd keep her key wherever she liked, and he could stick one up his nose if he didn't approve.

She slammed the door, feeling as if she'd had a narrow escape. No way was she going to let that bossy, overbearing, gorgeous cop past her defenses!

NATE KNEW he shouldn't have watched her go up the stairs. He was going to be plagued by erotic daydreams about the sway of her cute little bottom as she climbed. Her legs looked even better in shiny hose than they had in tight black jeans. Fortunately for him, she had a prickly personality and no interest in coming on to him. She was trouble. If he let her get close, it would be Margo all over again.

He stomped into his apartment, pooped from pulling a night shift that went into overtime. He wasn't looking for a new girlfriend. In fact, his personal life had been pleasantly uncomplicated since Margo dumped him six months ago for an old man with big bucks. He wanted it to stay that way.

Margo! She was on his mind again after his hard struggle to forget her. It was his new neighbor's fault. Her need for protection and counsel reminded him of Margo's helplessness. He'd lived with Margo for nearly two years, twenty-four months of trying to balance her hopelessly messy checkbook and to keep bill collectors from hounding her. He'd loved the diminutive perfection of her body and her silky blond hair. In the beginning, he'd been charmed by her bubbly personality, but by the end he'd been fed up with rescuing her from one crisis after another—not to mention her maddening habits. She was never on time, never remembered to do household chores, and she couldn't make a simple decision without going into a panic.

If he ever fell for another woman, he wanted a tall, leggy brunette he could kiss without bending over, a competent adult who wouldn't bring turmoil into his life. Not that he minded taking responsibility, but enough was enough. As the oldest of four kids, it came naturally, although his two brothers, both cops now, had always been pretty independent. His flighty little sister was another matter.

He tried to put Rebecca Ryan out of his mind as he stripped for a shower. He was tired enough to sleep ten hours, then he wanted to putter around his new apartment. She had done him a good turn, telling him about the vacancy. He felt totally at home in the three oversize rooms with high ceilings and glossy hardwood floors. Maybe someday he could do her a small favor to even the score. No doubt the woman he'd nearly arrested had plenty of little problems needing a commonsense solution.

He strolled naked into the tile-floored bathroom, which had the only jarring colors in his otherwise tranquil living space. The landlady had remodeled it before her husband's death, unfortunately going with the trendy sixties color scheme of avocado and orange. But he appreciated the walk-in shower and the hot water that gushed out in only a minute if none of the other apartments were running their taps.

Most of the time he didn't hear anything from the two rear apartments, one of which was occupied by Mrs. Vander Polder, but muffled sounds from above sometimes let him know what Rebecca was doing. He could tell when she was up there, but she didn't keep him awake—not usually, anyway.

She'd beaten him to the hot water, but he was too tired to wait. He settled for a fine spray of tepid water and soaped up, humming to himself as he washed away lingering reminders of the smoky squad room and the disinfectant mustiness of the jail.

The water pressure abruptly increased, stinging his back and washing away the last suds. He turned off the faucet, but instead of the usual squeal from the pipes, he heard a bloodcurdling scream.

His cat burglar neighbor was shrieking her head off!

He raced to the bedroom and grabbed his rumpled trousers, struggled to pull them over his wet legs, and zippered on the run. After instinctively grabbing his gun from the bedside drawer, he ran out of his apartment and up the stairs.

"Rebecca! Are you all right?" He pounded on her door, wondering if he'd have to force entry.

The door opened. He saw the broom first, held like a club for riot control, then he noticed that Rebecca's short yellow robe was tied so tightly around her waist, her nipples pushed against the fabric.

"It's in the bathroom!"

She led the way, still holding the broom like a weapon, the silky wrap clinging wetly to her bottom.

When she stopped abruptly in the doorway, he nearly knocked her over.

"In the tub," she gasped, maneuvering around him to the shelter of his back.

A green shower curtain with big yellow fish was drawn around a claw-foot tub. He braced himself to encounter anything from a prowler to an escaped pet boa.

He gingerly pulled aside the curtain and saw... nothing.

"I nearly stepped on it," she said.

He moved to the edge of the tub and looked down at a rubber mat on the bottom.

"It's pretty big, isn't it?" he asked, laughing at least partly from relief.

"It's not funny! I hate spiders! If I'd stepped on him..." She shuddered and hugged herself.

"I won't need this." He laid his revolver on her sink counter, plucked a couple of tissues from a nearby box and scooped up a hairy brown spider the size of a half dollar. One flush took care of the intruder.

"Get a glue board," he advised. "I had a cricket at my last place. Kept me awake chirping, and I couldn't find it. The trap worked right away."

He pretended to look around for other insect invaders just to keep his eyes safely occupied. The tightened sash of her robe made her breasts swell invitingly, and one glimpse of the creamy skin between the lapels was enough to show him where the real danger lay.

"I can't thank you enough."

"No trouble."

Except women who needed rescuing should invest in sensible flannel robes!

"I'm really grateful. It was silly to scream, but I have a phobia about spiders. The darn thing really scared me."

"Hey, I understand. Glad to help."

He looked directly into her eyes and felt mushy inside, like an adolescent with a crush. Crazy, since he was only doing a neighbor a favor.

She walked into the living room, then turned to thank him again, catching him looking her over. The little wraparound thing was clinging like a second skin with big wet spots between her shoulder blades and across her bottom.

"Well, I'd better—you know—get dressed," he said.

He didn't know which felt sillier, carrying a gun to exterminate a spider or getting hot and bothered over a woman he wanted to avoid.

Back in the sanctuary of his apartment, he peeled off his damp slacks in the living room and hit the shower for the second time that hour. Turning on the cold water full force, he let it pelt his body until his skin was a field of goose bumps.

That was it. They were even. She'd helped him to get this apartment and he'd gotten rid of her spider. He didn't owe her anything else. He knew her kind of woman: needy and clinging. If he gave her a chance, she'd dump all her problems on him. He'd been down that road before, and he'd vowed to steer clear of messy relationships.

Was it a Chinese tradition that said if you saved a

person's life, you were responsible for the rest of it? Well, all he'd done was flush a nonlethal spider to a watery end, and that didn't make him his neighbor's guardian angel. If he didn't watch himself, they'd soon be snuggling on the couch, and he'd find out if she ever wore a bra. He had a strong suspicion he could fall hard for Rebecca with her wide-eyed innocence and little-girl breathiness. His best defense was avoidance.

SHE SHOULD HAVE offered to cook dinner for her new neighbor, Becky thought. She owed Nate something for disposing of the spider and being so nice about it, but common sense had made her hold back the invitation. Mostly she was too embarrassed about screaming for help to want to face him again. She hated her phobia almost as much as she loathed creepy, crawly, detestable spiders. Considering she'd grown up on a farm where the ants were big enough to carry off an ear of corn and grasshoppers could qualify for the Olympic high jump, she was as mystified as her family about the cause of her arachnophobia.

Unfortunately she hadn't been too frightened to notice the open snap at the waist of his pants or that they'd clung to his damp body like plastic wrap. Having him in the apartment, bare-chested with silky dark whorls disappearing under the zipper flap, was too much. And darned if his bare toes weren't cute! She couldn't say that about many men, not that she'd made a study of lower extremities.

He wasn't for her, but she wasn't going to feel guilty about feasting her eyes on his big, gorgeous body. It was art appreciation, like admiring a giant hunk on a lobby poster at the movie theatre—just a little harmless fun.

She stayed home that evening, catching up on the little jobs that added up to a big yawn: tweezing her eyebrows, washing panty hose, balancing her checkbook. Around ten she was thinking about an early bedtime when her buzzer sounded.

Mrs. Vander Polder's security mania didn't extend to paying for modern devices. Becky couldn't push a button to open the door down below. Instead she had to trot down to the entryway and check out the visitor the old-fashioned way. In lieu of an intercom to screen visitors, the landlady had installed a peephole.

The young woman standing outside the door was definitely a stranger. She was tall and exceptionally pretty with curly dark shoulder-length hair and a perfect oval face that, if life were fair, would have had zits or moles.

Puzzled but curious, Becky opened the door...and saw the baby.

"Are you Nate Dalton's neighbor?" the lovely young lady with the flawless skin asked.

"Yes, I—"

"Your name is on the little card by the buzzer. Rebecca, right?"

"That's me," Becky said, distracted by the very young child sitting in a car seat on the front porch. Dressed in a pink cotton sleeper with white fuzzy bunnies dancing across the front, she had to be a girl. She had her mother's dark hair, already a curly cap on her head, and her tiny hands were clenched.

The baby stirred and opened her eyes, and Becky could see they were heavenly blue—an oddly familiar shade.

"I rang and rang Nate's buzzer, but he must be working. This is so like him. Never available when I need him."

Becky remembered he'd been there when *she* needed him and made a halfhearted attempt to defend him. "I guess he has to work long hours," she said, tearing her attention from the baby to determine who this woman was—ex-wife, former girlfriend, abandoned lover? It was none of her business whose baby this was, but Nate had just rented a new apartment—a bachelor pad, as far as she knew.

"I don't know what I'm going to do," the visitor wailed. "This is terrible! I was counting on him!"

Becky noticed a taxi stopped by the curb, lights on, the driver obviously waiting for the woman. Apparently she wasn't there to move in.

"You can use my phone to call him at work," Becky offered, responding to the desperation in the woman's voice.

"Oh, dear." She sounded tragic. "The meter is running. This is my worst nightmare. Why couldn't he be home when I need him?"

He has to earn a living, Becky thought, but decided the situation didn't call for a barbed comment. The baby made a little cooing noise, and she ached to pick her up.

"Could I ask a huge favor? Can I leave a message with you?"

"Sure. Come up, and you can write a note. I'll see that he gets it."

Becky tried to sound helpful, but she wasn't eager to deliver a message, not if it meant seeing Nate and facing his threatening charm again. But how could she refuse?

"Can I help you carry something?" she asked, noticing a bright-red bag sitting on the porch.

"Thanks. It would really help if you wouldn't mind carrying the diaper bag."

She handed Becky a nylon pack heavy enough to contain stolen gold bars. Her mother used to warn her about letting strange men into the house. What was no-key-under-the-mat Dalton going to say about taking in this woman—maybe *his* woman or, at least, one of them?

"Come on up," Becky repeated, leading the way, curiosity outweighing caution.

"This is my daughter, Lucy," the woman said, setting the car seat on the braided rug in the center of Becky's living room.

"Hi, Lucy." Becky dropped to her knees, fascinated by the miniature person solemnly looking her over. "Oh, there's a pad and pencil by the phone," she said, pointing at the counter that divided the kitchen and living room areas in her efficiency apartment.

While she cooed at the baby, the mother wrote a note, folded it, and gave it to Becky.

"I'm in such trouble, I just have to ask you this," she said. "I was counting on Nate, and he's left me in a terrible bind. I can't take Lucy with me. He has to take care of her." She was sounding definitely teary.

"But—but he works."

What could she say to the mother of a blue-eyed angel, a mother with luminous brown eyes—definitely brown. Becky couldn't deny the obvious: Nate, baby, beautiful woman frantically searching for him.

"I can't wait until he gets home," the woman said, sobbing now. "The cab...my bus...you see, I don't have any choice. Could you possibly—oh, I know it's too much to ask a stranger."

Uh-oh, Becky thought, bracing herself. The woman was going to ask whether it was too much or not.

"Could you possibly take care of Lucy until Nate gets home? I'll be glad to pay you." She patted at wet tears streaming from her eyes.

"Oh, I couldn't accept money." Becky's better judgment was screaming no, no, no! But the woman seemed so desperate. "How do I know Nate will take her when he gets home?"

"Of course he will! Family is terribly important to him. Please!" She looked at her wristwatch. "I wouldn't dream of leaving Lucy if I weren't so desperate. And you live right above Nate. It's not like you're a total stranger. Please say you'll watch her until he gets home."

The woman was sobbing into a damp wad of tissues she'd taken from the pocket of a cotton knit sweater she wore with a short flowered skirt and a lacy white camisole.

Becky felt a rare flash of envy. The woman was beautiful even when she was bawling—icing on the cake in a life that included a baby like Lucy.

"If you won't take her, I don't know what I'll do," the mother cried dramatically.

Becky knew she'd been had. She had terrible visions of Lucy abandoned in a service station rest room or left in a cart at the supermarket. The woman could be deranged. For the baby's sake, she had to keep her safe until Nate got home.

"All right, I'll watch her," she reluctantly agreed.

"Everything she needs is in the bag. She'll probably go back to sleep if you give her a bottle. I can't possibly thank you enough. And be sure to give Nate the note."

"Nate will definitely get the note," Becky said dryly.

No long farewells for the suddenly tearless mother, she thought disgustedly as the woman quickly kissed Lucy on the top of her head and hurried back down the stairs to her waiting cab.

"Well, Lucy," Becky said, lifting the baby from her seat, "whose little girl are you?"

She had a sinking feeling. Those bright blue eyes surely came from a macho policeman's gene pool.

3

SHE DIDN'T WANT to be awake! Becky pulled the sheet over her head and curled into her favorite going-back-to-sleep position, determined not to be dislodged by a few howls. Wise to Ozzie's ploys for attention, she wasn't going to jump out of bed because her pampered pet felt like playing.

Unfortunately her wonderful dream faded away, forgotten as the noise persisted. She rolled to the edge of the bed and reached down, exasperated enough to toss a slipper at her feline tormentor.

"Oh my gosh!"

She bolted to her feet, reality coming back in a rush: the baby, not the cat, was the source of the crying in the bedroom.

Lucy was still safe in the seat that had doubled as a bed, but she wasn't the contented cherub Becky had fed and changed a few hours ago.

"Hey, sweetie, don't worry," Becky crooned, picking up the little bundle of fury and cuddling her en route to the kitchen. "There's a nice bottle in the fridge."

Becky had sat with little nieces and nephews enough to know the microwave drill, but she'd never had to do it at the crack of dawn with her eyelids at half-mast and her brain barely functioning.

"Five o'clock," she moaned, staring unhappily at the digital clock on the microwave's control panel.

She'd waited up past two for Nate to come home, sure that she'd heard him leave for work in the middle of the afternoon. If he'd worked the three-to-eleven shift, why the heck hadn't he come home? She'd finally scurried down and left a sticky note on his door telling him she urgently needed to see him the minute he got home.

So, where was he?

It was the spider's fault! Nate probably thought she had some inconsequential crisis not worth checking.

Jerk was the nicest name she mentally called him while she was getting the bottle ready, balancing Lucy on one hip.

Maybe he still wasn't home. Wouldn't that be typical behavior for a man who played hit-and-run in the baby game?

Lucy's gorgeous blue eyes were reproachful, so Becky quickly changed her before giving her the bottle, bagging the discarded diaper in a plastic garbage sack and dropping it beside the door with the two already there. The way she felt about Dalton, she'd like to bombard him with soggy diapers when he finally came up those stairs.

Lucy downed the bottle and nodded off, substituting thumb for nipple after Becky put her to rest in the car seat. Becky's own bed beckoned. Three hours' sleep was just enough to transform her into a zombie-chick.

A loud noise downstairs distracted her from returning to her cozy bed. No one could accuse him of sneaking in quietly. She charged out to the hallway, in the mood to slay a giant.

Sounding as insistent as she could in a mock whisper, she called out, "Dalton, get up here right now!"

"Don't tell me you have another spider."

He looked rumpled and weary, a pale-green dress shirt hanging out of khaki slacks and his jacket bunched under his arm. He stared up at her with sleep-deprived eyes, his chin darkly shadowed with prickly-looking bristles.

She must have been temporarily deranged to let him become her neighbor. Even when he looked like a street-corner derelict, he was drop-dead sexy.

"No spider," she said with exaggerated dignity, knowing self-righteousness wasn't her style but too disgusted to play it cool. "This time it's real vermin—a two-legged rat."

She enjoyed the puzzled look on his face as he came up the stairs, dragging his feet in reluctance.

"In here," she said curtly, leaving the door open for him to follow. "Anyone you know?" she asked in a husky whisper, pointing at the slumbering baby when he walked into the room.

"Lucy!"

He rushed over to the baby, his face rigid with anger or disapproval or some negative reaction she couldn't quite define.

So he knew the kid. No big deal to her! Maybe she had been nourishing a feeble little hope that it was all a ghastly mistake, a soap opera mix-up he could clear up with a logical explanation. It didn't matter to her if he fathered a dozen blue-eyed cherubs. Only it was a shame if little Lucy didn't have a father willing to help raise her.

At least he didn't deny knowing the baby. Admitting it showed he had some character, however flawed it might be.

She reminded herself he was only a neighbor—and that was all she wanted him to be. The man of her dreams was gentle, soft-spoken, gallant and considerate. Nate Dalton didn't qualify on any count.

"What are you doing with my niece?" he demanded to know.

"Your niece!"

"Who did you think she was?" Then apparently it dawned on him. "You thought she was mine?"

How could he look so shocked? It was the most likely explanation.

"What was I supposed to think? Lucy was dropped on my doorstep because you weren't home."

"On your doorstep?" He looked ready to throttle someone, and she was the only handy scapegoat.

"Not literally! Her mother rang the buzzer downstairs. I answered. I saw those big blue eyes and—"

"You assumed I was her father."

"It may have crossed my mind," she answered defensively, annoyed because he was intimidating her again. "Look, Detective Dalton, all I did was agree to take the baby because I was worried about her. The mother seemed like..." She stopped herself from saying a basket case. "Your type."

"My type? How do you know what my type is?"

She felt like stamping her foot in frustration. If this

was the way Mr. Macho Cop treated people who tried to help, she'd be better off getting arrested. At least he'd taken time to listen to explanations when he thought she was a criminal.

"She was very nice-looking—gorgeous, actually. But I change my mind about your type. You deserve a lady wrestler or a female marine who can break your arm when you get bossy!"

"Sorry, just my cop instincts kicking in."

"Well, kick them out! She seemed like a nice person, but she was really upset."

"Has to be Freddie."

"Freddie?"

"My sister, Fredericka. My parents thought she'd be their fourth son, so they picked the name Fred and stuck with it. What did she say? I can't believe she left Lucy with a perfect stranger."

"At least you admit I'm a *perfect* stranger, not a common criminal. She begged me to keep the baby until you got home. Your sister knew an honest face when she saw one."

"You took a big chance, accepting a child from a stranger. What if I didn't know her?"

"I thought of that," she lied. "But the baby has your eyes."

He scowled. "Yeah, blue eyes, a real rarity."

"Where's the baby's father?"

She had no intention of telling him how special his eyes were—not just blue but sparkling azure pools that could mesmerize a gullible girl. But not her! No way! She was through with men who radiated sexuality like heat from the summer sun.

"He took off right after Lucy was born, seven months ago."

"Why did your sister leave the baby with you?"

"My brothers both live out of state, and my parents are finally taking the big cruise they've dreamed about for years. Anyway, I'm the one who's always bailed her out of jams, even when she was a kid. What did she say to you?"

"Not a lot. Oh, I forgot. She left a note."

"Let me have it!"

He was anything but soft-spoken.

"Keep your voice down. You'll wake the baby. She just had her 5:00 a.m. bottle." Becky whispered just to let him know she was in charge here.

She handed him the note which, of course, she'd read in the wee hours waiting for him to get home. A sealed envelope was private, but how could a folded note be confidential? Anyway, it could have been something urgent like a ransom note or a blackmail demand.

"What does it say?" she asked, feeling a bit guilty because she already knew.

"Just that she had to get away for a while to sort things out. She wants me to take care of Lucy until she gets back. One part I don't understand, though."

"What's that?" Becky asked, wondering if her voice sounded stagy when she put on an innocent act. Subterfuge wasn't her game. Usually she erred on the side of being too outspoken.

"She doesn't want our mother to know I have Lucy." He frowned at the note as if it contained some hidden clue.

"Strange," Becky agreed. She'd already wondered about that part herself.

"That's Freddie, always waving a flag for independence, especially if she can get me to take care of her problems while she's off being her own person."

"I wouldn't call Lucy a problem."

Lucy must have sensed that her favorite uncle was there. She opened her eyes and took one of his big, hard fingers in her chubby fist.

"No, she's my godchild and I adore her, but taking care of her is going to be a big problem. I do have to work for a living. What am I going to do with her?"

He stood and looked pointedly at Becky, but he didn't ask the question she sort of expected: could *she* watch Lucy? Why did she feel let down when he failed to suggest it? She didn't run a baby-sitting service, and she certainly didn't want an excuse to see more of her too-sexy-for-her-own-good neighbor.

"I'll just have to work something out," he said, tossing his jacket on the closest chair and bending over to pick up Lucy.

The man does have a nice backside, Becky thought, annoyed at herself for noticing and still just a little hurt that he didn't consider his temporarily unemployed neighbor a qualified caregiver. He probably didn't want someone he'd almost arrested as a burglar watching his precious niece.

Nate did know baby language. Circling the living room several times carrying a contented Lucy in his arms, he sweet-talked his niece into showing him a big grin.

"I don't suppose you could help me until I can hire

a good baby-sitter?'' he asked suddenly, the solution finally dawning on him. ''I'd pay you, of course.''

A lukewarm offer if she'd ever heard one. Becky was tempted to refuse outright, but how could she let him give this adorable baby into the care of just anyone?

''Maybe I could help out a little,'' she said with exaggerated hesitation, ''but I wouldn't need to be paid.'' His attitude had made it a matter of pride, and hers was a bit prickly right now.

''We'll talk about that later.'' He seemed to think it was his decision.

''Fine.''

''You're getting to be a big girl,'' he said, smiling at the baby and ignoring Becky.

''I'll get her bottles from the fridge,'' Becky said. ''They should take you through today, but you'll have to get more formula for tomorrow. Her mother has her on soy milk.''

''Hey, I haven't slept yet.'' He was giving Becky his full attention now. ''Tomorrow—I guess it's today—is my day off. If you could take the first shift...''

''Just a minute. I waited up past 2:00 a.m. for you to come home, and Lucy got me up at five. I've hardly had enough sleep to count as a nap. By the way, it's none of my business, but did you work all day and all night?''

''You're right, it isn't your business, but I worked overtime, then caught the tail end of a bachelor party for a fellow officer.''

''Must have been some tail.''

"I got there in time for the exotic dancer, if you're worried about it."

Thinly veiled sarcasm was still sarcasm.

"I'm not worried about anything, but you look as if you spent the night in a bear cage at the zoo. I feel a certain responsibility for Lucy...."

"Point taken."

He jostled Lucy in the crook of his arm and ran his hand over his chin.

"I don't mind bristles," she said, "but your eyes are fluorescent red with black accents." Dang, this man annoyed her just by existing!

"Just for the record—not that I need to explain myself to you or anyone—I pulled a ten-hour shift and spent the rest of the night in a smoky room. If I'm hungover, it's from inhaling whiskey fumes, not drinking the stuff. I had a few beers and a bowl of popcorn—and, no, I didn't score with the girl who jumped out of the cake or anyone else."

"Interesting, but more than I wanted to know."

"So, about Lucy..."

"We could toss a coin."

"Never mind. She's my problem."

"Well...I suppose I owe you one for the spider. Noon—I'll watch her until noon."

"Deal." He brushed the baby's forehead with his lips and handed her over. "You said there's enough formula. What about food?"

"Her diaper bag was packed full of stuff. There should be enough jars of baby food for today."

"Great. I appreciate this, Rebecca."

"Twelve o'clock sharp," she reminded him.

"Noon, right." He touched Lucy's soft pink cheek with the back of one finger. "See you later, sweetheart. You be good for the nice woman."

For one silly second, Becky was jealous of the baby.

NATE WAS DREAMING about a girl who jumped out of a cake, wearing three tiny daisies and nothing else. She started gyrating to the loud beat of a drum, and he caught the first daisy she tossed. There was something familiar about the curve of her hip and the thrust of her breasts, but when he moved closer to check her out, the fantasy slipped away.

But the noise continued, not the beat of an imaginary drum but an insistent pounding on his door.

He sat up, realizing he'd kicked off his shoes and collapsed on the couch fully dressed. He had to start getting more sleep!

"Open up, Dalton. I know you're in there!"

"G'way," he called out, loosening the belt buckle that had indented his belly while he slept.

Now he knew the identity of the dream girl in the cake, and he'd bet his pension she was the one trying to embed her knuckles into his door.

She pounded some more, and he reluctantly looked at his watch, remembering his promise to take Lucy off her hands at noon. It was 1:13, and this wasn't going to be his lucky day.

He lurched over to the door, tugging his belt out of the loops and tossing it aside. He needed at least a gallon of coffee before he started dealing with his sister's problems, not to mention his neighbor.

How the devil did Rebecca get into his pleasantly

erotic dream? He was determined to keep her out of his life—and out of his head. He had a sister who couldn't get her act together. He had an ex-girlfriend who hadn't been able to make a move without him. He certainly didn't intend to get involved with another helpless-little-girl type!

He flung open the door and faced two very unhappy females—his howling, red-faced niece and an angry, pink-cheeked neighbor.

"You'll have the landlady on our case." It was a dumb thing to say, but he was too groggy to deal with crying and recriminations.

"She plays canasta on Saturday afternoon, and it is after noon, Dalton, in case you haven't noticed."

"Yeah, come in." He stepped aside reluctantly.

"You promised to take Lucy at noon. I gave you an extra hour and then some."

"Thanks." He took the baby, car seat and all, out of her arms. "Just put the bag anyplace."

"We had an agreement. I have things to do."

"Sorry, I fell asleep on the couch before I remembered to set my alarm."

How could she look so perky on a couple hours' sleep? She was wearing a pink-striped tank top, and he was having a heck of a time pretending not to notice the way her nipples pushed at the taut cloth. If she were his woman, he'd insist on baggy shirts and armored bras.

"Lucy needs diapers—check out the empty package for the size—and don't forget, she'll run out of formula this evening. Just follow the directions on the can when you mix it. The food will last another day or so, but you'd better stock up on that, too. I don't know Lucy's favorites, but beets are usually on the most-hated list. Plan on one green and one yellow—''

"What are you doing the rest of the day?"

It slipped out; he didn't need or want to keep track of his neighbor's activities.

"I have my own errands, and I definitely need a nap or I'll fall asleep on a first date."

"New boyfriend already?" He immediately wished he hadn't asked and busied himself with Lucy so he'd seem indifferent to her answer.

"No, but one of the assistant managers at the garden center where I'll be working asked me to dinner."

"Doesn't seem too smart, dating management at your new workplace."

He soothed Lucy, wondering what he'd do with her the rest of the day.

"He's not one of my supervisors. He's quiet, polite and he doesn't come across as a bossy macho type," she said pointedly. "Now, not that I'm eager to get rid of Lucy—she's a doll—but I have things to do."

"Just keep your eye on her while I shower, then I'll play superuncle for the rest of the day."

Before she could refuse, he unbuttoned his shirt and tossed it in the general direction of his belt, then unsnapped his pants and started inching them over his hips, wondering how far she'd let him go.

"Okay, okay, keep your pants on! Fifteen minutes and not one second more."

She grabbed Lucy and fled.

He headed toward the shower. Funny, he was feeling a lot more energetic already.

4

WHEN THE KNOCK CAME, Lucy was on her tummy on the carpeted floor, doing a good imitation of a sand crab on a slippery slope. She managed to cover amazing distances with a total lack of technique, leaving Becky to follow in her wake.

"No, sweetie, don't chew the TV cord," she begged, trying to substitute a stuffed creature with a head like a carrot. Scooping up the baby, Becky rushed to answer the door.

"The cavalry! You're just in time for Lucy's full-fledged assault on my electrical cords. Watch out, she likes to chew on them."

"I'll try to remember that," Nate said.

"Remembering isn't optional," she warned, wondering how a quick shower had left him smelling so yummy.

He took Lucy, grimacing at the string of drool that dampened his arm.

"Don't kids this size stay in pens or something?"

"That's up to the caregiver—in this case, you."

Lucy expressed her opinion of playpens by grabbing the chest hairs showing in the unbuttoned flap of Nate's polo shirt. He yelped and tried to loosen her grip, but all he got for his efforts was another streak of drool on the front of his clean navy shirt.

"Hey, Lucy, say hello to Mr. Carrot Head," Becky said, flipping the toy until the baby grabbed for it.

"Thanks." He grinned and belatedly buttoned his shirt. "I was in a hurry to get here—fifteen minutes, you said."

"Well, you made it, and she's all yours now." Becky picked up the seat and the diaper bag. "Don't forget—you'll need formula and diapers today."

She made the mistake of looking directly into his heavenly blue eyes. True, they were still darkly shadowed after his too short sleep, but it wasn't her fault he'd sat around all night ogling female flesh with his police buddies. No way was she going to let herself feel sorry for him! She was not going to get emotionally involved with her cop neighbor.

Lucy was making happy noises, apparently delighted by the prospect of spending the rest of the day with her gorgeous uncle, but then, what female wouldn't be? His broad shoulders were designed for cuddling—and not just with babies.

"Thanks for watching her. I don't know what I would've done without you," he said, now fully loaded with baby gear and trying to fend off Lucy's attack on his nose.

"You're welcome. Have a nice day," Becky chimed as they said their goodbyes, pretty sure Lucy still had a few tricks left for her uncle.

HER ERRANDS were no big deal: return some library books and mail a letter at the post office. She could have waited until Monday and taken a longer nap, but she wanted to test-drive her car. It had been working fine for a while, but the last time she used it, the dashboard had lit up like a video game. She was hoping it was only a hiccup in the electrical system.

It wasn't.

When she got home, she retrieved the manufacturer's manual from the glove compartment and carried it upstairs, hoping she could pinpoint the trouble by reading it. Mostly she hoped the car would keep going until she started getting regular paychecks again.

She gave up when she couldn't focus anymore. Unfortunately, she wasn't good at napping. Genes inherited from work-addicted farming ancestors kept her wide-eyed until it was time for her to get ready for her date. Her wakefulness couldn't possibly have anything to do with visions of Nate crawling around on hands and knees trying to keep Lucy occupied and out of trouble.

Not in a first-date mood, she compensated by wearing her summer best, a flirty, filmy pale-peach dress. Josh Milwood was on the short side, so she wore white flats, not that she was ever taller than anyone she dated. She was trying to work up enthusiasm for an evening with a future fellow garden center employee when she heard high-pitched wails, followed by an urgent knock on her door.

Lucy was in fine form, red-faced from screaming. Her uncle was a little red in the cheeks himself.

"I can't figure out what's wrong," Nate said. "I fed

her, changed her, did all the right things, but she won't stop crying.''

"Give her to me," Becky said, instinctively putting the baby over one shoulder and patting her back.

Lucy let loose a burp worthy of a frat boy.

"Just gas," she explained, kissing the baby's forehead and handing her back to Nate. It was then that she noticed the warm, wet spot on the front of her dress.

"Yuck." She plucked the dress away from her waist.

"Sorry," Nate said sheepishly. "I don't know why she sprang a leak. I just changed her."

He held the soggy baby at arm's length as her diaper slid slowly downward until it bunched above her ankles.

"I thought if I got them big, I wouldn't have to change them as often. She grabbed at the little cartoon characters on the front."

"They're just the thing for a toddler who refuses to be trained, but twins Lucy's size could share one of those. Didn't you think they were a bit large when you put this one on?"

"She was wiggling a lot. Hey, I'll be glad to have the dress cleaned for you."

"It's washable, and so am I. But you'll have to stay here and answer the door for my date while I take another shower and change."

"But Lucy is leaking."

"I'll throw you a towel," she said from her bedroom door.

Nate felt like an idiot, holding a soggy baby wrapped

in a bath towel and listening to muted shower noises coming from behind the closed bedroom door. Who knew all diapers weren't alike?

And why was he on edge because she was naked behind that door? He was crazy to stand there imagining the water cascading over her shapely breasts, down her taut little belly.

He was sweating. Didn't she use the air-conditioning? Lucy was wiggly, so he held her closer, hoping the towel wouldn't soak through, too.

The water shut off. She was probably drying herself at top speed, rubbing the towel across her shoulders, down her back, across her cute rear, down her legs…oh man!

The buzzer shrilled. He had to run downstairs and let her date in. He maneuvered Lucy over his shoulder and let the towel drop down to cover his front. He'd embarrassed himself enough today without letting her date see he was turned on by the sound of shower water and his own out-of-control imagination. He had to do something about his sex life before he did something really stupid—like letting Rebecca get under his skin.

"Hi, I'm the neighbor," he said, opening the door and greeting the puzzled-looking guy standing outside. "Rebecca asked me to get the door for her. She'll be ready in a couple of minutes. You can go up to her apartment to wait."

He was dying to see Becky's reaction to this broomstick in a suit, but his niece had other ideas.

None of my business anyway, he reminded himself as he entered his apartment after discovering Lucy had left her mark on his shirt. If Rebecca didn't have enough sense to avoid the duds, there was nothing he could do—wanted to do—about it. Better anyone else than him.

Nate had solved part of the problem of what to do with Lucy by borrowing some equipment from friends whose kids had outgrown it: a playpen that doubled as holding tank and crib, and a collapsible wheeled thing they called an umbrella stroller. He figured eight o'clock was a reasonable baby bedtime and even managed to give Lucy a bath of sorts, letting her splash in his kitchen sink until he ran out of patience and was as wet as she was. At the rate he was going through shirts, he'd run out of dry clothes pretty soon.

"Now, young lady," he said with mock sternness, "it's sleepy time."

Lucy had other ideas. She made a shambles of the makeshift bedding in the playpen, managing to pull the comforter that was supposed to serve as a mattress into a jumbled heap. Worse, she sprang another leak, one that necessitated another trip to the kitchen sink and another clean outfit. Her clothing supply was dwindling down to nothing, too, so he quickly threw a sackful of dirty laundry into the washer.

"Enough is enough." Nate sighed, trying another approach. As he walked the floor with her, he sang made-up songs in what he hoped was a soothing tone.

"Don't let your kid become a cop;
The bad guys never want to stop;
If you don't catch them, you're a flop;
Please go to sleep before I drop!"

He could have sworn Lucy giggled.

What she didn't do was sleep. All he had to do was lean over the pen on his way to laying her down and she'd start howling. The kid had to sleep sometime! He decided to tough it out, to let her howl until she cried herself to sleep.

That lasted about three minutes. Then he had an inspiration: let her nod off in the stroller. He was sure he'd seen babies zonked out that way.

Nate needed to run, but he'd have to settle for a walk with Lucy. Fitting her into the stroller was like working a jigsaw puzzle, but at last he had a chubby leg in each big opening and the belt secured around her middle.

Lucy loved the walk. She grabbed at bushes and tried to eat the leaves, cooed at dogs big enough to swallow her whole, and looked around wide-eyed and sleepless. Nate figured he covered about three miles before her head finally slumped.

He was a block from home when he saw two people get out of a car and walk up to the porch. It was Rebecca and the stickman. He walked slower to give them time to go upstairs or do the thanks-for-the-date ritual in the hallway. He definitely didn't want to interrupt any vertical foreplay.

''What the hell, I live there, too,'' he said after slowly counting to a hundred.

He carried Lucy, stroller and all, up the porch steps, used his key to open the front door, then pushed the baby, still sleeping in her stroller, into the hallway.

The guy was grabbing Rebecca! She was shrieking! Nate acted on instinct, yanking him away and propelling him toward the wall.

"He's choking!" Rebecca cried out. "On a peanut! He wouldn't let me do the Heimlich."

Nate got behind the guy and pressed his midsection, dislodging the foreign object from her mortified date, who tried to sputter his thanks between gasps for air.

"We went to a roadhouse—you know, line dancing, peanut shells on the floor. Josh filled his pockets when we left," Rebecca explained. "He tried to kiss me with a peanut in his mouth."

She started giggling, probably a nervous reaction to nearly losing a date the permanent way. Nate had to cover his mouth with his hand to hide his amusement. The poor guy was humiliated enough without ridiculing him.

"Josh, come up and I'll get you something to drink," she offered, managing to stifle her nervous laughter.

"Thanks, but no. I'll just be going. I owe you big time, buddy," he mumbled in Nate's direction. To Rebecca he said, "I'll call you sometime."

"I had a nice time," she called after Josh as he beat a hasty retreat. "It could happen to anyone!" she declared, turning back to Nate.

"Sure," Nate said mildly.

"He's a nice guy," she insisted.

"Nice time, nice guy. I'm not doubting your word."

"Well, I guess I should thank you for saving his

life," she said. "He kept clutching at me. I couldn't get behind him to do it myself."

"He thanked me himself. It isn't your fault he was trying to do a lip dance with stolen peanuts in his mouth."

"He didn't steal them! They were there for the taking. Oh, never mind! I know he isn't a big macho he-man like you and your police buddies, but he's..."

"Nice. Yes, you told me that."

"Very nice, low-key, polite. Not that it matters. No chance he'll ask me out again after that fiasco."

"You'll see him at work when you start your new job."

She gave him a look that could freeze mercury just as Lucy let out a horrendous howl. They were tag-teaming him!

"How was *your* date?" she teased, bending over to coo at the baby.

"Lively. Lucy has a thing for dogs—big dogs."

"I didn't notice the storm."

"What storm?" He knew he shouldn't ask.

"If you haven't been through a tornado, you must be having a very bad clothes day."

Okay, he deserved that after all his "nice" remarks. But he couldn't look suave going through a week's worth of clothes in one day. Anyway, his faded maroon sweatpants cut off to midthigh had a few more years left in them. Better a little dog slobber on the front than teeth tears and blood.

"What time are babies supposed to sack out?" he asked.

She laughed, not one of those dainty put-on chuckles women used when they wanted to score points, but a robust, throaty belly laugh.

"I just asked." He picked up Lucy, a little annoyed by Rebecca's amusement. "I think the kid is colicky. Or maybe she misses her mother."

He held Lucy on his shoulder and patted her back, hoping for a little cooperation so he wouldn't look like an idiot in front of this grinning woman. Hell, how complicated could it be to make one pint-size female happy? He just had to get into a routine, then it would be a piece of cake.

Lucy shut off the tears but not before soaking one shoulder of his ratty ancient Rose Bowl T-shirt.

"Has she had her bedtime bottle?" Rebecca asked.

"No, she ate a big dinner. I didn't think she'd have room for one."

"She's probably used to a little liquid snack to put her to sleep. Here, I'll hold her while you fix a bottle."

She took the baby. He couldn't do a thing unless he wanted to play tug-of-war over the kid. So he opened the door and let her go ahead of him into his apartment.

"Whoa! You *were* caught by a tornado!"

"I wanted to catch up on some paperwork after Lucy went down. Only she didn't conk out, and I made the mistake of putting her on the floor for thirty seconds while I got my key. Anyway, the polite thing would be not to mention it."

"I stand corrected." She didn't look the least bit chastised. "Just shows you how handy it is to have a key under the mat. By the way, your answering machine is blinking.''

"Guess I'd better check it."

"Don't mind me. I won't listen."

Unlikely, since she was standing with Lucy less than ten feet from the machine, showing no sign of leaving. Why did this woman make him feel self-conscious about listening to a message? It wasn't as if he subscribed to phone sex or had amorous females calling his place all the time.

"Go ahead," she said when he hesitated. "I grew up with three older brothers. Nothing shocks me."

"Nothing shocking here," he grumbled, hoping he wasn't getting called in to work overtime. This was his weekend off. He needed both days free to figure out what to do with Lucy.

He activated the message tape.

"Nate, don't you ever stay home?" Freddie said in her usual rapid-fire way. "I really owe you big for helping me with Lucy. I wanted to be sure you got my message about not telling Mom you have her. I'll come for her as soon as I work some things out. I promise! I'll owe you forever! Give Lucy a big hug and kiss for me, and tell her Mommy loves her a bunch. Thank you, big brother! Thank you, thank you, thank you!"

"Now you know everything I do," he said morosely.

But his sister hadn't told him a damn thing. Why the devil was he supposed to keep Lucy's whereabouts a secret from her doting grandmother? When were his parents due back, anyway? He'd have to check his date book, but to his recollection the cruise should be over soon.

Rebecca had put Lucy on the floor and was kneeling beside her, coaxing her to grab some pointy-headed doll. They were both ignoring him.

"I know Freddie," he said, even as he wondered why he had this strong urge to justify his sister's actions to Rebecca. "She's crazy about Lucy—you couldn't ask for a more conscientious mother. And she's always been responsible about taking care of her, even if she's a little dippy about other things."

"She probably had a good reason for leaving her with you," Rebecca agreed, absorbed in playing patty-cake with the baby.

"She hasn't had much luck with anything she's tried, but she keeps moving on to new things. She must have strong motivation for leaving Lucy and disappearing."

He was trying to convince himself. Surveying his baby-infested digs, he indulged in a brief revenge fantasy. Freddie had gone too far this time.

"Her pajamas are wet." Rebecca stood and picked up Lucy, thrusting her in his direction at arm's length.

He groaned, wondering how long it would take to dry the load of baby stuff in his washer. He took the handoff, holding Lucy well away from his shirt.

"Did you get the right size diapers?" Rebecca asked.

"Didn't have time. I used tape to take up the slack."

She raised one eyebrow, a cute trick and probably her way of telling him he was an idiot.

"Go get some. Buy-Right is open twenty-four hours a day. Be sure to check the chart on the package. Have you had dinner?"

"No time for that, either."

"Well, get those diapers and then we'll see about dinner. Meantime, I'll unwrap Lucy and see about getting her dry."

LATE EVENING was a good time to go to the supermarket. Nate zipped down the aisles, buying three packs of diapers in different sizes and throwing a few more baby food jars in the cart, just in case.

He made the trip in record time, letting himself into the apartment with vague dread. Somehow he had to get Lucy down for the night. He'd leave the mess until tomorrow and hit the bed himself the minute her eyes closed. He'd drag all next week if he didn't catch up on his sleep.

"Shush!" Rebecca pointed at the open doorway to his bedroom. "Lucy zonked out after you left. I moved her into your room so you could use the living room without waking her."

"The diapers…"

"I pleated the legs on one of the giant ones. It should hold while she's sleeping."

He must have fallen into a time warp. In the short time it had taken to run his errand, everything had righted itself: no scattered pages; no toys to trip over; the dryer purring in the kitchen closet that served as a laundry room; the mouth-watering scent of frying onions wafting toward him.

Frying onions?

"What's cooking?"

"Steak and onions—my version of a Philly sandwich, although it'd be better with real cheddar instead of those bland slices you have. They're about as tasty as their cellophane wrapping."

"I don't have any steak...."

"Doggy bag, courtesy of Tommy-Bob's Roadhouse. Don't order their house special unless you want a side of beef."

"I didn't see—"

"It was in my shoulder bag. It looks so tacky to carry around a bag of leftovers. I hope you don't mind eating my leavings."

Mind? He could kiss her!

She went to the kitchen and puttered around in bare feet, deftly covering toast with steak and onion strips, adding cheese, and sticking it under the broiler.

She knew her way around a kitchen. If good things came in small packages, she'd be at the top of every guy's Christmas wish list.

Don't be suckered in! his head warned him. Fried onions and a gorgeous body—many a fool ended up hog-tied and branded with less tempting bait.

"The only healthy food I found was carrot sticks." She transferred the open-face sandwich to one of his thick china dinner plates and added some washed baby carrots.

"You'll have something with me, won't you?" he asked.

He was hungry, all right. And not just for food. What could be tastier than nibbling on those full, pink lips.

"No thanks. Um...my date—um—insisted on ordering for me," she explained. "He overdid it."

She couldn't remember her date's name! He wasn't the only one sensitive to the supercharged atmosphere in the cozy kitchen with dancing spoons and knives on the yellow wallpaper.

He couldn't remember the guy's name, either.

"Your steak will get cold," she said.

"Wouldn't want that to happen."

He was rooted to the spot. He didn't know how to feel about a woman like Rebecca bustling around his bachelor kitchen.

"Well, I'll be going."

"No! I have a bottle of red wine. A gift—not my usual drink. Stay and have a glass with me."

"I don't think..."

"It's a good idea?"

He knew damn well it wasn't, but he'd just noticed her chin, pert but not pointy, and her long spiky lashes, and the way she moistened her lower lip with the tip of her tongue when she was undecided.

He made the decision for both of them, getting the bottle from the cupboard over the fridge and locating his only corkscrew—also a gift, but he'd seen no reason to throw away everything what's-her-name had given him.

"The last time I tried this, the cork stuck, and I ended up chopping it out. Little pieces got in the wine. Had to strain it."

"I hate it when that happens." She sounded out of breath. "But I should be going."

"Stay a couple of minutes in case Lucy wakes up."

"I guess—oh, by the way, hope you don't mind I put the wet clothes in the dryer."

"Thanks."

"I hope you don't think I'm, you know, being pushy. I had to do something while you were gone."

"I appreciate…"

They both heard a little whimper and raced toward the bedroom where the makeshift bed was pushed against the edge of his oversize one.

Rebecca got there first, and without meaning to, he sandwiched her with her knees bending into the net siding of the playpen.

"False alarm," she whispered, looking down at the slumbering baby in the dim light filtering from the living room. "She's still sound asleep."

She turned to leave just as he pressed closer with some idea of straightening the light flannel blanket covering the baby.

"Sorry." They said it together; he was lying and hoped she was, too.

Her body was so inviting. Unconsciously he pushed his knee forward between her parted thighs, then drew back with a jerk, realizing how close he'd come to initiating something he might not be able to stop.

He backed up just as she tried to squeeze past him, and they collided, front to front.

"Don't you ever wear a bra?" Was that raspy voice really his?

"I'm wearing one now."

Stalemate. Neither of them had enough space to move clear of the other.

"No way."

"So what makes you an expert?"

"Experience and…"

She demurely pulled her soft cotton shirt off her shoulder just far enough to reveal a lacy peach strap.

He touched it, slipping one finger under it, testing the elasticity without snapping it against her.

"Seen enough?"

"I stand corrected. Front snap or back?" His tongue felt thick.

"In your dreams!"

"Just curious."

"I bet."

She squeezed past him, flattening her bottom against the wall to get past his hip.

"This definitely wasn't a good idea—bringing Lucy in here," she said in a breathy voice that made him long to slide his fingers down her cleavage.

She padded, still barefoot, into the living room, her bottom wiggling slightly under the tangerine-colored skirt. He needed sleep worse than he'd thought. Sleep deprivation was causing all kinds of uncomfortable fantasies.

"You'd better look for a real baby-sitter," she said.

"Yes, I will."

She slipped into her shoes, abandoned by the door, snatched up her purse, and got the door open in one sweeping movement.

"You need help," she said.

"Yes."

He was desperate for help, but it had nothing to do with Lucy. What he needed was to get this woman out of his mind. Sure, Rebecca was cute and sweet and sexy, but he'd nearly made a big mistake in the bedroom. She was too—he could only think of her favorite word—*nice*—too nice for just-for-fun sex. And he was too old and jaded to play house with his neighbor. He didn't need her to straighten his place or cook his meals, and no way would he let her get the wrong idea!

He knew women's tricks. Let one into his kitchen, and pretty soon her toothbrush would be in the holder beside his—and he'd be straightening out all her troubles.

"Good night," she said.

"Thanks for helping."

"You're welcome."

He didn't watch her walk up the stairs.

5

FROM NOW ON, Becky decided, she'd focus on career success. She'd be starting out in inventory control for the lawn-and-garden department, but who knew where pesticides and fertilizers could lead? Today plant food, tomorrow CEO of the corporation? That had been her reason for coming to Grand Rapids. If all she wanted out of life was a man, she could have stayed on the farm and gone husband hunting at co-op dances.

She'd had a narrow escape with Nate. He looked better in rummage sale rejects than most men looked in formal wear, and when he'd cornered her in the bedroom—or maybe she'd set herself up—she'd been a nanosecond away from making the big mistake.

He even had cute knees, although it was hard to say why his were sexier than the average knobby specimens.

She'd retreated to her apartment Saturday night only to find that the delectable aroma of fried onions had wafted upward into her apartment, lingering there while she let her imagination run wild, playing out torrid love scenes with the sexy-as-sin cop that left her weak with longing.

But not so weak that she couldn't actively avoid him

all day Sunday, much as she would have enjoyed seeing more of Lucy. For a baby, that girl had personality to spare. She also had her uncle's number, putting him through a vigorous initiation into substitute parenthood.

Monday evening was a fiasco. Her best friend, Zoe, was obsessed with becoming cookware queen of the year and had talked Becky into working a couple of home parties under her supervision—make that dictatorship. Becky sold one set of saucepans, three no-stick cookie sheets and a frying pan at a party of gossiping strangers that lasted until nearly midnight. After the company took their profit, the hostess got her payoff and Zoe took a unit-commander's cut, Becky estimated she'd made $7.20.

She was in the mood for a late-night horror movie and a big bowl of strawberry ice cream when she got home, but fate intervened. She came through the front door just as Nate was struggling to open his door with Lucy sleeping on his shoulder, a diaper bag hanging from his arm and a collapsed stroller balanced between his legs.

"Need help?" She felt she had to ask.

He'd gotten smarter—Lucy was resting on a flannel blanket folded over the shoulder of his sport coat.

"Oh, it's you."

"Spare me your friendly greeting."

"I just spent the last hour tracking down my sister's kid. I left her with a cop friend's wife, but her father was rushed to the hospital, so she took Lucy to a neighbor's. I had to find my friend at a robbery scene to locate her."

Uh-oh! She was starting to feel sorry for him. He did look beat in a yummy sort of way. His brow creased, making her want to smooth it out. Danger signal!

"What you need is a reliable baby-sitter."

Should she volunteer for the job? She'd love to take care of Lucy until her new job started, but was she up to seeing Nate twice a day, every day? She might end up washing his shorts and changing his sheets, then who knew what? Fortunately she remembered how bossy and overbearing he was just in time to refrain from offering. Hey, she was only looking for an excuse to avoid more cookware parties.

She wasn't going into that apartment, not even if he begged her.

"Three child-care agencies are sending me women to interview in the morning starting at 9:00 a.m. Plus, I put signs up at a couple of grocery stores. So I'm going to need all the sleep I can get."

He didn't slam the door in her face, but it sure felt as if he had.

"Well, good luck." She turned away from him, wondering if she could make a dignified retreat climbing the stairs.

"I'm not sure what to ask them," he said.

It cost him something to admit that; she was feeling all mushy inside again.

"Want some help?"

If he said no, that was the last time she'd offer to do anything for him—ever.

"I'd really appreciate it. Just come down around nine?"

"Okay."

Not okay! Hadn't she learned anything from Stalnaker? Kevin had started out sweet-talking her into little favors and flexing his muscles at her. Before she knew what hit her, she'd been stuck in that miserable, windowless office trying to straighten out his shoddy accounting practices.

"Thanks, Rebecca." He managed a weak grin.

"I wish you'd call me Becky. When my mother said Rebecca, I knew I was in trouble."

Come to think of it, she probably was up to her ears in trouble now. If men knew how appealing they looked with babies draped tenderly over their shoulders, the bars would be full of borrowed kids.

"Becky, I never did open that wine. If you'd like to come in…"

"No, thank you."

She started backing toward the stairs. When her heel hit the bottom riser, she nearly did a pratfall. Why was he standing there watching her?

Then she made a big mistake. She looked directly into his eyes.

Bam! Pow! Whammy! She could drown in those neon-blues!

She turned and hightailed it up the stairs. His was a strip-you-naked look if she'd ever seen one!

She fumbled for the key in her purse; she'd let him spook her into not leaving one under the rug. When she finally got inside her apartment, she slammed the door and put on the chain, something she neglected to do most of the time.

She was out of breath and could hear her heartbeat. If this was a hormonal rush, she'd better find an antidote quickly!

Before she went to bed, she made a list of questions to ask potential caregivers. A neighbor had asked her to help hire a suitable employee. She had good business sense, learned by watching her parents in the complex management of a modern farm. Why not use it to help a casual acquaintance?

"And he's going to stay a casual acquaintance!" she warned herself. Getting romantic ideas about Dalton was as dangerous as putting her head in a bear trap.

In the morning she kept waking up and checking her clock: 4:17; 5:02; 5:56; 6:35. At seven she got up and went over her list of questions again.

Just so Nate wouldn't think she was eager, she waited until 8:57 to go down to his apartment. To her amazement, the front door was propped open with a chair. A sign resting on the seat said Interview Apartment One in bold felt-pen letters. On his door a second sign invited the applicants to enter.

She entered.

The only difference between the group in his living room and the one she'd faced at the cookware party was the noise level. This all-female gathering was muttering, not enjoying themselves.

She caught a glimpse of Nate through his kitchen door. He was pouring coffee into an odd assortment of mugs.

"What did you do?" she asked in a whisper. "Round up all the usual suspects?"

"I wanted a good selection," he whispered back defensively. "Thought I'd give them a cup of coffee, then call them into the kitchen one at a time."

"You don't have to serve refreshments at a job interview. Where's Lucy?"

"In the bedroom. I gave her some measuring cups and spoons to keep her occupied until this is over."

"While you talk to all those women? In your dreams! We'll do the interviews in the bedroom—see how Lucy reacts to each of them."

She led the way, stopping to deliver instructions to the crowd of applicants. "Please come in the order you arrived," she said. "I'll call the first person in a minute."

"I can't interview in here," Nate said in an urgent undertone when the bedroom door was closed.

He had that right! The unmade bed and scattered clothes on the floor weren't employment incentives.

"Hi, Lucy," Becky said, leaning over the playpen to dangle a set of plastic spoons on a ring. "Make your bed, Dalton."

She was proud of herself. She could be tough. The old Becky would have straightened the room for him.

He was fast; she had to give him that. In two minutes the room looked less like bachelor quarters, even if it was a little casual for a job interview. At least the door closed, giving an illusion of privacy.

She took her list of questions out of the pocket of her just-above-ankle-length blue denim jumper. Worn over a yellow tank top, it was decidedly casual, but compared to Nate in his frayed khaki shorts and faded black University of Iowa T-shirt, she was dressed for success.

"What's that?" He pulled a straight-backed wooden chair close to the bed.

"My list of questions for the applicants."

They were talking very softly. Funny how whispering made everything sound more urgent.

"I interrogate people for a living. I'll just wing it."

"You asked me to help!"

"Sure, I can use your help picking the best one. I thought a woman's viewpoint would be useful."

"I'm supposed to sit still, keep quiet and listen?"

"And maybe keep your eye on Lucy."

At least he had the grace to look uncomfortable.

"I'll jot down their names and phone numbers," she said, resigning herself to a secretarial role. "Shall I usher in contestant number one?"

He gave her a scathing look, probably deserved since she definitely wasn't in the mood for nicey-niceness.

The first prospect was pleasant but sloppy-looking. Her knee-length T-shirt worn over baggy-legged shorts either doubled as a cleaning rag or she'd fallen front-first into a breakfast buffet. She said she'd seen one of Nate's signs.

"Have you ever been arrested or served time in prison?" Nate asked after a perfunctory greeting.

"Nate!" Becky stood and pulled him into the walk-in closet across the room, shutting the door and hissing at him in the dark. "You can't ask questions like that."

"Yes, I can. Do you want Lucy in the hands of a criminal?"

"Check for arrest records later, if you must. Ask about child-care experience. You need to find a pleasant, efficient person who loves kids."

Candidate number one obviously didn't. She was picking at her fingernails and totally ignoring Lucy when they emerged from the dark closet. Becky wound up the interview in a hurry; the din from the living room suggested the natives were getting restless.

Candidate number three was the first to coo at Lucy. She was young and perky, a part-time student at the local community college who was studying child development. She brought references neatly arranged in a manila folder. She also had a tiny diamond stud in her nose, a beaded silver wire through her eyebrow and huge gold hoops in both earlobes. Or maybe it was her zebra-print miniskirt that made Nate's face wrinkle with distaste.

"She has good references and likes kids," Becky pointed out before calling the next person.

"I can see Lucy yanking on those ear hoops," he said.

Becky sighed and ushered in the last applicant, a square-jawed woman with steel-gray hair and half-lens glasses perched low on her nose. She introduced herself as Mrs. Lorenzo.

"Do you have any references?" Nate asked.

"Yes. I've mostly cared for my own kids and grandkids, though. I'm alone now—just thought I might have some usefulness left in me."

Amazingly, supercop seemed satisfied with her answer. Becky would have asked to see some wallet photos. They chatted awhile about formula and schedules, then Becky walked her to the front door, returning with the chair and signs.

"My vote's for the child development student," she volunteered. "She's young and enthusiastic."

"Maybe, but I don't want to come home and find a boyfriend or a party. I think Mrs. Lorenzo will do."

Becky was skeptical, but she couldn't give him any solid reason to reject the older woman. Mrs. Lorenzo looked sensible in her brown tie-up shoes and lavender polyester slacks, and fit enough to handle an energetic baby.

"You're going to hire her just like that? No FBI check, no police lineup?"

"The agency is supposed to screen applicants. Since I need her to start today when I go to work at three, I'll have to trust them on this."

Becky still had some doubts, but it was his decision.

"Thanks for helping," he said.

She picked up Lucy, hugged her, and set her loose after her long confinement in the pen.

"Anytime you need someone for crowd control, just let me know."

THE REST of the day dragged. Becky wasn't looking forward to another cookware party, but Zoe was desperate. She'd gotten a twenty-four-hour flu bug and couldn't do the gig. It was out in the suburb of West Grand Rapids, and Becky's car was obviously malfunctioning again. She only hoped it would get her there and back.

Fortunately she got there and made it home safely, too. As for what had happened between trips, she could only hope to block it out of her memory someday. A flame-haired shrew dominated the party, complaining about the no-stick baking sheet she'd bought at another party. The hostess served stale gingersnaps out of a box, and the cauliflower for Becky's steamed-vegetable demonstration had turned black in spots. She might have made ten dollars.

From outside the Victorian house, she could see Nate's apartment was brightly lit. It was nearly midnight, and his car wasn't parked in his spot. The three-to-eleven shift seemed to work a lot of overtime.

She couldn't help wondering if the new sitter had had trouble getting Lucy to sleep. It was none of her business, but as long as Nate wasn't home, she didn't see any harm in checking on Mrs. Lorenzo.

She knocked softly, but it wasn't the steel-haired sitter who opened the door.

Her landlady stepped out into the hallway and closed the door, but not before Becky got a glimpse of Lucy sitting on the lap of an older woman with silvery-blond hair.

"That so-called baby-sitter came to my apartment— left Lucy all alone while she did," Mrs. Vander Polder fumed. The landlady was wearing a flowered housecoat over her ample form and pink mules on her feet.

"Who's the woman inside?"

"She showed up after the other one—what's her name—talked me into coming down."

"Mrs. Lorenzo."

"That's it. Said she had an emergency, and would I come watch the baby. Well, I wasn't born yesterday. Emergency, my foot! Well, I got the truth out of her. Some sitter! She didn't even have the sense to lock the door!"

"Why did she leave?"

"She got a call from her bookie! Swore she'd never done anything like this before but won some big money and had to collect immediately. Guess it was lucky she bothered to get me."

"Who's the woman in there?"

"Says she's the baby's grandmother, but I stayed anyway, just in case. You never can tell about people."

"That's for sure," Becky had to agree, wanting to throttle Nate for being suckered in by gray hair and oxfords.

What good were his police "instincts" if he hired a woman like Lorenzo? Of course, he had been right when he let Becky go instead of taking her to the police station, so she couldn't be too hard on him.

"I was dozing in front of the TV when that woman came to the door. I like to watch Leno, but darned if I can stay awake most nights. I need my sleep."

Becky got the message. "I'll stay until Nate gets home. You can go, Mrs. Vander Polder. I'm sure he'll be really grateful to you for helping out."

Becky entered Nate's apartment and quietly shut the

door. The woman inside didn't give her a chance to say a word.

"I'm Margaret Dalton, Lucy's grandmother. There's no reason for you to stay. I can just take Lucy to my house. It's only a half-hour drive, and I have a room all set up with a crib for my grandchildren."

"I'm sure Nate will be home any minute. He'll want to see you."

Becky didn't know whether to offer her hand, bow from the waist or run for her life. This woman was mega-intimidating! At least now she knew where Nate—and his sister—got their good looks. His mother had wonderful bone structure: high cheekbones, finely chiseled features and a perfect oval face. Her eyes were a striking blue, and she knew how to dress to emphasize them. Her knit top was a soft periwinkle-blue worn with a white denim skirt. The years had been kind, with only a few fine lines adding character to her face.

"Do you know anything about this missing babysitter?" Nate's mother asked her.

"Only what Mrs. Vander Polder told me."

"How long had she been taking care of Lucy?" She stroked the baby's head lovingly, softening her question somewhat.

"Today was her first day."

"Where did he find her?"

"Through an agency. She had good references."

Not answering was unthinkable. Mrs. Dalton was a pro; her interrogation unnerved Becky, and she was only an innocent bystander.

"Didn't he do a background check himself before hiring her?"

Becky shrugged—mentally, at least. No one had put her in a position like this since she'd seen a couple of boys in her sophomore high school class spray paint a school bus during a football game. She'd told the truth then, even though some kids called her a blabbermouth for the rest of the year.

"He needed someone right away," she defended.

"His father and I got home this morning. Nate knows I wouldn't let jet lag stop me from taking care of my granddaughter. He should have called me instead of trusting a gambling addict."

Freddie had asked Nate in a note and again in a phone message not to tell their mother. What was going on here? Becky wanted out, but Mrs. Dalton made her feel as if she needed permission to leave!

Just then Nate opened the door and stepped into the room. He couldn't have been more welcome if he'd been a knight in battle armor.

"*Mom*—you're back. Becky, what are you doing here?"

"Do you know…about Mrs. Lorenzo?"

"I saw her down at headquarters." He looked decidedly ill at ease. "She and her bookie walked into a sting—illegal gambling. She told me Mrs. Vander Polder was watching Lucy when I threatened to slap a child endangerment charge on her."

"That settles it," his mother said, standing and holding a sleepy Lucy against her shoulder. "Get her things together, Nate. Lucy is coming home with me."

"Freddie left her with me."

Nate was standing his ground, legs apart, hands on his hips. Becky sensed a battle of the titans and wanted out, but he was blocking her escape route.

"I've been over this with your sister before. A baby needs a stable home situation. Your father and I are best able to care for Lucy until Freddie does some growing up."

Mrs. Dalton was trying to use Freddie's absence to get custody of Lucy! The situation suddenly became crystal clear to Becky.

"Mom, I'm keeping Lucy temporarily for Freddie. She's a good mother—after all, she learned from you."

"Do you even know where your sister is now?"

"No, but—"

"You left this child with a criminal!"

"Mother, it was her first offense," Nate said.

"You know Lucy would be safer with me than with a stranger, Nate."

"You're a wonderful grandmother, but this is Freddie's child. Everything concerning Lucy is *her* decision."

"You always did stick up for her, but this time you're wrong. Who will take care of her while you're working?"

"I will," Becky piped up.

She was meddling, interfering, sticking her nose where it didn't belong. But she couldn't stand by and not help Nate.

Now that she had their full attention, Becky suddenly realized she was still wearing the cookware apron Zoe had loaned her. It was yellow polka-dot tulle with Zoe's name and the company logo embroidered in swirly purple flourishes. It was bad enough alone, but she was wearing it over a bright-green cotton-knit tunic with cream-colored tights—Maid Marian cooking for the Sherwood Forest gang!

"Who is this woman?" Mrs. Dalton asked.

Lucy had gotten bored with the discussion and fallen asleep on her grandmother's shoulder.

A jolt of astonishment at Becky's offer made Nate slack-jawed for a moment, but he recovered quickly.

"Mom, this is Rebecca Ryan. My...fiancée."

His mother was too surprised to notice Becky's shocked reaction.

"Isn't this a little sudden?" the older woman asked in a bewildered voice.

If she only knew how sudden!

6

"WHY DID YOU tell your mother we're engaged?" Becky asked as soon as they were alone and Lucy was put to bed.

"Do you think she would have left quietly without Lucy if I'd said, 'This is a woman I met when I nearly arrested her for breaking and entering'?"

"Entering, not breaking!"

"You surprised me by volunteering to take care of Lucy, but my mother came here to rescue her. And when my mother makes up her mind, it takes something major to distract her."

"*Major* is the word—major problem! I know mothers! She'll expect to see a ring. She'll want me to meet your father and the rest of your family. She'll expect to meet my parents. She'll start shopping for a dress for the wedding—that means telling her what kind of ceremony we're planning and when! She'll need to know the color of my bridesmaids' dresses. Oh, brother!"

"All we have to do is stall until Freddie shows up."

"You don't know when that will be."

She had him there. His sister hadn't given him a clue. His only hope was that Freddie would miss the baby so much, she'd be back soon.

"No, I don't," he admitted. "Meanwhile, you did say you'd take care of Lucy."

"Only until my new job starts."

"That's understood. I'll pay you, of course. The standard rate, if that's okay."

"That's the least of my worries now. What are you going to do about our so-called engagement?"

"I guess it will be a short one."

He grinned, at least partly from embarrassment. He'd goofed big time twice in one day. Becky had urged him to go with the college student, but he'd ignored her advice. Now he was waiting for her to rub it in. This wasn't the first time he'd stuck his neck out for his ditzy sister, but the results were certainly the worst. Suddenly he had a fiancée and a baby to take care of, not to mention parents who were probably dancing with joy at the prospect of marrying off their rogue son. Freddie had better have a good reason for getting him into this!

"It's already lasted too long!" Becky insisted, pouting.

She was cute when she was petulant. When her lips were puckered that way, they looked soft and kissable, but this was no time to let his imagination kick into high gear.

"One good thing," he said. "I think my mother is secretly relieved that Lucy will have good care without her having to assume responsibility."

"Remind her of that when I break your heart."

"I'll let her down easy. Maybe your long-lost husband can show up."

"Sure, you can explain how he was trapped in the

belly of a whale until the great beast burped him up on a deserted island in the South Pacific.''

''We'll have to work on our story. Seriously, Becky, I really appreciate your offer to watch Lucy. Freddie and Mom are always at odds. Whatever this is about, it could get sticky if I don't keep the baby. And why are you wearing that yellow thing?''

''It's an apron. A friend talked me into doing cookware parties.'' She untied it and wadded it into a ball. ''It was a fiasco. I hoped to earn some money to repair my car, but my commissions from two parties hardly add up to an oil change. I'd watch Lucy for free because she's adorable, but...''

What a choice! She could make some desperately needed extra money and all she had to do was be in daily contact with the sexy neighbor she was trying to avoid.

''I wouldn't let you.''

''Well, anyway, it's better than asking my father for money. He'd give it to me, but not without a lecture. He'd like to see me settle down with a farmer's son so he can have a bumper crop of grandbabies.''

''Then we have a deal. You're my baby-sitter and temporary fiancée.''

''Only until my new job starts.''

''Agreed.''

''This is only an engagement for convenience,'' she said, frowning with skepticism.

''Of course. We hardly know each other.''

''And that's how I want it to stay. You're not my type.''

''Definitely not—whatever your type is.''

"No playing house."

She knew how to play hardball, but it was okay with him. The last thing he wanted was another entanglement. He had enough trouble with his sister.

"Maybe it would be better if you don't date while our engagement lasts," he suggested.

"What about you? You're more apt to run into someone you know since you grew up in the area."

"I'm not seeing anyone right now."

Considering the men she attracted, he was doing her a favor by taking her out of circulation for a while.

"So, is no dating for either of us part of the deal?" he pressed.

"Okay—why not? There's no danger Josh will ask me out again. Anyway, I need a vacation from the dating rat race."

Exactly his sentiment! He was only thinking of her as a neighbor, of course. He didn't want a lot of traffic in the building where he lived. He especially didn't want to lie awake nights, wondering what was going on in the apartment above his.

"What about your ex-boss? Any chance he'll come around?"

"If I never see Kevin Stalnaker again, it will suit me perfectly."

He couldn't argue with that, but he didn't like the little flicker of relief he felt.

"Now, about our breakup…" he began.

"That's your problem, but *I* get to break up with *you*. I'm not going to be dumped twice in two months, even if it is pretend."

"I'll take the flak, don't worry. Oh, there is one little thing."

"What?"

"We're invited to dinner on Saturday."

"At your parents'?"

"'Fraid so."

"Couldn't you think of an excuse not to go?"

"I was fresh out of fabrications. Anyway, my last bright idea got us engaged."

"True, but how can I have dinner with your mother and father and keep up the charade? They'll ask questions—hard questions."

"That is a problem. They'll both grill us. Dad's a retired cop. Mom can be relentless when she wants to know something. I don't like lying, but the alternative is letting Freddie down and surrendering Lucy to my mother. All we can do is be cool."

"And evasive." She looked as unhappy as he felt.

"I'll take the blame if it comes to that."

When she left, his key in hand, she seemed resigned to the ruse, but he didn't feel any better about it. He was acting like a jerk, involving her in his family's problems. If he could think of a way to backtrack without selling his sister out, he'd feel a lot better. But if she didn't get in touch with him soon, this would all unravel.

He checked on Lucy, glad to see one female who wasn't giving him a hard time at the moment, and envied her innocent sleep. He couldn't stop thinking about the folly of pretending Becky was his fiancée. What if she started to like the idea? What if *he* did?

"No way," he muttered. "Not my type."

Still, he couldn't seem to stop thinking about her.

"I CAN DO THIS," Becky said to Ozzie the next day when it was time to go down to Nate's and baby-sit. "I'll say hello, then he'll leave for work, and Lucy and I will have a great time."

Certainly it was more appealing than the manual she was studying for her new job. Whoever had written it should get The Snoozer Award for the book most likely to put the reader to sleep.

But first she had to dress for failure—as a fiancée, not a sitter. In the drawer reserved for potential cleaning rags, she found a pair of military-green shorts, cast-offs one of her brothers had worn in junior high. They fit her like a potato sack. She completed her ensemble by wearing charcoal anklets with her Keds and a baggy red T-shirt with an Iowa State University logo. Naturally she was wearing a bra; the man with the X-ray eyes couldn't miss that.

The worst thing about reporting for work at two-thirty in the afternoon was stewing over it all morning. She'd compiled all the pros and cons of her "assignment" on a mental seesaw. Good care for Lucy: positive. Seeing Lucy's uncle every day: negative. Money to repair her car: positive. Fake engagement to Nate: negative—no, double negative. Helping a woman she'd met for five minutes: undecided.

What really tipped the scales against getting involved with the Daltons was her firm belief that Nate was another wrong number on her romance hotline. She'd had it with domineering handsome hunks; she didn't want a man who'd take her life and try to mold it to his satisfaction. Better she should settle for a guy like Josh.

"Heaven forbid!"

The truth, now that she admitted it to herself, embarrassed her. She'd tried to like Josh—after all, she'd be seeing him at work—but everything about him was limp: his too pink lower lip, his mousy brown hair, his sweaty handshake, his long, boring stories.

But that didn't make Nate Dalton any less of a threat. He was wrong, wrong, wrong!

And you'd better remember it, she thought on the way down to his apartment.

He was foaming at the mouth when he opened the door.

"Sorry, I'm still shaving," he said, bare-chested with most of his face masked by white lather. "Lucy just went down for her nap."

"Shaving. That would have been my guess," she said, trying to pretend she didn't see his sexy chocolate-brown nipples and the way his biceps bulged even when he wasn't flexing them. Wouldn't it be fun to spray her initials on his chest with shaving cream!

She was losing it! She didn't want to play games with a pretend fiancé. She wanted a warm, loving, funny, sexy, for-real husband, someone just like Nate but without the attitude.

She was glad when he finally left for work.

Conversation with Lucy was limited to a few one-syllable sounds, but the baby sure was a great listener.

"What am I going to do about your uncle?" Becky asked Lucy over strained green beans and pears at dinnertime. "I can't get him out of my mind."

Lucy giggled and a dollop of green mush trickled down her chin.

"You're no help at all, but I adore you anyway."

AS THE WEEK progressed, a routine started to take shape. Mornings weren't difficult. Nate was always in a hurry to get to work. It was the midnight or later homecomings that sapped her resolve not to get emotionally involved with him. He reminded her of a warrior home from battle, a gladiator victorious but drained. She had wild impulses—to cradle his head on her lap, to kiss his droopy eyelids, to cuddle on his lap, or to whisper sweet nothings in his ear.

This was insane! He deserved a kick in the pants for getting her into this engagement charade, not tender loving caresses. She had to build a wall between fantasy and reality, and the *real* Nate was everything she didn't want: macho, bossy, controlling, cocky and too good-looking for her own good. He could be a poster boy for a branch of the armed services; he'd have women lining up to enlist!

Friday night was the worst.

Nate came home, hollow-eyed and visibly drooping. She'd already learned that cops didn't talk much about their work except with brother officers, but he looked as if he'd been flattened by a bulldozer.

"Rough night?" she asked.

"It's a living."

"But you're big and tough. You can handle it."

She should bite her tongue! Now he'd think she wanted him to need her. How many days until she could begin her new job?

"Pretty much so."

He turned the full blast of his neon-blues on her. She felt petty and mean. She had no right to snipe at him.

To her surprise, he laughed.

"Women!" he said. "Let one through the door, and you're expected to bare your soul."

"I was just making small talk," she said, offended by his cavalier attitude. "If you're so supersensitive…"

She headed toward the door, but he was too quick, blocking the entryway so she nearly plowed into him.

"Hey, I'm sorry. You caught me in a foul mood."

She didn't want him to apologize; she wanted to be mad at him. Anger was good! Anger pushed away all the sappy ideas he seemed to generate in her head.

"At least we're not really engaged," she said, at a loss for a snappy comeback.

"You do remember about tomorrow night, don't you?"

"Of course—dinner. I've been dreading it like a root canal."

"My parents are pretty civilized. It won't be too bad."

"I'd rather they were rotten and evil. Then I wouldn't feel bad about lying to them."

"Okay, we'll forget the whole thing. My mother will rush over and demand to take Lucy. If I refuse, she'll never forgive me. If I let her take my niece, the battle with Freddie will heat up. Mom might even seek legal custody on the grounds that Freddie deserted her child. The family will choose sides. Even my dad won't be able to stay neutral."

"You should be writing for the soaps," she said unhappily, feeling trapped and confused.

How could she sort things out when he was standing close enough to steam up her sunglasses, if she was wearing them?

"My family is fairly normal compared to the ones I meet on the job," he said.

"Yeah, I guess."

"Sorry I blew up. Hey, look at me." He cupped her chin and gave her a crooked little grin that should have been outlawed on the grounds that it was mind-altering.

"Time to go," she mumbled without conviction.

"I really owe you a big one for this. I couldn't straighten out this mess without you."

"I'm just the hired help," she said with an uneasy twitter.

"You're more than that."

His lips came to rest on hers, warm and firm and smooth. She could feel his pulse beating where they touched—or maybe it was hers. If this was a thank-you kiss, she wanted to wallow in his gratitude.

She gasped when he put his hands on her shoulders and put pressure on her mouth, kissing her so soundly it would have been rude not to kiss him back just a little. Okay, maybe a lot, but how often did a girl get a world-class smooch?

"Ah—thank you," he said, breaking the kiss to breathe.

"You're—" the words stuck in her throat "—welcome."

"I guess I shouldn't have done that."

"No, probably not," she agreed.

"I shouldn't do this, either."

He wrapped his arms around her, making her feel all mushy and protected, then kissed her so soundly her toes left the floor.

"Even pretend engagements should be sealed with a kiss," he said, releasing her but not moving away.

"You made that up." It was a halfhearted accusation.

"Do you want me to admit I've wanted to do that since I caught you breaking and entering?"

"Just entering!" She backed up and felt for the doorknob behind her. "I have to go."

"I guess so. Thanks...for doing such a good job with Lucy."

They were back on safe ground. She told him a cute baby story and then beat it out the door.

Why couldn't a man and a woman be friends without their hormones kicking in and confusing things? Fortunately, with Nate, that was all it was. She'd had enough lessons on the folly of playing second banana to a male ego. Maybe she had gotten a little buzz from his kisses; it didn't have to mean anything.

BECKY WAS READY on time Saturday evening. Nate had to give her credit for always being prompt. She also scored high on her outfit—a tan cotton skirt, not as short as he'd like but definitely a parent pleaser, and a short-sleeved knit navy top with little white buttons up the front. She was wearing panty hose with her sandals—as if her legs needed improving!

"It's really hot," he said as he settled in the driver's seat after loading Lucy in her car seat in the rear.

"Stifling."

"Storm weather."

"Feels like it."

"I guess that's enough weather talk," he said. "We can find another safe topic."

"Of course. Lots of things we can talk about."

"It's less than an hour's ride unless we get tied up in traffic."

"Shouldn't be heavy at this time on a Saturday."

"Once it took me over two hours. There was a snow-storm."

"Oh, stop it," she said.

"Right, no more weather."

"How are things going at work?"

"Usual cop things."

"There's a conversation stopper if I've ever heard one," she said.

"Sorry."

"I doubt it."

"I've already apologized for kissing you, haven't I?"

"Did you? I've forgotten."

"Liar."

"Just practicing for your parents."

"Nothing to it. We'll eat, chat, leave."

"That middle one bothers me."

"Let me worry for both of us."

"Sure, you're the big, strong he-man. Poor little me will just follow your lead."

"If you like."

How could one pint-size female be so irritating? At

least if his parents saw this side of her, they shouldn't be too shocked when they broke off the engagement.

The rain started before they got there, big sheets whipping across the business loop of the expressway, forcing traffic to a cautious crawl except for a few lead-footed idiots.

"Can we talk about the weather now?" she asked, sounding apprehensive.

"Let's not."

He frowned through the windshield. His mother had a phobia about tornadoes. Her family's home in northern Iowa had been destroyed by one when she was a young girl. She'd probably serve dinner in the basement in case there was a tornado warning.

When they arrived at his parents' house, one door of the attached garage was open with space for his car, so they didn't have to get soaked getting inside.

"There's a good chance of twister sightings west of us nearly to the Minnesota border," his mother announced upon their arrival. "We're sure to have one."

"I've got the radio on," his calm, burly father said. "We'll get plenty of notice if one is headed our way."

Becky and his dad hit it off at dinner and seemed to have a great time challenging him and his mother at darts. It was a game that had to be played in the basement.

The rain subsided, but only temporarily. There were tornado watches until 2:00 a.m., and the prospect of more severe weather seemed like a sure bet.

"You'll have to stay over." His mother said it as a statement of fact.

"That's too much trouble," Becky quickly protested. "We'll leave when the storm seems to be moving away."

"It's no trouble at all. My children and grandchildren stay often, so the guest room is always ready. I can loan you nightclothes, and anything else you might need is in the bathroom."

Nate had been down this road before. Even without Lucy, his mother was too paranoid about big storms to let them leave without a really ugly scene.

"No problem, darling," he said to Becky, surprised at how easily the endearment came. "Lucy's already asleep in the nursery Mom keeps for the grandkids. I'll take the couch in the living room."

"I guess it does make sense not to take the baby out in stormy weather," she said dubiously.

"I won't have Nate trying to fit himself on my short couch," Margaret insisted. "You two can share the guest room. I'm old, but I'm not totally out of it yet."

"That's okay, Mom. The couch is fine."

"No, I'd feel guilty for keeping you two apart. I know you have separate apartments, but when you're practically married..."

"Not exactly..." Becky began, but Nate distracted her by putting his arm around her waist and bumping his hip against her.

"Don't let me keep the rest of you awake," his mother said. "I'll just keep the radio on until the watch is lifted."

"Really nice to meet you, Becky," his father, Joe, said, giving her a bear hug at the bottom of the stairs before they went to bed.

There was no need to ask Dad if he liked his fiancée.

He'd been beaming from ear to ear since they arrived. Nate already dreaded having to tell him when the "engagement" was over.

Nate ushered Becky ahead of him, smiling at the rigid set of her shoulders. He was going to catch hell when that bedroom door closed on them.

"I'm not going to sleep with you!" she whispered angrily as soon as they were alone.

"I don't remember asking you."

"Oh! You know what I mean. You'll have to sleep somewhere else."

"I can't—not until Mom gets the all-clear on the weather news. Believe me, she'll stay up until the watch is over. Don't worry, I'll sleep on the floor."

"I've never heard of a woman insisting her son share a bedroom with a woman!" she wailed.

"It's a shock to me, too, but she really wants us to think she's liberal and understanding. You should take it as a sign of her approval."

"Great."

"We'll pay more attention to weather forecasts before we come here again."

"Again? With a little luck, I can dump you before it's necessary."

Nate used the bathroom first, deciding to sleep in his stiff new jeans rather than making Becky madder by stripping down to his shorts. He used the comforter and one of the pillows to sack out on the floor, and when Becky crawled into bed he was feigning sleep in the far corner of the room.

"At least you don't snore," she said to his back. "Unless you're faking."

He grinned but kept quiet.

7

BECKY TRIED KICKING away the cocoon of cloth that was making her hot, but she still felt trapped. By the time she was fully awake, she realized why. There was enough terry cloth in the borrowed robe she was wearing to stock a health club with towels.

What was she doing here? She remembered, of course, being hustled off to bed in the same room with Nate, but how did she get herself into a mess like this?

At least he doesn't snore, she thought again, glancing at the makeshift bed on the floor, but it wasn't his quiet sleep habits that made the room so still. Just enough light from the streetlamp was filtering through the closed blinds to see that he was gone.

Fine, that was just what she wanted. Nate was sacking out somewhere else. She could go back to sleep. Or could she? Her eyes were wide-open. She couldn't get comfortable in the heavy robe, but tossing it aside and lying under the sheet in her panties did nothing to lull her back to sleep.

Checking to be sure the door was closed all the way, she slipped out of bed and padded barefoot over to the spot where Nate had bedded down. He'd been wearing a wonderful aftershave, and she picked up his pillow, curious whether the scent lingered on it. She buried her face in the cotton percale and inhaled deeply, hugging the pillow against her bare breasts.

And then hugging it some more.

It was too bad they were so wrong for each other. There were worse fates than waking up every morning in the arms of a man who smelled so darn good.

Reality took that moment to intrude. If he came in and found her cuddling his pillow, she'd die of embarrassment! She tried to put it back exactly as he'd left it, even punching it with her fist to make a head indentation.

Suddenly restless, she wondered if fiancées rated kitchen privileges. A glass of milk might induce her to go back to sleep, especially since the luminous face on the bedside clock showed it was only 2:37.

She crept downstairs, just able to see, thanks to a night-light in the bathroom. The living room was dark, but light was coming from the kitchen and family room area. She tiptoed toward it, not really wanting a woman-to-woman encounter if Margaret was still awake. She peered around the corner, hoping a lamp had been left on accidentally.

Nate was sitting in a Boston rocker, holding Lucy in his arms, his head bent as he watched her. Becky saw Nate's mother move toward them from the kitchen, stopping beside the rocker and pressing a kiss first on the baby's forehead, then on Nate's.

"You should be able to put her back to bed now," Margaret said softly.

"Think I will. Night, Mom. You get some sleep. The weather report says this area is all calm now."

"Good night, dear. I'm really glad you decided to sleep over."

Nate rose from the rocker and walked directly toward her. Becky lost her chance to retreat without being seen.

"Becky! Did we wake you?" he asked, shifting the baby to his shoulder without waking her.

"No, I was too warm."

"Come in and talk to another insomniac," Margaret said, clad now in a pale-blue satin robe that softened her face. "You go back to bed, Nate."

He looked a little uncertain for a moment—as well he should, leaving her to carry on the charade by herself. Then he left.

"Once a mother, always a mother, I guess," Margaret said with a smile. "I was just going to get a glass of milk. Would you like something?"

"Milk would be nice, please." Becky was so uneasy being alone with Nate's mother, she would have said yes to a glass of turpentine. Margaret stood by the kitchen counter and filled two tall glasses.

"Come sit for a little while," the older woman said, carrying both drinks to the heavy oak chest that served as a coffee table in front of the brown-and-tan plaid couch in the family room. "I wanted to thank you for taking such good care of Lucy. She adores you."

"I love being with her," Becky said, seating herself in a large brown leather armchair that made her feel like Goldilocks in Papa Bear's chair.

"I realize we've only just met—and under some very odd circumstances—but I know you'll be a wonderful wife for Nate and a wonderful mother when you two decide to have a family.''

"Thank you," Becky managed to say.

She was practically mute with guilt. How could she disappoint this kind, sweet woman by dumping her son? First thing in the morning she was going to tell Nate that he had to be the bad guy. He had to be the one to break the engagement!

Fortunately Margaret was exhausted from her storm watch. She soon said good-night and went to bed.

Creeping slowly up the stairs after she was sure Margaret was in bed, Becky hoped to sneak into the guest room without waking Nate. She'd been touched by his mother's tenderness toward him, but she didn't want to be influenced by it. She had to remember this was only a temporary engagement. It wasn't even for real!

She closed the bedroom door and let her eyes get used to the darkness. She felt tired enough to sleep through a tornado now, but the question was: where?

Nate was sprawled out in the middle of the bed.

"You, sir, are no gentleman," she accused him in a whisper.

He was lying on his back, and his soft snoozing sounds couldn't be fake. Bare to the waist, he had the sheet draped decorously over his bottom half, as though he'd tried to arrange himself in the sexiest possible way without total exposure. Even if she was imagining his intent, she was right on target about the effect.

She was sooo tempted to crawl in beside him. Her cheek ached to feel the tickle of his chest hair. Her head would fit very nicely in the crook of his arm.

"You rat!" she whispered, sure he was trying to

make her miserable. Not only was he hogging the bed, he looked so cuddly and sweet she almost lost it.

Disgruntled and disgusted, she plopped down on the floor and punched his abandoned pillow a few times. This whole situation was getting out of hand. Why couldn't she meet a nice, normal man, date him in the usual way, and get engaged for conventional reasons? First Kevin had exploited her, now Nate had involved her in a bogus engagement. Her initial impression was confirmed. They were both alike: big handsome studs who thought women existed for their convenience. And she'd had just about all she could handle.

Twisting and turning in the bulky robe, she finally curled up, determined to drop off. Nate was sleeping just fine! He didn't seem to see anything wrong with their strange arrangement. He wasn't lying awake, wondering how it would feel to be together for real, her smooth skin pressed against his body, his big hands busy here and there. He was sleeping like a baby!

Darn you, Nate Dalton, she thought unhappily. You're too bossy! You're too macho and full of yourself! I'm not even sure I like you! All I want is my independence. I want to make my own decisions and live my own life.

Wouldn't it be great if she could have all that and still crawl up on his bed!

SHE WOKE UP in a sunny room the next morning with the sound of the shower in the adjacent bathroom drumming in the background.

She allowed a few moments to think of Nate happily soaping down his gorgeous hide, then stood, combed her hair with her fingers, and arranged the borrowed robe into what she hoped were regal folds.

He came into the room a few minutes later, wearing a borrowed chartreuse tank top that was her least favorite color in the world and looking spectacular. Unshaven with his damp hair a rich, dark shade of brown, he had presence. Unfortunately he also had attitude, and he was scowling like a man who'd just swallowed a vinegar-and-lemon-juice cocktail.

"Sorry." He didn't sound it. "I didn't mean to wake you. Use the shower if you like."

"Thanks, I will, but first we have to talk."

"Whenever a woman says that, it means a gripe session."

"I hate it when you do that!"

"Do what?"

"That 'woman' business, lumping all the females in the world into one narrow category. Maybe you've known thousands of women—"

"Not in the Biblical sense."

He smirked, and that irritated her even more.

"May I finish?" She crossed her arms over her chest, making sure the robe was fully closed from her neck to her calves.

"Please do. I'd like to hear your take on this mess we're in."

He moved close, forcing her to look up at him, no doubt another of his clever interrogation techniques.

"A mess you created with your big mouth!"

He shrugged, his open-palmed hands raised innocently at his sides. She wanted to kick him in the shins.

"If it weren't for Lucy, I'd call off this fake engagement this minute," she said.

"You agreed to it. Isn't your verbal assent binding?"

"You're the law enforcement officer. Does it count if we didn't shake hands?"

He did the worst possible thing: he smiled. Until now, she realized, all his good-humored grins had been reserved for Lucy. A sunny, happy Nate was a stranger to her.

"What are you staring at?" he asked, shifting his feet self-consciously.

She shook her head, well aware of how seductive his eyes were when they crinkled with good humor.

"You are so..." he began, stepping toward her even more, too tall for her to see his face without tipping her head back. "Short."

"Short! I'm over five feet tall. That's perfectly normal."

"How much over? An inch?"

"Well, yes, but I have very good posture."

"I can see that."

From where he was standing, probably all he could see was the top of her uncombed head, but she clutched the front of the robe even tighter and backed up, slipping on the pillow on the floor and reaching out to regain her balance.

He was there to steady her, taking both her arms in his hands.

"Careful."

"If I were the cautious type, I wouldn't be in this

mess,'' she grumbled. "I hate having to face your parents again. They're so nice.''

"Yeah, this isn't my proudest hour. I'd like to wring Freddie's neck for putting me in this position. I wish I knew why she was being so darn mysterious. She trusts me with her kid but not with a little information. Well, I'm not ready to have her declared a missing person yet. She called once. Maybe she'll call again soon.''

"If she doesn't...''

He released his grip on her arms and stepped back.

"I can't be responsible for Lucy indefinitely. If I didn't have you to baby-sit...''

"And I won't be available forever. The garden center will open in a couple of weeks. I think we should put a time limit on how long we'll pretend to be engaged.'' She was whispering now, not knowing where his parents were or how thin the walls of the house were. "I don't want to make your sister look bad, but the truth will come out sooner or later.''

"How about officially breaking our engagement when your job starts? I'm not leaving Lucy with another criminal caregiver. I'll have to turn her over to Mom when you can't sit anymore.''

"Sounds reasonable, I guess.''

She wanted it to be over, but he didn't need to sound so enthusiastic about getting his official freedom back. Of course, he wasn't her type, and sexy bods didn't make for good relationships. How well she knew that! She couldn't possibly be feeling hurt because he sounded eager to get rid of her, could she? Becky knew it was only a business arrangement, but wasn't it nat-

ural to feel some emotional attachment when an adorable baby was involved?

"One thing, Dalton. *You* have to dump *me!*"

"We agreed—"

"Oh, no. You gave me the choice. I choose to make
you the bad guy. You explain to your parents why
you'd break up with a great girl like me."

"They aren't going to like it," he said, frowning.

"I don't want your mother to think I'm a flake."

Like you do, she almost added, realizing he still
thought of her as the blue-haired ditz who'd tried to
steal a check from an ex-boyfriend in the middle of the
night.

"If that's what you want, what choice do I have?"
he asked, looking grumpy again.

"None whatsoever."

Unless, of course, he wanted to make the fake engagement real.

As soon as Nate walked into the kitchen, he realized
there wouldn't be a quick getaway. His mother was
working on a big-event breakfast, the kind usually reserved for Christmas or large family reunions. The waf-
fle iron was out, the sink was filled with bowls, and a
pan full of freshly baked muffins was cooling on the
stove top.

"Mom, why are you making such a huge breakfast?
I thought you'd sleep in."

"It's the least I can do for your future wife," she
said, taking crisp bacon strips out of the microwave.
"I certainly wasn't a very good hostess last night."

"Becky understands about your phobia," he said, snatching a slice and nearly burning his fingers.

"You told her I have a phobia? Really, Nate!"

"I didn't use that word." Okay, he did. "Are those blueberry muffins?" he asked, changing the subject.

"Is Becky up?" his mother asked, ignoring his question.

"She's taking a shower."

His mother slapped his hand when he reached for a muffin. Some things never changed.

"Set the table for me. Your father's back is bothering him."

"Has he been going to therapy?"

"Off and on. You know how stubborn he is."

"Yeah."

"He was a captain with only four years to retirement. Why did he take such a big risk?"

Nate just shrugged. His mother was a good cop's wife in most ways, but she was fixated on the idea that his father wouldn't have fallen through rotten planking in a warehouse bust if he'd been more careful.

She wasn't going to like it when he called off his fake engagement. Not one bit. But he didn't have to live with his mother anymore; a wife could be a whole lot bigger problem. Probably two-thirds of the guys on the force had divorced at least once—some several times. Given his weakness for helpless, dependent types like Becky—he meant Margo—it was a good thing he didn't have any marriage plans.

Breakfast lasted a long time, and he didn't need the food. Since he'd taken responsibility for Lucy, he'd put on three pounds, mainly because he didn't have time to run.

His mother kept pouring more tea as an excuse to linger at the table, and Becky cozily chatted away as though she wanted nothing more than to get better acquainted with her future mother-in-law. His father read the morning paper at the table and talked baseball with him, but Nate couldn't work up any interest in the spotty win record of the Cubs.

Yep, he was going to look like a big jerk when he broke off the engagement. By this time tomorrow every relative from Grundy Center to Dubuque would start looking for a wedding invitation, and his mother would flip when she had to explain to a legion of close and distant connections on both sides why it was off.

"Don't forget about the tickets to that shindig of yours next Saturday," his father said, interrupting the female tête-à-tête about using children in weddings. His mother was just relating to Becky how Freddie had held up one of their aunts' weddings when she was a flower girl. She'd insisted on scattering rose petals down the aisle one petal at a time.

"That's right," his mother said. "The hospital fund-raiser."

"With this back of mine, there's no way I'm going."

Funny how his father's back acted up when he wanted to duck out of doing something.

"This works out perfectly. Nate, you and Becky can use our tickets. I'm not the cochair this year, so I don't have to be there."

"Mom, I don't think—"

"I'll baby-sit Lucy. You'll have a wonderful time."

In his opinion, mingling with his mother's social set was almost as entertaining as Thanksgiving dinner at the county jail. Add to that a barrage of congratulations from her marriage-happy friends, and it was an evening meant to be avoided.

"Thank you, but we really couldn't take your tickets," Becky said.

He caught a look of dismay on Becky's face and decided to watch her squirm for a while.

"You'd be doing us a big favor," Margaret said. "You see, whatever the ball raises on tickets will be matched by the Reinhart Corporation, but the tickets have to be signed and turned in at the door to count in the final tally. Not the way I would have done it, but I wasn't on the fund-raising committee this year."

"Thanks for small favors," his father said under his breath.

"Oh, I'm really sorry, but we're busy next weekend," Becky insisted, giving Nate a look that screamed for backup.

Since she was going to make him look bad when they broke up, maybe she deserved a hard time before they called it quits.

"I don't think there's anything we can't reschedule," he said, enjoying the baffled look on her face.

"But, Nate, our friends…"

Considering their only mutual acquaintances were Lucy, the landlady and a criminal nanny, she was on shaky ground.

What the heck! It might be worth putting on a monkey suit for an hour or two to see Becky in some hot little evening dress.

"Don't you have to work next weekend?" She was making a last-ditch stand, and he was loving it.

"Nope. We'll go. I'll dust off my old wedding tux—I've been a best man nine times, did I tell you, honey? Finally got smart and bought the blasted thing."

"It's not black-tie," his mother said, fortunately not noticing Becky's stricken look. "It's a costume affair."

"Costume?" he asked. The joke was over.

"You won't be able to wear your father's outfit. He's put on too much weight around the middle. And I planned to be Martha Washington, not at all right for a pretty young woman. I know how busy you are, so I'll go to that costume shop over on Hutchins Street and pick out something for both of you. You can change here when you drop Lucy off."

His father gave Nate a smug nod; he'd gotten out of going. His mother beamed, and what could he do? He might as well go along with her little scheme. She wasn't going to be a proud mama when he dumped his golden-haired fiancée.

For that matter, he wouldn't be too happy, either.

8

"WOMEN GET ACCUSED of talking too much, but you're the one with the big mouth!" Becky said as they pulled into his parents' driveway the evening of the costume ball. "I can't believe I'm doing this."

"Haven't we had this conversation already? I offered to cancel." Nate handed the baby to Becky, then hefted the car seat under one arm and grabbed the well-stocked diaper bag with his free hand.

"I hope your mother rented a gorilla costume for you."

"She wouldn't. She thinks I'm cute."

"Maybe thirty years ago you were. How old are you, anyway? We're engaged, and we haven't even exchanged vital statistics."

"I was thirty-two on February tenth. Six foot two, 183 pounds before I became a nanny—this baby-sitting puts on the flab. I haven't seen or played a sport I don't like, and my favorite color is red."

"I guess that's as much as I want to hear." She wouldn't give him the satisfaction of knowing she was interested or that she didn't see an ounce of excess fat on his lean midsection.

"And you?"

"You've already pointed out that I'm short. I weigh less than you, and I'll be twenty-six August fourth."

"You're just a child—I'm practically robbing the cradle. What else?"

"Favorite color, blue." She only said that because his baby-blues gave her shivers. "Favorite sport, badminton."

"Badminton? I've never met anyone who played badminton."

"We had a net at the farm. It was the only game where I could beat my brothers."

"I'd like to hear more, but I see Mom waiting for us in the window. Smile and pretend you're thrilled to be going on a date with her fair-haired son."

"This isn't a date!" she said, pretending she was talking to Lucy.

"Of course, it is. I plan to open car doors, give you my arm, and kiss you good-night."

"You wouldn't!"

"You don't want me to open doors for you?"

"Not the door part! Oh, you're impossible."

"I think you mean irresistible."

Margaret was so excited, you'd think she was going to the ball herself, Becky thought as they exchanged cordial greetings. Darn, she wished Nate's mother was nasty and unpleasant. Being treated like a future crown princess made her feel like a real criminal.

"Your costumes are up in the bedroom. There wasn't a whole lot left to choose from, especially in Nate's size, but I'm pleased with them. Lucy and Granddad and I will have a wonderful time, so you two go on home afterward. We'll keep Lucy until tomorrow afternoon and bring her to your place. That way you can sleep late after your big night.''

Becky could swear she heard Nate snort. As far as she was concerned, they'd turn in their tickets and leave. She was grateful they wouldn't have to come back and report to his mother.

"The theme of the ball is A Thousand and One Desert Nights," Nate's mother called after them as they went upstairs.

The costumes were lying side by side on the bed like two giant paper doll outfits. Nate swore when he saw them. Becky was speechless. She was supposed to go as a harem girl; his belonged on someone who lived in a lantern.

"They don't fit," he said gruffly.

"We haven't tried them."

"I'm already sure mine won't fit."

He picked up an emerald vest resplendent with faux glass jewels.

"At least you have a shirt," she pointed out. "Part of my costume seems to be missing."

"Yeah, you need a jewel for your belly button." He picked up her harem pants and held them to the light. "Transparent. I kind of like these."

"I can't wear them!"

Nate picked up a wicked-looking saber and lunged playfully at her, resting the point between her breasts.

"You're my prisoner. Put on that costume or I'll run you through."

"Rubber," she said, pushing the sword away. "Some little boy could have a lot of fun.

"All right, I'll put on the costume, but only if you

wear each and every part of yours.'' She picked up a
fake gold armband and spied him through it. ''If you're
not too chicken, that is.''

''Trying to goad me, are you? It won't work.''

''You are too chicken! You're afraid of looking
silly.''

He grumbled; she had him.

''Well, I'm going into the bathroom to get dressed,''
she said. ''If you're not changed when I come out, you
can tell your mother we're not going because one of
us doesn't have enough nerve to wear *his* costume.''

''My mother rented the wrong costume for you. She
should've gotten something with a pointed hat and a
broomstick.''

She raised her chin and scooped up all the parts of
her costume, including jeweled slippers and a flowing
see-through veil attached to a small hat.

''We don't want to disappoint her,'' she said before
locking herself in the bathroom.

She couldn't believe her future mother-in-law—
oops, Freudian slip—had picked out the teeny purple
bikini panties and billowing transparent slave-girl trousers. The halter top was skimpy, too, a pseudovest in
bright-blue velvet heavy with glass jewels. Her little
cap was gold with the veil sewed on to cover the lower
half of her face. All she needed was a bottle, and she
could star in a sitcom revival. As if she didn't feel
conspicuous enough, the waist of the trousers ended
well below her navel, and no amount of tugging could
bring it higher.

It was fun teasing Nate in the privacy of the bedroom, but she wasn't sure she had enough nerve to walk into a public gathering in this getup.

Nate's reaction was emphatically reassuring.

"I don't believe it. You look terrific!"

"You're not half bad yourself."

He was substantially less exposed than she was. His trousers fitted comfortably around his waist and were opaque yellow satin. On the plus side, most of the material in the filmy white shirt was in the puffy sleeves; the front was an open slash down to his waist with his brawny chest beautifully displayed. His emerald-green vest was stiff with gold trim and jewels and looked too snug for comfort, but it set off his broad shoulders and slender waist almost too well. Women would be lining up to dance with this giant genie.

"I look ridiculous," he said.

"You may feel ridiculous, but I'm sure a lot of women would like to rub a magic lantern and have you pop out."

"Flattery won't get me out in public in this outfit."

"What if I said, 'Please don't disappoint your mother by not going after she went to so much trouble for us'?"

"I guess I owe her that much, considering what a louse I'm going to be when I dump you."

"Well put. Let's go."

"Just to turn in the tickets," he insisted.

"We have to be seen. It sounds like your mother's friends will be out in force."

"I like you least when you're right," he admitted glumly. "Let's get it over with."

After surviving Margaret's gushing admiration upon

seeing them in their harem wear, they left the suburban sprawl behind and drove to the country club. Becky was impressed by the well-watered fairways and greens behind the building, although, farmer's daughter that she was, she thought the water would be better used to grow corn and soybeans. The clubhouse sprawled at the end of a curved road just beyond impressive stone gates. The long hours of summer daylight made it possible to see the tan brick facade and the not-quite-matching wooden siding. Becky wished it was dark—midnight-dark with a power failure for good measure—so her costume couldn't be seen.

"Want me to drop you off at the entrance before I park?" Nate asked.

"Don't you dare! I'm not standing in plain sight under the searchlights they have beamed on the door. Besides, you might abandon me."

"I wouldn't do that. I'll be right beside you—if you're nice."

"Why do *I* have to be nice? This is all your fault!"

"My fault! I think if you dig a little deeper, you'll come up with the real culprit."

"Your sister," she admitted. "I may never answer the door again."

"I'm glad you did. For Lucy's sake," he quickly added.

When they got inside, the ticket taking was being supervised by a blue-haired woman who personally had to witness their signatures on the tickets, even though four other volunteers were hovering around her, looking for something to do. The guests waiting to enter all seemed to know each other, and Becky felt like the guest of honor at an Aztec sacrifice. She was sure a plump woman in a Cleopatra costume with a black wig loathed her because her husband, a knobby-kneed Caesar—or maybe Marc Antony—was leering. She wanted to loudly proclaim that the costume was all her future mother-in-law's fault, but instead she squared her shoulders and put her hand in the crook of Nate's arm.

He looked surprised and grinned at her.

At least the golden glow in the main ballroom was better than the stark white neons in the entryway. The muted lights were covered with dark-yellow gels, apparently to simulate desert sun. Big cutouts of palaces and minarets, inspired by Hollywood versions of the Arabian Nights, stood along the walls, and long strands of beads hung over the band's raised platform. They were playing elevator music, but no one was dancing yet.

"It looks like we won't win the prize for the silliest costume," Nate said, grinning at a woman with a wig of limp cotton snakes. "Isn't she the one who supposedly turned men to stone?"

"Yes, Medusa. But only if they looked at her."

"Guess I'd rather look at you," he teased.

"Eyes forward," she warned, though she liked the way he was studying the more intriguing details of her costume. The evening wasn't wasted if she could heat him up just a little—not that anything could possibly come of it, even though she *did* enjoy seeing him in his sexy get-up.

Nate's mother was one of the few who thought the desert theme called for outfits straight out of an Arabian fairy tale. Cowboy seemed to be the costume of choice for a lot of men, probably because they could wear their own jeans. Some women went along with the western theme and wore everything from short fringed skirts to calico gowns. Becky's favorite was a sunflower with legs; her partner was either a raccoon or a rat—the latter, judging by the way he gave Becky The Look.

She was separated from Nate when a dragon lady in a mandarin costume cornered him. Circulating in a crowd of strangers wearing half a costume was Becky's idea of purgatory, so she drifted toward the refreshment tables which offered a cash bar at one end and a huge spread of finger foods at the other. She wasn't hungry for stuffed grape leaves or lobster puffs, but she'd love a cup of punch to occupy her hands.

The serious eating hadn't started, but a knight in a cardboard-and-tin suit of armor was trying to set a record for the most appetizers ever piled on a single disposable plate. Beside him, Guinevere tried to snatch tidbits from his plate, manage her long train, and keep her pointed hat from falling off.

Oh, no! Becky recognized that velvet-covered rear. Worse, she knew the tin man stuffing whole grape leaves into his mouth. What was Kevin doing at a function like this? With Courtney!

Her first instinct was to disappear. So was her second.

Nate picked that moment to sweep down on her, rubber saber flapping at his side.

"We might as well eat as long as we're here," he said.

"I'm not hungry!" She grabbed his arm and tried to steer him away from the table.

His feet were firmly planted, and it would have been easier to tug a locomotive off its tracks.

"Mom will want a report on the food. She swayed the committee to pick the caterer."

"Maybe a little later!"

Too late!

"Becky, what are you doing here?" Kevin called over. He clunked toward her, taking the plate but leaving Courtney behind.

"Who's that?" Nate asked.

"Kevin Stalnaker." She hated admitting it.

"Ah."

"What do you mean 'ah'?"

"Stalnaker," Nate said, stepping closer to him. "I've been wanting to meet you." He stuck out his hand, forcing Kevin to do a juggling act with the plate and his cardboard shield.

"You have?"

Kevin looked at Becky for a clue; Courtney waddled over to them, ogling Nate.

"Nate Dalton," he said, introducing himself. "Becky's told me a lot about you. I owe you for bringing us together."

"How's that?" Kevin was a great conversationalist—if fertilizer was the topic.

"Nate is just kidding," Becky quickly said.

"I'm her fiancé," Nate volunteered.

"Oh."

This was going too far!

"Why are *you* here, Kevin?" Becky asked.

No point in being subtle with her ex-boyfriend.

"One of my customers had tickets and couldn't go, so he gave them to me. Did you say engaged?"

He looked at her, taking in her skimpy costume or, rather, all the parts it didn't conceal. Was that a fleeting look of regret on his face? Nah, couldn't be! She had to get into some real clothes!

"I'm Courtney."

"Hello, Courtney," she heard Nate respond.

Courtney's cleavage was reminiscent of watermelon breasts covered with a sheen of perspiration. Only she would wear fifty pounds of heavy velvet to a summer party.

Becky expected Nate to gape. Instead he slipped his arm protectively around her waist, hugging her close as he made inane chitchat with Kevin.

Men had a special language. They could talk to each other any time in any circumstances, as long as some team somewhere had done something in the last few days.

"Kev, honey, I'm really hungry," Courtney whined. "I'm dying to try those little round puffy things."

Kevin ignored her. He was talking to Nate, but weighing his chances of getting into Becky's good graces again; she knew that look only too well! What had she ever seen in him? She was embarrassed she'd ever been taken in by him and regretted Nate had met him. This costume ball was a disaster beyond her worst fears.

"Her fiancé?" Finally Kevin got the message.

Courtney said she had to have a drink from the cash bar.

"That's right," Nate said, hugging Becky against his side. "Her fiancé."

All men were naturally competitive; Nate was only marking his territory, never mind that she wasn't his to stake out. But darn, it felt good to have him on her side, rousting Kevin and sending him on his way, disgruntled and rejected.

"I told you that suit would make a racket," Courtney said as Kevin clunked away by her side.

"People are starting to dance," Nate said, leading Becky toward the music without mentioning food again.

He didn't say a word about Kevin, and there was so much he could have ridiculed.

"You really do look terrific in that costume," he said, drawing her into his arms to dance.

He was a foot taller than she was. They should have made a lousy dance team, but they didn't. He had natural rhythm; she loved to follow a man who moved with the music. He didn't try to dance cheek to cheek, all hunched over the way some tall men did, and the fingers that held hers were gently seductive, caressing between her fingers, thumbing her wrist, stroking nothing but her hand and arm but sending pleasurable shivers throughout her body. As for his hand on her bare waist, his fingers slid lower, toying with the elastic that held up her low-slung trousers.

"It's not such a bad party," he said in a dreamy tone she'd never heard him use before.

"No, not so bad."

One finger breached the elastic boundary and tickled the hollow below her spine. This shouldn't be happening on a dance floor. It especially shouldn't be happening with Nate!

"You're naughty," she whispered, more playful than reproachful.

He backed her into a dark corner, deserting the dance floor and the milling crowd.

"I try."

"Nate, what are you doing?"

"I thought it was obvious."

He covered her mouth with his and oh-so-gently drew her lips between his.

This was more than kissing! He was branding her mouth; she felt light-headed, giddy. She was kissing him back, their chins meshing, his lashes flicking against her eyelids, his breath warm on the curve of her cheek.

"I didn't intend to do that." He straightened and stepped back.

"I didn't intend to let you."

"You made a decision about something I hadn't done yet?"

"You're a man. It was always a possibility."

"You hoped I'd kiss you."

"No, of course not!"

"But it wasn't bad, was it?"

"Do you always ask your dates to rate your kisses?"

"Are you my date?"

"We're here in a social setting. What would you call me?"

"I told Kevin you're my fiancée."

"He didn't much like it, did he?" She giggled. Suddenly everything seemed terribly amusing.

"I wanted to boot him where his tin cans didn't cover, but I guess Courtney is punishment enough," Nate said.

"I had a lucky escape."

His hand was locked around hers. It felt right, but she didn't know when it had happened.

"Guess we can leave now. We've put in an appearance," he said, dropping her hand but still keeping her cornered.

"Yes, there's no reason to stay."

"Courtney was holding her breath to make her bust look bigger for my benefit."

"She wasn't!" Becky pushed at his chest with the flat of her hand. It was warm and fuzzy; she pushed again.

"Let's go." He linked her fingers with his again.

"WE FORGOT TO EAT," Becky said in the car when Nate left the rural setting behind and approached the outskirts of the city.

"Courtney zapped my appetite," he lied, knowing his mind had been too full of Becky to care about food.

Damn that costume! Why had his mother, of all people, chosen to send Becky out in public half-naked? It was almost as if his mother wanted to give him extra incentive to go through with the wedding. Why did she think his libido needed a boost? Sometimes that woman was clairvoyant!

"I guess we could stop at a restaurant for dinner," he offered halfheartedly.

"In these costumes? We look like a nightclub act that bombed."

"Well put," he said dryly.

"I know what. I'd love a chili dog and a giant lime Slushee. You could run into a Quiki Mart. Their food isn't half bad."

"And you could stay hidden in the car."

"Well, there is that," she admitted with a grin. "At least you're not wearing see-through pantaloons."

"If more women looked like you do in them, they'd become the latest fashion rage."

"I believe you just gave me a compliment, kind sir. At least I'll take it as one."

Maybe a chili dog with onions was just the thing to cut down his frustration level. He might get indigestion, but that was better than having the hots for a pint-size siren who looked like she lived in a bottle.

"Tell you what," he offered. "If you'll go into the convenience store, I'll grant you three wishes."

"Wow! I could have fun with that. I could have you jog twice around Butterfield Park in leopard-print bikini underwear, then—"

"I was thinking along the lines of washing your car or doing your laundry."

"My laundry! I don't think so."

"Guess I'll have to go in myself."

At least he'd tossed the saber on the back seat. He looked ridiculous enough without that rubber thing slapping against his leg.

He spotted a Quiki Mart with only a couple of vehicles parked between the gas pumps and the store. He could be in and out in three minutes. If he gave some bored clerk a laugh, it wasn't a big deal.

The pickup truck packed with kids pulled away, leaving the place practically deserted.

The time was ripe to move.

"Look, what is that woman doing?" Becky asked, pointing at the remaining vehicle. "She's pounding on the window of that compact as if she's trying to break in."

"Stay in the car," he cautioned her, coming to a stop and jumping out.

She listened like his sister; the door on her side slammed shut an instant after his.

"I can't get into my car!" the woman called out hysterically. "My little boy is in there!"

"Did you lock your keys inside?" Nate asked, hurrying over to assess the situation.

"I popped the trunk and tossed them on the dash while I loaded my bags."

The woman pounded on the driver's side window again, her face close to the glass. "Open the door, Andy! You're too young to drive!"

Nate peered in at a self-satisfied little squirt energetically trying to turn the locked wheel of the car.

"How old is he?" Becky asked, standing beside Nate's elbow.

"Three," his mother said. "Do you know how to open the door?"

"Not without a tool," Nate said. "Can't you talk him into opening the door?"

"I've been trying! He always says he wants to drive. He managed to unbuckle his car seat and crawl into the front. He locked me out before I got the trunk closed. I'm too old to be the mother of a three-year-old!''

She banged on the window again, pressing her face frantically against the window. "You're in so much trouble, Andrew Harrison Matthews! I'd better call the police!"

"I'm a police officer, ma'am," Nate said, ignoring her skeptical glance at his costume.

"I've heard of going undercover, but you're dressed like a cartoon character. Maybe I should call a real policeman."

"In a situation like this where the motor isn't running, you have to call a locksmith," Nate explained.

"Is your son capable of putting the key in the ignition?" Becky asked.

"He hasn't noticed my keys yet, but I wouldn't put it past him. He took my vacuum cleaner apart last week and hid all the parts," she said wearily.

"Nate, do something!" Becky insisted.

He rapped on the window to get the little guy's attention, but the towheaded kid was too busy trying to turn the wheel.

When this kid was sixteen, Lucy might go for him. The thought was scary! He made a mental note. If he ever had a daughter, he'd keep her in an isolated cabin until she was thirty!

"We'll watch him," Becky reassured the woman. "You'd better call a locksmith."

"My husband is going to have a fit!" she said, but she scurried into the convenience store to make the call.

"One good thing," Nate said, pointing to the interior. "The car has handles to roll down the window. If we can get the little pip to roll one down just enough to get a hand in..."

"I'll run and ask his mother what would tempt him to open up."

She hurried toward the store, and he wasn't so concerned about the kid that he didn't notice the enticing wiggle of her bottom through the harem pants. She hadn't hesitated about going inside when a child's safety was involved. He liked that.

When she came back, she was laden with goodies: a frozen slush, a big cookie and a car magazine.

"A car magazine?" Nate asked.

"He loves his big brother's car magazines, according to his mom."

Becky tried the cookie first but all she got was a wicked little grin. The slush and the magazine didn't entice him to roll down the window, either. She tried tapping the cookie on the glass, but he was more interested in the ring of keys on the dash. He obviously wanted them, but couldn't reach them without leaving his position of glory in the driver's seat.

"Quick, dangle your keys at the window," Becky told Nate.

He shook the ring, making the keys dance against the glass. Little Andy was definitely interested. One chubby little fist reached for the handle, and Becky was there to slip her slender arm into the opening as soon as he managed to lower the window a few inches.

After Becky managed to unlock and open the door, Nate scooped the future race car driver off the seat and into his mother's waiting arms.

"Andy, you're so naughty! Don't ever lock me out again!" his mother said, hugging and reprimanding at the same time. "I'm so grateful to both of you! What can I do to repay you?"

"I'd like the Slushee, please," Becky said. "This rescue business is thirsty work."

"I wouldn't mind the cookie," Nate said a little sheepishly.

It took almost longer to get away from the mother's effusive thanks as it had to rescue her son. As soon as he could, Nate ran inside for chili dogs, daring the amused clerk to comment on his costume with narrowed eyes. He could be intimidating when he wanted to; it was a job asset.

They wolfed the dogs in the car. He'd bought five, and they ate every last bite and laughed at themselves for being piggish.

He hadn't had this much fun in a long time. Too bad they were all wrong for each other. Like oil and water...

When they got home, Nate was still keyed up and not ready to call it a night. He toyed with the idea of going for a run, but he was too full.

"You don't have to walk me up," she said when he started to follow her to her door.

"You were a big help tonight. Maybe I can do something to even the score—change a lightbulb or something," he suggested.

She was climbing the stairs ahead of him, the see-through trousers torturing him to no end. It was time to say good-night, his saner self warned, but her hot little body in that outfit had been making him feverish all evening. What harm could there be in one quick good-night kiss?

By now she had her door open, and it was easy to slip in behind her and ease it shut with his foot while she reached for the light switch on the wall. When the dim bulb in the entryway came on, they were so close he could see a minuscule speck of chili on one of the faux gemstones on her vest.

"You spilled," he said, pointing at the glass bauble with his index finger, then moving it up to brush her lips when she inclined her head to look.

Their lips came together as if they were magnetized. It was good—supergood. Her breathing hammered in his ears, and he knew this was what he'd wanted—needed—all evening. She stepped lightly onto the tops of his feet and melted against him, molding her curves to his body and pressing against his erection until he felt ready to explode.

He scooped her into his arms and carried her with their lips locked together into the bedroom. This wasn't rational. He wasn't prepared, and he was making a major mistake. But he wanted her naked and panting and crying out under him. He wanted her, period.

Her arms were around his neck, her tongue returning his thrusts. He was poised to lay her gently on the bed and straddle her luscious form when a flying ball of fur dashed between his legs and knocked him off balance. He tripped forward onto the bed, bouncing Becky on her back and landing with his chin poking her stomach.

"That damn cat!" he said, trying to scramble into

some semblance of a dignified position. "I nearly broke my leg!"

"Ozzie, bad cat!" Becky scolded, her giggles taking the sting out of her reprimand. "Are you okay?"

"Just what I was going to ask you," he said, his voice ragged.

"I'm fine."

"Yeah, me too."

He stood, glared at the cat who was challenging him from the doorway, and realized their unceremonious flop on the bed had cooled him down enough to think rationally.

"I wanted to…"

He couldn't say what he was thinking. He wanted to make love to her. It was the best and the worst thing that could happen between them.

"Me, too," she said.

"But I guess…"

"Yeah, we owe Ozzie."

"Of course, there's no reason why we shouldn't— we are consenting adults," he mumbled.

"Engaged, too," she said, pulling up her knees and resting her chin on them, studying the one slipper still on her foot.

That was the problem. They couldn't enjoy a little recreational sex when they were engaged. She might start believing she was really his fiancée. Their breakup could get very sticky.

Not only that, he could get her pregnant. He'd been disappointed in Freddie for conceiving a child without any commitment from the guy. Nate was older than his sister and should know better, but he'd been about to risk making the same mistake she had.

"I guess this is a good time to say good-night," Becky said as if reading his mind—or his face.

"Yeah, well, good night."

The cat followed him to the door.

Becky didn't.

"Blasted cat," he groused under his breath.

9

"WHY DID I let it happen—almost happen?"

Nate was gone. Becky sat on the bed, talking to her feline companion and hugging her fat bed pillow, trying to make sense of what had just happened—almost happened.

Ozzie jumped up beside her and presented his soft underbelly for some tender stroking.

"A lot you know about it, cat," Becky complained, obliging him with some petting. "You don't have to fool around with all this complicated boy-girl stuff. I know, you didn't choose to be neutered, poor boy, but love isn't one long romantic high, you know."

Love! Why was she thinking about love? She wasn't going to hand over her heart to another man, not for a long time—and certainly not to that cocky cop!

She tossed the jeweled halter on the floor, kicked off the remaining slipper, and fell asleep in the harem trousers.

MONDAY BEGAN a new week and a new arrangement. Nate started working days, beginning his job at the inhuman hour of 7:00 a.m. and getting home in late afternoon. His early departures meant neither of them had the time nor inclination for chitchat. When he got home, she made it a point to escape up to her own place with the speed of light.

Soon her career as a nanny would be over. She was looking forward to working in panty hose instead of spinach-stained T-shirts. Sure, she'd miss Lucy, but it would be a relief to end the pretend engagement with Nate.

His mom called more often than hers did, and both her parents were sure she couldn't get through a week without some down-home advice.

"Have you spoken to your mother about lunch, dear?" Margaret asked as Becky held the phone with her shoulder and wrestled Lucy into a dry diaper. "I thought we could meet halfway in that wonderful little tea room I told you about. It's in a converted post office, and the gift shop alone is worth the trip. She doesn't mind driving, does she?"

"No, not at all. We can set a time as soon as she gets back from my brother's. She's helping out because my sister-in-law just had a baby."

Her mother was, fortunately, off doing a stint as grandma-in-residence. Otherwise Margaret surely would have called her for a little get-acquainted talk over the phone.

Becky hated the elaborate network of deceit. Why was she going along with it? she wondered, and not for the first time. Maybe Freddie was an unfit mother and deserved to lose her adorable baby. Maybe Margaret would do a better job of raising Lucy. Nate told her his sister had called again, but nothing Freddie said explained her long absence.

"You're just hired help," Becky reminded herself,

transferring another load of baby clothes from the washer to the dryer.

At least she'd restrained herself from doing Nate's laundry. She was a temporary nanny. Nothing more! The fact that he hadn't mentioned their feline interruptus encounter made that painfully apparent. And she'd stick her tongue in the garbage disposal before she'd bring it up first.

It was nearly four o'clock, and theoretically Nate should be home. Was he working overtime or having a beer with the boys?

Good grief! She was thinking like a wife! And she didn't plan to be the kind of spouse who expected an accounting of every minute of her husband's day.

No wonder Nate didn't worry about being late. He knew her social life was on hold, and it had little to do with their agreement not to date during their bogus engagement. Her phone was mute witness to her lagging social life of late. Zoe wanted to change that. She wanted Becky to go on a blind date that Saturday with her boyfriend's cousin, but Becky wasn't tempted.

"He wouldn't be bad-looking," Zoe had told her with scary honesty, "if he'd have one tiny mole removed from his upper lip and buy some sharp-looking gold-framed glasses instead of wearing heavy black plastic things. Those are details you can work on, if you like him."

Ha! She'd much rather spend an evening with Cary Grant. She could check out one of his movies at the video library and watch it with Ozzie. Where else would she find a witty, suave, urbane, sophisticated, considerate man?

She wished Nate would get his cute little butt home on time for a change, but not because she had any interest in how he spent his off hours. She'd just like a chance to do a few things for herself. After eight or nine hours of playing with Lucy, feeding, bathing, changing, rocking and generally riding herd on her, Becky was pooped. Not that any one thing she did was hard work; it was just the constant vigilance that wore her down. When that girl walked, make way for Hurricane Lucy!

The buzzer sounded, so Becky propped the baby on her hip and went to the outer door. Nate never forgot his key, and Becky sincerely hoped Margaret wasn't making a surprise visit. She eyeballed the peephole— something she conscientiously did now that she was responsible for Lucy's safety. A frizzy-haired blonde was just giving the buzzer another impatient punch. She was almost as young as Freddie, but unfortunately this wasn't the missing mother. Becky opened the door.

"Hi, I'm Margo. Did I push the wrong button?"

Becky had heard the term sex kitten, but this lively embodiment was the first she'd had the misfortune to encounter. Her breasts—could they possibly be real?— were poured into a shimmering violet dress, if something that ended at the panty line could be called a dress. Her face was all lips, big pouty ones plastered with purple lip gloss. Odds were *she* never sat home alone on Saturday night.

"Not if you're looking for Nate Dalton," Becky replied sweetly, in no hurry to explain what she was doing in his home with a baby.

"Well, who are you?"

Nothing subtle about grape-lips.

"A friend." She nearly said his fiancée, but she wanted a little more information first. This could be a friend of Freddie's with news.

"I'm Margo, an old, old friend." She actually purred, setting Becky's teeth on edge. "I'll bet that's Nate's niece."

She poked the fat under Lucy's chin with one silver-nailed finger. Lucy did not appreciate it. The baby retaliated with a large glob of drool that sent the visitor searching in her trendy little shoulder bag for tissues to dry her hand.

"I'm in town visiting, so naturally I thought of Nate. We were really close."

If this bimbo thought she could make Becky crazy-jealous, she'd better do her homework.

"He isn't in residence at this time," she said in her best imitation of a high-class butler.

"When will he be back?"

Like I'd tell you! Becky wanted to say. What was wrong with her? Just because Lucy had refused to nap, pulled over a table lamp and smeared strained carrots in her hair didn't give her a right to be rude to Nate's old friend—if Margo really was a friend.

"He's still at work, I guess," she said just as the man himself pulled into the drive.

"Oh, wonderful, here he is!" Margo obviously recognized his car.

Becky retreated to Nate's apartment, telling herself she wasn't interested in witnessing a big reunion scene.

It was several minutes before he entered the apartment with his visitor. Becky was on her hands and knees trying to get the carrot-faced doll that was wedged under the couch, while Lucy chomped on the latest TV-listings magazine. Becky scampered to her feet, feeling as exposed as someone who'd just mooned a football crowd.

"This is my neighbor, Becky," Nate said offhandedly to Margo. "She's baby-sitting while I have Lucy."

Margo nodded at her. Becky nodded back. Exactly what had happened to her fiancée status?

"Becky, could you possible stay a little longer—if you don't have any plans, that is. Margo is meeting a cop buddy of mine for dinner. They just started dating and want me to join them just to show I don't have any hard feelings about them getting together. I don't want to be a poor sport."

"I don't have plans."

"Wait, you could come with us," he suggested magnanimously, "if we had a sitter."

"I *am* the sitter," she reminded him.

To his credit, he looked sheepish.

"Listen, I'm going to take Lucy to my apartment since I have things to do, but you have a nice time," Becky said, scooping up Lucy and her always-ready diaper bag, making what she hoped was a dignified if indignant exit.

MIRACULOUSLY, Lucy ate her dinner with a minimum of mess and conked out on a quilt in Becky's living room shortly afterward, the carrot-headed doll firmly clutched in her chubby little fist. Nate's niece was a living doll, but what a responsibility! Becky knew she was up to it. She would love having children of her own, but, of course, she was currently missing the main ingredient: a partner.

Gazing affectionately at Lucy, Becky realized that a person didn't know what peace was until a napless baby settled down for the night. Even Ozzie was worn out from his time spent around Lucy. He curled in a ball on Becky's bed, and was immediately deep in feline dreamland.

Alone now, watching the hands of the clock continue to tick away, Becky became increasingly annoyed. A fiancée—okay, pretend fiancée—should not be expected to baby-sit for a dozen hours straight so Nate could go out with that sex symbol personified. What did men see in a woman like Margo? Anyone could look the way she did. All it took was nerve and incredibly bad taste.

She could look like Margo, too. All that was needed was a little imagination and a quick makeover. If she truly were Nate's wife-to-be, she'd fight fire with fire in a situation like this. It would serve him right if she turned into a helpless little tease, then dropped him as soon as he started panting. She was tired of being taken for granted.

Besides, this could be fun!

After checking on the baby, she shampooed her hair—the smear of strained carrots would be a definite turnoff—used her curling iron, then fluffed it into a frizzy halo.

When Nate came for Lucy, he wouldn't have any doubts about whether she was wearing a bra or not.

Old girlfriend, ha! She was starting to believe there was no buddy involved!

While under the delusion that she'd be marrying Kevin, she'd bought a gorgeous peignoir set to save for their honeymoon. The transparent peach gown had thin straps and a matching robe, equally see-through and trimmed in marabou like something in a 1930s movie. She poured herself into the gown, then strutted in front of the mirror with the robe hanging halfway down her arms in a classic vamp pose. For makeup, she brushed on lipstick until her mouth was a pouty pink bow and darkened her lashes with jet-black mascara from a sample kit she'd won at a co-op picnic eons ago and never used.

Her only concession to modesty was to slip on a pair of bikini panties. Her fuzzy mules were shabby, so she put on a pair of spike-heeled pink satin shoes she'd been forced to wear as a bridesmaid in a friend's wedding. The color wasn't exactly right, but the effect was. She looked like a femme fatale, easily as tacky as Margo—only *her* legs, visible through filmy fabric, were much better, if she said so herself.

She wasn't doing this because she was in any way jealous of Nate's old flame. Nope. No way. Not her. Never. She just wanted to have fun with him. He deserved some payback for drafting her to do double duty.

She checked the results of her makeover in the full-length mirror on the back of her bedroom door.

"Maybe this is a terrible idea," she said to Ozzie, who'd ambled over to see why she was disturbing his before-bed nap.

Suddenly she didn't feel up to being a sex kitten. Nate might take her act seriously. What would happen if he didn't see the joke? She'd never been a tease, and experimenting on Nate seemed like a very bad idea.

Before she could change, which she emphatically intended to do, the downstairs buzzer sounded. It wouldn't be Nate; he certainly had his key with him. Most likely it was Zoe, dropping in to lobby for her blind date candidate, or Mrs. Vander Polder, who always had the courtesy to buzz instead of using her master key.

She didn't want either of them to see her seductive outfit, especially not Zoe. She'd laugh about it for a month!

Becky did the only thing that came to mind—she yanked on her yellow rain slicker and snapped it shut on the way down the stairs. She probably looked even sillier, but all her body parts were modestly concealed.

Busy concocting an explanation for her friend, she opened the door without looking through the peephole. Big mistake!

"Hi, babe!"

"Kevin!"

"Hey, you looked so terrific at that costume bash, I couldn't stop thinking about you."

He whisked right by her into the apartment. It was hard to outmaneuver nearly two hundred pounds of muscle and gall.

"Kevin, what are you doing here?"

Her door was open. She had no choice but to follow him into her living room where Lucy was still soundly sleeping.

"Hey, who's the kid?"

"I'm sitting for a neighbor." She'd tell him the whole story when Ozzie learned to bark.

"In a raincoat? Last I looked, it was about ninety degrees and dry enough to ruin lawns. Good for my business."

Kevin didn't understand the concept of shyness or reticence. Before she saw it coming, he ripped open the row of snaps and slid the bulky raincoat off her shoulders, then hung it in the closet with the familiarity of a man who thought he was welcome there.

She quickly crossed her arms over her semiexposed breasts, but he got the picture anyway.

"Oh, babe, you are looking fine."

"Go home, Kevin."

"You expecting someone? You never fixed yourself up like that for me. We might still be together if you had." He pouted like a spoiled little boy. Once, she'd found him beguiling. Now he had less appeal than a chimp begging for a banana.

"Leave, Kevin."

"Honey, I know you're ticked at me. I deserve it. But I still care about you. It's only sex with Courtney. You're a class act. I was a dope to let you get away."

"Why are you here, Kevin?"

She knew him too well. For someone who had little or nothing worthwhile to say, he could take a long time getting to the point.

"There's no chance we could…"

"No."

"But we're still friends, right?"

"Good buddies," she said, forgetting Kevin never recognized sarcasm.

"Hey, my replacement seems like a good guy. Bartender at the party said he's a cop, right?"

He was wrong about Nate being his replacement, but she wasn't going to encourage him by denying it.

"Yes, he's on the force."

"What a coincidence. I've hit a streak of bad luck. I'm close to having my driver's license pulled. In fact, I got a speeding ticket last night. May give me enough points to lose it."

She stared at him coldly, getting the drift but unwilling to be drawn into a discussion.

"Then you'll enjoy having Courtney as your chauffeur."

He groaned. "The only time she stops griping is in bed. There I give her no reason."

"That's more than I want to know about your sex life."

"Please, babe…"

"Don't call me babe!"

"Please, Becky, ask your cop friend if he'll fix my ticket. For old time's sake."

She was so disgusted, she forgot to keep her arms crossed.

"He's a detective. He investigates felonies. He doesn't have anything to do with traffic offenses."

"But he must know—"

"No."

"You're turning me down, just like that?"

"Yes."

"You're trying to get even. Do you want me to apologize? I had the hots for Courtney. It's chemistry. It happens. It doesn't mean I don't still care for you.''

''I wouldn't get your ticket fixed even if I could, and I can't.''

There was no arguing with Kevin. She didn't have the energy to try.

Darn, but he was quick! He heard a knock on her door and opened it before she remembered how she was dressed.

''How are you?'' Kevin said, offering his hand to Nate. ''Come in. We were just talking about old times.''

''No, we weren't!'' Becky crossed her arms again, but not before Nate saw her getup. She hated to imagine what conclusions he was drawing.

''Looks like I interrupted,'' Nate said with attitude.

''No, you didn't! Kevin came by uninvited hoping I'd get you to fix a traffic ticket.''

''A bum rap if there ever was one,'' Kevin piped in.

''What did you tell him?'' Nate ignored Kevin and looked at her with icy blue eyes devoid of amusement.

''No. I told him no—emphatically.''

''Good answer.''

Kevin was as tall as Nate and a little heavier. But he was a cream puff—a jellyfish—when confronting another man. Becky imagined Nate's toe connecting with Stalnaker's fleshy backside and bouncing him down the stairs step by painful step. Nate might have had something like that in mind, but Kevin was expert at saving his own skin. He backed out the door, arms raised so his hands were just above his shoulders, the universal sign of surrender.

"He's a lover, not a fighter, I guess," Nate said after he watched Kevin turn and hightail it out the front door, not pulling it shut so it would lock.

"He's neither."

"Well, it's a good thing I got home early."

"I didn't need you to rescue me from Kevin. All he wanted was a ticket fixed!"

"Judging by your costume for the night, you must have been disappointed."

"I didn't know he was coming, and if I had, I wouldn't have opened the door."

"But you did."

"I didn't use the peephole. I thought it was a friend—a female friend. So arrest me, cuff me, send me down the river…or is that up the river—whatever!"

"Why are you made up like a bimbo?"

"This is my home! I can wear whatever I choose— or nothing at all."

"You knew I'd be coming for Lucy."

He had her there, but she wasn't going to play true confessions. The more he looked her over, the sillier she felt. Women like Margo probably had a special gift for looking sexy in odd outfits. Obviously, she only looked ridiculous to Nate.

He was still standing in her open doorway.

"Oh, go home," she said crossly. "I've had enough of men for one night."

"Are you lumping all men in one unsavory package? Seems I got my ears blistered for doing the same thing with women not too long ago."

"Take Lucy and go home!"

"No, I'll take her," a female voice said.

They'd been so involved in arguing, they hadn't noticed two people coming up the stairs.

"Freddie!" Nate said.

His sister rushed past both of them and scooped up the sleeping baby. "Oh, Lucy, honey, I've missed you so much! Say hello to Daddy, sweetheart."

Becky and Nate turned and looked toward the hall. Neither of them could think of anything to say to the tall, gangly blond man hovering on the threshold.

10

"YOU CAN HOLD HER," Freddie urged, holding up her baby for the young man's inspection. Lucy stared at the stranger with sleepy disdain.

He reached for the baby with the trepidation of a demolition expert defusing a bomb. Lucy eyed him suspiciously, but she must have seen something she liked. She gurgled winningly instead of howling.

"Freddie!" Nate said in a tone that demanded her attention.

"Nate, this is my husband, Brad—Brad Kenyon."

"Your husband?"

Becky had to suppress a giggle. Nate couldn't have looked more dumbfounded if he'd been slapped in the face with a wet diaper.

Freddie was beside Brad, cooing over Lucy, the three of them clustered in such an intimate knot that Becky wanted to creep away and leave them alone— which wasn't practical since it was her apartment and she was draped in transparent nylon.

"Brad's in the army," Freddie said. "He was overseas and didn't know about Lucy until I wrote last month and sent him pictures. He fell in love with her long distance."

"She's cute." Brad might be brave under fire, but he was one nervous papa right now.

"I can't thank you enough, big brother," Freddie said, turning to give Nate a whopper of a hug. "I couldn't get Mom all excited for nothing in case things didn't work out. You know how she gets wedding fever if I so much as date the same guy twice."

Nate looked slightly nauseous.

"Anyway, Brad was due to fly home, but things were tense where he was, so he didn't come and didn't come. I practically camped out at the St. Louis airport! I was afraid I'd lose my nerve—we hadn't seen each other in so long—and I wanted to be sure we wouldn't be getting married just for Lucy's sake."

"Why be so mysterious?" Nate asked, restraining his enthusiasm—if he had any.

"I didn't want to disappoint. I wasn't a hundred percent sure until Brad walked through the arrivals door, then I knew I couldn't live without him!"

"You could have told me where you were," Nate said.

"No, I had to put my life on course first. You've always been there to help me out of scrapes. This was one time I couldn't let my big brother smooth the way for me. We went to Brad's folks in Kansas City and tied the knot there. He's being transferred to North Carolina, and I'm going with him as soon as I see Mom and Dad."

"Well, welcome to the family, Brad," Nate said.

"Thank you, sir."

Becky tried not to snicker. Maybe military men called everyone sir, just to be on the safe side.

The younger man thrust out the hand that wasn't supporting Lucy, and the two men had a brief hand-squeezing match, a ritual Becky thought must go back to the cavemen. Grab an enemy's spear-throwing paw, and he couldn't attack on the sly. The new brothers-in-law sized each other up. Nate blinked first. It was going to be all right. His sister's seducer would get clan status.

"Drop the sir stuff," Nate said.

"I'm his fiancée," Becky said impulsively, wishing she could perform a little genie magic and transform her sexy gown into jeans and T-shirt. To his credit, Brad had hardly looked at her.

But Nate gave her a look.

"This is Becky—Rebecca Ryan. I couldn't have taken care of Lucy without her help."

"We met when I dropped off Lucy," Freddie said. "I can't thank you enough, Becky, but why didn't you tell me you were Nate's fiancée?"

"It didn't come up...."

"Happened suddenly," Nate said.

"This is wonderful!" Freddie hugged Becky enthusiastically, then threw herself at Nate. "When is the wedding? What a relief! Mom will be too excited about yours to obsess over missing ours."

"We haven't set a date...." Becky began.

"Not rushing into anything," Nate said, not looking at Becky.

The newlyweds were doing a group hug with the baby, and Becky felt like an intruder. She was going to miss Lucy, but it meant the end of her forced association with Nate. That was what she wanted. She should feel elated.

She didn't.

Freddie laid Lucy and the pad from her diaper bag on the floor and started to explain the art of diapering to her young husband.

"I'll gather up Lucy's things," Becky offered.

"I'll go downstairs and bring up the rest," Nate said.

Brad played with Lucy's stubby little toes while Freddie prepared the baby's bottom for travel. Becky ducked into her bedroom and did a quick-change act, emerging in jeans and an all-concealing sweatshirt, never mind that it was winter weight.

Dang, she felt weepy! Maybe she'd enjoyed being substitute mom to Lucy more than she'd realized. Or maybe the prospect of not seeing Nate anymore— *No, don't go down that road,* she warned herself.

Nate returned with Lucy's things, grim-faced and quiet. Why wasn't he dancing with joy? His little sister had made a big decision, and the new groom didn't seem in any way objectionable.

Becky waited anxiously for Nate to tell Freddie the truth about their engagement. Instead, he and Brad exchanged some crucial male stats: which team they wanted to go to the World Series, and whether somebody or other would get traded next season. Men! Why didn't they talk about something important, like what kind of father Lucy needed or how Brad felt about his sudden marriage?

Then Freddie's little family left in a flurry of hugs and thanks, leaving Nate and Becky to look across the room at each other in awkward silence.

"Brad seems nice," Becky finally said to break the ice.

"Yeah."

"It's wonderful that Lucy will have two parents."

"I'll miss the little rascal, though," Nate admitted.

"Me, too."

"About our engagement..." They said it simultaneously and laughed. Becky's was forced.

"I didn't want to tell Freddie all the details about what's been going on," Nate explained. "Her nickname at home is satchel mouth. She can be tight-mouthed about her own business, but..."

"I get the picture. You'd rather be the one to break the news to your mother that our 'wedding' is off."

"Definitely." He smiled broadly.

Did he have to look so darn pleased?

"I meant what I told Freddie about your help, Becky. Thanks—thanks a lot."

She shrugged. "I was between jobs, anyway."

"You taught me a few lessons about taking care of a baby."

"Well, I hope it comes in handy someday."

She instantly wished she hadn't blurted out such an obvious attempt to find out how he felt about fatherhood. Time to change the subject.

"So how was your dinner with Margo? And her new boyfriend." She tried to sound casual. There was no reason for her to care but, darn it, she did.

"My friend didn't show. Maybe he never intended to. I left early. Margo and I didn't have much to say to each other. I didn't expect to find Stalnaker here when I got back. He can't be dumb enough to believe I could fix his ticket if I wanted to."

She wasn't going to elaborate on Kevin's intellectual shortcomings. She felt dumb enough for having had a crush on his muscles.

"Well, I'll leave so you can have some peace and quiet," he said.

"I guess you're my ex-fiancé now."

"Yeah." That made him smile! "I can't thank you enough for helping me, Rebecca."

Was 'Becky' suddenly too intimate?

"No problem." *Go home, Nate,* she thought.

"I owe you."

"No, you don't."

"Anytime you need anything…"

"Go home, Nate." This time she said it out loud. Did he plan to hang around until she bawled?

"I'm on my way." He didn't move. "Are you sure you don't want to be the one to dump me?"

"Yes, I'm sure."

"All right. I started it. I'll finish it."

Did he have to sound so blasted cheerful? If he said, "It's been fun," she was going to deck him!

"Well, thanks again," he said on his way out the door.

Alone again, Becky thought miserably. But at the same time she couldn't be happier for her one-time charge.

Lucy belonged with her mother, and it was wonderful that her father would be with her, too. Aunts and uncles and grandparents should be icing on the cake,

Becky told herself, the image of the baby she adored fresh in her mind.

She picked up and folded the quilt Lucy had been using to sleep, and something fell from the folds—the carrot-head doll, Lucy's favorite toy.

Becky's eyes filled with tears, and she closed them tightly, willing away the deluge building behind her lids. She hated to cry! It was even worse because she wasn't sure why she was doing it. She was going to miss Lucy, but she adored her little nieces and nephews, too. Leaving them after a visit never made her cry.

"It's Nate you're going to miss, you dope!" She didn't even pretend she was talking to Ozzie, who'd had the good sense to hide somewhere.

She'd gotten used to having Nate around; that was the trouble. She certainly didn't need him to kill spiders or rescue her from dopey ex-boyfriends.

He'd needed her, too, for a while. Maybe he still did, but she couldn't imagine the self-reliant cop admitting it to anyone, especially not to her.

She caught herself hugging the silly doll. Tempting as it was to keep it as a souvenir, she couldn't deprive Lucy of her favorite plaything. She'd have to take it down to Nate. He could return it to the baby while Freddie was at her parents' house breaking the news.

Fixing her tear-reddened eyes wasn't easy. She was a messy crier, and the cold cloth she used to make her crying jag less obvious left a pink band across the top of her face. She gave a final sniff and left to return the doll.

"Three knocks, and I'm out of here," she promised herself when Nate didn't open up on her first attempt.

He didn't respond to her second summons either, but why should an unencumbered bachelor hang around his place now that he didn't have a baby—or a fiancée, albeit fake—on the premises?

She gave one more perfunctory rap, prepared to leave the doll by his door and get on with her own life. She was startled when the door burst open.

Nate sported a freshly showered look, damp whorls of hair curling on his spectacular chest. He was clad only in baggy gray sweats riding low on his hips, and his feet were bare.

"Freddie forgot this," she said, practically throwing the doll at him. She had no intention of torturing herself by hanging around her half-naked neighbor.

He caught her hand before she could get away.

"Come in a minute."

He put his secret weapon into play, tenderly massaging the inside of her wrist. His hands should be registered as lethal weapons—they were certainly too dangerous for her peace of mind.

"Thanks, but I have to…"

She couldn't think of a single thing she needed or wanted to do at that moment.

"No, you don't." He didn't let go.

"Nate!" Darn! How did she get inside his apartment? She didn't remember moving, but Nate pushed the door shut behind her with his foot. How many men could clutch a doll with a pointy orange head and still look seductive?

"I'm really grateful to you for helping me keep

Lucy. I've never seen Freddie so happy. She's finally got her act together, and you helped make it happen.''

"All I did was a little baby-sitting."

"Lucy adores you."

"Thank you—I'm glad I could help."

Time to go! her saner self screamed, but she was rooted to the spot, mesmerized by the circular motion of his thumb on the sensitive underside of her wrist.

He pulled her close. She didn't resist—didn't want to. When he tossed aside the doll and wrapped his arms around her, she knew he was the one not wearing underwear this time. Then she stopped thinking. And melted.

His first kiss was long and slow and tender, teasing her lips apart until she felt dizzy with longing. His back was smooth and firm under her fingers, and there was a rhythm to their next kiss—and the next and the next—that made the hard pressure of his lips sheer delight.

"Can't thank you enough," he murmured.

"Keep trying," she encouraged.

His magic hands were under her sweatshirt, massaging her shoulder blades and the small of her back, circling around her waist and moving slowly upward until he cupped her breasts.

"No bra," he whispered, then his tongue began stroking her mouth.

He was hard against her. Her fingers found him through the thick cotton of his sweats. One of them groaned—maybe both of them did.

"Take...them...off." His voice was husky, his fingers working at the denim covering her.

"You first."

She slid her fingers under his waistband over his sleek, hard hips, her little fingers grazing the creases between his thighs and bottom.

He kissed her so emphatically, her ears rang.

No, no, the ringing was as real as it was unwelcome.

"Ignore it," he said, capturing her hands and guiding them back to where he wanted them.

"Yes." She'd agree to ignore an avalanche if he'd keep kissing her.

The caller was persistent. Becky wanted the phone to stop. Who would let the phone ring and ring and ring?

"Maybe you'll have to answer it."

"Could be an emergency at work," he admitted.

"Or Freddie calling about the doll."

"Remember where we were," he said, as if she could forget!

He picked it up and mostly listened.

"Yeah…sure…fine…okay, bye.

"Freddie," he said, hiking up his sweats so the elastic circled his waist. "Lucy was wailing, so they're heading back for the doll. Freddie realized it was missing."

"She likes that doll."

Becky felt like leaving it on the lawn for Freddie to collect.

Nate leaned down and kissed her forehead. "I really can't thank you enough."

A terrible thought occurred to her. "Is that what this is all about? Your way of thanking me?"

"Of course not! What do you take me for?"

"I'm not sure. I really don't know what to think."

"I've wanted to make love to you since Day One—you're on my mind twenty-four hours a day. Can't we talk about this after Freddie gets the doll and leaves again?"

"I want to talk now! If all you want to do is scratch an itch—"

"Now I see. You're scared. You're starting a fight so you have an excuse to turn tail! You wanted this as much as I did!"

"*This!* Do you mean sex, lovemaking, playing around—"

"My point is—"

"There is no point! I'm going home!"

"Fine. Go."

"Fine. Goodbye."

She slammed his door and ran upstairs to her own little haven.

OVER THE NEXT two days her haven felt more like a prison. She only left the house when she was sure Nate was gone; in fact, Nate watching became her pastime. By standing on tiptoes and looking out the upper half of the window over the kitchen sink, she could see a small slice of the parking area, enough to eyeball the dusty trunk of his car or get a brief glimpse of his comings and goings.

Her self-imposed isolation wasn't lonely. On the contrary, her phone rang so much, she considered starting an answering service. Everyone she knew was on the horn, maybe because a sweltering Iowa heat wave was driving people indoors. Nate wasn't one of her callers. Darn, she wished she could stop thinking about him.

He'd slid a check for her last few days of baby-sitting under her door. As satisfying as it would be to shred it and sprinkle the scraps outside his door, she needed it to pay her electric bill.

The start of her new job had been delayed, something about supplier problems. She'd canceled the newspaper to save money, but she bought one at a convenience store to see if more details about the garden center opening had made the papers. There was no news in the issue she bought, but she read the Help Wanted ads, almost willing to settle for a lower-paying job if it would get her out of the house.

The cold, hard truth was that she missed Lucy. But she especially missed Lucy's maddening, macho, sexy uncle. Nothing offered in the classified ads could distract her from thinking about him, and she did nothing about looking for another job.

Her parents had invited her to come to the farm for a big bash when her new little niece was baptized, something that normally would have excited her. She probably would attend, but in her current funk she didn't make any promises.

Then she got another, more alarming, invitation when Nate's mother called.

"We're having a reception for Freddie and Brad, even if we did miss out on their wedding," Margaret told her. "It's the perfect opportunity to get acquainted with your parents. If you'll just give me their phone number and address…"

"What did you say?" Becky asked in a loud voice, clicking the phone repeatedly. "I can't hear you!"

She broke the connection and turned the ringer off so Margaret couldn't call back.

What was happening? Was it possible Mr. Big Strong Police Detective Dalton didn't have the nerve to tell his mom that he'd dumped his charming, vivacious fiancée? Thanks to Nate, she'd been reduced to acting like a cheesy sitcom character, faking phone trouble to avoid a sticky situation.

She shuddered, imagining her parents' reaction if they were invited to meet a fiancé they didn't know existed.

Well, Dalton better have a stellar explanation, or she was going to blow the whistle on his ill-conceived engagement.

SATURDAY WAS her first opportunity to confront Nate. She could see the rear of his car through her apartment window. Water was puddling around the rear tires, so it didn't take a detective to deduce he was out washing his car.

She was so mad, she didn't bother to stop Ozzie when the cat sneaked out with her on her way to the drive.

He was bent over, scrubbing a front tire, his running shorts taut across his round, firm rear. Naturally he was bare-chested. Didn't the man ever wear a shirt? And he'd had the gall to comment on how often she did or didn't wear a bra!

Ozzie scampered around her feet, saw something he didn't like, and arched his back menacingly.

"Fight your own battles," she snapped at him. "I have problems of my own."

Nate straightened when he saw her. She didn't give him a chance to say anything.

"I have a question for you."

"What's that?"

He pulled off his sunglasses and shaded his eyes with his hand. Good grief, the man even had sexy underarms! She had to vent her anger and get away from him before she melted into a pool at his feet.

"You were supposed to tell your parents our engagement was off. Why didn't you?"

He shrugged. "Just haven't gotten around to it," he said casually.

"Spiffy! Your mother just called and asked for my parents' address. She wants to invite your future in-laws to a big party for Freddie and Brad."

"What did you say?"

"I pretended my phone wasn't working. You made me lie and look silly! I don't know which I hate more."

"Call her back and tell her we broke up." He replaced his sunglasses and turned back to the car, hosing the tire he'd just lathered.

"No way! *You* were supposed to be the bad guy and tell her you dumped your kind, sweet-tempered fiancée."

"What does it matter who does it?" He released the sprayer and laid the hose on the ground, then turned his attention to the front grill.

"No way am I going to answer a ton of questions. I'm not going to break your wonderful mother's heart by telling her we're not getting married."

"She'll get over it."

"That is so callous! You promised you'd be the one to tell her!"

"I will—when the timing is right."

"When you decide it's right? What about my parents? Your mother could be calling information this very minute to get their phone number."

He didn't answer. He was more concerned with scrubbing bugs off his grill than keeping his word about their phony engagement.

Just then, Ozzie streaked past her and up a big old maple, spooked by what had to be one of the neighborhood's bigger dogs.

Becky picked up the hose and directed the spray at the menacing canine's front paws, soaking Nate in the process. The dog lumbered away like a bear making tracks. She dropped the hose and rushed over to the base of the tree, joined by a soaking-wet Nate.

"You're wicked with a hose," he said, grinning. He was so wet, his running shorts stuck to him like plastic wrap.

"Quick, call the fire department," she ordered.

"Why? You didn't quite drown me."

"They'll bring a ladder."

His sigh could probably be heard in the next county.

"Just get a can of tuna and coax him down," he said, trying to wring out his nylon shorts.

"That won't work. I've tried it before."

"Well, aim your trusty hose in his direction. Cats hate water, don't they? He'll scurry down on his own."

"I can't do that. He might lose his balance and fall."

"I've never heard of a cat falling, but don't call out the National Guard. I'll rescue him."

He leaped up, caught one of the lower branches, and got a toehold on the trunk.

"Wait! You can't climb a tree in rubber thongs! Go put on some sneakers!"

He gave her a real-men-don't-need-shoes look and continued scaling the multilimbed tree, cursing under his breath.

"Be careful!" she shouted.

Ozzie had crept out on a limb sturdy enough to hold Nate's weight. He crawled out after the cat while Becky watched, her heart in her throat because heights always made her nervous.

"Got you, you mangy furball," Nate said, snatching Ozzie by the collar and transferring him to the crook of his arm.

Becky relaxed a little. Coming down was easier than going up, wasn't it?

Moments later, as Nate lay sprawled on the ground, Ozzie's nine lives still intact, Becky reconsidered that last thought.

11

"SIT RIGHT THERE," she ordered, scooping up her infernal cat. "I'm taking you in for an X ray. Oh, and thanks for rescuing Ozzie. I did tell you not to climb in flip-flops."

"I know, I know."

She took her time getting back from putting the cat in her apartment, but at least it gave him a chance to maneuver onto his hands and one knee and pull himself upright, clutching the tree for support. Intense pain radiated from the red balloon that used to be his ankle.

"I picked up your car keys from the kitchen counter," she said, hurrying back, a stack of clothes in her arms. "We could go in my car, but I'd have to stop for gas. I'm down to fumes. Are your shorts nearly dry?" She fingered the cloth clinging to his thigh, diminishing him to little-boy status and fueling his anger. Since when did *he* need rescuing?

"Here, I'll open the door, and you can sit on the edge of the seat."

Giving detailed instructions, she worked a pair of cotton khaki shorts over his damaged ankle and up his legs, then held up a knit shirt so he could slip into it.

"There," she said in the tone she'd used when she'd

finished diapering Lucy. "Don't look so crabby. Everything's going to be just fine."

She drove him to the emergency room, insisted on getting a wheelchair, and pushed him into the building. After a long wait and a short examination—with Becky hovering off to the side—he was X-rayed, admonished, and loaned a pair of hospital crutches.

On the way home she stopped for a prescription and went over his instructions.

"Keep it elevated. That's really important."

"I have it here in writing." If he sounded sullen, he was.

"You say that now, but will you follow directions Monday morning? You have to stay off your feet for at least two days. Your ankle is sprained, not just strained."

"Like you know the difference?"

"You bet I do! My brothers played football when they weren't busy maiming each other. Anyway, this will give you time to call your parents and tell them you're an unencumbered bachelor again."

"I'll wait until I see them."

"So meanwhile, I screen all my calls in case your mother calls?"

"I guess so. I really think I need to tell them in person."

She insisted on settling him on the couch with his foot propped up on two pillows, ice water by his side, and the TV controls and phone near at hand.

"That should do it," she said, using her Lucy-voice again. "I'm going. Do you want me to lock the door?"

"No."

The worst of it was, he didn't want her to leave. He wasn't hurting so much that he didn't love watching her. She was wearing white shorts, and her legs were silky smooth from her creamy thighs to her delicate ankles. Her navy tank top made her breasts look smaller than he knew them to be, but she looked terrific in anything.

Unfortunately, he liked a lot more than her sexy little body. Even when she was trying to give him orders, like right now, he felt a warm glow just from being around her.

"Well, call me if you need anything. And stay off your ankle!"

"Bossy female." He meant it affectionately.

Ten minutes after she left, he remembered the prescription for painkillers she'd filled for him on the way home. It was still on the floor on the passenger side of his car. He could get it himself. He was no stranger to crutches, but he was hurting. The least she could do was hustle down to the car for him, considering she'd let her blasted cat get loose.

Dummy! he thought. Maybe he could use an excuse like that on her, but it was getting harder and harder to fool himself. He liked having her around. He wanted to see her, talk to her, touch her. A sprained ankle was trivial compared to the emptiness he felt when she wasn't near him.

He picked up the phone.

Becky was in and out the rest of the day. So was he—literally. The two pills he'd swallowed sent him to la-la land, and in his lucid moments he decided to toss them out and take a couple of over-the-counter pain-killers.

He was only vaguely aware when she freshened the ice pack, brought him cold drinks, and sat quietly watching him. But by the time she started fixing dinner, he was fully alert and enjoying her attentions, even though he was finding it difficult to make small talk.

"You don't have to cook for me," he said gruffly to mask the emotion he was feeling at the moment.

"You have ham, cheese and onions. I have eggs, green peppers and bread for Texas toast. Between us we have the makings of a good omelette."

"I get the picture."

"Of course, if you'd rather I run to the store for you..."

"No, an omelette would be great."

So would a little cuddling. From the knees up he ached to take her in his arms, but he wasn't nuts. He didn't know how she'd react if he revealed his true feelings. Feelings he'd tried so hard to ignore. But from what he had sensed she could hardly wait until their engagement was history.

"Anything else you need?" she asked a while later, after they'd eaten and she'd cleaned up the kitchen.

He needed to be deep inside her, to fall asleep with their bodies spent but still joined. He needed to wake up every morning with her bottom nestled against him and her hair tickling his nose.

He needed to wait for the perfect moment to tell her how he felt, and now was not that time.

"Hello...Nate, are you there? Have those pills made you spacey? I don't think you even know I'm here," she said. "I really need to leave if there's nothing else you need."

"No, nothing."

He knew she was there, all right. And before long he'd tell her what he really wanted.

BY THE TIME he dragged himself home from work a few days later, he was tired, cranky, and in pain.

He sniffed as he quietly closed the door behind him. His apartment smelled like an Italian restaurant, reminding him he hadn't bothered with lunch. Call it stubborn pride, but he hadn't wanted anyone at work waiting on him, bringing him food. Nor had he wanted to make a spectacle of himself by going out on crutches. Or maybe he just didn't want to admit he'd been felled by a furball, not a felon.

"Rebecca?"

"What happened to taking the day off?" she asked.

"I wasn't expecting any breaking and entering in my own home," he said to avoid her question.

"Just entering, and you can't arrest me. I still have the key you gave me. Sit down. All I have to do is boil the pasta. The spaghetti sauce is simmering."

"You don't have to cook for me."

"Aren't you grouchy! I bet your ankle hurts like crazy."

He started to make a sarcastic crack, but looking at her took his breath away. She was pink-cheeked from the heat in the kitchen, and little ringlets of hair clung seductively to her forehead. Her short denim skirt was like a million others, but the fabric tie made him think of untying it and letting it slide down her legs. Her pale-blue tank top had thin shoulder straps that confirmed her braless state, not that he couldn't see her nipples outlined under the stretchy cotton. If she'd come to seduce him, she was a genius at picking her outfit: simple, sweet and sexy...because she was wearing it.

He was in pain, all right, but getting the weight off his ankle wouldn't alleviate it.

She was adorable. He wanted her. And even when she was irking him, he needed her.

He tossed aside one crutch so he could reach out to her, circling her bare upper arm and drawing her close.

"The pasta..."

He dropped the other crutch, balancing on one foot, and wrapped his arms around her.

"Dinner is nearly ready," she said in a husky little voice.

He nuzzled her throat, knowing he had to kiss her and sure he couldn't kiss her only once. He found her mouth, soft, sweet and willing, her lips parting with only a little persuasion from his tongue. He stopped thinking. He was light-headed, even giddy, from the intensity of his need.

She wrapped her arms around his waist, taking him by surprise and nearly toppling both of them. He caught himself, and she broke away from him.

"Maybe we'd better eat."

Why was she whispering? Didn't she know how sexy and beguiling she was when she let words slide over him like hot oil?

"Not before an appetizer." Ouch, how corny could

he be? She was making him think and say things that surprised even him.

Instead of making the smart remark he expected, she put an arm around his waist and offered herself as a leaning post as he staggered to the couch. His hormones were on full alert. He pulled her onto his lap and crushed her mouth against his.

"Oh, oh, oh…"

He loved the tiny sounds she made between kisses. He shivered when she unbuttoned his shirt and slid her fingers over his nipples, tormenting him by doing exactly what he wanted her to do.

Her back was warm and smooth under his hand, and he was surprised how satisfying it was just to be kissing her and touching her skin. He didn't want her any less, but he wanted to savor every wonderful part of her. There was so much to learn about this woman, he'd need two lifetimes to tap the surface. Imagining the moment when he joined his body to hers was almost more pleasure than he could handle at one time.

"Thank you," he murmured in her ear, teasing her lobe with the tip of his tongue.

"For what?"

"Helping me…making dinner."

He immediately regretted saying anything. The last time he'd thanked her during a heated moment, she'd misinterpreted his intentions. He wasn't looking to seduce her with words, but he needed the reassurance of talking, of reaching a meeting of their minds. Whatever else she was, Becky was special.

But she dumbfounded him. He lost all ability to say what he truly wanted.

"For making dinner?" She sounded drowsy in a lazy, satisfied way.

And what he wanted most was to satisfy her, to love her. He slid his hand under the little bit of skirt hiked high on her thighs. He found the silkiness of her panties and stroked gently, feeling the moisture there.

"Oh, Becky…"

She wiggled, clamping her thighs around his hand. He pushed into her just a little, suddenly wanting to be rid of all their clothing.

"If you're auditioning for the role of real-life fiancée, you—"

"If I'm *what?*"

"That didn't come out the way I meant.…" What was he thinking? Had he been about to propose?

She sat upright and pushed away his hand.

"Do you know what your trouble is? You don't know what to do with an independent female. That's your problem! You have to be the big male protector. You have to play hero. Well, I'm not helpless, and I don't need anyone to protect me. You and your big ego need to get a clue."

"My big ego?" That hurt!

"Admit it! You want the nice, safe, comfortable role of protector. That's what you've been for Margo, Freddie, even little Lucy."

"You don't know what you're talking about!" He stood, forgetting about his ankle until pain made him wince. How could she think that he wanted her helpless and needy? Her independence, her caring and compassion, were just a fraction of what he loved about her.

"You can't give up control," she continued. "You have to be in charge! You're afraid to be vulnerable."

"Did you rehearse that speech or was it just ad-lib?" he said defensively.

"Enjoy your dinner!" she said, storming out of his apartment.

He was trembling, physically trembling. He was out of control, and it scared him. But it wasn't the kind of fear that came from risking his life or facing danger. He was afraid he'd blown it with Becky before he'd even seized his chance.

12

"WHY, why, why?"

Two days had dragged by, and Becky still didn't know why she'd blown up at Nate, ruining any chance of having a relationship with him.

Ozzie ignored her. She had to stop talking to her cat.

"He just irritates me so much sometimes," she fumed, resuming her one-sided conversation. "He's stubborn and maddening, and I love him so much I could burst!"

There, she'd said it out loud, never mind that only her indifferent pet had heard.

Soon she'd be starting her new job—finally. It would help to be busy all day, but keeping track of grass seed and rakes was no substitute for nestling in Nate's arms. If only she'd kept her mouth shut, he might have admitted how he felt about her.

But no! Thanks to the bossy, domineering, pushy brothers she'd adored all her life, she had to assert herself. She had to let Nate know what was bugging her, and she'd jumped down his throat at the worst possible moment.

He'd never forgive her. She'd never forgive herself! But how could he suggest she was "auditioning" to be his real fiancée?

She paced, tormented by all the things she *hadn't* said to him. Namely, that she loved him. She shouldn't have stormed out and left so much hanging in limbo.

Her buzzer sounded.

Please, please, please, don't let it be Nate's mother! He was due home from work anytime now. He should be the one to break the news to her.

She debated not answering, but curiosity won out. She crept downstairs as quietly as possible. This time she was going to check the peephole. If it was Margaret Dalton, she wasn't going to open the door.

Even the distorted image Becky saw through the tiny hole couldn't disguise the fact that Lucy was adorable. She didn't hesitate to throw open the door. Lucy was just the cure she needed for post-Nate blues.

"Hi, Becky." Freddie held out her daughter, and Lucy toppled into Becky's willing arms. "Say hello, sweetheart! We wanted to surprise Nate, but I guess he's not home yet."

"Is your husband with you?"

"No, he's bonding with my dad—both of them have their noses pressed against the TV screen. Baseball or something. It's a guy thing, you know."

"Yes," Becky agreed, even though she was beginning to believe she didn't know a darn thing worth knowing about the male sex. Otherwise, how could she have messed up her relationship with Nate so badly? "Well, come up and wait in my place. It's about time for him to get home."

Freddie and Lucy were just the company she needed. All she had to do was nod occasionally while Freddie carried the conversation. And playing with Lucy, cuddling her and nuzzling her downy-soft head, was a tonic for Becky's sagging spirits.

"Oh, I hear the door. Must be Nate," Freddie said, interrupting a long story about how she'd met Lucy's father. "I'll run down and see. Would you mind watching Lucy for a minute? She's getting heavy to lug around."

"I'd love to," Becky said, absorbed in Lucy's antics as the baby tried to coax Ozzie out from under the couch.

Freddie left the door open, and Becky heard the two siblings, Nate obviously still hobbling on crutches. She picked Lucy up, giving her a goodbye hug in anticipation of her mother's return.

Instead Freddie called up the stairs.

"Nate's here, Becky. Would you mind bringing Lucy down?"

Yes, she would mind! She'd been avoiding confrontation with Nate for forty-eight hours, and it might be forty-eight years before she worked up the courage to see him again.

She walked out to the top of the stairs, intending to tell Freddie to come get her child herself, but the downstairs entryway was deserted. Freddie had once again assumed someone else would take care of Lucy. How did Nate get such a self-absorbed sister? she fumed, but carried Lucy downstairs.

At least Freddie was too busy chattering about her belated wedding reception to notice that Nate didn't speak to Becky.

"Oh, Mom told me to be sure to get your parents' address, Becky. She'll express-mail their invitation.

She tried calling them, but no one was home. Don't your parents have an answering machine?''

''Not on their home phone,'' Becky said, not offering her father's office number.

Though she'd suspected from Freddie's behavior that Nate had yet to tell his family the ''engagement'' was off, Freddie's request for parental information confirmed her suspicion.

Now why hadn't Nate ended the charade once and for all?

Especially given their last encounter?

''I need to run some errands. I wonder if I could leave Lucy with you for just an hour or so?'' Freddie asked her brother.

''You do plan to come back today?'' Nate teased, making his sister laugh.

''Her daddy is so crazy about her, I wouldn't dare go home without her! I really should ask you, Becky. Nate can't lift her on crutches. You don't mind, do you?''

She minded a whole lot!

Nate looked directly at her for the first time. She looked at him. They were daring each other to say yes.

Becky blinked first.

''Sure, I'd love to watch Lucy,'' she said, meaning it but wondering how to avoid spending another minute with the baby's uncle.

Freddie breezed out after planting a noisy kiss on Lucy's forehead.

''It's silly for both of us to baby-sit,'' Becky said without looking at Nate. ''I'll do it.''

''All right.''

That was all he said: *All right.*

"Take the diaper bag," Nate said. "Call if you need help."

"I won't need help."

"Becky..."

"What?"

"Nothing."

She could feel his eyes on her all the way up the stairs and into her apartment.

EVEN WITH THE BABY and Ozzie for company, it was the loneliest hour Becky had ever spent. If Nate wanted things to be right between them, wouldn't he have insisted they both watch Lucy? Obviously, he'd written her off. They couldn't even go back to being friendly neighbors.

Freddie returned as promised. Maybe marriage was making her more responsible, but it wasn't Becky's concern. The prospect of never again seeing Lucy was depressing, but she could console herself with her brothers' growing families.

"Now promise you and Nate won't wait until the reception to come see us," his sister said. "North Carolina seems awfully far away right now."

"You'll love it! No Iowa winters," Becky assured her.

Freddie wasn't going to be distracted. "Promise you'll come see us! And I'd better not go home without your folks' address."

Becky wrote it on a scrap of paper, trying to calculate how long it would take for the bombshell to explode on her parents. Sprained ankle or no sprained ankle, Nate absolutely had to tell his mom he'd dumped her. If he didn't, she would have to.

Only problem was she couldn't face going to his apartment to deliver her ultimatum. Her heart and hormones took over every time she got too close to him, and this time she needed a cool head to insist he fess up.

Maybe shock treatment would work. She picked up the phone.

"Nate," she said as soon as he answered. "I'm counting to a hundred, then calling your mother. If you plan to keep your word and do it yourself, that's how long you have to dial her number before I do."

She hung up the phone before he could say anything.

"One, two, three…" She counted as slowly as possible, dreading the call she had to make if Nate thought she was bluffing.

"Thirteen, fourteen, fifteen…" She was so agitated, it was hard to remember the number sequence she knew as well as her own name.

"Twenty-two, twenty—"

A clomping on the stairs seemed to shake the whole building. Nate was coming up on crutches, and she'd forgotten where she was in the count.

A loud racket startled her so much, she dropped the phone she'd been clutching. For one terrible moment she thought he'd fallen down the steps.

"Becky, get my crutch for me, would you?" he called out. "Please!"

No way would she run out there, not even if the Society for the Prevention of Cruelty to Cops Who Break Girls' Hearts came after her.

He called out again, then there was a long, eerie silence. Had he gone back down, maybe sliding silently on his bottom?

No such luck! His single crutch thumped up to her door, followed by several loud knocks.

"Go away!"

His vigorous pounding only got louder.

"If you won't get my crutch, I'll keep pounding, even if I have to spend the night on your threshold!"

What was he trying to pull? His knocking got louder. Was he trying to get both of them evicted?

She picked up the phone, brandishing it like a weapon, mad enough now to read him *her* rights. Reluctantly, she opened the door.

"Put down the phone!" he ordered in a tone calculated to scare the resistance out of dangerous felons. He pushed the door shut with the rubber-tipped steel crutch.

She backed up until her calves collided with the edge of the couch.

"Drop it now!"

She obeyed, letting it fall from her fingertips onto a couch cushion.

"Come here."

She obeyed again. How could she resist the command of a cop on a crutch, especially a cop she was crazy about!

He swept her into his arms, letting his remaining crutch fall to the floor.

They were off balance, swaying and in danger of toppling over.

"Your crutch! You'll fall!"

"I don't need them anymore."

"Then what was all that business on the steps?" She squirmed but he only held her tighter.

"I wanted—no, I needed—attention from you."

"You needed…"

He shut her up in the nicest possible way, bringing his lips to hers for a long, slow, utterly delicious kiss.

Nothing had ever felt so wonderful!

"Not so fast." She was trembling. "Tell me that part about needing me again."

"I need you, in oh-so-many ways. And I've wanted you for so long. I was an idiot not to admit it to you—or myself."

They kissed again, his tongue caressing and sliding against hers, curling and uncurling, until she was lost in her feelings for him. Totally caught up in the moment, giddy with the wonder of being held by the only man she'd ever really loved, she wasn't even surprised when Nate swept her off her feet and carried her toward the one destination on both their minds.

In the bedroom he managed to sweep aside the pink-flowered comforter on her bed and lower her to the sheets without a single jarring movement.

"Your ankle…"

"Forgotten." He lay beside her, one leg pinning her to the bed—not that she had any intention of trying to escape.

"That macho, high-tolerance-to-pain attitude will get you nowhere," she teased.

"Okay, it aches like a tooth being drilled, but with a little help from you, I'll forget all about it."

She reached out and pulled his head down to hers,

closing her eyes and kissing him with all the love in her heart.

"Forgotten," he whispered, brushing her eyelids with his lips, making her tingle with anticipation.

"Lie still," he said.

"Still giving orders, Detective Dalton?"

"No, requesting permission to love you."

He lifted one of her arms and trailed kisses from the inner crease of her elbow, down to her wrist, letting his tongue flick against the supersensitive skin of her wrist. Then he pressed his lips against the lines on her palm and kissed the pads of every finger.

Putting that arm to rest, stretched above her head, he turned his loving attention to the other.

Who knew knuckles were erogenous?

"Don't move," he urged, slowly working her shirt over her breasts, bunching it around her throat, then carefully sliding it over her face and up her arms. He did the same for her bra, groaning in admiration when her breasts were exposed.

"I knew you'd be spectacular," he murmured, touching her with awe, then taking one nipple between his lips and gently suckling, igniting a network of hot wires that made her wet with desire.

She reached out to him, impatient with the clothing that separated them.

"Not yet."

His beard was slightly rough against her soft midsection, but she hugged his head, his hair soft on her arms, and pulled him even closer, delighting in the gentle movement of his tongue on her breasts.

"Love me," she gasped, not knowing she said it aloud.

"Wait," he said more to himself than her, spearing her navel with his tongue and making her crazy with need.

He stood and stripped off his own clothes faster than her eye could follow. She loved him so much, it hurt to look at him. She felt more virginal than she had before Kevin, half afraid and half fascinated by Nate's maleness.

He went down on his knees beside the bed, surprising her with sensations she'd never dreamed of. He peeled off her panties, rolling them torturously downward inch by inch, pressing hot kisses on her exposed flesh.

"Tell me..." He sounded short of breath. "Tell me if you don't..."

"I do."

How could she feel wildly stimulated and deprived at the same time? She needed only one thing to be completely happy: to meld with Nate and be one together.

She reached out, clutching his shoulders. He was torturing her, using his hands and his mouth, kneading her thighs, using his finger and then his tongue until she thought she'd go crazy from wanting him. She shut her eyes tight and surrendered to sensation, needing him so much she was struck dumb.

It seemed eons before he straddled her hips and lowered his body toward hers.

"Darling, sweet darling..." A stream of tender endearments flowed from his lips. Never had she felt so loved and cherished.

Their joining was a delicious shock, heightened by a kiss so passionate her lips quivered. He slid into her and stopped, giving her time to brace herself, legs wrapped around him, and become fully sensitized. He slid his hands under her shoulders, and she clutched at him, raising her head and rocking her hips.

Something happened.

Something good…wonderful…unbelievable!

She was out of control. In only moments, so was he. How could anything feel so tremendously great and keep getting better? She was streaking down an endless slide, and then she soared.

Nate was there to bring her back to reality, and it was beautiful.

"I never knew…"

He laughed with happiness.

"It's every man's dream to be the first."

He made her feel a bit guilty. "Not exactly…"

"The first to make the world rock for someone who's…"

"You did!" Did he ever!

"I've never known anyone like you."

He rolled to his side, carrying her with him without breaking their union. His chest was damp against her cheek, firm but still cushioning. She could hear his heartbeat and feel the silky hair clinging to his chest. Drowning in contentment, she never wanted to leave his arms.

WHEN BECKY WOKE UP, the pale light of dusk showed Nate still beside her, sleeping on his tummy with his arms pillowing his dark head. It was the first time he'd ever seemed boyish, and she loved him even more because of it. His bottom was even cuter than she'd imagined, two perfect round globes, and his long legs sported powerful calves and thighs. She could hardly keep her hands off him, but she didn't want to wake him, not quite yet.

She needed to think, but her mind was like a whirlpool, sucking away every thought before she really had a handle on it.

The truth was, she needed to talk. Even with her limited—boy, was it limited—experience, she knew something special had happened between them. She just wasn't sure how Nate felt.

She thought of several interesting ways to wake him but hesitated, content for the moment to watch him sleep.

"Aren't you going to wake me?" His voice didn't sound the least bit groggy.

"How long have you been awake?"

"Longer than you. I wondered what you'd do when you woke up."

"I didn't do anything."

"Yes, you did." He rolled over suddenly and pulled her down on top of him. "You were eyeballing my bod."

"Was not!"

"Did you like what you saw?"

"Garden-variety hunk."

"Nothing special?"

"Seen one, you've seen them all."

"Liar! Anyone before the knight in tin cans?"

"No." She was a bit flustered. This wasn't at all the conversation she wanted to have.

"Do I still have to tell my mom I'm dumping you?"

"Is that why you—why we…" She wiggled free of his arms and sat upright on his midsection, glaring down with mock anger.

"No, this is about me being blind and stubborn. About seeing you with Lucy today and realizing how much I was missing you whenever I wasn't with you. About how much I'd like to make a baby with you— maybe a whole houseful some day."

"Did we?"

"No, I took care of it."

"I didn't see you."

"You weren't looking. Some things are even better with open eyes. Trust me, darling, I'd never take a big step like that unless you were one hundred percent in agreement."

Darling! She loved the sound of that word.

"I do trust you." She loved him, too, but she wasn't going to be the first to say the magic words.

"Kiss me," he murmured.

"No, I don't think so."

He moved so fast, she never had a chance. He tumbled her onto her back, then slid to the floor on his knees.

"What are you doing?" She sat up, self-consciously crossing her arms over her breasts.

"I'm begging your forgiveness."

"I might believe it if you weren't laughing."

"I badly misjudged you, right from the beginning.

You may be a shrimp, but you're one tough, strong-willed, independent woman."

"A shrimp!"

"Don't interrupt."

"Don't give orders."

"I'll try not to. It's sort of a habit."

"A bad habit."

"Don't think you can reform me overnight."

"I wouldn't even try. I think you're a hopeless case."

"I need you, Rebecca."

There was nothing she could say to that, so she just enjoyed the warm glow.

"No witty quips? No smart remarks?"

He pulled himself up and sat on the bed beside her. It was nearly dark, but she was totally aware of the expression on his face. His voice gave him away.

"No," she said meekly.

He reached across her and turned on the little bedside lamp she used for reading when she couldn't sleep.

"Becky, darling, will you marry me?"

"So you won't have to tell your mother you dumped me?" She could hardly absorb what Nate had asked.

"Believe me, this isn't about anybody but you and me. Tell me I have the rest of my life to make you happy."

"I already have. We are still engaged, aren't we?"

"For real," he said, bending his head and softly kissing her mouth. "I want us to pick out a ring— today. I love you, Becky. I love you too much for words."

"I love you, too." She didn't mean to say it in such

a tiny, soft voice. The way she felt, she should shout at the top of her voice. Just to get a grip on herself she added, "I'll take Ozzie to the farm. I know you don't like him."

"No, Ozzie stays with us. I love you so much, I might even get to like the little furball."

"About our children—and grandchildren—promise you won't tell them you almost arrested me."

"For breaking and entering."

"Just entering!"

"Only if you kiss me again."

"And again and again and again."

As Becky kissed her future husband, she couldn't help but marvel at the lessons in love they'd learned, thanks to one sweet little baby.

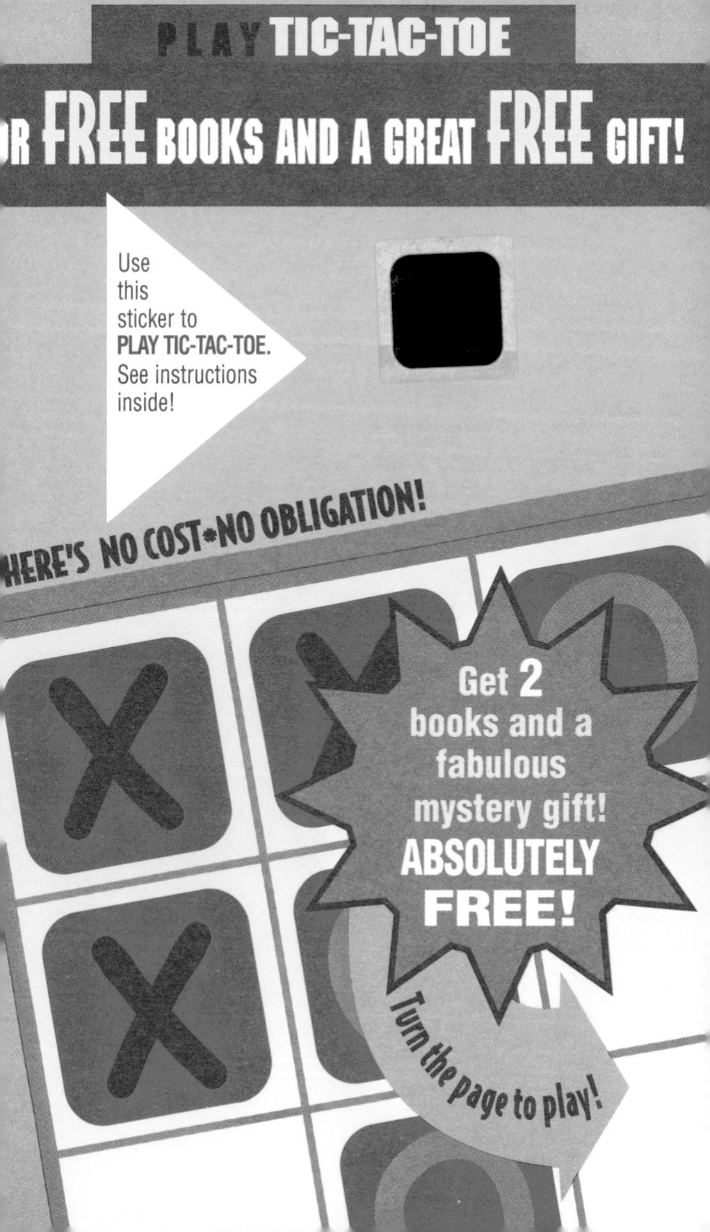
PLAY TIC-TAC-TOE
R FREE BOOKS AND A GREAT FREE GIFT!
Use this sticker to PLAY TIC-TAC-TOE. See instructions inside!
HERE'S NO COST•NO OBLIGATION!
Get 2 books and a fabulous mystery gift! ABSOLUTELY FREE!
Turn the page to play!

Play **TIC-TAC-TOE** and get **FREE GIFTS**

HOW TO PLAY:

1. Play the tic-tac-toe scratch-off game at the right for your FREE BOOKS and FREE GIFT!

2. Send back this card and you'll receive TWO brand-new Harlequin Duets™ novels. These books have a cover price of $5.99 each in the U.S. and $6.99 each in Canada, but they are yours to keep absolutely free.

3. There's no catch. You're under no obligation to buy anything. We charge nothing — ZERO — for your first shipment. And you don't have to make any minimum number of purchases — not even one!

4. The fact is, thousands of readers enjoy receiving books by mail from the Harlequin Reader Service® months before they're available in stores. They like the convenience of home delivery, and they love our discount prices!

5. We hope that after receiving your free books you'll want to remain a subscriber. But the choice is yours — to continue or cancel, any time at all! So why not take us up on our invitation, with no risk of any kind. You'll be glad you did!

YOURS **FREE**
A FABULOUS **MYSTERY GIFT!**

**We can't tell you what it is…
but we're sure you'll like it!**

A FREE GIFT—
just for playing
TIC-TAC-TOE!

The Harlequin Reader Service® — Here's how it works:

Accepting your 2 free books and gift places you under no obligation to buy anything. You may keep the books and gift and return the shipping statement marked "cancel." If you do not cancel, about a month later we'll send you 2 additional novels and bill you just $5.14 each in the U.S., or $6.14 each in Canada, plus 50¢ delivery per book and applicable taxes if any.* That's the complete price and — compared to the cover price of $5.99 in the U.S. and $6.99 in Canada — it's quite a bargain! You may cancel at any time, but if you choose to continue, every month we'll send you 2 more books, which you may either purchase at the discount price or return to us and cancel your subscription.

*Terms and prices subject to change without notice. Sales tax applicable in N.Y. Canadian residents will be charged applicable provincial taxes and GST.

If offer card is missing write to: Harlequin Reader Service, 3010 Walden Ave., P.O. Box 1867, Buffalo, NY 14240-1867

BUSINESS REPLY MAIL
FIRST-CLASS MAIL   PERMIT NO. 717   BUFFALO, NY

POSTAGE WILL BE PAID BY ADDRESSEE

HARLEQUIN READER SERVICE
3010 WALDEN AVE
PO BOX 1867
BUFFALO NY 14240-9952

NO POSTAGE
NECESSARY
IF MAILED
IN THE
UNITED STATES

KATE
THOMAS

Too Lucky
for Love

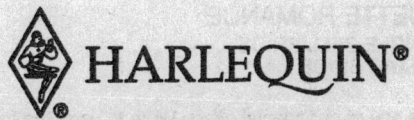

HARLEQUIN®

TORONTO • NEW YORK • LONDON
AMSTERDAM • PARIS • SYDNEY • HAMBURG
STOCKHOLM • ATHENS • TOKYO • MILAN • MADRID
PRAGUE • WARSAW • BUDAPEST • AUCKLAND

Dear Reader,

When asked to explain why I write romantic comedy, my only defense is that I'm just following the first rule for authors: write what you know.

For example, my husband says he didn't fall in love with my beauty, wit or charm. The first time he saw me, I was blowing bubbles in class and he thought, "Now, there's a smart aleck I want to meet!"

The romance continued. We spent our first anniversary in bed—with the flu. Our fifth found us bundled in coats, watching a man repair our furnace. And my beloved gave me my engagement ring for our eighteenth anniversary, claiming he hadn't realized before then that I liked diamonds.

Our happily-ever-after has included a daughter who, when nagged about dawdling, offered to drive herself to kindergarten so I could get to work and not be late.

She was serious. With my life, I can't be, which is why I'm so thrilled to share with you this story of a man who's *Too Lucky for Love*—and the woman who saves him from such a terrible fate.

Kate Thomas

Books by Kate Thomas

SILHOUETTE ROMANCE
1123—JINGLE BELL BRIDE
1357—TEXAS BRIDE

Don't miss any of our special offers. Write to us at the following address for information on our newest releases.

Harlequin Reader Service
U.S.: 3010 Walden Ave., P.O. Box 1325, Buffalo, NY 14269
Canadian: P.O. Box 609, Fort Erie, Ont. L2A 5X3

To the REAL heroes—those who, despite not knowing how, are willing to try. You know who you are.

1

TYLER HARDING STRODE through the morning rush-hour throng, ignoring it, his attention riveted on the interview ahead. If everything went as expected—and it would, thanks to his usual thorough preparation—today he'd achieve Step 3-B of the career plan he'd formulated seven years earlier on the day he received his architect's degree.

Right on schedule, too.

Automatically, Ty sidestepped to avoid a woman who'd stopped to repair her bouffant hairdo.

He wanted this job, he would get this job. Life was so simple, really: set a goal, work toward it, achieve it.

Ty planned to spend the next four years with Krako, Iverson and Delaporte, Phoenix's leading architects. Then he'd open his own firm, specializing in designing classic, tasteful homes for wealthy, discerning clients.

A couple more years to establish himself and he'd be ready to reap the rewards for his hard work and drive. He planned to acquire a sports car, a house and a wife.

Not that he intended to fall in love. As far as Ty was concerned, love was an illusion. He just wanted companionship, a stable relationship with someone calm, reserved, normal. And sex—he was a fully functional American male, after all.

He had their life all planned, too. They'd entertain, travel, maybe take up golf. If the woman insisted, perhaps he'd agree to one child, as long it was well behaved and quiet...

Ty shuddered as he recalled the chaos of his own

childhood, growing up in the middle of six rambunctious brothers and sisters. On second thought, no kids.

"Whoa there, buddy." An arm blocked his progress.

Ty looked up. Cars and trucks jockeyed for possession of the pavement in front of him. *Oh, yeah. Intersection.* "Thanks, man," he told the guy who'd stopped him.

"No problem," the man replied before strolling onward.

Balancing on the edge of the sidewalk, Ty checked his watch. Perfect. His appointment was in ten minutes and his destination only a block away. Absently, he glanced around as he waited for the light to change.

Lord, is it Halloween already? he thought, noticing an old woman on the other side of the street. *All she needs is a tambourine and a crystal ball.* She already had the ruffled blouse, full skirt and jingling jewelry.

For some reason, Ty's gaze followed hers as she leaned out to look at the oncoming traffic.

A block down McDowell Avenue, a bus pulled away from the curb. The street in front of it suddenly cleared; the bus accelerated. Out of the corner of his eye, Ty saw the old lady tense, pause, then gather the ends of her fringed shawl in one gnarled fist. Dammit, what the hell was she doing? He looked wildly around. A little dark-haired sprite seemed to be frantically pushing her way through the crowd, but it was clear she'd never reach the old lady in time.

Suddenly, the old woman stiffened her spine and stepped into the street—right in front of that speeding bus.

Although Ty knew he was too far away and it was too late, he launched himself without thought.

That's when Fate finally quit screwing around and went proactive.

Well—it has to work with what's available, too. Ambitious young hunks. Depressed elderly gypsies. The mathematical forms of the laws of physics.

To wit: at 8:17 a.m. Mountain Standard Time on the

second Tuesday in June, right there in downtown Phoenix, Arizona, Einstein's Theory of Relativity became Tyler Harding's reality.

A simple process really, once you wade through the math.

Basically, as Ty went airborne and accelerated, time slowed.

Slowed so much that he could observe his muscles bunch, then stretch as his body floated horizontally across the pavement. He saw the bus draw closer—in majestic slow motion—and the initially blank faces of the onlookers gradually acquire expressions of shock. Ty even had time to reflect that the old woman had been smiling as she stepped into the street, but as he approached, her smile faded. Weird.

In fact, he decided as he converged on his target, the whole thing was weird.

Still, thanks to that stuff about inertial systems and the equivalence of mass, energy and dimension and so forth, Ty had plenty of time not only to wrap his arms securely around the strangely costumed old lady, but to thoughtfully twist in midair so that his own body would take the brunt of the collision with the sidewalk which was rising slowly to meet him and the nice little grandmotherly woman he'd just rescued.

As the outer surface of his summerweight, Italian gray wool suit contacted the first molecules of cement, Tyler smiled, anticipating the sweet, fluttering thanks she'd give him. Then he recalled his personal agenda and frowned. He hoped this unscheduled incident wouldn't interfere with his job interview.

Ty made a mental note to avoid having impulses from now on, even heroic ones. Better to stick to his normal behavior pattern. Careful investigation and thorough planning were, after all, more—

Phu-whoomf! Ty's body-in-motion experienced rapid and painful deceleration as it impacted the sidewalk's concrete. Time snapped back to its normal state. The bus blew past.

The old lady struggled to her feet, digging an elbow into his stomach and jamming a bony knee into his groin in the process.

Ty lay on his back, the breath knocked out of him. Every bone in his body protested the crash landing. And his physiological claim to manhood just plain hurt like hell from its violent encounter with the old lady's knee.

"Estoopid man!" the old woman hissed, leaning over to glare at him. The summer sunlight flashed on the gold coins dangling from her headscarf, blinding him.

Ty closed his eyes and tried not to groan. He was *never* going to do anything impulsive again. Ever.

The old lady continued to mutter angrily above him. It sounded like a severe case of bronchitis, but there were vowels mixed in here and there, so Ty figured it was probably a string of unflattering epithets in some strange language.

What he couldn't figure out was why she was mad. Hadn't he just saved her life?

Slowly Ty's lungs began working again and the pain receded to bearable levels. Just as he was about to open his eyes, sit up and assess the damage to his suit and his timetable, something pushed gently against his chest.

"No, don't move yet," said a soft voice. "You might be hurt."

Still short of oxygen, Ty inhaled deeply. And caught a whiff of light scent that reminded him of autumn moonlight.

Did you crack your head on the sidewalk, Harding? What the hell does moonlight smell like?

Shifting his weight gingerly, Ty opened his eyes—and looked straight into two pools of warm amber. Surrounded by a cloud of midnight silk. It was the little sprite he'd noticed just before trying to play superhero. The air between them seemed to sparkle and Ty felt dizzy.

Before he was even aware of it, his hand was lifting. Apparently intending to plunge his fingers into the mass of ebony curls, to cup her head and bring it close enough to brush his mouth across her soft, full lips. *And then...*

"Are you sure you're okay, Nadja?" the sprite asked her elderly companion. His chest heated up where her hand still rested.

"Yah, yah," grumbled the old lady over the jangling of coins.

Though Ty's knee-battered male physiology was suddenly revitalized, he sank back on the sidewalk, bemused by his response to the costumed kook's companion.

Who now asked, "Can you move your legs, Mr.—?"

"Harding," Ty supplied automatically. Only half his brain seemed to be functioning in normal mode. The other half appeared content to watch the morning sunlight strike blue sparks off that midnight hair. "Tyler Harding. And you are—?"

"Estoopid!"

Reluctantly, Ty looked past the sprite. The old woman he'd rescued stood glaring at him, arms akimbo, the coins on her scarf dancing. "Estoopid fool," she repeated. "How dare you interfere?"

"But Nadja, he saved your life," the young woman protested, then turned back to Ty. Her big brown eyes had flecks of gold and fire in their depths, he noticed almost dreamily. A man could get lost there and like it. "Thank you so much, Mr. Harding. We were—"

"Who asks him to save me?" the old woman interrupted angrily. "I decide. I will do. No *gadjo* shall stop me!" she declaimed with one arm raised as if to rally the troops.

"We were on our way to the Salvation Army," the sprite continued her explanation softly, her eyes still wide. Her hand still warming his chest. "To fill out a missing person form on Nadja's grandson. I wasn't sure this was the right stop, so I went to check the street sign.

I turned around, saw what was happening, but—I couldn't reach her in time."

Her distress had Ty sitting up, ready to put his arms around her and comfort her. *Hey—no more impulses,* insisted some pragmatic brain cells. Other testosterone-soaked cells voted for comforting. Unanimously.

"Bah!" The old woman tossed her head, sending the coins shivering again. "The Romany are not lost wallets," she declared. "If Nico does not wish to be found, iz hopeless. Iz reason—" The old woman flourished the end of her shawl toward the street, indicating her method of solving...well, whatever problem she thought she had.

Ty's attention drifted back to the crazy old lady's companion. He'd always thought he was partial to tall blondes. Besides, if today's appearance was anything to go by, this little sprite was not at all reserved. Hell, she was wearing some kind of bright T-shirt dress with about eighty-seven colors in it and pink plastic shoes!

But damn—with that glowing dark hair, those sensuous lips and some slim but definitely female curves, the woman attracted him. *The way a porchlight attracts a moth, Harding. Do you want to get burned?*

"Is your grandmother..." Ty lowered his voice, although for the moment, the old woman was ignoring him, adjusting her shawl and muttering in that bronchial language again. "Er, does she have spells like this often?"

"Huh?" Marisa blinked. Oh, dear. Gazing into Mr. Harding's eyes again, she'd forgotten Nadja's dilemma, her own...*everything.* Really, the man ought to wear sunglasses and hand out cards warning people about the risk of overexposure to those blue depths.

The color reminded her of the sky in an Italian Renaissance painting she'd seen once in a museum. A pure, rich, clear blue. Of course, some women might find his thick, dark brown hair more fascinating. Or his golden-tanned skin, or his magnificent athletic build, which his superbly tailored suit elevated to Greek-god status.

Well, what was left of the superb tailoring. That left sleeve was a complete write-off.

Marisa smiled, recalling the way he'd leaped from nowhere to save Mrs. Costeceaseu. Handsome *and* brave—a storybook hero!

"I have only grandson," Nadja declared belligerently and Marisa remembered that Tyler had asked a question. And this was real life, not a fairytale.

"We're neighbors," she explained with a quick, apologetic smile, then lost her breath when Tyler Harding smiled back. Lord, he should ration those, too! "My name's Marisa…Marisa Corelli. And this is Nadja Costeceaseu." Whose body language said she expected to hear the rest.

Marisa paused, then shook her head at the futility of trying to escape her bad luck. Of course within minutes of meeting such an incredible man, she'd have to humiliate herself in front of him.

Face it, Corelli. Her life—which hadn't been that great to begin with—had turned to dog dirt since Roving-Hands Ruben's mother had given her the evil eye.

This was just one more example, like all the jobs she'd lost in the last three months—through no fault of her own.

Nadja cleared her throat. Meaningfully.

Well, regardless of the luck issue, a man like Tyler Harding was out of her league anyway. So, taking a deep breath, Marisa dutifully added, "The Queen of the Gypsies."

One side of Tyler's mouth quirked up. "Gypsies? In Phoenix?" He chuckled, a deep, sexy sound in his throat that turned Marisa's bones to oatmeal. "Now I've heard everything."

"You do not believe?" Nadja screeched.

Marisa bit her lip. Oh dear. The Costeceaseu temper was legendary. Hadn't she single-handedly rid the neighborhood of Phoenix's worst teenage gang after one of them tried to snatch her purse?

"Now, Nadj—" she began soothingly.

The old woman ignored her. "I teach you, Mr. Estoopid Tyler Harding! I teach you to doubt the powers of the Romany," she declared, brandishing her finger like a bony sword. "I, Nadja Costeceaseu, Queen of the Gypsies, hereby place a curse upon you."

Marisa gasped. "Nadja! How could you? The man saved your life."

At least somebody appreciated his effort. Ty grinned as he climbed to his feet and checked his watch. Too bad Ms. Corelli hadn't been the one he'd wrapped his arms around. Those curves would nestle just—

"Hey, wait a second!" the sprite exclaimed, fisting her hands on her hips and frowning as she tilted her head to one side. "If you can put a curse on Mr. Harding, why can't you remove the one Mrs. Pachenko put on me?"

Lord, she was adorable! But he was six-foot-two and she couldn't be five feet tall. They'd look ridiculous together. Besides—if Marisa Corelli bought into this curse baloney, she was as crazy as her elderly friend.

The old woman spread her hands wide, palms up, then shrugged. "Professional courtesy," she said shortly.

Ty groaned silently. The look on Marisa Corelli's face as she stared at the old lady reminded him of a kicked puppy. He'd better leave before he did something stupid. For the second time in one morning.

As he brushed off his suit, Ty forced a laugh. "Well, if I believed in gypsy curses, I might be worried. But since I don't—"

The old woman focused piercing black eyes on Ty. "You will," she proclaimed. "I see inside you, Tyler Harding, and so I curse you with the one thing that will bother you most. I curse you with good luck!"

Marisa bit her lip, but took a step forward. "Nadja," she said sternly. "Mr. Harding doesn't deserve that kind of treatment."

He could fight his own battles, thank you, but it was a sweet gesture.

"Don't worry about it, Marisa," Ty said. Darn, she was cute, sexy and kind-hearted. But unlike the rest of the Hardings, *his* plans and schedules were not subject to change at every whim. "I don't believe in luck," he repeated past an odd twinge of regret. "Good *or* bad."

The old lady rattled her bronchial tubes again. "Believe, no believe. Makes no difference. Luck iz like electricity. Exists, works—whether believe or not. You will discover," she promised.

With a shake of his head, Ty murmured goodbye to the adorable but unsuitable Marisa Corelli, smiled wryly at her crazy old friend and strolled down the street toward his interview.

A few minutes later, as the receptionist showed him into Mr. Krako's office, Ty chuckled aloud. Even if it was true— Even if Nadja Coste-Whatever *was* the Queen of the Gypsies, even if a person's "fate" could be changed by a few words—how could *good* luck be a terrible curse?

TWO WEEKS LATER, he had a pretty good idea.

First of all, despite showing up late, his face streaked with dirt and his suit torn, Ty had gotten the job with Krako, Iverson and Delaporte. After a five minute interview. At twice the going salary.

That was Tuesday. On Wednesday, his car was stolen—and recovered an hour later without a scratch. Ty's insurance company was so happy about it, they lowered his premium.

On Friday, he'd gotten a raise.

The second week was even worse.

Ty inherited a mansion in Paradise Valley, the most exclusive section of Phoenix, from a college classmate he couldn't remember, accidentally captured a pair of bank robbers for the FBI—and won eighteen million dollars in the lottery.

Without even buying a ticket. Some guy at work handed them out instead of cigars when his wife had a baby.

Feeling ridiculous, but determined to prove to his reeling brain that there was absolutely nothing to this curse nonsense, Ty bought a ticket with the same numbers for the next drawing.

This time, he won twenty-six million dollars.

That's when he hired a private investigator. Once the guy located Nadja Something-or-other, who spoke some bronchial language and pretended to be a gypsy, Ty intended to confront her. Demand an explanation for all these coincidences. Then construct and implement a plan that would return his life to normal.

To help the investigator get started, Ty described Marisa Corelli. In exhaustive detail.

While he awaited results, he began his first assignment for Krako, Iverson and Delaporte: designing a computer-lab addition to an elementary school. As he worked up the mechanicals, it occurred to him that, while he understood how to plan for the *use* of electricity, he never *had* grasped some of that theoretical stuff. Like light being both a particle and a wave....

That's when Tyler Harding made his first concession to the inexplicable. He didn't believe in luck or curses or gypsies—or even in changing plans in midexecution unless absolutely necessary—but he did believe in being prepared.

So he went home and dug out that crystal thingy one of his younger sisters had given him last year. Just in case.

2

AFTER ANOTHER WEEK—during which the gypsy's curse continued to spread through Ty's life like a Type-A flu—the PI produced a single phone number that *might* lead to Marisa. No clue at all to the whereabouts of the gypsy queen.

While the detective was scribbling down the phone number, Ralph Krako stuck his head into Ty's work space. "Come by my office later, Harding," the man boomed jovially. "Gonna make you an offer you can't refuse!"

Ty hurriedly wrote the investigator another check and told him to keep looking. Then he ducked out the back way and spent the afternoon at the movies. Hiding. Because Krako's secretary had already told him about the offer. They wanted to make him a partner—after three weeks. Dammit, they couldn't do that! Not yet. He'd only submitted one preliminary design for one project!

What good was success if you didn't earn it? he fumed. How could you enjoy it, if you hadn't proven, at least to yourself, that you deserved it?

Slumped in the darkness while soothing explosions, car chases and gunfire filled the screen, Ty tried—again—to make sense of the lunacy of the last three weeks.

What had happened? He'd always been the steady Harding. The one who knew where he was going and exactly how he was going to get there. He always got there, too. Right on schedule. And he liked the sense of accomplishment that gave him. But now—

Dammit, he felt like a helpless victim on a runaway train.

His brothers and sisters were the ones who thrived on chaos and upheaval. They floated through life direction-less, letting events shape them—instead of vice versa.

A helicopter crashed through a building and exploded, raining fire and glass shards on the city below.

The fire reminded him of Marisa's eyes.

Ty fingered the piece of paper he'd stuffed in his shirt pocket, then jerked his hand away.

Dammit! How could five minutes of gazing up at the wrong woman feel so right? Marisa Corelli was not in his plans. Not yet, not ever. She was too short. She be-lieved in these crazy curse things. *She smells like moon-light and her hair's like flowing black silk....*

Once again, Ty felt the soft pressure of her hand on his chest, heard again the concern in her low voice. Con-cern for him.

On the screen, in slow motion, a driverless truck slammed into an oil refinery, setting off a string of spec-tacular explosions, complete with sub-woofer sound ef-fects that shook the cement floor of the theater. Face it—they were nothing compared to Marisa Corelli's effect on Ty Harding.

Maybe he *would* call. Ask her out for a drink. Prove to himself that—animal magnetism aside—they were completely incompatible. That would get her out of his system for good. Then he could concentrate on straight-ening out these ridiculous coincidences. Return his life to its normal stable, predictable state.

At last. He could relax now. He had a plan. With a happy sigh, Ty settled in to enjoy the rest of the movie, an artistic classic called *The Boston Killers' Rampage*.

MARISA WRESTLED THE philodendron through the apart-ment house door, tucked her chin over a leaf stalk so she could see better and headed for Nadja's place down the block. This was her sixteenth trip; she'd saved Baby for last.

"I'm going to miss you," she assured the huge plant, "but you're too delicate to survive living under a bridge and that's where I may end up."

Taking a deep breath, Marisa tried to swallow her anxiety. Emotional turmoil upset the plants. Being moved and saying good-bye would be hard enough on them.

On me too, she admitted silently. *But I'll survive— even if I do end up under a bridge.* That was one thing she'd learned at an early age: survival.

With a sigh, Marisa adjusted Baby's pot in her arms. All those years growing up without one, she'd longed for a home and a family of her own.

Now, just because she'd refused to dance with Roving-Hands Ruben Pachenko at the St. Gerald-of-Poughkeepsie church festival, she'd be lucky to keep a roof—of any kind—over her own head much longer.

*Luck…*Marisa groaned. She had all the luck she could handle right now.

All of it bad.

Last week had been typical of the weirdness overwhelming her life since the showdown with Ruben and his mother.

Her landlord had raised her rent again—just when she lost another job.

How, Marisa wondered, was she supposed to know the DEA had Alfredo's Bar targeted as a drug distribution center and would close it down? On payday. *Before* they handed out the paychecks, of course.

So now she was giving her beloved plants to Nadja and moving to a tiny, dark room in a boarding house. And from there?

Well, there was always hope. The rented room was cheap. If the next job paid minimum wage and she kept it for at least two weeks... It was probably silly, but Marisa planned to hire a *curandero* to remove the evil eye—since the Queen of the Gypsies, her very own friend, refused.

Professional courtesy, ha! Nadja Costeceaseu was a fake.

I knew it—she's just an old woman trying to make her lonely life seem exciting and special. If only her grandson Nico would call and tell her he's okay....

As she turned up the walk to Nadja's place, anxiety over her own future swamped Marisa for a moment. Deliberately, she turned her attention to job options instead. At least unskilled positions were plentiful. Although she dreamed of attending college, she'd had to support herself since she turned eighteen and so far had only managed to take a few extension courses.

First things first, Corelli. Employment now. Dreams later.

"There's always a night manager at a convenience store," she told herself as she mounted the low steps leading to the gypsy's front door. A little dangerous maybe, but better pay than the last few positions she'd held.

Besides—with her luck these days, any job posed a threat. Hadn't she lost her reading glasses in the muffin vat at the Lenin-Ho Revisionist Bakery last month?

Your eyes aren't that bad, she reminded herself. And since the public library had barred her after that computer incident...

Too bad she couldn't find employment wherever Tyler Harding worked. *Now there's a fringe benefit,* she thought with a smile. Imagine being able to ogle those rich blue eyes and that hard muscular body every day!

Balancing on one foot, Marisa kicked lightly on Nadja's door with the other. "It's me," she called, knowing the old lady's attitude toward strangers. Mrs.

Costeceaseu made the CIA look like a welcoming committee.

The Queen of the Gypsies flung open the door. "No more! Go away!" she yelled, even as she stood back to let Marisa in. "Listen to me—the Romany are nomads. We do not stay in one place."

Marisa set Baby down beside a worn, maroon velvet sofa, next to a small table covered with a fringed cloth. She frowned at the glass sphere on the table. It couldn't be a crystal ball.

Could it?

"I tell you we are not farmers! You must take theez jungle—"

"I can't, Nadja," Marisa cried, unable to keep up the pretense any longer. Even for Baby's sake. "I can't! I have to move. And you know why."

The old lady nodded. "Mrs. Pachenko's evil eye," she agreed dolefully. "The woman is powerful witch. Second only to me in neighborhood," she added magnanimously.

Marisa chewed on her lip. This is where she always got confused. Magic and witches and spells seemed silly, but wonder and surprise and hope were the very things that made life bearable. Where was the dividing line between hope and illusion, between dream and fantasy? "The new place has no room for my plants," she said quietly.

"Find better place."

Marisa looked steadily at Nadja. "Where?" she asked. "How?"

"Okay, okay." The old lady held up her hands in surrender, then folded one arm across her chest and tapped her chin with her free index finger. After a long moment, she looked up. "I do something about Mrs. Pachenko and you take plants away?"

"Agreed."

"Good." Nadja's sleeves fluttered as she made shooing motions. "Take plants now."

Marisa shook her head. "When you remove the *mal ojo*," she said firmly. Well, almost firmly. If Nadja *could* lift the spell, who wanted to tick her off?

And if she couldn't… Marisa didn't have the heart to destroy her friend's illusions. *Sometimes they're all we have.*

Like my ultimate dream of a loving home, a husband to share it with and babies….

Right now that looked as realistic as Nadja's claim to royalty.

"Iz not so easy," the old lady announced with a disgruntled look. "Iz not simple matter of chanting little jingle, you know. Takes time." She began to mutter in her own language, then she smiled suddenly. "Okay. Leave estoopid plants. Come back tomorrow."

After saying goodbye to Mrs. Costeceaseu and her plant family, Marisa walked back toward her barren apartment. *If Nadja really could halt this run of bad luck,* she thought wryly, *I'd be tempted to ask her for a love charm—and directions for working it on Tyler Harding.*

She'd thought about him—too often, really—since the day he'd saved Nadja from that bus. Such a heroic hottie. Wouldn't he make a wonderful husband? *And what a great father!*

Marisa tripped on the broken sidewalk just thinking about the process of Tyler Harding becoming a dad. She'd reached the end of the block, so she grabbed at the street sign to regain her balance.

Unfortunately, it was the one the garbage truck had clipped last week. The pole broke off at ground level; as it fell, it knocked loose the locking nut atop the fire hydrant. A spume of water rose from the hydrant, drenching her as she just stood there, appalled by the damage her fantasizing had caused.

After a few minutes, as the neighborhood kids rushed

out to cool off in the impromptu fountain, Marisa walked
onward to find a telephone and report her mishap, still
elaborating on her daydream starring Tyler Harding.

Of course, she really ought to find out more about the
man—like how he felt about kids—before she invested
any more time and energy in romantic reveries about
him. No sense wasting a perfectly good fantasy on the
wrong guy.

TAKING A DEEP BREATH, Ty dialed the number the investigator had given him. Listened to it ring. Waited to
hear Marisa's soft, low voice.

"Da Cactus Barrel Japanese Bath House 'n' New Age
Hoibal Shop," rattled off a hearty male voice with the
thickest New Jersey accent Ty had ever heard. "Dis is
Bert. What can I do ya for?"

"Uh…" It wasn't that he was disappointed. Exactly.

"Look, I ain't got all day here. You wanna resoive a
bath or you gotta question about hoibal remedies?" the
gruff voice demanded.

Ty cleared his throat. "I…I'm trying to locate a
woman—" *A little sprite, really. With warm-brandy eyes
and curling, midnight hair.* "—named Marisa Corelli."

"Don't know her," New Jersey Bert said. Too
promptly for Ty's taste. "But I been in Tibet da last six
months, studyin' astral projection. Hold on—da mezuzah
might know her."

"Excuse me?" Ty felt beads of perspiration form on
his upper lip at the conversation's unexpected turn. How
could a Jewish religious object be helpful in locating a
woman you met on a Phoenix street after you rescued
the Queen of the Gypsies from a runaway bus?

"Beverly." The man sounded impatient. "Da mezuzah. Ya know—da person dat gives da body rubs."

Masseuse! Weak with relief, Ty blurted out a question
that three weeks ago he would never in a million years
have asked. "Does she know anything about gypsies?"

"Gypsies?" the man repeated in a disbelieving tone. "Listen, man, da Queen of da Gypsies herself used to read palms down here on Saturdays.... But she retired awhile back."

"Wha-what was her name?" Ty asked, feeling faint.

"Nadja," Bert said, interest percolating through his accent now. "Nadja Costeceaseu. Talk about your *drabarní!* You lookin' for a fortune-teller?"

"No! I do not believe in that stuff. Not in any of it," Ty said through gritted teeth. All these...happenings were not caused by luck or fate or a damned gypsy. It was impossible. Irrational.

It was also screwing up his life Plan. Royally.

When he got back from the movie yesterday, they'd made him a partner—over his vehement protests. And the cat he'd rescued from that ledge at his apartment building... Why did it have to belong to the mayor? And why was a television crew present to film it? *Now everybody in Phoenix knows my face and my name,* he thought wistfully. *But as usual, nobody knows* me. *Nobody understands....*

Ty rubbed frustrated fingers along his jaw. He didn't need understanding; he *needed* to regain control of his life!

Bert was nothing if not perceptive. "You sound kinda upset," he said. "But whatever's botherin' ya, it's just your karma, see."

Karma. Geez. Another kook. "Well, this is more along the lines of a curse," Ty snapped without thinking. Was everybody in Phoenix crazy?

"Oh, man, I'm sorry. Curses are pretty tough to beat...." Bert fell silent for a moment, then said thoughtfully, "Your best bet is probably yin and yang."

Ty groaned. But he was desperate: his perfect Plan currently cruised the toilet. "How does that work?" he asked resignedly.

"You never hoid of yin and yang?" Bert sounded

shocked. As if it was something ordinary like—*electricity*. Recalling Nadja's comment on *that,* Ty almost missed the bath owner's explanation. "Ya bring opposites together so they can, like, neutralize each other. To restore da cosmic balance."

In a crazy kind of way, that made sense. If you were crazy.

Which he wasn't yet. "I'll, uh, keep it in mind," Ty said insincerely. "But…could you give me Nadja's address and telephone number if you've got it?" He'd ask the old lady how to contact Marisa. She owed him that much for saving her life. *And getting cursed for it.*

"Ax da expoit—great idea!" Bert exclaimed and provided the information.

Conscientiously, Ty made himself complete the side elevation drawings for the school addition before calling Nadja. Then, as he picked up the phone, he heard Krako booming his way down the hall.

"Sure, take all the photos you want. I'm a big fan of your magazine. Don't forget to mention I'm the one who hired him—makes me look like a genius, doesn't it?" Krako's laughter was coming closer, accompanied by what sounded like two or three other people. Or more.

Ty hightailed it out of the office in world-record time.

He'd visit Nadja in person, he decided. Get this curse mess straightened out—now. Then he'd remove the tantalizing images of Marisa Corelli from his system. The ones that were disrupting his sleep and trying to lure him toward the chaos called love.

That done, he'd be able to get back to his orderly, rational, well-planned life. He'd work. He'd prepare. He'd achieve.

And he would never, ever, *ever* yield to another impulse. The next old woman who wanted to orchestrate her own demise could go right ahead.

Ty spent the drive to Nadja's neighborhood structuring his explanatory speech. Filling it with reason and rationality. And some good, old-fashioned groveling, just in case.

But when the door opened and, instead of an old lady in her crazy costume, Marisa Corelli stood there—wearing faded jeans that fit like a second skin and a thin white T-shirt—looking up at him with those soft amber eyes, Ty Harding's speech center blanked. He couldn't remember any English at all.

So he kissed her.

Fireworks exploded around them. For safety's sake, he threaded his fingers through Marisa's silken, ebony curls and held on. Her mouth was soft and warm and moist. He wanted to explore its depths for a month or two, wanted to slide his hand down her back and cup her—

What *was* that raucous cackling sound? Reluctantly, Ty broke the kiss to look around.

Oh, Lordy! Nadja stood in the center of a room straight out of some bad foreign movie. Laughing at him. And Marisa—she'd pulled away, had her back pressed against the open door and was staring at him as if he was some kind of sexual deviant.

Ty covered his eyes with his hand and groaned. What had he done? And why had he done it? Lowering his hand, Ty looked at Marisa's full mouth, her tousled hair, her sweet curves. Remembered those fireworks. Well, he *knew* why. He wasn't a eunuch, for heaven's sake!

"Uh, hello, Marisa," he said, wincing at how ridiculous he sounded. "What are you doing here?"

"I tell her to come," Nadja barked, motioning toward a threadbare velvet sofa. "Enough socializing. Sit. Both of you."

After a moment's hesitation, Marisa did as ordered. Ty followed suit, silently wondering how anyone could live like this. The place looked like a cross between an overfertilized rainforest and an exploding silk factory.

"Well?" Nadja demanded, while Ty tried to remember exactly how the speech he'd planned began. "Why have you come?"

"Nadja—" Marisa protested, only to be cut off with another hand gesture.

"I ask him question. You—remember promise." The old lady sank into a nearby overstuffed chair and fondled a glass ball as she glared at him. "Well?"

Ty sighed. After that crazy, impulsive, incredible kiss—and Marisa's reaction to it—he wasn't about to admit he'd come looking for the little sprite in order to get her out of his system and get his life plan back on track.

She'd probably call the cops. He probably deserved it, too. But if he got out of here today without being arrested, he might rethink the marriage part of his Plan. Not all feelings, he realized, were bad. Six years without kisses like that—and what came next—suddenly stretched like an eternity.

"You come to beg forgiveness, eh?" Nadja asked with a smirk. "Curse iz too much."

"Of course not," Ty snapped. He'd never fallen for any of that mystic stuff; he wasn't changing his mind now.

Marisa inhaled sharply.

Right. The Queen of the Gypsies didn't handle differences of opinion well. "That is...I did come to *discuss*—" He couldn't say the word. "Let's call it the recent chain of unbelievable coincidences," he suggested.

The old lady leaned forward to peer sharply at him. Ty intended to meet her gaze, but his eyeballs kept aiming sideways to see if Marisa was still appalled by his earlier behavior. Dammit, if she'd let him, he'd apologize for frightening her. But not for that kiss.

Because he wasn't sorry for it. In fact, he wanted to try it again. Wanted to discover how such a brief contact packed such a big wallop.

"Bah, you still no believe," Nadja said, straightening and turning away. "And in that case—iz not possible to just—" she raised her arm over her head like a dancer and snapped her fingers "—lift curse."

Ty stared at the old lady and wondered which one of them was crazier. "Then what do you suggest?" he asked dryly.

Nadja's wrinkled face suddenly framed a smile. She pointed at Marisa. "Take her—and her plants. Go home. Live together until next blue moon. Curse will be broken."

Two full moons in the same month, right? How often did that happen? Which meant plenty of close, personal contact with the sprite. Every male cell in his body screamed YES!

Before he could respond verbally, though, Marisa jumped to her feet.

"No!" She started to add a scathing remark about self-interested busybodies, then remembered that if she made Nadja angry, her plants would be homeless before she was.

But this was ridiculous. No, it was *dangerous*. "Absolutely not."

"Why not?" Ty and Nadja asked simultaneously.

"I have my reasons," Marisa replied shortly. Reasons she wasn't about to share. In the first place—aside from that glorious kiss, they were complete strangers and she'd vowed at eighteen never to live with another one. In the second place—for all she knew, he already lived with someone. *Someone female.*

And finally— Marisa shrugged. Although she didn't necessarily believe in the whole evil-eye thing, she refused to expose a hero who belonged in the Kissing Hall of Fame to the perils that surrounded her these days.

"Look, Mr. Harding…"

"Call me Ty."

Heavens, his deep voice and that crooked half-smile

ought to be classified as addictive drugs. She already craved another dose. *Another kiss, too. Talk about a rush! Ty Harding made cocaine seem like baby aspirin.*

Marisa shook her head at the nonsense afflicting her brain. No doubt about it. The man should be declared a controlled substance and female exposure to him strictly prohibited.

"I'm not going to call you anything," she said doggedly. "Just because I'm having a little trouble..." *Homelessness is a minor inconvenience? Corelli, your optimism borders on the ludicrous.* "...is no reason to impose on you. This is just a scheme Mrs. Costeceaseu cooked up to get rid of my f—"

She was about to say "family." She could imagine how Ty's twinkling blue eyes would laugh at that pathetic revelation! "My f-ferns," she said quickly. "A-and my kalanchoes. My dracaena marginata. And of course, my philodendron Baby."

"Who? No—don't tell me. I don't want to know." Ty ran his hand along his firm, masculine jaw. "Let me ask another question. Why is *she* trying to get rid of *your* plants?"

Her scalp tingled, remembering his touch. So did her lips. "Because she doesn't want them," Marisa explained patiently.

Ty shook his head. "No, I mean—why don't you keep them yourself?"

"Because I..." She forced out half a laugh. "I've had to give up my apartment."

"Why? Is there something wrong with it?"

"Wrong with it?" She echoed. He couldn't be that naive, could he?

"You know—it's too small for your forest. Too far from the mall?"

Nadja chuckled.

Marisa had to agree. The man could kiss, she thought

as she shook her head, but he appeared to be a few bricks short.

"Then why give it up?"

Maybe he's one of those lucky people, Marisa decided, reaching over to stroke one of Baby's deeply-serrated leaves, *who's never moved unless he wanted to.*

"Because I can't pay the rent," she said, spelling it out. "One of the neighbors gave me the evil eye, so now I'm out of work and out of money."

"Evil eye?" Disbelief filled his voice. After a second's hesitation, he shook his head, dismissing the concept.

Marisa wished she could do the same. But three months of disastrous coincidences had shaken her belief in straight-up cause-and-effect explanations.

"Moving's expensive, too," he said, breaking into her philosophical musings. "Why don't you just borrow the rent money from someone until you get back on your feet?"

Marisa stared at him. What planet did this guy live on? Then she noticed the little embroidered crest on his shirt pocket. Oh. That explained it. He lived on Planet Affluent. And she'd bet the shine on his loafers that he had a safety net she didn't: relatives he could rely on if worse came to where she was right now. "Who do you suggest I ask?"

"Well—" Ty shrugged. Oh yeah, he did have magnificent shoulders. "—your parents? A sibling?" He flashed another controlled-substance smile. "Haven't you got a rich uncle around somewhere?"

"She is orphan, estoopid," Nadja hissed.

Those spring-sky eyes widened. "Aw, geez, Marisa," Ty said. "I'm sorry...."

Oh, no. She didn't take sympathy from gorgeous but apparently semimoronic hunks. "No need to apologize," she said briskly. "It wasn't your fault.

"And I don't need a loan," she went on, looking at

the gold-threaded tapestry hanging on the wall to avoid searching those baby blues for signs of pity. If she saw any, she'd have to hit him.

And she didn't want to strike him. A softer, slower, more sensually satisfying contact was what she wanted.

Oh, face factoids, Corelli. That kiss wasn't magical. It just felt that way. The man obviously honed his technique by kissing anything female. "I don't need to mooch housing off anyone. I need a job—one I won't lose right away." She transferred her gaze to her elderly friend, who became busy rearranging a bowl of wax fruit.

Marisa looked at Ty again. "Forget Nadja's harebrained scheme," she counseled over resurging anxiety. She'd figure out *something.* "If you don't believe in curses, I can't see any real advantage to it for you."

After tossing Her Gypsy Highness another you-ought-to-be-ashamed look—which she ignored, naturally—Marisa glanced back at Ty. He just sat there. Oozing masculinity. Not saying a word. Studying the pattern of the rug at his feet, one hand idly arranging the ends of his tie against the vast expanse of starched shirt covering his massive chest. No wonder his brain wasn't so sharp—the man's DNA had expended all its energy on turning out a professional-class heartthrob.

"But I can," he said eventually, just before flashing her another bone-melting smile. "Haven't you heard of yin and yang?"

Adamantly disregarding Nadja's snort of disbelief, Ty began spouting as much of Bert's mumbo jumbo as he could remember. And some he made up on the spot.

Clearly, his decision to have no offspring was a good one. He *shouldn't* reproduce. All these years he'd believed himself the exception to his family. Incapable of shooting from the hip.

Wrong. Apparently, he too carried the Harding nuttiness gene.

Because he was yielding to another impulse, and this time, he didn't care.

His carefully crafted Plan was already in shambles. Why not add a roommate with the silliest ideas he'd ever heard?

Cuckoo or not, the midnight-haired sprite needed help. And unbelievable as it sounded to him, she had nobody to turn to.

Ty could hardly comprehend it. True, his aging hippie parents, his pain-in-the-banana brothers and sisters, the whole extended throng of free-spirited Hardings and their cronies—none of them could be counted on to provide much practical help in a crisis, but at least they'd *be* there.

Marisa had only a grouchy Gypsy Queen.

And me.

"So you see," he finished up, "you'll be doing me a favor if you move in as Nadja suggested. And it's only until the next—"

The next what? Millennium? Century? Lifetime? Ty couldn't remember. As long as she didn't leave peanut butter smears on the furniture or disrupt his Plan—*and how could she?*—who cared? He'd see those silky jet curls over the breakfast table. Long enough to stop being enchanted by them. And maybe with her crazy ideas about evil eyes floating around the apartment, these ludicrous coincidences would cease, too. Stranger things had happened in the last three weeks.

"Until next blue moon," Nadja furnished.

"Right, right." Who knew when that was? And who cared?

Ty looked at Marisa. Okay, he looked pleadingly at her. "What do you say? I've got a big apartment—plenty of room for you and your plants."

"And an understanding girlfriend?" Marisa asked, gnawing on a corner of her full lower lip. Ty stifled a groan. As if he needed a reminder of that mind-boggling kiss!

Which *must* have been an aberration. Kisses between practically strangers didn't melt your socks and rattle your rocks.

Still—she didn't have to act as if she'd rather smooch a rattlesnake than Ty Harding!

"I wouldn't have kissed you if there was anyone else," Ty informed her in a low voice, looking into those golden eyes. Concern still lurked in their tawny depths.

For criminy's sake.

"And this is a purely platonic arrangement I'm proposing, anyway," he declared through a throat tight with regret. He wanted to see if a second kiss resulted in another detonation. "I don't expect anything in return for room and board except a chance to bring our extremes of luck back into balance."

"Ha!" Nadja cackled, marching to the door and yanking it open. "You share bed before month is out," she declared. "Now take plants. Go. Or I curse you both with mother-in-law like me."

They went. As far as the sidewalk in front of Nadja's apartment. Where it took him almost thirty more minutes in the broiling Arizona sun to get Marisa to agree to live with him for the next two weeks.

Then he loaded about eight hundred plants into the truck given to him this morning by a local auto dealer who loved cats. The rest of Marisa's worldly goods fit into two suitcases and a shopping bag.

See? he told himself as he put them in the back seat of the club cab, the woman has no sense of priorities. Too many plants, not a stick of stabilizing furniture. Completely unsuitable—except for that kiss. Lordy, kisses like that would rev a cloistered monk's engine.

And now that he thought about it, Ty didn't remember taking any vows of celibacy.

As he unlocked his apartment door and stood aside to

let Marisa, who insisted on carrying the green giant she called Baby, precede him inside, Ty sighed. Nadja Costeceaseu might be certifiably crazy, he decided, but she was right about one thing. He *was* "estoopid."

Despite the fact that there was no such thing as a good-luck curse—or an evil eye—here he was, filling his pristine apartment with a freaking jungle of drapey, droopy, undoubtedly messy plants. Owned by a little sprite with lunatic ideas about witches and spells, who kissed like the devil. And who only agreed to move in because he'd promised not to touch her. Estoopid, indeed.

That was the problem with making decisions on the fly instead of sticking to Plans. Impulses led to complications. Which led to chaos.

He'd simply have to clarify—diplomatically, of course—his need for order and quiet....

Ty carried the last suitcase inside. Looked up to find Marisa standing as still as the desert dawn in the center of his living room. "I guess you'll want the plants—" he began, only to be cut off by the sprite asking in a small voice what the rules were.

"Rules?" Sheesh, she made it sound as if she expected prison-style regulations. He wasn't that rigid. *Except during that kiss.*

"Everyone has rules," Marisa insisted, her amber eyes watchful. "I've learned that things go easier if I ask upfront."

Ty bit down on the questions—and the flare of irritation—that statement provoked. Flaky or not, Hardings treated visitors as guests, not miscreants.

"If rules make you more comfortable," he said quietly, "we'll invent some tomorrow."

THAT EVENING, HE insisted Marisa take the bed. He tossed and turned all night in a sleeping bag on the carpet in the extra bedroom, which he'd idiotically set up as an office because he'd expected to put in overtime to achieve Step 4-C: the partnership Krako handed him yesterday like a rubber toy tossed to a teething puppy.

At least, he thought he was tossing and turning there—until the sprite set off the smoke alarm and woke him the hell up.

It took eight stitches to close the cut.

Ty would have considered that solid evidence that Nadja's good-luck curse was a bunch of hooey—except for what happened when they left the emergency room.

3

COOL BREEZE ON HIS bare chest. Hard bus bench under him. Early morning sunlight stabbing through the narrow slits between high-rise buildings right into his eyes. Minor inconveniences. Ty wasn't moving—in fact, he thought he just might sit here until a pigeon declared him a statue and the hospital stuck a plaque on him.

"Ty? Are you sure you're okay?"

Ridiculous, but even now, numb with fatigue, that low, soft voice stirred him. Thank heavens, he'd had the sense to pull on loose, cotton-knit pants with a drawstring waist before he sacked out last night. Otherwise, his, ah, stirring would be obvious. A mile away.

"I'm so sorry, Ty," Marisa said, between nibbles on her lower lip. "I swear—I didn't think Nadja's plan would work like this!"

Ty rubbed a hand over his unshaven jaw. Didn't help. Her statement remained a mystery. "Huh? You can't call eight stitches good luck, can you?"

"That's what I mean." She tilted her chin stubbornly. "Last night *you* suffered the consequences of *my* bad luck."

Ty covered his eyes. That was him groaning, too. Holy macaroni—how could someone so cute be so nuts?

"There is no such thing as luck," he declared. "Or evil eyes. Or curses. Or elves or gypsies. Or witches. Or—"

"You don't need to shout," Marisa interrupted quietly, lifting her adorable little chin another half inch. "I get your point."

"I'm not shouting!" Ty…er, shouted. *Okay.* He took a deep, calming breath. *Don't pop your stitches.* He wasn't going back into that quack shack any time soon.

Marisa leaned close to study his eyes. Hers looked the way he'd first seen them—brandy warm and filled with concern. *For me,* he thought, his mouth curving into a fatuous grin.

He forced it to form a frown. His Plan did not include involvement with a midnight-haired, petite stick of sensual dynamite who believed in…*nonsense.* Even if she kissed like blue blazes.

But he *was* involved with her, thanks to Nadja Costeceaseu. At least until she found a job—or the next blue moon, whichever came first.

"Your pupils are equal," she announced doubtfully, straightening away from him and looking down the long hospital drive leading to the street. "They said they checked you for concussion, but…"

She chewed on her lower lip, driving everything above a breathtakingly primitive level right out of Ty's melting brain cells. "You do remember what happened last night, don't you?" she asked casually, pretending to watch the sparse early-morning traffic glide slowly past.

Ha. As if he'd fall into that trap—his mother had used it for years.

"Some of it," Ty admitted cautiously. The predominant mental picture he retained from the night was the vivid image of a pair of long, sexy legs extending from the hem of a short, purply-red satin nightshirt number; he knew better than to mention that!

"What don't you remember?"

Ty hesitated again. His clouded brain sensed something tricky in the question, but he couldn't quite figure out what. So he did what any normal male would in similar circumstances.

He stalled.

"Well, I—" Then suddenly, he did remember. Everything. In full Technicolor vision and Dolby sound.

He'd thought he was awake, tossing and turning, but he must have fallen asleep. Apparently ending up with his head beneath the metal base of his drafting table. Dreaming of holding Marisa when—

SCREEEEEEEEEEE!

Jerking upward, adrenaline pumping wildly, his head had connected with something hard. Something sharp. Naturally, he'd slammed backward into the carpet....

And then Marisa *was* in his arms, murmuring his name in her soft, low voice. That felt good. Right.

SCREEEEEEEEEEEE!

The dreadful sound continued, but Ty lost interest in it. He distinctly remembered moving his head so his lips could nuzzle her neck....

He frowned, recalling the next part. He'd just gotten started with his exploration—her skin *was* velvety soft—when she'd wrenched away from him.

By the time Marisa had returned, the damned *SCREEEEEEEEEEE!* had finally scraped every nerve ending raw....

"You're bleeding," she'd explained, pressing a towel against his temple, then lifting it away to show him what she meant.

And hell yes, there'd been blood. All over the white terry cloth. *His* blood.

He'd gotten a little whoozy then. She must have called 9-1-1—he vaguely recalled an ambulance ride. Handing over his insurance card. Then they'd spent a couple of eternities with their rear ends molded to plastic chairs in the emergency room waiting area. While gunshot wounds, firecracker injuries and possible heart attacks jumped line and disappeared into the treatment arena.

Until the sweet little sprite beside him turned into Hitler Junior around 3:00 a.m.

Ty choked back a laugh.

She'd marched up to the desk and knocked over the In-tray as she demanded that he be treated immediately. The clerk glared at Marisa as he gathered the papers that had snowed out of folders to the floor—then Ty saw him blanch, hurriedly shuffle a couple of pages between two charts and race through the double doors shouting, "Hold it, Doc, hold it! Barnes is allergic to antivenin!"

Minutes later, they'd ushered Ty into an examination room where a yawning intern stitched him up.

"Oh, yeah," he said now, fingering the tape and gauze covering his temple and half his forehead. "I remember what happened. But *why* is the mystery." And how. How could a fire start in that apartment? No candles, no incense, no smoking. No clutter, either.

Okay, maybe it *was* a little on the austere side, he conceded, recalling the impact of Marisa's jungle against all that bare-wall beige. "What set off the smoke alarm?"

"I did." Marisa's sigh came from her toes. She owed Ty a new end table—and a copy of the book resting on it. Which, with her luck, had been a priceless first edition. *It's charcoal now.* Wet charcoal.

"But…how…?" He sounded confused and she could hardly blame him. He wasn't used to these disasters the way she was.

"I got worried about Baby, so I—"

"Who?"

"My philodendron," she said patiently, wishing as she had all night that Tyler had put on a shirt before the EMT's arrival. Despite hours spent in proximity to it, she still wanted to ogle his broad, muscular expanse of bare chest.

Talk about eye-candy! Even the deliciously dangerous-looking dark beard stubble shadowing Ty's firm jaw flooded her bloodstream with endorphins.

Knock it off, Corelli. It's what's inside that counts, she she reminded herself piously before the endorphins gurgled, *And what a package Tyler Harding wraps that inside in!*

With an effort that deserved a Congressional medal,

Marisa dragged her attention back to the conversation. "I got up to talk to her."

"Why on earth would you talk to a plant?" Ty asked, blinking his baby blues at her.

There now—see? she pointed out to herself. *Beautiful is as stupid sounds.* "I was afraid she'd be frightened in a strange place and thought a familiar voi—"

Geez, even his snort of disbelief was sexy. "You thought your plant might be scared?"

"Many people believe plants have feelings," she said stiffly. "Studies have shown that plants respond to music an—"

"Why didn't you try the stereo, then, instead of the smoke alarm?"

Marisa ignored his sarcasm. Eight stitches and a night in the ER—anybody'd be cranky. "I didn't want to wake you by turning on a lamp, so I used a match." She shrugged at the inevitability of what happened next.

"I held it too long...dropped it.... The next thing I knew, the book's burning, the table's smoldering. I doused the fire with a pan of water—and the smoke set off the alarm.

"Luckily—" She shuddered at the term. "Those were the only things damaged. Of course, I'll replace them—"

"Forget it," Ty growled. Sheesh, with those darned lottery winnings, he could purchase end tables for everyone in North America. Might as well—damned if he'd spend money he hadn't earned on himself.

He tried to change the subject. "Any ideas how we're getting home?"

"I called a cab while you signed yourself out," Marisa replied, tilting her chin again. And again, impulse seized him. A sudden urge to cup that adorable facial feature with his palm, angle his mouth over hers and see if another kiss would blow his socks off the way the first one had.

As Ty fought the impulse, she stubbornly insisted, "I will buy you a new—"

"I said forget it," he repeated. "It was an accident."

"An accident?" Marisa's eyes widened.

He wanted to dive into their bronze depths. Submerge in them. Drown in them.

God help him. He'd met plenty of women since formulating his Plan. Not one had tempted him to deviate from it. Not one of them had set off nuclear blasts with a little kiss, either. Until this one.

This one drew him like the Sirens or whoever lured Greek sailors to their destruction.

What made Marisa Corelli so special? True, she was beautiful. Sexy in a unique, satiny-nightshirt way.

"Oh, Tyler, how can you believe that after what happened last night?"

And nutty as a pecan log.

Marisa let out a long sigh. "I should have known Nadja's plan wouldn't work right," she muttered.

Totally bonkers. Which ought to be an effective antidote for desire, Ty thought, staring at the nutcase sitting next to him. *But so far, it's not.* Every cell and hormone in his body still wanted to haul her into his arms and repeat yesterday's nitro-kiss. Then go on from there.

"Just think, though," Marisa said, warming his aircooled skin with a thousand-megawatt smile. "With Nadja's cure a failure, you'll have good luck for the rest of your life."

Nuts. Completely, utterly nuts.

"Come on, Marisa," he argued. Mostly to keep from breaking his platonic promise right here in public. *Where's your famous calm control, Harding?* "Even you can't classify a night in an emergency room and eight stitches as good luck." Although it hadn't been so bad, really. They'd passed the time making up outrageous stories about the other occupants of the waiting area and turning Headline News reports into bad rap lyrics.

Ty smiled, remembering how her moonlight scent surrounded him as she kept pressure on his cut. And the way she'd held his hand while the intern stitched him up.

Yep, if you had to endure a medical emergency, Marisa made it bearable, Ty thought, noting a taxi turning onto the hospital drive and picking up speed as it headed straight toward them.

"It's not!" she agreed. "It's Mrs. Pachenko's evil eye sloshing onto you."

With a groan, Ty clutched his head. "You can't honestly—"

Squealing brakes drowned the rest. The taxi's nearside passenger door swept open before the vehicle halted completely.

What emerged was... Well, in Marisa's opinion, calling her beautiful would be like calling Elvis a moderately successful musician. The tissue she held to her chin couldn't hide the fact that she was everything Marisa wasn't. Tall. Blond. Sophisticated. Elegantly dressed. Perfectly coifed.

And agitated.

"Help me!" she cried, thrusting some money at the driver, then gliding gracefully toward them. "I need a doctor!"

Praying Ty would be okay on his own for a few minutes, Marisa jumped up to run inside and summon help.

"Oh, wait," the woman said in a completely normal voice. "I know you. You're that guy, aren't you? The one who wo—"

Marisa spun back around just as the woman jerked the tissue from her face, wet her lips, shook back her hair, and smiled at Ty. The only sign of injury was a tiny drop of dried blood on the underside of her chin.

"Who saved the mayor's cat," the blonde finished, turning the last word into two breathy syllables. Flashing another dazzling smile, she added, "I'm Lisette Daniels."

When neither Ty nor Marisa responded immediately,

the blonde batted thick eyelash fans. "The Intriguing Woman," she prompted.

"Oh. Yes." Marisa nodded, finally recognizing the face that, in glossy black and white, represented the year's most popular and expensive perfume.

"And of course, nobody lets me forget I was Supermodel of the Year two years ago," Lisette added with a light, expectant laugh.

"Of course." That sounded inadequate for such an achievement, so Marisa nodded again. Ty was no help—he just sat there like a lump. Stunned into worshipful silence, no doubt. "Yes, well… You're even more beautiful in person," she concluded lamely.

Accepting Marisa's compliment with a flick of pearlescent acrylic nails, Lisette addressed Ty. "I saw it on TV. How sweet of you to save that darling kitty!"

Tyler still sat there, mute. Marisa wondered what was going on inside him—beyond a flood of glandular excretions. She also wondered what had happened to Ms. Daniels's life-threatening emergency.

Stop it, Corelli. She's admiring the man's bravery. While you gave him eight stitches to exercise it on.

"I couldn't believe it when they said you'd won the lottery recently, too. How incredible!" Ms. Intriguing wet her lips again, then laughed, a low, throaty sound guaranteed to activate male erogenous zones. "And to think," she teased huskily, "the rest of us have to work for a living."

Marisa couldn't have duplicated any of it in a million years. The laugh, the flirting, the poise, the polish. Even Lisette's "casual" outfit—the T-shirt alone probably cost more than Marisa's whole wardrobe.

Which consisted of cheerful but nowhere close to elegant thrift-store purchases like the outfit she'd pulled on before the ambulance arrived: a now wrinkled pair of orange nylon soccer shorts and a blue workshirt with the name of a local muffler shop embroidered above the pocket.

"Take me, for example," Lisette purred, fluttering her lashes in Ty's direction again. "I've been standing around for simply hours, looking beautiful—first under a full, desert moon, then at sunrise." She sighed dramatically. "It's practically slavery, don't you think?"

When Ty didn't respond, Marisa nudged his shoulder. The touch seemed to rouse him from his coma.

"Huh? Oh, yeah. Definitely exploitation of the worker," he answered absently. Well, he was slightly distracted. Like Saul was "distracted" by that little revelation on the road to Rome or Damascus or wherever.

"Of course, there *are* benefits," Lisette conceded, combing her platinum mane with her nails again. "Travel. Fame. Getting to meet a genuine hero like you."

"I'm no hero," Ty disagreed, mentally ka-whamming himself upside the head.

What was wrong with him? Here was a woman who fit his Plan, who matched his ideal. Shouldn't he feel some attraction to her?

He should. But he didn't. Nothing at all was, ah, stirring. Not even a little.

"I'll be in town another week or so," Lisette declared, whipping a pen and business card from a pocket, scribbling on the card. "We're shooting the fall collection of a major designer. I'd love to buy you a drink sometime." Her head swiveled toward Marisa, then back to Ty. "For saving the puppy. Um, cat."

Absently, Ty took the card. Stuffed it in his pocket.

What the hell was wrong with him?

The cool, elegant, apparently perfect Lisette Daniels left him unmoved. While visions of and longings for the superstitious, possibly lunatic, absolutely wrong Marisa Corelli—*her dark, tousled hair tumbling around her creamy, bare shoulders*—danced through his brain like manic showgirls.

He didn't want to be hot for a short, crazy woman; she had no place in his well-Planned life.

He still considered marrying for companionship and sex a good idea. He didn't believe in love and he'd decided years ago that casual sex was too meaningless to bother with.

But that firestorm of a kiss yesterday still rocked him and now he wondered if a little passion was such a bad thing. And if it came only with amber eyes and ebony curls and a scent like autumn moonlight....

All right, already! Even perfect Plans required periodic reevaluation. So gypsy curse or no gypsy curse, he wasn't letting the sprite out of his life until he'd explored this sudden interest in passion—and its source.

Rising to his feet, Ty smiled gratefully at the Daniels woman for unintentionally guiding him back onto familiar ground. Once again, he had a clear-cut, defined goal.

Which meant he'd soon have his life back to normal.

Eager to get that accomplished, Ty put his arm around his sprite's shoulder. Noted how neatly her petite frame tucked against his side. How quickly her nearness warmed his skin. "Mind if we use your cab, Lisette?" he asked, guiding Marisa toward the vehicle.

A tiny crease appeared between Ms. Intriguing's arched brows. "But...you will call me, right?"

As Marisa climbed into the cab, Ty nodded solemnly. "Oh, sure. I'll call real soon. But we'd better let you go now. That cut on your chin—"

He didn't even have to finish the sentence. Lisette whipped the tissue back against her face and tore through the automatic doors leading to the emergency room.

With a sigh of relief, Ty followed Marisa into the taxi. Gave the driver his address and leaned back against lumpy upholstery. Gazed out the window as bits of Phoenix slipped past the dusty glass.

Building...strip center...pocket park...building, building, building... *His mouth trailing hot, moist kisses over Marisa's satiny skin—*

"I'll call Nadja." The sprite shattered the silence, and

his fantasy, like one of those Japanese monsters stomping Tokyo. "Tell her it's not working."

"What?"

"I'll find someplace else to stay by tonight. My plants—"

"Are not going anywhere," Ty said, folding his arms over his chest. He'd hold the stupid foliage hostage if he had to. "You said you'd stay with me two weeks." No way he was letting this woman walk away before he understood her attraction and, hopefully of course, freed himself from it.

"I refuse to cause you any more pain." Marisa shook those ebony curls.

"*You* didn't hurt me," he protested. "The drafting table did."

Her curls jiggled again. "Ty—pay attention! For three months, terrible things have been happening to me. Nadja said living with you would change that, but— don't you see? Now the terrible things are happening to you!"

Ty opened, then shut his mouth, unable to produce any reasonable argument to counter such insanity.

He settled for malarkey. "That means the yin-yang deal is working. It probably just takes a little time for the process to, like…adjust its swing."

Dolt! That sounds more like golf than mysticism.

Her curls flew back and forth. "I'll start packing as soon as we get to your apartment." Her brave smile couldn't hide a wistfulness that made Ty want to rip sheet metal. "Do you think I could borrow your truck to move my plants?"

Momentarily incapable of speech, he uttered some feral sound.

Marisa lifted her chin and turned it toward the side window. "You're right," she said woodenly. "With my luck, I'd probably wreck it. Well, I'll figure out something."

"No!" Dammit, she couldn't leave until he answered

those questions about passion. Tasted a few more hot kisses. But he couldn't say *that*. He needed something else, something really persuasive to stop her departure, but what? He groaned with frustration. Where was Nadja's good luck when he needed it?

"Ty—what's wrong?" Marisa touched his bare forearm and the electricity nearly jerked him off the seat. Didn't she feel it too? Dammit, he *had* to find the source of this voltage and understand its meaning, weigh its importance before he lived the rest of his life by the wrong Plan.

Suddenly, he caught sight of a white blob in the cab's rearview mirror. What—? Ah-ha! His bandage.

Well, give him an opening big enough to drive a Hummer through and even Ty Harding can sense an opportunity. So what if he didn't have any brilliant reasoning, any powerful arguments, any slick presentation techniques?

That left only the most effective, most persuasive tool known to man (invented by mothers). Guilt.

Ty willed himself to look pale and pathetic. "Oo-ooh," he moaned. And excellently, too, thanks to years of playing the ax murderer's victim in the Harding Halloween haunted houses.

"Tyler? Are you—?"

He moaned again.

"Oh, dear. Maybe we should go back to the hospital."

"*We.*" Ha. Ty smelled victory.

"N-no," he murmured weakly, lowering his lids to half-mast so he could study her reaction through his lashes. "The doctor said I just needed rest."

He tried a broken sigh. It sounded more like a broken radiator hose, so he hurried on. "Of course, he said I might get a little dizzy sometimes. Nothing serious…as long as there's someone around to keep an eye on me…."

Another sort of swooning move.

Marisa bit her lip to keep from laughing. Ty Harding

couldn't act his way out of a voting booth. What was this gorgeous hunk trying to pull with his helpless-invalid routine?

"Won't you stay and help me? I really think it's starting to work...."

Oh, puh-leez. His quaver sounded like that cartoon character who chased the silly wabbit. But what the heck—she didn't have any great ideas about where to go next. She could get there just as easily from Ty's apartment as from anywhere else. And he'd be safely home. "The yin-yang thing?" she asked, trying to keep a straight face.

"Uh-huh. I'll bet the evil forces of fate are being neutralized as we speak."

Maybe he *was* concussed.

Of its own volition, Marisa's hand moved toward his forearm. She jerked it back. That's how dangerous the man was. Her libido, which had apparently been in a coma for the past twenty-three years, was wide awake now, yelling out urgent messages to her nervous system. *Touch him. Kiss him. Run your hands all over that hard, smooth body.*

Forget it. One night under the same roof and already she'd given him a concussion. Wasn't that enough damage inflicted? Besides, between blood-blotting and calling EMS, she'd seen all the awards and diplomas on the wall.

The man's a highly skilled professional. I'm sure he wants more than a former poodle-washer living under a bad star—and he's been offered more, remember?

"You just met Ms. Intriguing," she pointed out gently. "Lisette Daniels gave you her phone number." *She practically threw herself at you and you looked ready to play catch.* "I don't know a man in America who wouldn't define that as good luck. Proving that Nadja's curse is still working. Perfectly."

There. Let's see him get out of that one.

"Coincidence, nothing more," Ty shot back, anxious to the point of foolish exasperation.

As the taxi turned into the apartment complex and stopped near the stairs leading to his abode, Marisa arrowed her index finger at his heart. "I'm not a charity case, Ty. If you don't believe in Nadja's curse, you don't need Nadja's cure. There's no reason for me to stay."

Spit. She had him. Logic—applied by a kook. It was the lowest form of treachery.

Which, Ty figured, gave him the right to exercise his own form of low, scummy trickery.

"Then go," he said, handing the driver some folded bills before crawling out of the taxi. "I'll be okay..." He gave a ragged sigh as he turned and stumbled up the first step. "...alone."

Marisa catapulted from the cab and raced to support him. Ha. Aha.

He pushed her away. Feebly, though. And still noted a tingle from the brief contact. "Don't worry," he sighed, touching the gauze covering his temple. "I—I'll be fine."

"Let me call someone to come stay with you." The sprite didn't even notice his gesture that sent the cab speeding off.

He administered the topper in a suitably pathetic-trying-to-be-brave voice. "There's nobody to call."

"Nobody?" she repeated, following him up the stairs to his apartment, watching as he fumbled the key into the lock and opened the door. "You don't have anyone?"

"Not a soul," he lied cheerfully—er, woefully, then wobbled over to collapse on the sofa.

Sympathy and doubt chased each other across her expressive face, so he patted his bandage again. Sent his eyes lolling backward to remind her that head injuries could be tricky.

Good, good—now she's chewing on her lip as she studied him closely. Maybe he *was* a little pale.

And it *was* her fault.

"You did promise Nadja," he coaxed...er, croaked, when she continued to hesitate.

"I suppose I did," she said doubtfully and Ty almost grinned with triumph. Until she smiled and added, "And it's only for a couple of weeks."

"Yeah," Ty agreed. "And I'm sure the worst is over."

He was sure, too, that the Marisa-attraction would die a natural death in two weeks. Sure he'd discover that passion was more trouble than it was worth—once he had just a little more evidence to judge by.

"You need to be in bed."

A tsunami of desire crashed over him. "Oh, yeah."

Without warning, the sprite grabbed his arm, slung it around her neck like a boa constrictor and slipped her arm behind his back. Her fingertips tickled his armpit and he jerked upright.

"That's it. You just come along and get some sleep now," she said.

Sleep? That wasn't what he had in mi— He practically cracked his jaw yawning. Hmm. Maybe he could use a few hours' rest. Maybe that's all he needed to regain proper Planned perspective.

'Cuz something told him Marisa Corelli wasn't the jump-into-bed kind—and he hadn't done any serious dating in years. He wasn't sure his high-school courtship techniques worked on adult women.

"Here we are," Marisa said, turning back the comforter and fluffing the pillows.

Obediently, Ty crawled into bed. As Marisa leaned close to tuck the covers around him, he caught a whiff of her autumn-moonlight scent.

"Sleep tight," she murmured. "I'll be here if you need anything."

Ty smiled. He had to admit he liked the ring of that. Maybe he *had* carried this aloneness stuff too far.

He frowned. He thought he heard Nadja cackling *"you share bed"* as Marisa quietly left the room.

Not today, your Royal Gypsy-ness.

A soft thud from the direction of the living room. Then the sound of breaking glass.

"Marisa?" Ty fumbled for the edge of the covers, already forming a plan of action. Find his keys, head back to the hospital. Don't faint if there's blood.

The bedroom door opened a crack. Midnight curls frothed through the opening. "That, um, dangly glass thing on the coffee table—was it really valuable? An irreplaceable heirloom?"

Ty fell back against the pillows. "Nope." He'd only kept the thing to avoid hurting Ronnie's feelings. Hmm—maybe he should dig out that ceramic monstrosity Sandi had given him for Christmas....

"I refuse to apologize. I warned you," she reminded him. "I'll clean up the mess—and I think I can get the ink out of the carpet." She backed away from the door and pulled it gently closed.

Drawing on every ounce of self-discipline he possessed, Ty stayed in bed.

Don't ask, he decided. Don't tell. The next two weeks would teach her the foolishness of believing in luck, and curses, and fate... *And passion?* he wondered as he let go of consciousness.

A WEEK AND A HALF LATER, Ty wasn't ready to actually concede the foolishness of *not* believing in curses and karma, but—the continuing coincidences were starting to creep him out.

He slept most of that first Saturday—and won a cell phone for *not* attending an Independence Day weekend fireworks display.

Sunday, Marisa visited Nadja, circled want ads, and rearranged her plants while Ty did laundry and watched golf, baseball and tennis.

On Monday, he went to work.

Marisa went, too. Four jobs the first week. Three more in three days the next.

Ty couldn't explain it. They were all simple jobs. All far beneath the intelligence she displayed at home, where mealtimes became the highlight of his day, involving lively discussions ranging from art to aardvarks.

Yet every job turned into a disaster—and Marisa got the fallout.

She unpacked books for a signing—and was fired when outraged fans discovered the last chapter missing in every copy.

She waitressed at the Way-Cool Organic Café and Laundromat—and was dismissed after serving soup to a restaurant critic highly allergic to the coriander in it.

She didn't mislabel the steam valve in the health club's sauna, either, but....

At home, the pattern took a more Nadja-esque twist. Marisa's efforts to help around the apartment back-fired—but somehow Ty benefited from each debacle. She misplaced his checkbook; he recovered his favorite mechanical pencil when he moved the sofa to look for it.

He found his college ring in the bend of the U-joint when he dismantled the disposal to remove shredded plastic. And the files she deleted from his computer when she dusted it were obsolete—taking up needed storage space.

Tuesday, she broke the microwave while making cold cereal—he couldn't begin to figure *that* out—so he took her out to breakfast. They ate free, even though they'd actually finished their meal just before the bomb scare cleared the café.

That night, she crushed the remote control with the vacuum cleaner, so he kissed the Olympics goodbye until next time.

And sure enough, when he waded through the legal papers connected to the mansion he'd inherited—and refused to even drive past, since he hadn't earned so much as one doorknob of the damned place—Ty discovered a clause that eased the tax burden on the thing.

One piece of good luck continued to elude him, though: an acceptable excuse for another close encounter with the sprite's lips.

But maybe the yin *was* getting to the yang, he thought on Thursday when Krako informed him he'd made a small mistake on his school-addition drawings.

Ty practically hugged the man. His elation at the return of seminormalcy diminished a tad when he stopped at the dry cleaners on the way home and won a big-screen TV for being their one-millionth shirt.

But that gave him an idea. A hackneyed one, true—but classics were classics for a reason. After posing for pictures with the dry cleaner, Ty headed home with a chop-socky video, a pizza, and a six-pack of beer.

"I thought you said the tropical fish store closed at seven," he called when he walked in and heard whirring coming from the kitchen.

"They told me I could leave after I fed the drowned goldfish to the homeless kitties in the alley." Her voice sounded odd.

Probably getting despondent over the job thing. Well, Chan's Ultimate Rumble—and a little necking on the couch—will take her mind off her problems.

Tossing his keys and the video on the coffee table, Ty headed for the kitchen. Something purple dripped from the ceiling. He ignored it. "So—how long you been home?" he asked as he popped the pizza in the oven.

"Long enough."

At her tone, Ty glanced up. Man, she looked... *passionate!* Her eyes sparkling, her hair crackling, her breasts heaving above her folded arms.

Her toe tapping.

Huh? "Long enough for what?" he asked carefully, though he had nothing to hide. They hadn't changed the law to make XXX-rated *thoughts* a criminal offense, had they?

"For the phone to ring. Twice."

Ty peered into the refrigerator. What *was* that blue stuff? On second thought, he didn't want to know. "So who called?" he asked, setting the six-pack on a shelf, then pulling out one long-necked brown bottle and twisting it open.

"Ms. Intriguing."

She'd called before. Ty dismissed Lisette with a languid wave of his bottle. "Who else? Anybody interesting?"

"Oh, yes. *Very* interesting." If he'd missed the significance of the tapping toe, the chill in her voice should have warned him.

Sheesh, the chill in her voice should have had him checking for frostbite.

Still preoccupied with his upcoming plan to cuddle on the sofa, Ty just shrugged those magnificent shoulders, lifted the beer to his mouth and took a swallow. "So— who called?"

The crumb. The worm. The lying son-of-a— Marisa ground her teeth. "Your brother."

The slime-bucket merely waggled his brown bottle. "Which one?"

4

"WHICH ONE?!"

The scumbag had the gall to scrunch his eyebrows together. "Did he leave a name?" he asked. Laconically, yet! "Want me to call back? What?"

"Ooh, you, you *gadjo!*" Marisa sputtered, scanning the room for something to pulverize. Where the heck was that yin-yang stuff when you needed it? Like, a loose ceiling chunk thwapping him on the head, courtesy of Mrs. Pachenko's *mal ojo.*

"Gezundheit," he said and blithely swigged beer.

"I didn't sneeze," she ground out. "I called you a...a non-Gypsy in Romany. It's the worst insult Nadja knows."

Ty cocked a hip against the counter. "You have to borrow insults?" Eyes wide—and blue, darn it, so blue—as he set down the beer bottle to fold back a still-crisp pale pink cotton cuff.

"People in my position can't afford our own," Marisa shot back, refusing to eye the crinkly hair on his knotted forearm. "We have to rent or borrow everything."

His eyes narrowed now, Ty folded back the second cuff. "When are we getting back to which brother called? Or am I supposed to guess?"

Pressing fingertips to eyelids, Marisa started counting to ten. At two, she still shook with fury over the jerk's deception. Around five, she was waffling, flattered to think he might have lied to keep her from leaving. By nine, her silly, newly awakened libido had her completely distracted, wondering if he made love with the same relentless focus.

Annoyed at herself, she dropped her hands to her hips and answered his questions. ''Now. Don't bother. Andrew.''

''Dru, you mean.''

''Isn't that what I said?''

''It's D-R-U. Short for Druid, not Andrew. Can you believe it?'' The moron chuckled. ''No wonder he went into athletics,'' he mused.

Marisa ground her teeth.

To think she'd been entertaining felonious fantasies about Ty Harding for weeks! Wasting hours of valuable sleep time reliving that amazing kiss. Practically idolizing the man because he never got upset, no matter what disaster she perpetrated.

You're not cursed, Corelli. You're a nincompoop.

Well, thank heaven she hadn't really believed Nadja Costeceaseu's cure could fix what was wrong with her life.

Because she now knew for pure, absolute certain that her elderly friend was a fraud. No Queen of the Gypsies had cursed Ty with good fortune. The jackass had been born lucky.

''Wonder what he wanted.'' The doofus placed his hands beside his hips and hoisted himself onto the counter, sat there casually swinging his feet.

''What is the matter with you?'' Marisa demanded. ''Call him back this minute and find out!''

One broad shoulder lifted, then dropped. ''There's no hurry,'' Ty insisted, sky-blue eyes twinkling, one corner of his oh-so-sensually talented mouth lifting.

Oh, no, Corelli. His charm left her cold. Icy. *Polar-glaciated.*

''No big hurry.'' Marisa stared at him. ''He's your brother!''

Laughter rumbled in that broad chest beneath the

starched shirt. "Like I said," the moron repeated with patent patience, "he's *one* of 'em."

Marisa grabbed fistfuls of her hair to keep from throttling the cretin. "How many do you have?" she demanded. "How many is so many you can be disdainfully unconcerned when one calls you?"

In slow motion, Ty slid off the counter, bracketed his belt with his hands, and blinked at her.

"Or are you just a self-absorbed, heartless..." Tears suddenly threatened; she fought them off.

She should have known better than to set him on a pedestal and spin romantic daydreams about him. So he'd saved Nadja. And he'd been understanding and patient with her. So he kissed like a dream and looked like some fitness magazine cover model.

"Heartless what?"

Shoot, even now, he sounded merely interested. Maybe he *was* a— "Well...heartless bastard," Marisa finished reluctantly.

"Nope." Ty crossed his arms over his magnificent chest. "My parents may be aging hippies, but they believe in commitment." *And so do I.* Casual relationships didn't interest him. He wanted—

Ty shook his head. No, he didn't. Not quite two weeks of living with Marisa and all the weird coincidences had scrambled his brain, that's all. Love equaled chaos. He just wanted monogamy. *Eventual* monogamy. Quiet, calm, *childless* monogamy.

"My folks were married three years before the first of us appeared."

"The *first* of you..." Marisa's voice trailed off. Her amber eyes turned to molten gold.

With a sigh, Ty remembered the old gypsy hissing, *"She is orphan, estoopid."*

Of course, she'd think it romantic; she hadn't lived through it. Ty rubbed his hand along his jaw. "Yeah," he said tiredly. "Four boys, three girls."

She looked at him like he'd just delivered the Holy Grail, postpaid. "You have six siblings?"

"Yes," he said impatiently. "Three older, three younger." *And me, lost somewhere in the middle.*

"It sounds wonderful."

"Trust me," Ty growled as gloom settled over him like night across the desert—thick, dark, complete. How could an orphan like Marisa understand how he'd felt growing up? "It wasn't. Most of the time it was a zoo."

"A zoo?" Marisa echoed, frowning.

For some idiotic reason, Ty tried to explain. "My parents encouraged individuality. Supported self-expression. So my siblings changed enthusiasms, interests and images the way other people change film in their cameras."

"People replace film when it's used up," Marisa said, waving a hand. His eyes followed the graceful movement like a snake hypnotized by a mongoose. "Is that what your brothers and sisters did? Finish exploring a subject and move on?"

Ty frowned. It sounded better when she put it that way, but— "None of them have normal jobs," he com—no, *ex*plained. "Or stick to any sort of normal schedule."

"Do they need to?" Marisa asked, tilting her head to one side as if fascinated by the strange creature before her.

"Of course they need to!" Ty shouted. "How can you accomplish anything without structure? Without discipline?"

Marisa simply looked at him.

Ty grabbed the beer bottle. Swigged. Set it down. "Yeah, I know. Different strokes."

"You called your parents hippies," she not quite asked.

"They were good parents," Ty said—because it was true. "It's not like we lived in a commune or anything."

"I did," Marisa said, studying the tops of her lime-green sandals. "Until the state pulled their accreditation."

"You were in foster care?" Duh. Despite their discussion about the rent, he'd assumed... "How many different places did you live?" he asked when she nodded. At least he'd always lived with the *same* nuts. In the same house, too.

"You don't want to hear about it," she assured him, lifting her chin with a jerk that set those midnight curls bouncing. Begging his fingers to bury themselves in the silken mass.

"Here's the number if you want to call your brother." She held out a slip of paper. Aha, the trade confirmation he'd been looking for.

But Ty wasn't as distractible as his siblings. "How old were you when—"

"I was three."

An image of Marisa as a tyke popped into his head. Lordy, she must have been adorable.

"My parents were killed in a car wreck. With no other relatives, I went into the state system and stayed there until I turned eighteen."

When he started to ask another question, she forestalled him. "You never stay anyplace very long," she said without a trace of self-pity. "You learn to pack fast, to live light. To find out the rules and fit in. You survive…"

"But you never feel like you really belong." Ty finished Marisa's sentence from his own experience: a quiet guy who liked order, growing up in what felt like the center ring of a hyperactive circus. "You get overlooked and outvoted."

Marisa hardened her heart. So he understood that sense of alienation, so what? Regardless of what she thought about them, Ty Harding had a family. A big one.

And he'd lied about it. "You should appreciate having so many close relatives."

"Oh, I do," he assured her sarcastically. "I've had all the family life I can stand."

Her face went white, as if he'd struck her.

Ty groaned, aching to fold her in his arms and beg forgiveness. Instead, he used every ounce of self-discipline he had to stay on his side of the kitchen.

Pure self-preservation: if he held her, he'd do more than beg forgiveness. And getting any more involved with a woman who canonized families the way Marisa did was just asking for trouble.

"They say you don't know what you have until you've lost it." Dammit, her soft, low voice still stirred him. "I hope for your sake you never find out how true that is."

Ty rubbed his jaw, helplessly puzzled at his own re-action to this latest system shock. He and the sprite were oil and water—a completely unsuitable combination.

She wanted what she'd never had. And he wasn't sign-ing up for any *Brady Bunch* sequel. His own dad had been a great father; Ty refused to saddle some innocent kids with a reluctant, therefore lousy, male parent.

So why was he standing here, still wanting her? Still itching to explore her passion, rouse it and release it with his own?

Searching for answers, he glanced at the number on the brokerage slip—and inspiration struck in defense of survival.

Casually, he strolled across the kitchen to finger the kalanchoe—the fat, round-leaf things were kalanchoes, right?—in the corner, while he tweaked his new Plan. Its goal: revive his allegiance to companionship while fading the Marisa-passion thing.

"Let me call Dru," he said, fighting down an inex-plicable aversion. Then, as if struck by a random thought, he added casually, "Maybe you'd like to meet him."

Of course she would. Everyone did; the guy thought

having fun was a Constitutional duty. "For a drink or something. How does that sound?"

It sounded like a kiss-off—except there was no relationship between her and Tyler Harding to kiss off. Going out with his brother might reinforce that fact to her enfeebled, infatuated brain. "Sounds great."

Apparently, Ty doubted her ability to get the message, because after rubbing one strong hand over his jaw a few times, he said, "We could double. You and Dru, me and Lisette."

"Perfect," Marisa pronounced grimly. Just perfect. Couldn't be any clearer than if he tattooed it on his forehead.

It *was* perfect. Who wanted to go all mushy and dreamy over some bozo who didn't appreciate the precious gift life had given him?

Dating said bozo's brother ought to get her waking up and smelling— "The pizza!" she cried as black smoke began seeping from the oven.

TY USED HIS CELL phone to arrange the double date for Saturday night after they left the apartment—the windows open to air out the pepperoni smoke—and headed for the nearest forty-seven-screen theater.

Marisa worried about someone robbing the place in their absence. Ty said, "They'll never get past the plant barrier," instead of "Not with Nadja's curse on the job."

A thunderstorm-induced power outage cut the ten dullest minutes from the movie—and management handed out free passes for the inconvenience.

Ty told himself *repeatedly* it was just another weird coincidence.

But on Saturday morning, when Marisa announced she might hit a few garage sales after she jobhunted, Ty muttered, "Busy," and split before he volunteered to tag along. Somehow, he could see it go down: she'd knock over some piece of junk and somebody—him, probably—would find a Rembrandt tucked behind it.

Not that he believed…anything. He just wasn't taking chances.

Or spending more time than necessary with a woman who attracted him the way no other ever had—and who doubtless wanted exactly what he didn't.

So Ty worked out, did laundry (finding twenty bucks and a lottery ticket in the dryer; he left it all there), then went to the office to correct the school-addition plans.

"YES, SIR," MARISA SAID. "I understand." Once more, she thanked the owner for his time, apologized again for tripping the customer—who turned out to be a disgruntled former employee with a grudge and a gun. He'd calmed down after his brief period of unconsciousness, agreed to get counseling and left with the paramedics.

But the shopkeeper was too upset to think about hiring anyone right then.

Still jobless, Marisa trekked to her favorite thrift store, determined to look as good as possible on—she consulted her wallet—three dollars.

Right, Corelli. Like you and the Second Chance can compete with Ms. Intriguing in her designer duds.

An hour later, Marisa headed home to get ready, dreading the night ahead. Ty's brother was undoubtedly a nice man, but she didn't want to date him. She didn't want to watch Ty dating Lisette, either. Didn't want to even imagine them kissing. *Wondering if they'd share the same fire we did.…*

WITH A SATISFIED GRIN, Ty placed a set of new, *perfect* school-addition plans on Krako's desk.

He'd been here all afternoon. Working—some of the time. And the rest—fighting off images of his amber-eyed sprite as a child, moving from home to home, family to family. An outsider longing to belong.

Dammit, he ought to be drooling over tonight's encounter with Lisette Daniels instead of sympathizing with Marisa Corelli.

As if she needed it; the sprite never bemoaned her fate. That was one of the things he admired about her.

Ty frowned as he shut down his equipment and left the office. If tonight's double date went well—and why wouldn't it? Lisette *was* Ms. Intriguing and Dru charmed ladies the way Garth Brooks sold CDs—his worries were over.

He'd be back on Plan. A little further along than expected, that's all. He *ought* to be happy.

But he wasn't, Ty admitted as he drove down to a car wash and put coins in the paybox.

Because with no curse to cure, Marisa would be moving out soon and, dammit, he enjoyed having someone to come home to. *Liar—you like having* Marisa *to come home to.* He liked to hear her humming softly in the other room. Or talking to the darned plants.

His stomach growled as he pulled into the wash bay. He hadn't eaten since breakfast, he realized with a shock. He never skipped meals.

Until the sprite.

Dammit, she'd turned his whole, carefully planned life upside down. Her and the Queen of the Gypsies, he corrected with a wry smile. Well, tonight, he'd just turn it back around.

Driving home in half the normal time—ahh, no rush hour on Saturday—Ty tossed his keys on the coffee table and headed for the kitchen to grab a snack.

"There you are." Marisa stood in the doorway of the office they'd turned back into a bedroom for her.

Thoughts of food ceased. *Thought ceased.* Primal urges surged. Hormones headed due south. Ready for action.

Ty stared at the sprite—who'd metamorphosed into every man's hottest, wettest dream. Long, sexy legs with bright, painted toenails peeping from strappy high heels. Feminine mysteries barely covered by a few inches of skirt that looked like wet rubber and a shimmery, short-sleeved, scooped-neck, navel-revealing top that looked like wet paper and plastered itself against curves so sweet they belonged in a red, heart-shaped box.

"If you're going to change before we go," she murmured, "you might want to get started. It's after six, already."

Change? Okay, he'd change. He'd reevaluate his ideas about putting off marriage and—

"Ty? Did you forget something?"

The question sliced through the sensual fog saturating him.

"Uh. Yeah, I did." He'd forgotten everything! Who he was. Who he wasn't. What he wanted. What he didn't want. Hell, the way this petite woman affected him, his precious Plan had an ice cube's chance in hell.

And Lisette Daniels might as well stay home and file her nails.

No! He wanted peace and quiet. A calm, orderly life. Not passion and heat and joy and—

"Is there something I can do to help?" Marisa asked, moving toward him.

Ty took a step back. If he smelled that moonlight, neither one of them would make it *back* into their clothes for at least a week. And they'd both regret it. Eventually.

"Shall I call Lisette and tell her we're running late?"

Late. Yeah, it was too late to change. Facts were facts. Lust led to love. Love—at least with Marisa—wound up with a family. And that equaled chaos. He didn't want, couldn't need any woman enough to develop a taste for chaos.

"What's your brother's phone number? I'll call him, too."

Brother. She's Dru's date, not yours. "No need." Ty bared his teeth. *But if he touches her, I'll kill him.* "Why don't you fix me a drink while I jump in the shower?" he asked, forcing his feet in that direction. *That's it. Relax. Forget these crazy thoughts. Stick to Your Plan.* "A finger of scotch, a little water. Couple of rocks, okay?"

"Okay."

Mechanically, Ty went to his room. Put his wallet on the dresser. Shoes in the closet. Belt on its hook. Unbuttoned his jeans. Shirt ditto.

A knock. "Your drink's ready."

Ty opened the door, accepted the blue plastic tumbler with mumbled thanks and shut the door. Shut his eyes, too. Lordy, those legs went on forever.

Tilting the glass, he took a healthy swig of liquid the color of Marisa's eyes.

Don't go there, either. Ty took another hefty swallow.

And another as he wrenched the shower controls. He had a plan. A good plan. Designed to keep both of them from ending up unhappy. Ty raised the glass a couple more times as he shrugged out of his clothes and in a fit of recklessness left them on the bathroom floor.

She must have used hot water and that made the ice melt, he decided, lifting the glass again and draining the last of what must have been twelve ounces of liquid as he stepped into the shower.

CAREFULLY, MARISA REPLACED the Chivas scotch in the cabinet. She hoped she'd mixed that drink right. She'd measured the length of her index finger, then poured in a bit more. Splashed a teaspoon or so of water into the glass. Adding two ice cubes, she'd walked it gingerly to his room.

And nearly dropped it when he opened the door with his shirt hanging open like some buff surfer-dude. One glance at that magnificent, muscular chest—and everything she'd learned the other night about Ty Harding went up in sensual smoke.

With a sigh, Marisa subsided on the sofa. She knew from her years in foster care that not all families were wonderful. She'd lived in her share of turmoil and discord.

But she still wanted a family of her own. A home. Babies.

And a husband to help her raise them. A guy with Ty's calmness, his structured approach to life.

Who needs Mrs. Pachenko? Marisa thought with another sigh. She was this far from falling in love with Ty, even though she knew that if she did, she'd doomed herself. He offered nothing but predestined unhappiness for a woman who'd waited her whole life for what he seemed to hold in abject disregard.

"There's m'sprite! Was lookin' f'you." The man in question swayed across the room, shirttails flapping. Nearing the couch, he stumbled and fell. Looking up from where he sprawled across her lap, Ty smiled crookedly. Fumes worthy of a distillery rose toward her as he slurred, "'M havin' li'l trouble wif ma buddons. K'hep me?"

Resisting an urge to run her fingers through the thick hair tickling her bare abdomen—and one to slip her hand inside his open shirt and stroke that smooth hard chest, Marisa pushed him far enough off her to wriggle loose. "You're drunk!"

Spying his keys on the coffee table, she scooped them up.

"Time t'go? Okay. 'S warm 'nough. Don' need buddons." Awkwardly Ty clambered to his feet. Stood swaying as he looked around for the door.

The idiot smiled triumphantly when he saw it. Lifted one foot—which swung like a cheap compass needle until it pointed in the right general direction and dropped.

Steeling herself as desire flamed through her, Marisa

put the key ring between her teeth and buttoned his shirt. Smoothed down the tails. Fastened, then straightened the cuffs.

"Gonna tuck it in, too?" He grinned goofily at her and held his arms out from his sides. Sucked in his already flat stomach. "Go 'head," he instructed. "Tuck me."

"No." Marisa knew her limits. Figured she'd passed them the day she'd let Ty and Nadja talk her into moving in, but she wasn't making things worse. If she touched him now, she'd take him. And she couldn't love his body without giving her heart.

"Come on," she said, suddenly eager to deliver Ty Harding to his supermodel date. "If you can't finish dressing yourself, we'll get your brother to do it. We're meeting him at the hotel, right?"

Ty nodded, losing his balance. Instinct overruled her head: Marisa intercepted his fall. He leaned into her heavily, fitting perfectly. His crisp scent filled her nostrils. And some stupid part of her didn't care if their goals were incompatible, it *wanted*. Wanted his body, his touch, his—

I am *delusional,* she thought, grimly leading him to the car. *In the hardware store, looking for bread. And I'm going to get hammered if I'm not careful.*

"Get in," she said, opening the passenger door. "I'll drive."

Ty obeyed. Had a little trouble wif his seatbelt. Snapped it jus' as his li'l sprite slid into the driver's seat and started the car.

They shot out of the parking space, then braked so hard he nearly went through the windshield. "Sorry," Marisa muttered as an SUV spurted past, horn blaring.

She tromped on the gas pedal again. More squealing brakes, more blaring horns. She cut the wheel; they drove over a landscaping bed and exited the complex right in front of a truck going twice their speed.

Her driving didn't improve over the next twenty minutes, but Ty's sobriety did. He also rediscovered the power of prayer and promised Anyone Listening that he'd update his will and try to lead a blameless life if he survived.

They wove through traffic like one of those worst chase videos, stopping so abruptly at the traffic lights that the smell of burning rubber filled the passenger compartment. Once, they clipped a tower of cartons stacked behind a delivery truck, sending cardboard flying and the guy in the brown shorts leaping for safety.

They took another turn on two wheels—

"Watch the pedestrian!" Ty shouted, already bracing himself for her assault on the brake pedal.

"S-sorry." Marisa's face mirrored his own terror.

Ty turned back to check on the almost-victim. Thank heaven, she seemed okay, smiling up at the man who'd pulled her out of harm's way.

"Have you ever driven before?" Ty asked at the next red light, eyeing the white knuckles rimming the steering wheel.

"I have a license, if that's what you mean." The sprite tried to lift her chin. It merely jiggled.

"Did you buy it on the Net?" Ty snapped, then stopped himself. Remembered Sunday afternoons—*lots* of them—with his dad, practicing in empty parking lots. Obviously, whoever taught Marisa hadn't taken the time or had the patience his dad had.

"Don't pay 'tention to me. I'm drunk, remember?" He summoned a reassuring smile. "You're doing fine. Really. The hotel's just a few more blocks. Ignore the horns. When the light turns green, press the gas pedal slow and steady."

Marisa did as instructed. Ta-da, no jackrabbit start. No whiplash. They pulled up the hotel drive smoothly.

Ty was congratulating himself on his heretofore unknown teaching skills when the parking valet—a teen-ager who thought himself immortal—leaped from his stool and stepped onto the driveway.

The sprite mashed the brake pedal; again Ty's seat belt stopped his forward momentum so abruptly it nearly broke his collarbone.

The car rocked to a halt with its bumper kissing the kid's trousers.

White-faced, the young valet froze until Marisa shut off the engine, then he tiptoed up to the vehicle.

"Sorry, ma'am," he croaked as he opened the door and extended one trembling hand to help her out of the driver's seat. "The boss warned us not to get too cocky. Now I know what he meant."

Marisa and the attendant exchanged keys and claim tokens, then Ty escorted the still-shaking sprite into the hotel. They both needed the one thing he didn't dare have tonight: a stiff drink.

Silently, they trudged across the lobby's Spanish tile past islands of lush plants to a seating area nestled behind ceramic saguaro cacti. An empty pilsner glass and a glass of white wine dregs sat on the low table in front of their respective dates.

"Marisa, this is my brother Dru," Ty said gracelessly. "Dru, Marisa Corelli."

The man—a deeper-tanned, lighter-haired, lankier Ty—stood. Extended his hand. "Pleased to meet you," Dru said with a smile. "My brother's taste is improving." His gaze flickered between Marisa and the blonde still seated on the brocade sofa. "Can't say the same for his judgment, though."

La Daniels remained seated, her pose displaying her flawless beauty and the elegant lines of her simple white sheath to perfection. She flashed white teeth. Also perfect, of course.

"You're late, naughty boy," she trilled at Ty, then interrupted Marisa's response to Dru with a no-trills "Hi."

Marisa returned the supermodel's greeting as the brothers shook hands.

Let the date begin, Ty thought, shoving his hands in his pockets and inventorying the stress points in the roof frame.

"Would you like something to drink here?" Dru asked Marisa and Ty dragged his attention from roof struts to Lisette—who quickly morphed her frown into a smile. "Or shall we adjourn to the patio?"

They adjourned and sat at a table under a palm tree, making stilted conversation. Water tinkled in a fountain nearby. A waitress brought their drinks, a bowl of salsa and a basket of chips.

Lisette insisted Marisa try the hot sauce.

Ty automatically shifted his chair back a few inches, out of range. Dru had taken the chair on Marisa's other side, so Ms. Intriguing got the full splatter when the chip broke and the salsa sprayed.

"Oh-oh-oh!" Lisette squealed, waving her hands as if drying her nails while she surveyed the damage to her dress.

"I'm so sorry," Marisa apologized, digging in her purse. "I've got some spot remover in here. If we use it right away, it might take out the stain," she added helpfully.

The blonde stared at her. "But it's an Escada original," she said, then circled Marisa's wrist with one perfectly manicured hand. "Fine. Come with me. If you'll excuse us."

She swept the sprite away before the men could get to their feet.

AFTER RECLAIMING THEIR seats, the brothers sat in companionable silence a moment.

"So." Dru grinned knowingly. "How do you like being a multimillionaire?"

Ty dipped a chip in the new bowl of salsa. "It doesn't change anything."

"It what? Oh, man—you are out there!" Dru exclaimed with a laugh, scooping salsa onto his own tostada. "Like always." After chomping the chip, he leaned toward Ty. "That money gives you freedom, you idiot. To do whatever you want. Or do you *want* to spend the rest of your life designing huge houses for spoiled rich people with no taste?"

Ty's hand, reaching for another chip, stilled. No. He didn't. He'd gone into architecture because he liked designing structures that lasted and finding creative solutions to difficult spatial problems. How hard was big?

With his usual short attention span, Dru changed the subject.

"So what's with you and Marisa?" he asked. "Any other guy tried to set me up with his live-in—especially a babe like her—I'd suggest psychiatric help."

"She's not my—I mean, we do live together, but—" Ty shook his head. "It's too complicated to explain." He grabbed another chip. "How'd you know about the lottery, anyway?"

"Besides blanket newspaper and TV coverage, you mean? Lisette mentioned it." Dru dismissed her with a flip of his chip. "Where'd a nerd like you meet a hot babe like Marisa? And how? She's not your usual style."

Ty growled. One wrong move and, brother or not, Dru was dog meat.

Mr. Puppy-Meal raised his hands, palms out. "Just pointing out the obvious, man."

Well, Ty could do that, too. "She's your date tonight, bro."

"Ha." Dru snorted as he reached for another chip. "Twenty bucks says I'm goin' home alone."

"You'd better," Ty growled before he could stop himself.

They'd settled down to a discussion of Diamondback pitching by the time Marisa and Lisette rejoined them.

Ms. Intriguing gave a tinkling laugh as she reclaimed her chair and scooted it closer to Ty. "Now tell me all about being an architect," she cooed. "What's the biggest house you've designed?"

Brothers exchanged glances.

Marisa remained silent. Lisette had been informative while they unspotted the Escada dress. Frankly stating that she planned to quit modeling soon via the time-honored retirement plan for beautiful females: marry wealth.

So here she sat, well informed, eventually making desultory conversation with Dru while Lisette charmed her retirement plan. And vice versa. By the time they strolled over to the resort's four-star restaurant, he had Ms. Intriguing simpering and regaling him with stories of globe-trotting for fashion's sake.

Well, hmph. Who wants someone who's attracted by shallowness?

Oh, meow, Corelli. Who's the shallow one here?

They ended the evening with a round of miniature golf on the resort's course, tucked between the driving range and the tennis courts. Both of which, luckily, were empty when the two men fished a squealing Lisette from the moat at the castle hole after she fell in while trying to duck Marisa's backswing. Claiming a twisted ankle, she insisted they carry her to her suite.

Actually, she suggested that Ty carry her there, but he suddenly remembered a bad back and Dru obligingly loaned him one of his own sports injuries as its cause.

The men linked hands to form a "chair" for Lisette and the three of them disappeared in the direction of the model's luxury suite.

Marisa waited in the lobby, where she passed the time by telling the desk clerk that the papyrus plants needed more light.

The men reappeared and almost immediately, Dru excused himself with some story about a headache, winking at his brother as he strolled away.

Leaving Ty where he wouldn't be without Dru's help. Where, he admitted now, he'd wanted to be all night: alone in neutral territory with his sprite. After hours of watching her smile, watching her ebony curls swirl, watching her amber eyes sparkle, he couldn't fool himself any longer. Unsuited, mismatched, yin or yang—didn't matter. Marisa and her passion attracted him, cool blond self-absorption didn't.

"Guess we'd better head home," he said, his voice husky with a new understanding of the term. Not merely an enclosed shelter from the elements, but a place shared with a person who mattered to you, a person, hopefully, who cared about you in return. But first—

"You going out with Dru again?" he asked as they waited for the valet to surrender the car.

"Your brother's nice," Marisa said softly, "but no."

Sheesh—the relief flaked him. "He's okay, I guess," Ty blurted, "but you should see the rest of 'em."

"Oh, shut up," Marisa sighed wearily. "If I have to listen to you whine again about your terrible misfortune of belonging to a large family, I'll scream.

"You are the luckiest man on earth, Ty Harding—*no* thanks to Nadja Costeceaseu—and you act like you deserve international aid."

"Dammit, you don't know my family!" he shouted, driven by an admittedly childish longing to be desired for himself rather than his parents' fertility, for Pete's sake. "They're not—"

"I know you!" she shouted back, freezing the valet in the act of handing her the keys. "And Dru. How did you two turn out so great if the others didn't?"

He hadn't formed the first syllable of his response when Marisa cut him off. "Lisette thinks you're lucky because you won the lottery. Neither of you appreciates that you're lucky because you have the one thing money can't buy—a loving family.

"You, Ty Harding, are a complete idiot."

Well, after that kind of royal ream-out, what could he do but snatch the keys from the teenage valet, tip him heftily and drive to the dark end of the parking lot. Cut the engine and reach for her.

Lower his mouth to hers and initiate another spine-tingling, mind-altering kiss.

Marisa initiated right back. Their embrace filled the car with explosive heat, erotic power, death-defying adrenaline, hormones and primal urges.

"Ah, sprite..." Ty breathed between ravishing her mouth and scorching her neck with hot, nibbling kisses. While his hands cupped her perfect breasts and circled the taut, satiny skin of her bared abdomen. "You're so—"

NUTS, SHE DECIDED while they waited for the police. Ty was an idiot, but she was nuts. Pressing her nose against the candy-store window. With or without any help from Mrs. Pachenko, she was going to get hurt here unless she backed off. Way off. Pronto.

Because hot kisses don't change anything. He doesn't want the one thing you need to be happy. And there's no compromise; plants aren't a family and you can't have half a baby.

"Let me get this straight," the parking attendant said. "You stopped here to check your receipt for dinner, accidentally hit the horn—and interrupted a rapist attacking that woman?" He pointed to the sobbing, blanket-wrapped victim clinging to the desk clerk.

"Uh...yes. That's about it." Marisa hoped her flaming cheeks weren't too apparent in the dim light.

She'd leaned on the horn, twisting around to give Ty more room to move one of his hands. That's when they'd heard the scream—and she'd come to her senses.

But she could still feel the heat of Ty's mouth on hers, his hand stroking her. Penetrating her flesh, her soul. Darn it, she could NOT fall in love with him. Not now, not ever.

Not much chance of avoiding it, Corelli. Unless...

Ty scrubbed exasperated fingers along his jaw, watched the cops drive away—and made another concession. He *didn't* believe in it, but something had to be done about this curse crap. And soon.

His plans weren't worth bug spit. Tonight's scheme: complete failure. He'd tried, but his residual interest in Lisette equaled his enthusiasm for getting a root canal.

Marisa, on the other hand— He wanted her no matter how wrong they were for each other. It was driving him crazy. He'd never failed to control his feelings for a woman. Until now. Until her.

If he wasn't careful, he might make them both miserable by trying to be something he couldn't.

"I'll be leaving in the morning," the sprite said after a silence that lasted most of the drive home. "There's no point to this any longer."

He should have hallelujah'd. Instead, his throat tightened. "B-but what about th-the curse?" he croaked. Dammit, she couldn't bail! Not yet. He still needed— one long weekend in bed with her to get her out of his system. Or a psychic overhaul to become Mr. Family Man.

Or...*a way to change the sprite's perspective.* Then maybe they could consider planning a future together. Ty smiled, imagining having Marisa around the house awhile longer. Maybe even permanently.

First, though, he had to convince her that the buzz on families wasn't all positive. 'Cuz he wasn't playing daddy to a bunch of hellions.

Well, maybe one little tyke with amber eyes and dark curls....

Impulse flared again. Impulse laced with panic, but

he'd better act on it or lose his only chance for something he'd never had—before he even knew for sure what it was.

"You can't leave tomorrow," he blurted. "I'm counting on you to help with the party."

5

ONCE AGAIN, TY didn't think he was asleep—until the metallic click of the front door closing shot him out of bed like the Space Shuttle given the Go-To-Launch command.

He hurtled down the hall, spun around the empty living room, then retraced half his steps and catapulted through the door to the sprite's bedroom. One nonranting brain cell noted the room's neat state; the rest of his mind simply gibbered until he showed it the small collection of rainbow-hued female clothes still in the closet.

Ty sidled back to the living room for another look. Gave his heart permission to beat: Baby sat in its corner, calmly producing chlorophyll. The sprite wouldn't evacuate without her pet philodendron.

Taking deep breaths to slow his heart, he padded into the kitchen in search of breakfast. Encountered an unopened box of cereal with a "Million Dollar Giveaway—Prize Inside" balloon on its front that made him hesitate before picking it up.

While he dithered, he spied a note from the sprite tucked beneath the box.

Visiting Nadja. Back midafternoon. Please give Baby half cup of blue liquid in fridge at ten. Thanks.

Which explained that blue stuff—sort of—and gave Ty four to six hours to ponder last night's impulse.

A party. What was he thinking?

Not thinking. Just responding like a hormonal teen-ager.

And facing facts.

Fact number one: two more mismatched people he'd never known. Appearance, attitudes, aptitudes—complete opposites in every way.

Not to mention fact number two: she idolized families as much as he didn't.

Despite their utter and eternal unsuitability, however—and leaving curses and gypsies out of it—*something* prevented him from simply walking away. Forgetting her. Reverting to his Planned solo existence.

That something was fact number three: Marisa Corelli touched some part of his being he hadn't even known existed until he lay flat on his back after saving her crazy friend. A cold part, warmed by her amber eyes. An empty part, filled by her smile. A sleeping part, wakened by her kiss.

He'd never felt like this before—and last night proved the feeling wasn't going away.

So, deal with it, Harding.

Or jettison those cold, empty, sleeping parts and go back to your original, lonely Plan.

Ty set a timer for Baby and located a bowl, spoon, and milk. Nodded, pleased with his renewed rationality. *And* last night's knee-jerk read of the situation. Wherever these impulses came from, this one's instincts had been right on. A party—with as many Hardings as he could corral—would reveal plenty about the possibility of a future with Marisa.

He'd teach her the equations that govern family life: enthusiasm over time becomes turmoil. Give her firsthand knowledge of how encouraging individuality multiplied by seven equals pandemonium.

Marisa had to understand that. And agree to avoid it. If she turned out like the rest of them, preferring noise and anarchy to quiet and structure, he'd then take steps to get over his fascination with her. Like move to the Moon.

Or let Nadja cast another spell.

Or—Ty shuddered—date Lisette Daniels again.

"Don't threaten yourself, moron," he muttered, thumbing the cap off the cow juice. "Just hope Marisa learns to dislike chaos and confusion the way I do. And don't tell me to get over it," he ordered...well, whoever he was talking to. "'Cuz I don't want to."

Don't want to or can't? asked a sprite-ish voice in his head.

"What difference does it make?" he challenged the voice, raising his own so the whole kitchen—and Baby in the living room—heard. He grabbed the box of processed grain flakes, tore back the lid, lifted and tilted. "Sheesh! Since when is falling in love, getting married and having kids the be-all and end-all of exis—"

A plastic-wrapped certificate plopped out of the box.

With two twitching fingers, Ty plucked it from the bowl. YOU'VE WON! HONEYMOON GETAWAY! screamed the certificate's heading.

He stared at it a short eternity. Then let it drop from lifeless fingers as he buried his face in his hands.

Time to get REALLY honest, Harding.

Within the noise and chaos and confusion of his childhood, Ty carried the image of his parents, too. Kissing in the kitchen. Laughing in the backyard. Holding hands in public and locking the bedroom door for "naps" on Sunday afternoons.

You'd like that for yourself, wouldn't you? Being in love, being married, on a permanent honeymoon...

Ty shoved aside visions of ebony hair spread over white pillows. This wasn't about sex and lust. This went deeper. And it wasn't about Marisa, not directly anyway. It was about him. About what kind of man he was.

He *wasn't* his dad. Jim Harding was a salesman, an

easygoing extrovert with the patience of Job and time for everyone who asked for it.

He, on the other hand, was an impatient introvert—who tried to turn limitations into virtues.

What a jerk. He didn't function well in chaos and clutter, so he bad-mouthed it. Love looked difficult, so he decreed it an illusion. Families—even couplehood—seemed complex, so he refused to participate.

DI-INNGG!

Ty flinched, then realized it wasn't Fate agreeing with his scathing self-analysis. It was the timer—reminding him of Baby's medicine or whatever it was.

Obediently, Ty measured out the blue stuff, carried it to the living room, pushed his way past Baby's deeply serrated fronds and poured liquid around the base of the plant.

Then he looked at the rest of the plants filling—and en*living*ing—his apartment. The little jar of wildflowers on the coffee table. The quartz-flecked rock by the phone. The bright, ripply striped afghan on the sofa.

All Marisa additions.

Geez, he wimped on even the small stuff—he didn't know diddly about home decor, so he lived in a sterile box.

Okay, so maybe he could stand to open up a little, let a little spontaneous, unplanned living into his life. Ty returned to his now-soggy cereal. Could he do it? Would Marisa help him try?

Elbow planted on the table, spoon suspended in mid-air, Ty asked himself another question, one that set his heart pounding like a judge's gavel in an unruly court-room.

If they discovered he could and she would, did he have a shot at the kind of happiness his parents enjoyed despite the overwhelming responsibility of raising all those kids for all those years…?

No, he wasn't capable of *that*. Unlike his dad, Ty

didn't multitask well. He could barely concentrate on his work with the sprite around, let alone if he had soccer schedules and school plays and piano lessons to worry about.

Okay. That meant the party impulse—er, *plan*—to wean Marisa from her family adulation had to work. And it would. All he needed was an excuse for the darned thing. Something guaranteed to bring the whole clan together. Something foolproof that would rope Marisa into the exhausting preparation process.

"I *am* a genius," he told Baby modestly when he'd showered, dressed, and granted himself permission to loll on the sofa and watch the ball game.

"No need to *explain* my objections," he informed the philodendron smugly while the play-by-play announcer murmured hypnotically. "I'll let her *experience* the hassle of running a big family. By the time the whole thing's over, she'll be willing to settle for just yours truly."

Ty gave himself a virtual pat on the back. "I tell ya, Babe-ster, this party thing's going to work out perfectly. For both of us."

"IT'S NOT WORKING, Nadja," Marisa insisted as patiently as possible. "For either of us."

"Give time!" the older woman shouted. "Curses are not cheap gum, getting stale and weak with few chewings. More tea?" she asked without pause between polemic and politeness.

"Sure," Marisa replied, handing over her glass. She'd drink a tanker car of the stuff if that's what it took to convince Nadja to develop another solution to her homeless, jobless dilemma. One that didn't involve further contact with the gorgeous, sexy and sweet Ty Harding.

After lying awake—and aching—all night, reliving that parking lot kiss, Marisa had risen early.

Tiptoeing past Ty's bedroom, she'd halted at his half-open door. One glimpse of tawny skin and tangled sheets—and she'd booked. Caught an early bus to visit Nadja the way she did every Sunday.

Having discovered a few months ago that her friend couldn't read, Marisa had begun dropping in to help with tasks that required literacy skills. Today, for example, she'd written out the money orders for the older woman's bills and addressed the envelopes, then asked if she'd heard anything from the still-absent Nico.

"I'll call the Salvation Army in the morning," Marisa had promised to ease the disappointment in the gypsy's eyes when she answered negatively.

After trekking to the neighborhood food pantry whose donated food supplemented Nadja's meager income, Marisa now fidgeted with the fringe on the pillow beside her as she begged Nadja to call off her cure.

Taking another sip of tea, Marisa tried an ingratiating smile. "I know it takes time." She ignored Nadja's snort. "But it's been two weeks and nothing's happening." Aside from her libido going into overdrive and her heart eagerly volunteering for a crushing letdown sometime in the near future.

"Nothing—ha. Iz funny," the Gypsy Queen cackled. "You are like complacent homeowner with termites eating away inside walls. Soon you will see." She passed her palm over the glass ball on the table beside her. "Sawdust."

Well, that was reassuring. "Look, Nadja, I can't keep living with Ty Har—"

"You can." The gypsy's hand circled the ball again. "You will."

If she didn't know better, Marisa would swear the globe started glowing.

"If you wish babies—"

Longing exploded within her. Longing for infant Tylers…and for the moments of ecstasy that led to them.

"You will stay with until blue moon. If not—" Nadja

shrugged. "Take chance," she suggested haughtily. "Iz only evil eye. Not as powerful as Gypsy curse."

Marisa blinked back stupid tears. Told herself this was only an old, lonely lady talking nonsense.

Nadja crossed her arms, fixed Marisa with an obsidian stare. "Decide," she ordered. "Fate hangs in balance."

For a second, pain tempted Marisa to sarcasm. But she held her tongue. Gypsy Queen or not, this elderly woman had little money, few friends and no relatives except the elusive Nico.

I can't destroy her dreams—they're all she has.

They're all you have, too, Corelli.

But darn, she just knew Ty Harding would be a terrific father—patient, fair, consistent, caring. And an equally wonderful lover. For the same reasons.

"Okay, if you're sure staying will change my bad luck," she said reluctantly. Surely she could resist him. She had to. Despite his flame-throwing, seductive kisses, the man sneered at the very things she wanted: a home, a husband and a couple of kids.

The old woman nodded, fingering a dark red stone the size of a small Post-it note that dangled from one of the garish necklaces she wore. "You make right choice." She crooked her finger, beckoning her guest closer. "Now I reveal secret."

Swallowing her skepticism, Marisa scooted to the edge of the lumpy velvet sofa.

"I tell Tyler Harding white fib," Nadja said with a chuckle. "Luck iz not like electricity. Iz more like faith. Believe—works. No believe—no work."

Light twinkled off a gold-capped tooth as the old lady smiled triumphantly.

Marisa's jaw dropped. "Are you saying that if I stop believing in Mrs. Pachenko's evil eye, I won't lose any more jobs?"

Nadja snorted impatiently. "You confuse luck and

fate.'' Her hand dropped from the red-stone necklace to the glass globe.

Which definitely glowed. Marisa shifted uneasily. They'd entered that weirdo zone again. The one that made logic and reason so hard to hold on to, faith and miracles so possible to believe.

''You listen, I explain.'' Nadja gazed at the glowing ball. ''The beautiful blond *gadje* who pants for your Tyler—''

Lisette.

''Her tall slender body, the cheekbones, the flawless skin—'' Nadja mercifully cut short her list of La Daniels's attributes with an encompassing wave of her hand ''—this iz luck only.''

Not as comforting as it sounded.

''But when she iz meeting soulmate at your party—''

''P-party?'' How did she know about that? Marisa wondered, her heart sinking. She was sure she hadn't mentioned it. ''I'm not having a party,'' she corrected faintly.

The Queen of the Gypsies ignored the interruption. ''—Iz *fate*.''

So even Nadja thinks Ty is Lisette's destiny, Marisa reflected an hour later as she waited for the bus to take her back across town to his place. Ms. Intriguing certainly did.

She'd been crystal clear about it last night. Ready to settle back and let the wrinkles begin, Lisette had her sights trained on Ty's good looks and lottery winnings.

And how could a mortal woman compete with a supermodel? Marisa wondered as the bus kawhooshed to a stop and she climbed on. *Give it up, Corelli.* Forget about happily-ever-aftering with Ty Harding.

Especially since he hadn't even suggested so much as a one-night stand!

Before she could sink into clinical depression, the bus blew a tire. Luckily for a pregnant fellow passenger, they disembarked to await a new vehicle a block from a hospital—just as she went into labor.

Or was that Fate? Marisa wondered as she walked the last three blocks from the bus stop, quietly let herself into the apartment and watched Ty slowly open his eyes.

"Hi, sprite," he said, giving her a slow, crooked smile that set her daydreams in motion again. "I was just resting my eyes. I'm watching the game." His hair stood in twisted tufts that begged her fingers to comb them straight.

"Sure," Marisa agreed as she downed the volume on the remodeling show. *I hope Ms. Intriguing appreciates this adorable, sexy man for more than his bank balance.*

Ty pushed himself into the full upright position, surreptitiously checking the corners of his mouth for napdrool.

Nadja's prediction echoed through his brainbox. *"You share bed within month."*

Now *there* was a plan! Waking up beside Marisa, kissing her, learning her curves with his angles, driving her wild with his hands, his mouth, his—

"I'm starved," Marisa said.

Me, too, Ty thought. But not for food.

She disappeared into the kitchen.

Marisa? The kitchen? Ty had his shoes on and his keys located by the time he heard the crash.

"Are you okay?" he called, analyzing the sound as he hurried toward it. China, he thought, not glass.

"I'm fine," said the sprite, so Ty's nerves detached his mouth from his brain and segued to the new Plan.

"Good—can't have my hostess incapacitated before the party. Don't move," he cautioned the figure sprawled attractively on the linoleum, surrounded by potting soil, broken greenery and shards of red clay. "I'll get the broom."

Marisa dismissed his diversionary cleanup offer. "You said that before. What party?"

It took some fancy talking and an hour of turning one battered kalanchoe into twelve new little plants to divert the sprite's attention from his ill-timed remark.

Ill-timed because he'd forgotten the darned weak spot in his Party Plan: an irresistible reason for it.

LUCKILY FOR TY, the usual catastrophes kept Marisa distracted for three more days—while he frantically sought a plausible party purpose.

Finally. It came in the mail Wednesday. Which he didn't look at until Thursday morning, also thanks to Nadja's curse.

Or was that Mrs. Pachenko's evil eye?

Ty shook his head as he pitched six credit-card offers into the trash, then studied the envelope addressed in his next-younger sister's scrawl.

Either way, he'd spent last night soaked to the skin—and Marisa was unemployed again.

He'd brought the sprite some Chinese for dinner just as a pipe at the day-care center burst. While the staff led the children to safety, he'd muscled shut the inflow valve.

Of course, Marisa volunteered to wait for the carpet squeegee crew. Ty helped her dry toys—and glowered at the crew boss when he hugged her for suggesting he charge the center less in return for enrolling his youngest in the toddler program.

They'd gotten home around one this morning; the sprite was still asleep. He'd been wakened by the Salvation Army relaying a negative response to Marisa's inquiry on Nico Costeceaseu. And by his lingering problem: a party excuse she'd buy.

Frowning, he slit the envelope. Read his sister's note and smiled. Here it was. The perfect excuse to test the sprite's determination to have a family. *Instead of just me.*

He checked the date. July 31. A little over a week away. Also perfect.

Pulling off a party this big, this complicated on such short notice would also prove irrefutably that Nadja's lucky curse and Mrs. Pachenko's evil-eye were—

Ty dismissed luck in favor of logistics. His parents lived in Denver, the sibs were scattered all over the country.

No problem—that stupid lottery money could buy a few plane tickets. Good use for it.

Finding paper and pencil, he settled on the sofa to start a list. Let's see, flying in and out would be silly, so they'd need to provide lodging, too. And a place to hold the shindig—the party room at his apartment complex was too small for a full-scale Harding convocation.

Wracking his brain for a site solution, Ty tapped the pencil against the notepad. It flipped out of his hand, hit the coffee table and rolled onto the newspaper lying there. Paradise Valley Zoning Debate read the headline.

Hmm. The house he'd inherited there *did* have the square footage. Should they—? *Wait till the sprite wakes up to worry about all that stuff.* The whole point of this was to get *her* overwhelmed…

He'd cover the easy part: inviting his unintentional co-conspirators.

Grabbing the phone and heading for the balcony so he wouldn't disturb Marisa, Ty spent the next couple of hours running up the kind of long-distance phone bill college freshmen usually produced. And, he admitted reluctantly, enjoying it.

See? he congratulated himself after lunch. Set a goal. Work toward it. Achieve it. Simple.

He'd said the magic words: ''parents' thirty-fifth wedding anniversary.'' Presto—Marisa agreed to help instead of jobhunt, at least today.

But now they'd stalled on the location thing.

After some lip-chewing that, ah, *stirred* Ty to the cold-shower stage, Marisa snapped her fingers. "Doesn't Dru manage a golf course?" she asked.

"Yeah," Ty enthused. "Country clubs have ballrooms, don't they?"

They do. They also have members. Busy, popular people holding meetings, getting married and showing off to their high-school class reunion.

"Love to help, buddy," Dru said when Ty called him, "but the members own the place. I just work here."

Ten hotels, eight resorts and about two dozen church halls later, Ty was ready to throw in the towel.

Marisa, on the other hand, buried her nose in the Yellow Pages. "Here's something," she said finally, looking up from her tantalizing cross-legged position on the floor. "Polly's Party Planning. A professional might have connections we don't."

Ty halted his restless fiddling with Baby. "Let's go," he said, digging for his keys and tossing them at the sprite. "Maybe my lucky curse works better in person."

Or not.

Polly Pendleton preferred plum. For her showroom displays, for her flowing faille gown, for the huge plastic frames of her eyeglasses. Even her shoulder-length bleached hair had a pink tinge to it.

"May I help you?" the party planner asked from her place behind a plum-colored counter as they came through the door.

Ty motioned for Marisa to speak. "We hope so," she said, smiling at Polly while she tugged her companion forward. "We're having trouble finding a suitable location for next Saturday evening."

Ms. Pendleton sniffed somewhat disdainfully. "I would imagine so," she proclaimed in round, er, plumish tones. "It's rather short notice."

"We know," Ty agreed, his fingers entwining with

the sprite's. "But we're only talking thirty, forty people."

Another sniff. "It's not the size of the wedding, young man, that creates the difficulty." Plum-rimmed glasses aimed themselves at Marisa's midsection. "Perhaps you two should consider postponing your nuptials a few months," she counseled.

Charged silence filled the plum-icious shop for a long moment.

Then, without looking at each other, Ty and Marisa exclaimed in unison, "We're not getting married!"

A sniff that would have turned a royal butler green with envy followed *that* disclaimer. "Then I fail to see what's so urgent. Everything is booked this time of year," the party planner drawled, patting her pink hair. "Has been for months."

"Thanks for your help," Ty said grimly as he dragged Marisa out of there. Damned if he'd acknowledge the little leap his heart had taken at Ms. Plum's erroneous conclusion. Marriage was not in his Plans. Not yet.

Not until Marisa accepted as valid his reluctance to get sucked back into the turmoil and chaos of family life. And that meant pulling off this stupid, *impulsive* anniversary party for his folks. In a week.

Without Polly's Party help. Without a venue. Without—

"We're toast, aren't we?" he asked when they reached the car. He motioned Marisa around to the driver's side.

She remained on the sidewalk, playing with the mirror on the passenger side. "There's always another option." She'd learned that from foster care.

"What? A picnic in the park?" He pointed to a bank sign down the street. "It's a hundred and twelve today. And it's supposed to get *hot* this weekend."

Marisa smiled as he stood there, rubbing his jaw. Obviously impatient, but controlling it to give her time to think. No wonder she'd gotten speechlessly dizzy back there in Polly's. Who wouldn't want a guy like Ty? Sexy and successful, calm and steady. Generous. Responsible. Reliable. Did I mention sexy? Everything she'd ever desired in a man. Except enthusiastic about the joy and security only a family of your own provided.

"We're going to have to think outside the box," Ty declared as his eyebrows nosedived.

As if she lived anywhere else!

"Let's get Nadja to curse a small convention or bar mitzvah into canceling," he suggested, catching the rearview mirror before it hit the sidewalk.

"You'd probably get luckier calling Lisette." Marisa blinked. Where had that come from? "Ah, because, ah—maybe she knows somebody who knows somebody."

When he actually pulled out his cell phone, Marisa wanted to hit him. And then kiss it—all of it—and make it better.

She was going nuts. No, she was already there. Crazy over Ty Harding. And bound to get hurt—a theory he proceeded to validate.

"Why not?" he said with a shrug. "I'll see if she's still in town, anyway."

Marisa would bet on it. *Who needs Mrs. Pachenko,* she thought wryly, *when you've got Ms. Intriguing?*

"I'll probably have to ask her if she wants to come," Ty mused as he pressed buttons on the cell phone, "whether or not she's any help." He cocked his head so a little strand of rich brown hair brushed across one eyebrow. "Anybody else we should invite to the party without a home?"

"How about Brad Pitt?" she muttered. "Or those cute pals, Matt and Ben?"

Ty shot her a look of confusion before turning his attention to the phone. In a very few minutes, he was telling it he'd see her Saturday night around sevenish and he'd let her know where.

"Lisette would love to help," he reported, pressing the disconnect with his thumb, "but she's a stranger here, so…"

He rubbed his jaw again, then flashed her a grin so hot it could evaporate steel.

Marisa's heart thudded. Another, feminine, location throbbed. *Focus on the party, Corelli. Leave the host to his fate.*

"I guess we'll have to check out my house," he said.

For a second, the Cone of Silence covered her, preventing speech. "Your what?" Marisa asked finally, her voice faint with disbelief.

"House."

She closed her eyes. "If you own a house, why do you live in an apartment?"

"I never asked to inherit it," Ty retorted—as if that answered anything.

"Spoken like a man who's never had to worry about having a roof over his head," she muttered.

He muttered back something about architects preferring their own designs. To which *she* muttered grave doubts that he'd designed the apartment building he occupied.

"Get in and drive," Ty said, ending the argument on a positive note. "We'll see if the place can handle a throng of partying Hardings."

"THAT MUST BE IT." Ty winced as he pointed to an oversized Santa Fe-style adobe structure that sprawled just beneath the crest of a hill.

"Why would anyone paint a house lavender?" Marisa asked as they pulled into the driveway, parked and got out.

"Beats me." Ty followed her to the front door: a custom-made, pretend-primitive door. Was that some kind of ironic symbol? he wondered. The urges that had spawned this party idea were as old as humanity, but they were brand-new to him.

Were they just another "estoopid" impulse? Or would they lead him to something vital, something he'd never planned for because he'd never known he needed it until now?

"Do you suppose the inside's purple, too?"

"Only one way to find out." Ty input the entry code on the keypad beside the rough-plank door. With a snick, the front door unlocked itself. Palming it open, he stood back to let Marisa precede him.

As she passed him, she brushed his arm. Heat seared through him. Visions of the sprite working that combustion technique on another, more southerly extremity dialed up Ty's thermostat about eight thousand degrees. Had it affected her, too?

Marisa took one step, another, then halted. Looked left and right. Overhead.

A second behind her, Ty did the same. Slid his shades down his nose, peered over them, then pushed them back in place. "Oh, my—"

"—goodness," Marisa finished, her voice fading on the last syllable.

Twenty feet above them loomed a Sistine Chapel-style ceiling—painted, apparently, by a Michelangelo on acid—displaying a pantheon of cavorting cartoon characters in neon colors.

Below the mural, dozens of baseball-style hats hung from nails in the walls, interspersed with to-do lists, appointments, phone numbers, even lines of computer code scribbled in black felt-tip marker on the bare Sheetrock.

To the right, an archway led to a large dining room containing a folding card table and a phone; its walls, too, had served as notepads.

Steeling himself, Ty investigated the archway opposite the front door. It led to an immense living room—sporting purple walls and an orange ceiling. Furnished with a green plaid lever-action recliner, a red-white-and-blue sofa, and the largest rear-projection TV made.

Marisa tiptoed past him to inspect the kitchen, open to the living room and connected to the dining room by another archway; it looked untouched since construction.

French doors led from all the public areas to a large courtyard of pebbled concrete containing a free-form pool and hot tub plus a built-in barbecue pit.

The house formed a U flanking the patio. A low wall at the far end enclosed the courtyard and ensured privacy.

With Ty leading the way, they explored the two arms of the U, groaning as they peeked into the bedrooms and baths, sighing with relief at the master suite at the far end of the west hallway, opposite the kitchen, then staggering back to the basketball court—er, living room.

The previous owner, a computer nerd Ty barely remembered from college, had obviously weirded out way before he went hang-gliding while stoned.

Aside from a king-size bed in the master suite and the items in the living and dining rooms, the house contained no furniture. Each bedroom, however, had been painted with the corporate colors and logo of a different fast-food franchise. Built-in shelves held massive collections of each company's give-away toys and merchandise.

"I never realized how closely linked clowns were to deep-frying in the American psyche," Ty said, fiddling with the TV. "Now what? We can't hold the party here."

Marisa tossed her ebony curls. "Sure we can," she insisted. He already knew the sprite was an amazing woman with an indomitable spirit.

But not even she could work miracles.

"We've only got a week," he pointed out.

"So? Hustle everyone through the house and out to the patio. I'll bring Baby and some other plants to dress it up. If the meal is good, nobody will—"

"Uh, meals," Ty corrected diffidently, realizing he hadn't exactly explained the party in *detail* yet. "Nothing fancy, of course. With a bunch of unruly kids, most of the focus'll have to be on crowd control."

His sprite's amber eyes flared. "Meal*s*? Plural?"

Man... He wanted to see those golden-sherry eyes flame with passion. Burn with desire. For his kiss, his touch. For *him*.

"Uh, well, the thing is..." Ty buried his hands in his pockets to keep from tangling them in her curls, cupping the back of her head and pulling her into his arms to kiss them both senseless.

"Dru's the only other Harding who still lives here in Phoenix. So the rest are...coming for the weekend."

He threw her a pleading look. She threw it back.

"How many?" she asked in a soft tone that made the hair on the back of his neck rise. "Exactly how many people are you expecting *for the weekend* next weekend?"

He started touching fingers. "The folks, of course. Chet'll bring his family—he's got three ankle-biters. Diane ditto. Bryce and his daughter Meg. Sandi and Ronnie can't get here until Saturday.

"That's when we'll have the official celebration. And the *big* crowd—Diane suggested we invite some of Mom and Dad's friends who live here and Sandi's calling some aunts and uncles." Ty gave her one of his knee-folding smiles. "So we only have to house and feed around fifteen for the whole weekend. But where? How?"

Get out of this right now, Corelli. Before your heart goes where it can't stay. "Don't ask me," Marisa said. "It's your family. Your party." There. Foot firmly down. Boundary firmly drawn.

Mr. So-Hot-He's-Incendiary ignored both foot and boundary. "I can't make this happen alone," he insisted, apparently forgetting the existence of his six brothers and sisters.

"I'm sorry, Ty. I can't."

"Why not?" he demanded, hands on lean, sexy hips, which only emphasized his broad shoulders.

Marisa turned away. Every cell in her body throbbed with sheer pathetic longing to be part of anything Ty belonged to—be it family, gang or chess club—but she'd vowed the day she left foster care to never again stand on the edges of someone else's life.

"Are you forgetting my bad luck?"

The numbskull dismissed that with a rude noise. "We have to be together to neutralize our curses, remember? Besides," he insisted, "any damage done to this place will only improve it."

He stuffed his hands in the back pockets of his jeans, which only emphasized his, ah, well-equipped masculinity. "Come on, Marisa," he pleaded softly, giving her the wide-eyed look usually employed by puppies in the adoption shelter. "I committed myself to this party, but I can't pull it off by myself. I need your help."

And she needed her head examined.

But of course, she agreed to his request. How could she refuse? Aside from the debt she owed him for keeping her and her plants off the street for the past three weeks, she knew in her bones that he loved his family. If she could reduce some of the stress surrounding this weekend celebration, he might remember how much.

Then he'd be free to—*meet his cool, blond fate, remember?*

"So where do you suggest we start?" he asked, watching her carefully.

"Well, the date's set," she replied. "The guest list ditto, the theme. That leaves the overnight accommodations, the party location, food and drink, any music or entertainment, a gift for your parents—unless one of the others wants to handle that."

Ty stared, admiration bubbling through him. Inside that wacky wardrobe lurked the soul of a planner. He waited while she chewed lip.

"Let's make lemonade out of this purple lemon," Marisa said.

"Huh?"

"Hold the party here."

"It's big enough," Ty agreed, "but the logos, the graffiti— There's no way we can paint over all of it in time, even if we draft Dru to help," he added, regretfully jettisoning a se-*weet* fantasy about Marisa in those little orange shorts and him removing dabs of paint from sensitive spots....

"Lisette said you won some money in the lottery. Enough to hire some painters?"

He nodded. Posed another objection—just to watch her problem-solve. Spectating the process was fun for a change. "There's no furniture except in the living room." *And in the master suite.* Hmm. He could make some plans for that bed. Plans that would play right into the Gypsy Queen's predictions.

Ty decided he could live with that.

"What if you asked everyone to bring sleeping bags? And we could cook hot dogs on the grill."

Nuts. He hadn't earned the house or the forty million from the lottery, but he could spend one on the other for his parents' anniversary. They'd been thrilled at the idea of having everyone together again. And he certainly owed them more than one little party.

More than he'd realized, probably, until Marisa came along.

Ty studied her big, amber eyes. They were full of longing, a wistfulness Genghis Khan couldn't have resisted. As much as he remembered how lonely he'd always felt, lost in the middle of the Harding crowd, he suddenly wanted to give the sprite a taste of the family life she'd never had. Even if she liked it.

"We'll rent furniture," Ty said, his mind made up. "And have the food catered."

As soon as he blurted out his decision, an odd feeling came over him. A sense of...fatefulness.

Well, so be it. If next weekend convinced Marisa she couldn't live without a huge, boisterous family, fine.

If, however, by that Sunday she saw the advantage to living with one quiet, dull architect, even better.

Polly Plumnoid might pull down some business after all.

FIRST THINGS FIRST, though. One Plan at a time.

The next day—Friday—party prep began in earnest. While Marisa contacted caterers listed in the phone book, Ty hired a crew of painters recommended by Krako's secretary. For the ransom he agreed to pay, they consented to neutralize the Fast-Food Mecca's interior by Wednesday.

At dinner, he discovered the sprite had another new job—at a flower shop featured in one of the catering ads.

"But—you're still signed on for the party, right?" he asked. Idly, since between Nadja's good luck and the ol' evil eye, she'd be de-hired before the first bouquet wilted. After all, he needed her help, so—

A little chill ran down Ty's back. Since when had he started counting on luck and magic to achieve his goals instead of planning and hard work?

"The owner, Mr. Abelard, agreed to give me some time off next week."

"Great, then," Ty said, covering his shiver of fear with a nonchalant tone. If one of these jobs panned out, Marisa would leave.

Unless he offered her a damned good reason to stay—and until next weekend, he wouldn't know if he could.

Thank heaven, his brother called with an invitation to play golf before he flew into full-blown anxiety.

And when Dru asked, Marisa agreed to meet them for lunch afterward.

"I'd love to," she enthused into the phone. "I'd like

to talk to your banquet staff about the catering. It seems everyone in the phone book's busy."

Ty went for a run while she and Dru chatted like old pals. He wasn't *jealous*—he just didn't want to risk any moves that might push Marisa out of his life before he knew what to do about the feelings that simmered between them like lava in a volcano. Actively seeking a fissure.

Moves like kissing her eyelids. Nuzzling her neck. Exploring those feminine mysteries...

Ty ran an extra four miles. In record time.

ON SATURDAY, WHILE Dru described his brother's course-record three holes-in-one to the sprite, Ty wandered over to look closer at the plants fronting the pro shop.

Scaly trunks, spiky leaves edged with a red stripe. Ty thought they had one filling a corner of the balcony. Bigger, of course. And healthier.

"Let's eat, bro," Dru called, then nearly lost a hand when he tried to guide Marisa toward the dining room.

Ty jostled his younger brother aside to place his own fingers on the small of Marisa's back. That little phfft of electricity sizzled his fingertips. Generating a pulsing need to taste her passion once more.

Only her mention of the upcoming weekend stopped him from sliding his hand possessively around her waist.

When she met the Harding bunch—would she connect to his reality? Or confirm her own G-rated fantasy?

"Come on, man, it's all good." Dru nudged his arm with the menu card. "Order something."

He did, then watched a deft, silent waiter work them down a short stack of plates while the sprite interrogated Dru's chef and banquet manager.

After which—another round of a now-familiar pattern. Marisa knocked the ice-sculpture off the dessert buffet. Ty set himself between her and the members who left their tables to circle the slush—until he noticed they were complimenting the men in white hats on the decoration and offering suggestions to prevent future tragedies.

The sprite ignored the whole thing; stayed focused on his party. Ty beamed.

"Breakfast can be self-serve," she announced as he led her to the car. "Lunch the same. We'll put out sandwich makings, chips, carrots, celery sticks and cookies.

"Dinner's the big problem." She chewed on that kissable lower lip and Ty went rigid with a nonfood hunger. Barely managed to follow her dissertation on the uninteresting subject.

"Ernie—the banquet manager—gave me a name, but he said even a basic dinner would run to some serious change, so maybe we should just fire up the barbecue. Throw on some hot dogs and chicken. With a salad and a nice dessert...."

"This is my parents' anniversary," Ty protested, more for her lower lip's sake than his folks'. Hey, his mom thought canned ravioli was a complete meal. "After thirty-five years, they deserve more than charred chunks o' chicken." He held out the cell phone. "Call the name and book him."

Well, sheesh—even without the lottery windfall, cost didn't matter. Not compared to the brilliance of Marisa's smile, the way her eyes glowed at him as she took the phone.

TY SPENT SUNDAY at the lavender mansion—supervising the painters and bagging collectibles.

Leaving a few sacks there for his nieces and nephews, he dropped the others at various charitable doorsteps and donation boxes on the way home. (Yeah. Remember the headline: Children's Home Auctions Rare Pez Dispenser to Fund New Building?)

Marisa put in her second day at the flower shop. Was

that yin-yang stuff actually working? she wondered when the day reaped only a couple of minor disasters—and she wasn't fired.

She delivered a dozen roses...with a (sorry, irresistible) *free bee* included.

And got the address for a mixed-bouquet delivery wrong.

The husband on Twenty-fourth Street couldn't believe what a difference a few short-lived blossoms made to his wife; he decided regular flower deliveries was a great marital aid. And the wife on Twenty-fourth Avenue had no flimsy reason this time to forgive the so-and-so's verbal abuse; she went home to mother.

Monday, Ty toddled off to Krako, Iverson and Delaporte after the sprite suggested he request time off at the end of the week.

Bull-oney. He *told* Krako he'd be out Thursday and Friday. Hey, they'd made him a partner—thanks to Nadja's curse or their own impetuosity. They could take the consequences.

Naturally, Krako didn't protest. Just punched him on the arm, declared families the bedrock of America and agreed to reschedule six meetings with potential clients.

Not that *any* of them wanted Ty Harding, the architect. They wanted the lottery winner. Or the cat savior. Or the day-care hero—since that made the papers too, somehow.

When Ty voiced chagrin at being chosen for his notoriety rather than his professional skills, Krako boomed, "Who cares what brings 'em in? Long as they bring a fat checkbook."

He must have read Ty's reaction on his face, because the older man har-har-harred. "Don't tell me you're in this business for the design challenges!"

He was, Ty realized. Although he hadn't consciously thought about it when he devised his original Plan, he wanted to be known for designing clever, elegant and compact dwellings with no wasted space. Large, expensive, sprawling houses offered little challenge.

Reeling, Ty left Krako chanting mantras about profit margins, overhead and the economies of grand scale.

Sheesh—had he Planned his life all wrong?

Had Nadja's curse and its fallout of fame really been a lucky break—saving him some unnecessary years at Krako, Iverson and Delaporte? Mumbling something at the receptionist, Ty fled the office.

But how did he *change* his Plan? What did he do next?

Bert's New Jersey accent echoed through his head. *"Ax da expoit."*

Automatically, Ty drove to the flower shop, seeking the expert sprite—who knew how to roll with life's punches. How to accept unexpected change without being defeated by it.

Unfortunately, Marisa was busy waiting on customers.

So Ty checked on the painters, then schlepped over to Dru's country club and invited himself to have a beer with his brother.

"You—wandering aimlessly around on a workday? What is it, bro?" Dru asked when they'd sucked down half a brew each. "Woman trouble?"

"It's not about Marisa," Ty snapped.

"Who named names?" Dru retorted with a knowing grin.

Ty rubbed his hand along his jaw. "It's not woman trouble," he repeated. Although maybe it was if he thought a woman who wanted a family could solve his problems. "It's…"

What the hell. He and Dru were only a year apart; they'd shared a room—and their darkest secrets—for years. The sprite wasn't available. And he needed to talk to *somebody*.

Taking a deep breath, Ty spilled it. "I had a plan, you know? A perfect plan that took everything into account! I had a schedule, I worked hard…."

Dru rotated the bottom of his bottle a few inches above the bar. "I had one, too," he reminded his brother. "According to mine, I'm supposed to be starting at second base for the Yankees now."

He fingered his left knee for a minute, then tipped the brown longneck and took another sip. "Plans change," he said, then shot Ty a sideways glance. "Stop me if you've heard this."

"I was so sure I was on the right path." Ty sighed. "But now... What do you do when—" he waved his bottle in a helpless arc "—things change?"

"What everyone else does." Dru grinned. "Muddle through. Remember what Dad always said—'Take it as it comes.' I'd say Mom's favorite advice fits here, too."

"'If you do your best, dear, that's good enough,'" Ty quoted in falsetto, then thanked his brother for his useless but somehow comforting advice, left his beer unfinished and went home.

Made breakfast for dinner: scrambled eggs, toasted English muffins, crisped real bacon. Put it on plates in the oven to stay warm until the sprite got home.

'Cuz, hell—who wanted to eat alone? Especially when facing more unexpected, unwelcome, *undeniable* facts.

Ty shambled into the living room and thumbed the new TV's remote. Fact number one—even the best Plans don't always work out.

Fact number two—knowledge comes *from*, not *before* experience.

Absently surfing the channels, Ty mulled his parents' wisdom.

How did you take things as they come? And how did a man live with himself if the best he could do *wasn't* good enough?

Ty's thumb stilled on a familiar game show. Was that why he'd rejected love so adamantly? Not from distaste for the resultant turmoil, but doubt that he could handle it, could do what needed doing?

A contestant spun the plyboard game wheel.

Architecture was so simple! A matter of math and engineering, applying proven principles of design.

But a woman—*especially* the sprite—deserved more than him fumbling around learning how to love. After her lonely and disrupted childhood, Marisa deserved more than he could give.

Are you sure?

"Huh? Who said that?" Ty looked over at Baby. Nah. Philodendrons don't ask incisive personal questions. But as the glitter-gowned cohostess touched letters, the question hung in midair, begging for an answer. *Before* he leaped to depressing conclusions about his inadequacy to successfully cohabit—*Now,* there *was a conclusion to leap to!*—with the sprite and her passion.

Soothed that he had a temporary direction, if not a decent plan, Ty settled back to solve the puzzle.

AFTER DINNER, MARISA sat on the living room floor, making lists and notes and plans galore to ensure the party he almost already regretted ran smoothly.

Ty sat on the sofa. Speechless. Brainwaveless.

"Have you decided on attire?" she asked, stretching out one long, smooth leg.

The crop top and short shorts she had on were fine by him. Or the purply-red satin nightshirt. He liked that, too.

"For Saturday night."

"Oh." Ty shrugged. "I don't know. Whatever you think."

Marisa gazed through her eyelashes at the cords of muscle in Ty's arms, the broad planes of his chest. Nude. She voted for nudity. Now.

"It's not my family," she said for the whatever-ith time aloud. The bazillionth time for her own benefit.

"Trust me," Ty said, shifting deeper into the corner of the sofa. "If you're in the house, you're family. That's how the Hardings think."

Except one Harding. The one she wanted—more every day.

Keep your focus, Corelli. Unless she played her cards exactly right—not something she'd give much likelihood—the next few days promised to be the most difficult of her life.

Thank heavens for her job! Evenings together were torture enough. A whole weekend with the man—*You'll be a goner, Corelli, no matter what happens between Lisette and her "fate" here.*

Marisa chewed on her lip, desperately seeking a way to exclude herself from the actual festivities—when Ms. Intriguing was destined to seal the deal. "Would anyone object to making the evening formal?" she asked, suddenly inspired. Ty had sisters. Surely they'd conditioned him to the classic "I don't have anything to wear."

"The women'll love an excuse to spend more time at the mall. We can rent tuxes for the guys." Ty frowned. "But what about the kids? Won't they run amok? Spoil everything?"

"You must have been a holy terror!" she exclaimed with a laugh. "Not all children are rambunctious little hellions."

"These are," Ty asserted, "if they take after the Harding side." Then he chuckled, a deep, sexy sound that made Marisa's insides tighten with longing. "Even Diane, who's with the DEA, had her water-balloon moments."

The heck with it. Marisa knew survival required accepting reality, but it might be years before she got over Ty Harding and his blazing masculine charm enough to settle for a mere husband who wanted the same things she did: a home and babies.

"Tell me about growing up with your outrageous, mischievous siblings," she urged. When he hesitated, she offered an added inducement. "Just a couple of f'rinstances and I'll reveal the secret of getting kids to behave when necessary.''

After a long, very blue gaze and a few absent strokes of strong fingers along his firm jaw, Ty clicked off the TV. Began sharing stories of some of the stunts he and his siblings had pulled. Adventures he hadn't thought of in years—like the time he and Bryce made Ronnie balance an apple on her head while they tried to shoot it off with toy arrows.

With the tales—and Marisa's delighted response—still percolating in his head, Ty called his folks to run the formal-dinner thing by them. ''How did you and Dad put up with all the stuff we pulled?'' he asked when his mother finished gushing about seeing her darlings all dressed up.

''We love you, silly,'' she said. As if that explained anything.

After phoning the rest of the family so the females could begin their clothing frenzy, he interrupted Marisa's good-night-Baby routine. ''What's the secret?'' he demanded, remembering her promise. ''To making kids behave?''

''Fear works,'' she said quietly, shadows darkening her amber eyes. ''But respect that flows both ways works better.''

Ty scowled until she laughed softly. ''This weekend? We'll let them wear themselves out in the pool.''

He took himself off for a long, punishing run. He didn't want to think about how Marisa knew about fear controlling kids. Or wonder again whether he was capable of applying love and respect the way his parents had, turning seven crazy kids into fairly decent adults.

''Nuts. There's more to it than that,'' he muttered as sweat soaked his T-shirt somewhere in mile three. He seemed to remember a few tuition bills. Braces. Some wrecked cars. Sandi and that prison penpal…

''Okay. I'm a chicken,'' he admitted to the last stoplight—which flicked to green, of course, as he reached the intersection. "But what kind of man takes on a responsibility he's not sure he can handle?"

Marisa lay awake until she heard him return. Reminding herself that a couple of kisses do not a commitment make and that she was a commitment-committed woman.

So she lusted for Ty's body. Appreciated his kindness and generosity. Envied him the cocoon of relatives wrapping his childhood in love. So what?

Twenty years of being an orphan—hadn't she learned anything?

A person with no support network can't afford fantasies. *It's simple, Corelli. Fall for Ty, fall apart when it's over. You have nobody to help put you back together, so don't be "estoopid." Protect yourself.*

SHE REPEATED THE hard wisdom so many times before falling asleep that the next morning, she managed to shake her head when Ty asked if they were going grocery shopping tonight or what.

"You're right. We should do the furniture rental first. I'll pick you up—"

She shook her head again.

Ty dropped toast remains on his plate. Narrowed his eyes. "Are you bailing on me?"

"I'm not..." Yes, she was.

"Why?"

Why indeed?

"Come on, Marisa—please? I *need* you."

Who on earth could resist a plea like that? she wondered as she nodded her surrender. Not a woman who didn't remember ever being wanted let alone needed, who'd always been a burden, an unwanted package to be stored one place or another until she could be pushed out on the street to fend for herself.

For once in her life, Marisa wanted to pretend she

belonged. Not forever. Just until Sunday. Six days. Like a fantasy baseball camp.

"Okay—but if Mrs. Pachenko's *mal ojo* wreaks havoc with your parents' anniversary, it's on your head."

"Warning noted," Ty said, flashing a grin as he drained his coffee cup. "I'll see you tonight. Pick you up at six?"

"Make it six-thirty. Mr. Abelard's going to show me how to swipe credit cards."

She'd kept the job three days already, but apparently Nadja's "termites" were making sawdust at the flower shop, too.

Luckily, Ty arrived in time to operate the fire extinguisher. The credit card company agreed to send someone out the following afternoon to install newer equipment *and* reconcile the credit records free of charge. Mr. Abelard was ecstatic.

The same good-bad pattern repeated itself at the furniture rental place. Marisa tripped on an area rug, knocking over a floor lamp which broke a glass coffee table.

The crash lured a lost child from hiding and Ty returned the toddler to its mother.

"It's gotta be the yin-yang balancing out," he insisted as he drove the truck donated by the cat-loving auto dealer around to the loading dock to pick up what bedframes they had in stock. He had to admit the vehicle came in handy at times, even if he hadn't bought it.

They were scheduled to shop for linens after work on Wednesday; Krako burst into Ty's office late in the afternoon, nearly incoherent about a new client who wanted to come in at four.

"B-but it's Turrell!" Krako gabbled when Ty refused the meeting. "Turrell 'The Fleet' Foote—the Cardinals' first-round draft pick! He just signed for a bushel of bucks and he wants *you* to build him a house here in Phoenix."

"Me?" Ty asked. "Why?" Damned if he really

wanted to go shopping, but *any* time spent with Marisa was more enjoyable than explaining unworkable design concepts to locomotive-sized men used to expressing themselves in a physically aggressive manner.

Krako's face reddened. "Turrell's superstitious," he confessed. "And he read about the little lost kid and you winning the lottery and the kitty...."

Phooey. Ty stalked out of the office. Pulled Marisa out of the cool case where they stored the flowers. Fed her, then stormed the mall and bought enough textiles to send the Cotton Council or whoever into fits of ecstasy.

Which was where he wanted to go, too. With Marisa. If only she'd forget that family stuff...

"You sure we've got enough?" he asked as they lugged sacks of sheets and towels, bathmats and comforters, pillows and toothbrush holders into the lavender mansion by moonlight. "What if one of the kids wets his bed?"

"The utility room's fully equipped," Marisa pointed out with a laugh. "We'll just throw the sheets in the washer."

On impulse, Ty tried a little test. "I'm not doing somebody else's kid's laundry," he declared—an instant before remembering how Marisa had spent her childhood.

Dropping his bags, he enfolded her. "Ah, sprite," he breathed, his body thrumming with how right her soft curves felt, tucked against his hardness—which was getting harder rapidly. "I'm sorry. I didn't mean—"

She flunked him, anyway. "I'm sorry you can't see that a few wet sheets are no price at all to pay for the joy that children can bring." Her hair swirled like smoke in still air as she added, "I can't wait to have some—and I will as soon as I'm sure this bad luck thing is over."

She pointed. "Those bags go in the east wing. I'll do the west wing."

GREAT LECTURE, CORELLI, Marisa told herself as she stacked the last towel in the master bath's linen closet and returned to the bedroom to stare at the biggest bed she'd ever seen, imagining herself in it with its new owner.

His hands on her body, his mouth ditto. His sky-blue eyes hot with desire.

Too bad he probably didn't buy a word of it.

She sighed with frustrated longing. Why couldn't Ty, blessed with everything a person could want—health, intelligence and a large, loving family—want to repeat the process?

Agitated, she wandered around the room. Thinking about the magnetic attraction she felt for Ty, wanting to indulge it—despite all her self-warnings.

Undoubtedly, the sex would be great. The man's smile fizzed her hormones; his kisses sent them into hyperdrive. Completing the consensual act would probably launch her right past the galaxy's rim!

"But you want more than great sex," she reminded herself, sinking onto the raised stone ledge forming the fireplace's hearth. "You want love and children and forever.

"And Ty's never said a positive word about any of the above," she pointed out. "Let alone mentioned you in the same sentence with even one of them."

So no letting a one-sided attraction to Ty distract her from her life goals.

As soon as this stupid *mal ojo* lost its oomph and Ty's party was over, she would start looking for some bozo—er, great guy who wanted a wife and some little chips off the old DNA to carry on the Bubba name.

Unreasonably distressed, Marisa started to rise. Lost her balance. Grabbed for something to stop her fall.

Her flailing hand encountered a lever jutting out from the firebox wall.

The laws of physics kicked in, converting Marisa's

inertia of motion to energy acting on the lever: soot filled the room.

Hearing her cry, Ty raced toward the sound. Halted for a second in the doorway, then plunged across the now-gray carpet, tugging loose his shirttail. As he started to carefully wipe the sooty residue off her face, something winked at him from the pile of ashes fanning out from the fireplace.

Lane's Fine Jewelry was open late for its Moonlight Madness sale; the gemologist appraised the winking something as a flawless two-carat, marquise-cut yellow diamond.

Ty gave Marisa a quick, assessing glance.

"Don't even think about it," she muttered. "Finders are not keepers of rocks that size."

So he settled—on impulse—for having it set as the center of a ring surrounded by gemstones representing him and his siblings. After securing a solemn promise to have it ready on Saturday, he gave the jeweler Diane's number to contact for the other birthdays. Earning him another glare from the sprite.

Silent and exhausted, they went home together. To separate, uncomfortable beds where Ty tossed for hours....

REALLY, HE WAS pretty sure he was only dozing—until Krako woke him Thursday to not take no for an answer.

After apologizing and handing Marisa his credit card and car keys, Ty met with Krako and the gigantic Foote while the sprite supervised the delivery of the rest of the furniture, then went grocery shopping.

Having finally discouraged replicating the Taj Mahal, Ty excused himself to haul designated plants—and a suitcase apiece—to the lavender house. Finally got to meet Marisa at a well-known Mexican restaurant for dinner. *For our last evening alone together before the Harding Horde's onslaught.*

Impulsively, he hired the café's mariachi band to serenade his parents. Because Marisa suggested it, then softly disparaged her own idea as too romantic.

There's nothing wrong with romance, Ty informed her. Okay, he might have shouted it. 'Cuz he felt—again—like someone caught in a revolving door. Confused. Aroused. Willing. Lost.

But for one impulsive minute, he wanted to give Marisa what she longed for. The tender, loving union of man and woman in holy matrimony. A gaggle of relatives. Offspring—

Marisa carrying my child. The image lanced through the deepest part of him. Filling him with a longing he'd never felt before.

And sheer unadulterated terror.

"Let's go," he said, snatching the bill from the waiter's hand.

THREE BACK-BREAKING hours later, Ty let himself out on the patio.

While he'd scraped paint off windows and tile, Marisa had organized the kitchen and arranged Baby and its friends in groupings around the pool and through the house. Amazing what a difference a few green things made, Ty thought as he stretched his spine and rotated his neck to loosen sore muscles.

He smelled moonlight. Looked around.

There stood Marisa in those orange nylon shorts and a tight, blue tank top. Instantly driving him crazy. Again. Maybe she always would.

Maybe he should accept it.

As he stared, a crystalline drop of sweat beaded on her satiny skin and trickled down the V of her shirt.

"Looks inviting," she whispered huskily.

Body overtook brain. *Want her. Take her. Give... be...join....* Words failed him. "Arrk..."

"The water."

Ty pretended to examine the swimming pool. A lush, almost-full moon coming up over the garage tipped the gently lapping water with a silvery, sensual light.

"What are their names?" Marisa asked.

Ty blinked. Ripples had monikers?

"Go over your family's names once more," she pleaded. "I'm so afraid I'll forget one. Start with the children."

Was she deaf, blind and dumb? Here they were. Hot. Sweaty. Alone.

It was time for romance, for seduction, for sex. Not for kids.

"By tomorrow, you won't need names," Ty snapped, fighting to rein his desire. At least until he got a little encouragement. "You'll be yelling 'hey, stop it!' indiscriminately."

Marisa went still. "Don't you like kids at all?"

An image flashed through his mind. An image of an infant sprite with dark, curly hair. "I don't know," he said slowly. "Maybe it's just quantities of 'em I don't like."

He looked at the moonlight dancing across the pool, then at Marisa. "I'm sure I'd like the creation process."

She spun away, fiddled with Baby's leaves. Even in the dark, she didn't dare risk him seeing how much she wanted—*another fantasy, Corelli. Haven't you been listening?*

"With the right woman," he murmured, his deep voice suddenly next to her ear.

"Maybe you've already found her," Marisa said, picturing Ms. Intriguing's tall, cool-blond beauty beside Ty's dark, rugged handsomeness.

"Yeah," he purred, a deep testosterone-wrapped

rumble that made every feminine part of her shiver. "Maybe I have."

"W-well," Marisa choked out. "Th-that's nice."

He just stood there, so close she could feel his heat. She told her feet to move sequentially, taking her away from temptation. They refused.

"It's, uh, still warm, isn't it?" she said, desperate to break the mood before she did something really stupid. Like fling herself into his arms and plaster herself against his big, hard, male—

"Sure is." In one swift motion, he pulled his shirt over his head, exposing that extraordinary masculine chest she dreamed about every night. "Let's cool off in the pool."

Slick, bare skin? Floating in wet moonlight? "I...I don't—"

"Right. You don't need a suit," he whispered huskily, misreading her hesitation. "Nobody's watching—just dive in. I will if you will."

His hands went to his belt buckle, then the waistband of his khakis. When they moved to his zipper, Marisa fled to the steps leading down into the pool. She paused on the first step, still uncertain this was a good idea. Water sloshed around her ankles. It felt...wet.

Ty kicked off his shoes, then shimmied out of his pants, answering the boxers or briefs question.

Marisa slipped down a step. Water to her knees. Not high enough to cool the fire raging inside her at the sight of Ty's magnificent male body drenched in moonlight.

The third step put the wavelets dancing right where the fire burned hottest. Marisa glanced down, expecting steam.

When she glanced up again, he was there. His head bending, his mouth taking hers in a kiss that started tenderly. Built rapidly. To a fierce, hungry, demanding duel of lips and tongues. Heat and moisture. Moans and whimpers and deep, guttural sounds coming from both of them.

His arms encircled her. Then crushed her against the smooth, hard plane of his chest. One hand moved to tangle in her hair, holding her while the other sought her breast.

His thumb brushed her nipple—and need coursed through her like lightning. His mouth nibbled newly sensitive places on her neck, below her ear, her shoulder...

Finally. His mouth captured her breast. She was floating—on water or desire? Who cared?

All that mattered was the pleasure they were exchanging. He groaned encouragingly when her hands spread across his chest, stroked his back, caressed his buttocks and his muscular thighs, then found his hipbones and slowly cupped his undeniably aroused male, ah, mechanism.

Ty groaned again. "Careful, sweetheart," he murmured. He started moving toward the steps—somehow they'd drifted into the center of the pool during their feverish mutual exploration.

"Let's try out one of those chaise lounge things we bought," he suggested in a hoarse whisper, his hands supporting, stroking, kneading. "Let me love you in the moonlight."

His fingers found the edge of her shorts, slipped inside.

With Ty's touch spiraling her to heaven, Marisa couldn't make herself deny them both the chance to satisfy—

"GE-RO-NI-MO!"

The war whoop had barely registered when a huge wall of water crashed over the pair.

Ty cursed as he swiped water from his face. The force of the splash-wave and the element of surprise had stripped Marisa from his arms. She bobbed up a few feet away, her hair in long, ebony rivers just as the idiot who'd cannonballed at exactly the wrong time erupted beside his brother.

"I'm still the greatest, bum knee or not," Dru crowed, slugging Ty on the upper arm. "How's it going? I thought I'd come over 'n see if you guys needed any help."

"Thanks, but you've done enough," Ty growled, watching Marisa make her way to the edge of the pool, pull herself up and climb out in one graceful motion. "Dru—you have the worst timing known to man."

He began floundering his way to the steps.

"Or the best," Dru said softly, a hand restraining Ty's forward progress. "She's not the fool-around kind," he warned. "You want some advice?"

"No."

"Here it is, anyway. Don't get in too deep unless you're sure you want to swim."

Shrugging off his brother, who shrugged right back, then started doing noisy laps, Ty hurried after the sprite, who'd just about made it to the French doors nearest the east wing. "Marisa, wait!"

She halted, but didn't turn around. "What for?" she asked, her voice tight with...*something.*

"You're not mad, are you?"

"Mad? Why would I be mad?"

"Because Dru interrupted us before we could—" Puzzled but determined to clear this up, Ty said, "That *was* just the beginning, Marisa."

"Beginning of what?" Uh-oh. Bare foot slapping cement, arms crossed over her chest.

Well, dammit, he was frustrated too. Even now, he was tempted to ignore his brother and his common sense, sweep her up in his arms and carry her off somewhere private. Bury himself in her. Bring her to heights of pleasure neither one of them had ever known before.

Then do it all over again.

"Guess we'll never know," he spit out, shaking with denied desire. "From now on, we'll be surrounded by family."

"And what's wrong with that, Ty?"

"Are you nuts, woman?" He goggled at her. "Weren't you paying attention just now?"

Her hands formed fists, clenched against her thighs. Smooth, taut thighs.

"Yes!" she hissed. "And all I heard was an invitation to try out the lawn furniture."

Okay, so he'd been a little too eager to head for a bed. Was that a crime? What did she want?

A declaration of your intentions, you moron. "Aw, come on, Marisa!" Did she really think he was that kind of jerk? "You have to know I wasn't just looking for a casual sexual encounter.

"For heaven's sake!" he exclaimed. "We've lived together for weeks. I've never put that kind of move on you." Not that he hadn't wanted to, but he'd swallow his tongue before he admitted that. "Believe me, if all I wanted was recreational sex, I'd know better than to ask you."

He ignored her muttered, "Gee, thanks."

"I care about you," he said.

"And?"

"And I wouldn't do anything to hurt you." He had no idea what she wanted him to say. What more *was* there to say? He liked her, he wanted her, he was considering major revisions to his life-plans for a taste of her passion, he no longer dismissed her nutsy ideas about luck and *mal ojos.* Sheesh—he was even wrestling with having a kid for her.

Why couldn't she return the favor? Accept him the way *he* was?

If *she* cared for *him,* he and the way he was would be—

"I'm not sure that's enough," she said, turning

away. "And until I am... I—I'm glad your brother showed up when he did. Good night, Ty. I'll see you in the morning."

"You'll also see what I'm talking about," he retorted against the bitter disappointment suddenly burning the back of his throat. "You think a big family is wonderful and fun and fabulous—because you've never been lost in the middle of one. Well, tomorrow's your chance. Go for it.

"We'll talk...later," he said over the churning coming from the pool. Or was that his gut? "I want you, Marisa. Seriously, long-term want you. But you know how I feel about kids, about big families. And if you want me—that's the way you'll take me."

He turned and walked back to the pool area. Halfway across the patio, he heard the click of the door closing behind her. How, he wondered as he started sprinting toward the pool apron, could something going so right go so wrong so fast?

"GERONIMO yourself," he called out to his brother as he went airborne above the water.

The kerSPLOOMPH! of *his* cannonball gratified Ty's vengeful urges. And killed the last stirrings of his, ah, male equipment.

Until he was once again alone in a too-big bed. Staring through darkness at the ceiling of the mansion's master suite. Cursing Dru's lousy timing. Aching for his sprite, who was holed up a million miles away in the other wing.

And wishing—no, *almost* wishing he wanted children.

But almost didn't cut it. Unless he truly wanted a child and knew he'd be a good parent, it would be wrong to have one just because the sprite wanted one.

Why couldn't she see that?

Dammit, he refused to saddle a child with a father

who couldn't cut it as a dad. Better to let Marisa go now.

"You share bed before month is out."

"Which is Saturday," Ty muttered as he flopped over and pounded his pillow. "The day after tomorrow. So much for the Gypsy Queen's magical powers."

For the first time in his life, Ty Harding wished he believed in magic—*and* looked forward to being surrounded by his boisterous family. He needed distracting; they'd provide it.

As for Marisa—maybe seeing would be believing....

7

TY TRIED TO TALK to her again the next morning, but Marisa snapped a sheet at him in self-defense, told Dru—who'd apparently spent the night somewhere in the house—to have his brother finish making beds or vacuum or divvy up the fast-food toys among the children's rooms or go buy more food.

After which, she shoved the sleeping chart they'd worked out at one of the slack-jawed morons and departed for the flower shop, where she'd arranged to make centerpieces for tomorrow night's big dinner. In lieu of a paycheck—but Mr. Know-It-All didn't have to know that.

What was one more speck of ignorance in his ignorance-speckled mind? she grumbled silently as she stuck miniature roses into damp florist's foam. Ty Harding didn't have the brains God gave protozoa if he thought she'd give up her lifelong dream for a short-lived affair—no matter how wonderful.

"I want a baby, darn it," she muttered, jabbing button mums into the clay. "A family."

Which will never include Ty. Even if this weekend taught him to appreciate his family more, hadn't Nadja warned her that Lisette would meet her fate at the party? Who else could it be but Ty?

Ms. Intriguing had already passed on Dru; the other male Hardings were taken, although one wasn't bringing his wife, just his daughter.

His child. Tears blurred the arrangement's outline.

Marisa grabbed blindly for stems. Stuffed them into the shallow bowl.

"That looks great!" Mr. Abelard praised, coming over from the customer desk. "You have a real flair for color. Here—let me help you do the rest."

After completing the centerpieces, Marisa arranged for the caterer to pick them up the next day, then—since Ty had vetoed her absence from the formal dinner—she stopped at her favorite thrift store. Mrs. Pachenko's evil eye must have taken a smoke break: she hit paydirt.

At least now she wouldn't have to borrow something from one of his sisters; despite Ty's assurances, Marisa doubted any of them were "about your size."

Returning to the oversized lavender villa, she lurked in bathrooms scrubbing already-gleaming tubs, keeping out of Ty's way until she heard him leave for the airport to pick up the first arrivals.

Then she listened to Dru's fairway-mowing philosophy while rehearsing her Weekend Survival Strategy. Stay away from temptation—namely Ty Harding. Do everything possible to make his parents' anniversary party a success.

Remember that by noon Sunday, her debt to Ty would be paid.

So if Nadja Costeceaseu really was the Queen of the Gypsies and Ms. Intriguing met her fate tomorrow, Marisa could move on and survive.

Even if it felt like—

LIKE BEING IN A *blender at a Parrot-Head convention,* Ty decided. That's how he felt. Wound up. Insides fizzing. And why?

'Cuz he knew he was right, but that cold, empty, lonely part of him hoped he was wrong, he conceded as he craned his neck trying to spot Chet and Debbie in the crowd streaming off the plane. He and a family didn't mix.

I'm doing us both a favor. Hadn't Marisa admitted
the other day that she'd never stayed more than two
years in one place? She wouldn't want her kids mi-
grating between houses for alternate weekends with—

"Tyler!"

—a failure as a husband and dad. Sheesh, he hated
thinking of himself that way, but...*too much at stake
to take the risk.* His stomach whirled.

"Hey, man. Glad you could make it." Ty pounded
his oldest brother on the back, kissed Deb on the cheek,
and patted their oldest boy on the head. "Hello, Dex,"
he greeted the child, who gazed at him owlishly. "Boy,
have you—"

"Grown a lot since the last time you saw me. I
know."

His mother shot the boy a repressive look. Ty found
himself grinning. Heartily glad to be distracted—momentarily, at least—from his own gloomy thoughts.
"Guess that covers it, Dex. So what's your hot passion
these days? I think you were raising rabbits last visit."

To his surprise, the kid still kept animals.

"One-track mind," Chet said as they ambled toward
the gate where Bryce and his daughter were scheduled
to arrive in twenty-five minutes. "Like you. We're already saving for vet school."

"Nothing wrong with being focused," Ty retorted,
automatically defensive.

"Didn't say there was." Without missing a step,
Chet lifted the sleeping toddler from his wife's arms.
"Always envied you that. Knowing what you wanted,
going after it. Never quitting till you got it. I think we
all felt safer, somehow, with you so centered. Like we
had someone besides the folks to count on."

Definitely margaritaville, Ty thought, his jaw dropping.

He was saved from responding—luckily?—by the
four-year-old announcing an urgent desire to visit the

nearest bathroom. While Deb escorted Ryan to the restroom, the toddler awoke hungry—and proceeded to notify everyone in the airport.

Also luckily(?), Bryce's plane got in a few minutes early.

From then on, the pace became frantic. Well, almost frantic. After Ty herded the group of seven to baggage claim, out to the truck and through a meal at a family-friendly restaurant, he realized the one-to-one ratio of adults to kids had kept things actually pretty manageable.

When they arrived at the house, Marisa introduced herself before he could. And what was that about? Ty wondered.

Before he could ask, though, she escaped—showing Deb and the children to their rooms.

Ty braced for questions about the sprite, but Bryce merely lifted an eyebrow and Chet nodded at Dru as if agreeing about something. Then they all drifted into the living room. To talk jobs, sports, current events and crabgrass until midnight.

"This was nice," Ty blurted as the informal group broke up.

"Yeah," Bryce agreed with a rusty laugh. "You're not bad company now that you're no longer a snotty little brat messing with my stuff."

Chet lingered after the others left.

Here it comes, Ty thought, but his oldest brother didn't mention Marisa. Not by name.

"It's like training for a marathon," Chet said, then followed that non sequitur with, "just start small and work your way up."

"See you in the morning," Ty said, ignoring the blatant sales pitch.

Because a child meant eighteen years of responsibility. And kids didn't come with guarantees. *Or* instructions. What if he got a wildman like Dru or a restless rebel like Ronnie? Someone he didn't understand and couldn't help.

Ty headed toward the master suite. Lay awake a long time contemplating those disheartening facts.

Woke before dawn wondering if there was any solution to his dilemma.

He still desired Marisa. More than ever after their interlude in the pool.

But a child wasn't a car you could trade in, a job you could change. You owed it to the potential innocent victims to be sure of your capabilities *before* you started a family.

Pulling on swim trunks, he headed for the pool. A few hundred laps would help control the urges only the sprite could satisfy. Until Marisa got the full Harding experience. Then maybe they could sit down and calmly decide where their relationship stood.

WHEN HER WATCH said six-thirty, Marisa quit pretending to sleep. She showered, dressed and made the bed, then headed for the kitchen.

Started coffee and began setting out cereal boxes. Because life went on. Like a river rolling to the sea. People got hungry and had to be fed. Bills arrived and had to be paid. Birthdays came and went. Children grew up.

Maybe you should, too, she suggested, watching one of the Harding men tirelessly crawling the length of the pool while she cleaned and sliced strawberries into a blue-and-white bowl. *Accept life on life's terms, Corelli.*

Even when they stink.

She still had choices—ranging from lousy to worse. From rock to hard place.

She could have Ty for however long "serious long-term wanting" lasted. Until "sevenish," when Lisette *arrives to meet her fate, if Nadja and her crystal ball know anything.*

Or she could look elsewhere for the loving home, husband and babies she'd always wanted.

It shouldn't be as hard to choose as her stupid heart was making it.

Somewhere in the house, a door closed.

Mechanically, Marisa set out the dishes and cutlery they'd borrowed from Dru's country club for breakfast use. Lunch plans involved strictly disposable plates and utensils.

A yawn threatened to dislocate her jaw; she poured herself a cup of coffee and took a big, tongue-burning swig.

She'd spent all night, it seemed, reviewing that last, dripping conversation with Ty—and most of the others they'd had on the subject—and it boiled down to this: he didn't seem to want kids, hadn't used the L-word and wasn't offering anything permanent.

"I care for you." Bah. As a commitment, that was about as strong as dishwater.

The bowl heaped with strawberries went next to the cereal choices and pitchers of juice on the rented sideboard in the dining room. Other bowls held bananas and oranges.

She pulled some apples out of the refrigerator and began washing them. Intent on doing everything in her power to make Ty's party run smoothly.

Still dreaming, Corelli?

No—hoping. That Ty would enjoy himself today. That he'd see past a little noise and some confusion to the core issue: family matters. Hoping the weekend planted a seed.

Because the world needed all the good parents it could get.

And Ty was perfect father material. Calm, conscientious, caring.

Perfect at the fathering process, too—if Thursday night's tantalizing taste was any indication.

Marisa sipped more coffee and sighed. She didn't want it all; she just wanted Ty and a family.

But unless today's celebration magically changed his mind, it looked as if her choice was going to be Ty *or* a family of her own.

"It's too early to make decisions this difficult," claimed a cheerful voice from the threshold joining the kitchen and the east wing.

Heart firmly pressed against her tonsils, Marisa pivoted to greet—not a mind reader. Chet. Ty with more lines at the corners of his eyes, which were more sapphire than summer-sky blue. Same smile. Same brown hair. Shorter, a few pounds heavier.

And carrying a pajama-clad miniature of himself. Longing squeezed her heart as the man introduced the miniature. "I'm sure we met last night, but my memory's terrible. This is Ryan. He's four. I'm Chet, the oldest. And you are…?"

"Marisa," she said, smothering a smile at the frustration that flickered briefly in his eyes. "Marisa Corelli." She opened the freezer compartment. "Breakfast is self-serve. There's fruit and cereal in the dining room. We'll have muffins, too, in…" She consulted the box. "Eight to twelve minutes."

Chet lowered his son to the floor and aimed him at the living room. "Why don't you check out the cartoons, tiger?" the man said, giving the child a gentle pat on his bottom before straightening. He reached for the box of frozen pastry. "Allow me."

Breathing a sigh of relief—with her luck, the stove would explode—Marisa handed it over.

As he opened the package, Chet continued probing. "So you and Ty are…?" He paused, waiting for Marisa to fill in the blank.

Her chin came up. "Very happy you could come

celebrate your parents' anniversary." If he wanted a status report, he'd have to ask his brother.

"And we're very happy to be here," said a new, deep voice. Another, taller Ty—this one with solemn navy eyes and deep grooves bracketing his mouth. And that was Megan, who looked a little older than Chet's son, clinging to her father's hand. "I'm Bryce," he said, "the handsome one." His grin lasted about as long as a Phoenix winter.

"Good morning," Marisa said, then smiled at the little girl. "Would you like some juice, Megan?" she asked, bending so their eyes were level. "Or some strawberries?"

"I'll see to her breakfast," Bryce said, his tone clipped. His face closed.

Not antisocial. Hurting.

Chet frowned after him as he and his daughter disappeared into the dining room. Marisa made a bet with herself and started counting.

One thousand one. One thousand two. One thousand three.

Big brother tried again. "You and my brother—"

"Have worked like dogs to get this place ready," Ty said, coming into the kitchen from the patio. His hair wet, his broad chest ditto. Swim trunks plastered to his— Endorphins flooded Marisa's bloodstream, exhorting 'Pleasure—Now!' like some sixties' flower child.

He finished toweling off, his blue eyes not meeting her gaze.

That's the way he wants to play it, Marisa thought, *fine.*

Who knew? Maybe she'd discover he was right about the turmoil, change her mind about having a family of her own and sign up for that "serious long-term" option instead.

Unless she got anointed Pope first.

In the meantime, Marisa decided as she poured milk into a pitcher, she'd apply the lessons of her childhood: live in this moment only, let the uncertain future take care of itself.

And today, she'd darned well "live the fantasy"— thank you very much.

Bryce's daughter appeared in the archway from the dining room, a bowl piled with gridded grain squares in one hand. A spoon like a scepter in the other.

"Unca Ty!" She launched herself at him. Cereal went flying, so did the bowl. The spoon thonked Ty on the temple.

Chet deflected the bowl with his foot. Marisa got the broom and began sweeping up cereal. Bryce apologized for his daughter and Ty carried the little girl back to the dining room for another attempt at breakfast.

As Marisa reclaimed her coffee and sipped cool caffeine, Dru—wearing rumpled shorts and an unbuttoned Hawaiian shirt—sauntered through the kitchen to the living room, where he dove over the sofa and plucked the remote from Ryan's possession as he rolled past onto the floor.

With a shriek of delight, Chet's son jumped on top of his uncle. The TV blared as the two wrestled, their shouts punctuated with laughter.

Chet's wife, a lovely woman with short dark hair, entered the kitchen carrying one child and herding another. She nodded the older boy toward the dining room and sat the little girl on the counter while Chet poured her a mug of coffee. "Dexter's on his way to spill something," she confided with a wry smile, "but he insists on doing it himself."

"How old is Samantha?" Marisa asked, touching the baby's arm with a fingertip.

"A year last week," Deb said, "and still not walking on her own." With a laugh, she added, "This might be the day, though. Sam's our ham—I have a feeling she's just been holding out for a bigger audience."

As if on cue, the baby began squirming to get down.

Marisa held out her arms. "May I?" she asked. "Just, uh, so you can have a peaceful breakfast."

"She's all yours."

Debbie laughed as Chet chimed, "For as long as you can stand it. Bring her back when you've had enough."

Never, never, never, Marisa thought as the baby gurgled, put her arms out and let herself be lifted from the counter.

Ty sagged against the molding of the doorframe. Closed his eyes against it, but the image burned behind his lids. His sprite—glowing with a passion he'd never seen before. A gut-twisting mixture of wonder and awe and ecstasy.

He cursed silently. Hopelessly. *Uselessly.*

Because even *he* recognized that this wasn't garden-variety female nesting.

Nor a simple desire to give some kid what she'd missed.

This was *need.* Elemental, deep, *needful* need.

Children were like oxygen to Marisa.

And you want her to hold her breath.

He spun on his heel, grateful for once for the patented Harding turmoil. Covering his retreat. Until he shook off the bereft feeling clogging his insides.

Which was stupid. He hadn't planned to get married for years and years, remember? And he didn't believe in love. He absolutely didn't want to have children—not even with the sprite.

Because what Marisa needed, he couldn't handle.

Even if he wanted to, he couldn't be a decent father. No patience. No tolerance. No parental instincts.

Take Megan's rain of cereal just now. Perfect example.

Of course, he knew it was an accident, but his jaw had tightened. He'd started to tsk-tsk at her.

Give him some kids of his own and enough time and sooner or later he'd lose his temper. He'd rant and rave. Lecture. Impose disciplinary yard work. He'd probably dock their allowances for high crimes and misdemeanors like coming home late.

Ty went to his room, pulled on clothes, and returned to the dining room. Scooping some strawberries into a bowl, he covered them with Choco-Bomblasts. Drowned the whole thing in milk and slumped in the chair next to Bryce. Morosely prodded his breakfast.

"Hey, man—cut it out," Bryce said as he peeled an orange for Megan. "Moping's my territory."

"Oh, yeah, I forgot." Ty let a minute go by, then asked, "How *is* your wife?"

"The same," Bryce said, wearily. "That truck broadsided her car more than four years ago. It's not like the movies, you know. She's not going to wake up."

"I know. And I'm sorry, man."

"Yeah, me too." Bryce pushed back his chair and rose. "Let's go outside, honey." Carrying the sectioned fruit in a napkin, he led his daughter toward the patio.

After father and daughter left, Ty moved down to sit by Dexter, helped him finish wiping up the juice he'd spilled "on accident, Uncle Ty, honest" and ate his own cereal once it reached the proper mushy consistency.

Hurray for Nadja's curse, he thought as he carried his bowl and Dex's dishes to the kitchen sink. Lucky he'd seen how completely wrong he and the sprite were for each other—before they got too deeply involved to avoid somebody getting hurt.

So why did he feel so miserable?

Turning around, bracing his hands on the rim of the

sink, Ty scanned the scene before him. Just like old times. Chaos reigned. And he felt lost, also like old times.

The phone was ringing, kids shouting. Dru ambled through the kitchen, patting Samantha as she toddled around, fists clutching Marisa's fingers.

Ty checked his watch.

Marisa looked up. "It's almost time to get Sandi," she announced quietly. Chet covered the phone. "Do you want someone to go with you?" sprite and brother asked.

Yes, Ty shouted silently. *I want Marisa.* "No, thanks." He'd gotten used to the sprite's company, that's all. He had *not* been lonely all these years. He'd been alone. According to Plan. "I can find the airport by myself," he snapped.

"Oooh, somebody got up on the wrong side of the bed," Dru drawled as he poured himself some coffee. "Or was it the wrong bed entirely?"

"You're the one who can't keep his—"

"Knock it off, boys," Chet said, exchanging the phone for a hotpad to pull a tray of muffins from the oven. "Dru, keep your comments to yourself. And Ty—" He dumped the baked goods onto a plate. "You can carry that self-sufficiency stuff too far. Let the rest of us help. That's what we're here for."

"Sounds just like Dad, doesn't he?" Bryce commented, leading Megan in from the patio. "But he's right." With a sly grin, he added, "For once."

"For once?" Chet accepted the challenge with a grin of his own. "Try more times than you ever are. Who picked the last three Super Bowl winners?"

"Oh, like that's the true sign of intelli—"

Ty fled. They'd be bickering like that the rest of the day. And the more Hardings arrived, the worse it would get.

He hoped whatever happened wouldn't *completely*

derail the careful plans he and Marisa had slaved over, but he *knew* there'd be a monkey wrench thrown. With this bunch, it was just a question of who, what and when.

Try now. Sandi walked off the plane with a cowboy named Edgar.

"Hope y'all don't mahnd me taggin' along," Edgar drawled as they crossed the already-scorching parking-lot pavement. "But I jes cain't bear to let this li'l lady outta ma saht."

After taking a moment to translate, Ty glumly assured the cowboy, "The more the merrier."

Sandi elbowed her brother. "Say it like you mean it."

"I would if I meant it," he shot back as he unlocked the trunk. "I *had* a million things to do today. Now I've got a million and ten."

He freed Sandi's bag from her hand and leaned close. "Starting with where Mr. Rodeo's sleeping tonight. Want to give me a hint?"

Tipping her head to one side, Sandi looked at him. "Same old Ty," she said. "So busy cataloguing and controlling, he never gets around to *liv-ing*." She turned to the cowboy lounging against the SUV parked next to them. "I love him dearly, but this brother's thumb is stuck up his—"

"Easy, darlin'," Edgar said, tossing a sympathetic look in Ty's direction. "Iffen ya wanta eat steak, somebody's gotta run the feedlot."

AFTER THE THIRD OR fourth disaster—when the hot dogs exploded and soapsuds foamed across the patio from the hot tub—Marisa expected Ty to start shouting about her evil eye and asking her to leave his family, his party and his life before she ruined everything!

But he spent most of the day shuttling to and from

the airport and the others seemed to take the calamities in stride.

"Typical family get-together," one of them said, brushing off her apology for the luncheon delay while Dru called in a pizza order and somebody else—Diane's husband?—whipped up nachos to prevent starvation until it arrived.

Not exactly what she'd dreamed of all those years in foster care, living on the edges of other people's lives.

But close enough. Wonderful enough.

Because she wasn't on the sidelines today. The women included her in their discussions of school and soccer, fashion and jobs.

The kids clung to her legs and begged her to play with them in the pool.

The men teased her like a sister.

Except one. Once. And that was...

Unbelievable, Ty told himself late in the afternoon as he shepherded his parents through the house. *But not unexpected.* When he left to meet their plane, he'd noticed Dru refilling Bryce's margarita glass.

Now the drunken so-and-so had Marisa cornered between Baby and the barbecue pit.

A red tide of fury swept over him as he watched Bryce lift his hand to touch her—hair? Cheek? *Lower?* With a growl, Ty started to storm across the patio to rescue his sprite—who was backed against the philodendron, chewing on her lip.

His mother's hand on his arm stopped him. "No need to make a scene in front of the little ones, dear," she said calmly. "Let the others take care of it."

And to his surprise, they did. Quickly, efficiently and without bloodshed.

Sandi popped up between Bryce and Marisa. "I just found out these plants are yours," she declared at the top of her lungs, hooking one hand around Marisa's arm. Signaling unobtrusively with the other. "Tell me your gardening secrets."

Within seconds, Ronnie's (also uninvited but now very welcome) boyfriend was talking NASCAR to Bryce while she and Sandi escorted Marisa to the far side of the patio where they huddled with her for a few minutes.

Obviously explaining Bryce's unique circumstances—and his low liquor tolerance—because Marisa nodded, threw Ty's brother a sympathetic glance, then strolled over to help Diane with her NO-screaming two-year-old.

Ty sighed as gratitude for the others' swift and sensitive handling of a sticky situation replaced his initial rage. Now that the sprite was safe, he could almost feel sorry again for his lonely brother. Even decide Dru looked abashed enough to be spared dismemberment. Maybe.

"Such a lovely girl, your Marisa," Ty's mother said. His dad grunted agreement.

"She's not mine," Ty said automatically. Silently acknowledging that the part of him sick with jealousy a minute ago, the part unimpressed by logic and Plans and noble reasoning fervently wished she was.

Gwen smiled. "I'm sure you know best, dear."

"The caterers are here," Diane's husband announced. "Where do you want them to set up? And where do you want us while they— Oh, never mind, I'll ask Marisa." He walked away.

Ty's mother smiled at him again. "Go on, dear. I doubt if she does, but I'm sure you think she needs your help."

"Now, Mom," Ty protested. Sheesh, they all acted like he was some kind of control freak. "I'm just trying to see that everyone has a good time."

"We're going to," Gwen Harding assured him. "Your father and I are going to gather up the grandchildren and enjoy some quiet time before dinner while the rest of you do what you need to do.''

Ty's gaze went to his sprite, already in consultation with the caterer and Diane's husband. After hours of work and confusion, of being mobbed by kids, even after Bryce stepping out of line, she still glowed.

Just the way she had this morning, holding Chet's youngest.

Ty rubbed his hand along his jaw, then over his face. *See?* he thought wearily. *There's proof Nadja's curse is so much bull-pucky.*

'Cuz a *genuine* good-luck curse would have Marisa looking up. Giving him a private sign that she'd changed her mind, wanted to spend the rest of her life alone. With him.

Hmm. She *was* signaling him. Pointing to her wrist. Jerking her head to the side. Mouthing something.

Huh?

Pre-sent.

Ty checked his watch. Sheesh, he only had twenty minutes to get to the jewelers before they closed.

With a nod in the sprite's direction, he raced outside, pinwheeled his arms at the guy in the catering truck until he got the message and moved the vehicle so Ty could get his car out of the driveway.

He arrived at the store just in time to do CPR while the jeweler's assistant called 9-1-1. Maybe there *was* something to Nadja's curse, he thought shakily when the paramedics got there and took over.

''Another minute and this guy woulda been a goner,'' one of the EMTs told him. ''Good thing you knew the procedure.''

After collecting the ring from the jeweler's assistant, Ty drove back to the lavender house on the hill in a thoughtful mood. He'd been in the right place at the right time—by happenstance, not plan. Glad he could help, of course...

But was that any way to live your life? he wondered as he showered, shaved and changed into his tux. Being responsible meant being prepared, didn't it?

Ty fiddled with his bowtie. But, he guessed, you also had to, well, *expect* the unexpected once in a while.

"LOOK WHO'S HERE," Dru suggested as Ty strode into the living room at 6:45.

"Darling!"

"Oh. Hi, Lisette." Wearing white again. Didn't the woman know clothing came in colors?

Ty smiled, contemplating what his sprite would be wearing this evening. One of her rainbow outfits no doubt.

"That's better," La Daniels breathed. "For a moment, I thought you weren't happy to see me."

"Of course I am," Ty said, taking the cue she'd bludgeoned him with. Nodding like one of those auto-accessory, bobbing-head dolls, he looked around. Spotted some sisters and their men. "Come on, let me introduce you to the rest of the family."

Excusing himself a moment later and glad—again!—for the generous number of Hardings around, he left the supermodel impressing some of them. Headed for the patio.

Where the caterers—at Marisa's direction, no doubt—had transformed water-logged cement into a fairyland banquet setting.

Tiny white lights twinkled through the slowly gathering summer dusk. Tables draped with linen cloths floated above the pebbled concrete like snowy islands. China, crystal and silverware gleamed. Baby and the other plants sported festive bows.

The head of the catering crew hurried over to him. "Don't worry," he said. "These things happen. We're fixing it now. Nobody will notice and, of course, there will be a price adjustment."

Ty stared at the man. "What are you talking about? No, first—was anyone hurt?" He felt for his keys, his brain already working out the fastest route to the nearest hospital.

The caterer shook his head. "Nobody's hurt. Ms. Corelli asked us to rearrange some of the items on the appetizer buffet. When Ramon moved the shrimp tray, he stumbled...."

Closing his eyes against the inevitable, Ty said, "Go on."

"That's when we discovered that someone had accidentally loaded a tray prepared yesterday." Ty's lids sprang open. "The shrimp might still be good, but we don't wish to take the chance. So we're substituting sweet-and-sour meatballs. If that's okay with you—Ms. Corelli said you were the man in charge."

Choking back a laugh, Ty assured the man that meatballs were fine, then watched him scurry away. *I've never been less in charge of anything,* he realized.

He'd spent the day playing chauffeur. The sprite had kept the show running. Beautifully. Everyone seemed to be enjoying themselves.

I'll thank her during my speech, he thought, *when I present the ring to Mom.* Or maybe later, he'd demonstrate his gratitude...*privately.*

"I've always been proud of all of you, son, but this—" Ty's dad appeared, a drink in his hand. He lifted it in a toast. "The only return parents really want is to see their kids happy and self-sufficient. This—" He waved his glass to encompass the house, the patio, the celebration about to begin. "—is icing, son."

After squeezing his arm, his dad wandered off.

Ty rubbed his jaw, hard enough to remove a layer of skin. Muttered expletives right and left. None of which helped.

"What's wrong?" asked a soft voice.

"Thank heaven," he breathed as he turned toward its owner—then stood stock still. *Holy aspidistra!*

Only the magnitude of this latest disaster kept Ty from dragging this seductive siren in the low-cut, black-silk column of a dress away to the first room with a lock on the door and—

Every male particle in him shuddered with longing as it thought about what they'd do in that room. Together. So together they wouldn't be able to tell where one of them ended and the other began.

Reluctantly, he dragged her to the nearest corner instead. "So much for Nadja and her damned curse," he rasped. *And so much for my vaunted planning.* "What the heck are we going to do?"

"About what?"

Two soft words, a pair of warm amber eyes filled with concern, one whiff of moonlight. Ty's anxiety faded like a politician's campaign promises. 'Cuz the unexpected didn't faze Marisa.

"I just talked to my dad," he hissed. Glaring over the sprite's bare, sexy shoulder at the family members and other early guests filtering out of the house. Nibbling on appetizers.

"The present!" he shouted as quietly as possible, while Marisa soothed *and* aroused—just by touching his hand. "We've got the ring for Mom. But we don't have anything for my father!"

"I thought Diane was handling that."

Ty groaned. "She's so busy with those kids and her job with Drug Enforcement— When we found the diamond, I...I told her to forget it," he confessed.

"You forgot marriage involves two people?" Marisa's lips twitched.

"Well..." Ty squirmed. What was happening to him? To his careful planning, thorough preparation, hard work? Sheesh—he couldn't think straight anymore, he acted on impulse, depended on luck.... "Can we analyze my transgressions later? Right now I need a gift to present—'' he rotated his wrist ''—in an hour.''

Marisa tapped a finger against her lips.

Ty forced his gaze from her mouth. Had less success getting his mind off the kisses they'd shared in that pool only ten feet away.

''Why don't you talk to Ronnie?'' she suggested, trying to stay focused on Ty's dilemma, instead of on how brain-blastingly handsome he looked in that penguin outfit. ''She's traveled a lot. Then call the travel agency that booked this weekend's tickets. Have them courier over two tickets to someplace romantic and exotic.''

''Genius,'' Ty said and hauled her into his arms and kissed her soundly. ''Brilliant.''

He released her abruptly. Tugged on his dinner jacket—probably noticing Lisette glaring at them from across the patio. ''What would I do without you?'' he asked.

Whatever it was, he hurried away to do it. Without looking back, let alone kissing her again. *See, Corelli? You're dreaming. All by yourself. As usual.*

He'd spent all day too busy to talk to her.

So she'd stayed too busy to notice. Dispensing soft drinks and snacks. Picking up wet towels. Collecting empty glasses. She'd talked to whichever siblings were around. Played with the kids. Stayed useful. Never forgot she didn't quite belong, no matter how everyone treated her.

Just like old times.

Marisa blinked back tears. Nuts. What did crying change except the location of your mascara?

She'd get through the rest of the evening. She'd put out breakfast in the morning and help everyone get back on their planes or in their car.

Then, debt paid in full, she'd leave Ty Harding in

the dust. Go punch out Mrs. Pachenko if she had to. Get an apartment or a cardboard box to sleep in. Start hanging out…well, wherever young singles hung out. Date up a storm.

And eventually get what she wanted: a loving home, husband and babies. "Plenty of 'em," she muttered as she watched Ty extricate Ronnie from Mr. NASCAR's embrace and pull her into a corner of the kitchen.

"Marisa!" Dru called from the doors leading to the living room. "The mariachi group is here. Where do you want them?"

"Why ask me?" she snapped, watching Lisette begin to drift in Ty's direction.

Dru shrugged one shoulder. "Because I can't find the General and you're his second-in-command."

I'm not his anything, she thought. Despite her stupid heart desperately wanting to be. Idiotically craving Ty Harding and the magic of his kisses.

"Humor me," Dru insisted. "Mariachis go—?"

With a sigh, Marisa pointed. "Have them set up on the far side of the pool."

She'd turned around to check that the centerpieces were, well, centered on each table when, over the clink of cocktail glasses and the clatter of boot heels, she heard a gasp.

She pivoted. Just in time to witness Lisette Daniels meet her fate.

8

INSTRUMENTS IN HAND, the musicians were filing onto the patio, the silver trim on their short jackets, broad sombreros and narrow pants twinkling in the twilight.

The next to last one in line came through the French door, saw Lisette—and stopped, transfixed, his guitarón suspended in midair.

A corner of Marisa's mind noted Ty returning to the patio through another French door. Saw him freeze. Gradually, the other Hardings, too, halted their conversations and turned, as if sensing something extraordinary.

The air seemed to shimmer around the supermodel and the mariachero. No words passed between them as they slowly closed the distance separating them. Apparently, none were necessary.

The young Hispanic smoothed his mustache, then held out his hand. After only a millisecond's hesitation, the tall blonde nodded and put her hand in his. Their eyes held; they smiled incandescently.

The basso sexto player ended the magical moment— coming up behind the enchanted mariachero, murmuring something in Spanish and nudging the man, who still held Lisette's hand.

Slowly, with a dreamy smile, the mariachero nodded, then drew himself to his full height, several inches short of the towering supermodel, bowed and kissed her hand.

"Hasta luego, querida," Marisa heard him promise as he reluctantly loosened his grip and allowed the basso sexto to lead him away.

Lisette clasped her hands and touched them to her lips as she watched the young guitarón player join his fellow musicians and begin tuning his instrument. Soon soft Tejano love songs floated through the gathering dusk.

And Ms. Intriguing floated across the patio to gaze adoringly at the man her heart had apparently chosen at first sight.

Without conscious thought, Marisa's gaze found Ty—whose only visible reaction was a bemused smile. As she watched, he gave his head a slight shake, stepped around one of his nephews and engaged his brother-in-law in conversation.

Wild, crazy, foolish hope was flooding through Marisa as Ty's mother approached with a smile.

"That's the way it happened for Ty's father and me," she said. "We've been very lucky," she added quietly, confirming Marisa's earlier impression that the woman carried serenity with her the way other women trail perfume clouds.

"And we're very happy that Tyler's finally gotten lucky, too."

Marisa could only stare at the woman. Her cheeks flaming. Her heart was wishing it were true. Wishing Dru had stayed home two nights ago and she'd settled for loving on a chaise lounge. Instead of holding out for love, marriage and a baby carriage Ty might never agree to push.

"I always hoped it would happen that way for Ty," Gwen went on. "He's so quiet and reliable that most people take him for granted. I'm glad to see someone finally recognize his true value."

Oh, no, Marisa groaned silently. Was she that obvious?

"I hope you'll encourage *him* to recognize it, too," Ty's mom continued. "His only fault is a tendency to underestimate himself."

The woman smiled warmly. "Once he's committed to

a goal, though, he's very thorough in his pursuit. I've seen Ty look at you the way the slender blonde looked at the guitar player just now. So, take a mother's advice, dear. Expect a miracle."

With another warm smile, Ty's mother excused herself.

It would take a miracle, Marisa thought with a sigh, remembering Ty walking past the little boy a minute ago as if he was a lawn statue. So far, the weekend didn't seem to have changed Ty's attitude about fatherhood.

On the other hand, Corelli, the Queen of the Gypsies had been right about Lisette.

Okay, she'd leave the future—and her heart's desire—in fate's hands. Meanwhile, the rest of the dinner guests were arriving.

Happy to find a task to occupy her while, hopefully, ol' Fate hosed Ty's brain, Marisa hurried to the foyer to answer the door and direct the newcomers to the dining room for hors d'oeuvres.

Then, leaving the nonrelatives to inhale appetizers and drinks, she and the boyfriends took group photos of the Harding clan. Ty's parents with each child and his or her family. The siblings. The cousins. Mom with the girls. Dad with the boys. Reverse.

When the formal picture-taking ended, Marisa moved through the house and courtyard taking candid shots.

Including one of Lisette mooning over her mariachero, who returned her soulful contemplation while his fingers rippled over the guitarón.

As if nobody else exists, Marisa thought enviously, then looked up.

Thirty people and the swimming pool separated them—but when Ty followed the cowboy into the house, then reappeared on the patio, looked at her and patted his dinner jacket, Marisa knew and understood. With a nod, she signaled the caterer while Chet and Ty escorted their parents to their seats.

Within minutes, the crowd was circling the tables reading the placecards and the waiters began serving the first course.

Which tasted like cardboard to Ty. Because some idiot had switched the little name thingies and put Marisa at the table farthest from his.

With no sprite to talk to, Ty forked salad and pondered how long until he could touch, talk to, connect with her again. All day, the bigger the crowd grew, the more he'd wanted Marisa close.

Four more courses, then the gift presentation. An eternity. And then, they'd have to stand around and chat. With *others*. Sheesh!

Wait—they'd scheduled dancing after dinner. Brilliant.

Ty rolled his shoulders trying to dissolve the knot between his shoulder blades. Soon he'd know if his party Plan had succeeded. If they could resume and enhance what Dru had so rudely interrupted the other night. Or if—

"Oh, yeah! Children are a real joy," Ty's dad proclaimed to his old golfing buddy across the table, "—once they're all grown up!"

Ty laughed dutifully with the others. Beneath his laughter, though, ran a sudden twinge of sorrow for Marisa's parents, who'd died without knowing what a sweet, wonderful woman the sprite would become.

"You've got plenty to be proud of," the golfing buddy assured Ty's dad.

"Yes, I do," Jim replied, laughing. "And plenty of gray hair, too."

So why'd you have us? That's what Ty didn't understand. He knew Marisa's answer; but he still didn't have a good one of his own.

THE QUESTION CONTINUED to nag him forty minutes later when, with a big, yellow moon climbing above the garage to beam down on the proceedings, Ty stood, tapped his spoon on his water glass and signaled the waiters to bring out the final course—an elaborate wedding cake—and serve the champagne.

Chet led the group in a toast wishing the anniversary couple continued health and happiness.

Then, on behalf of all their grateful children, Ty presented the parental units with a two-week trip to Tahiti. While the other guests applauded and Mom wiped away tears, Dad leaned over to whisper, "Icing!" Ty couldn't help himself—he looked at Marisa.

When she smiled and nodded, he took a step toward her—but Chet popped up again. Insisted on another toast, this one to Ty "and his able assistant," thanking them for putting together the celebration.

Blue eyes met amber as the others saluted with their glasses; even Lisette enthusiastically lifted her crystal flute in the sprite's direction before returning to her mariachero-contemplation.

Dammit, he *had* to go to her! They had to talk. Touch. *Kiss...*

Impatiently, Ty watched the guests of honor cut the cake. Fidgeted as slices were distributed to the rest of the guests and waiters circulated with coffee. Then Dru announced that dancing would commence "on the Lido deck," and encouraged everyone to enjoy themselves or he'd do it for them.

At last! Ty pushed back his chair. Hellbent on finding Marisa, hearing her soft voice, inhaling her moonlight scent. Holding her—even if he had to pretend they were dancing to do it.

BY ELEVEN O'CLOCK, he still hadn't achieved his goal. Like a wily commando, Marisa evaded him, slipping away whenever he got close.

Finally, he saw her out on the dance floor—with Bryce no less!—but by the time he grabbed his mother and pushed her through the crowd like a shopping cart so he could cut in and claim the sprite—the song ended and she'd vanished.

Was she avoiding him or just doing what she'd done for the past week: wear herself out for his family?

I'll convey their appreciation, Ty vowed with a frown at Bryce.

Who toggled his head and said, "I just wanted to make sure she was okay with..." both men glanced at their mother, who was nodding one of her grandsons into dancing with a former neighbor "...things," Bryce finished with a helpless gesture. "Since I assume she's joining the family."

Over a suddenly giddy pounding in his chest, Ty opened his mouth to issue some caution about assuming.

"What the hell do you mean by that!"

Both men spun, then groaned in unison. Ronnie and her beau stood glaring at each other, toe-to-toe in the middle of the patio area reserved for dancing.

"I'll take Sis," Bryce volunteered. "You take Mr. NASCAR."

With a nod, Ty shouldered his way through the crowd, knowing they only had seconds before Ronnie got LOUD.

AND THAT, Ty thought hours later as he waved the limo carrying his parents on its way to the honeymoon suite at Phoenix's fanciest hotel and headed off to bed, proved his point about families. At least, this one.

Somebody was always getting their panties in a wad.

And too darned often, *he* got nominated to unwad 'em.

This time, he'd hustled Ronnie's race driver into the kitchen while Bryce herded their sister to the far side of the patio. Listened while Riff or Biff or whatever-his-face-was rambled on about misguided women taking a simple statement wrong. Fed the man coffee until he started getting rapturous about Ronnie's eyes.

He'd seen the two back on the dance floor later, shamelessly entwined, argument forgotten. But he'd lost his chance to dance—or anything else—with the sprite: the party had begun breaking up and he'd gotten caught in the farewells.

With a sigh, Ty locked the front door, then schlepped through the now-silent house to the master bedroom. Stripped off his clothes. Pulled on cotton drawstring pants—just in case somebody set something afire and they had to evacuate the place.

Flipping back the comforter and top sheet, he slid into the cool cotton haven.

"How about that, though? No major disasters," he whispered into the darkness as he drifted into a relaxed state. Too tired to sleep, really, but pleased that he and the sprite—mostly the sprite—had given his parents a weekend and an anniversary to remember. Now that it was over, he had to admit it *had* been kind of fun to see everyone again...

SOMETHING *SNICKED*. Ty sprang up in bed. "W-what?" His brain identified the sound. *The door latch.*

Someone was in the room, fumbling on the dresser.

Heart pounding, adrenal-gland secretions tearing through his system like a *Lethal Weapon* car chase. He peered into the darkness. "Who izt?" he demanded.

"It's me," whispered the sprite.

In the thin light coming through the door, Ty caught a flash of purply-red satin. His adrenaline switched its arousal goal from fight/flight to pleasure.

"Sorry I disturbed you," Marisa said in that same soft, low whisper. "I was just looking for your car keys."

"Keys?" Groggily, Ty swung his legs to the side of the bed. "What for?"

"Never mind," Marisa whispered, coming closer. A stream of moonlight slipped through the doorway behind her. Began caressing the edges of her ebony halo of hair, highlighting the slippery satin hugging her curves and outlining her long, long legs with silver.

The scent of moonlight drifted to his nostrils. Marisa's scent. The one that made him dizzy. And crazy. And *wanting*.

She turned away. "I'll try calling a taxi."

He couldn't seem to reason his way through that leap. So he went against all male instinct and asked. "Why?"

Satin shimmered as she shrugged. "Because we miscalculated the number of bedrooms we'd need."

"Huh?" How could she say things like "miscalculated" at such an ungodly hour after such a long day? All he had the energy for was... *Loving Marisa*. His already-aroused male component stirred a little more; he rearranged the comforter over it.

"There's no place for me to sleep," Marisa said, a tiny edge to her voice now.

"What are you talking about? We made a list. You were supposed to share with..." Ty rubbed his jaw. Somebody. Some *girl*. Who remembered at this hour? Especially with the sprite so near his bed. His arms, his—

"With Sandi," Marisa supplied. "But that was before Edgar." Moonlight silhouetted fists on sweetly curved hips. Causing more, ah, stirring. "I found my nightshirt, neatly folded, outside the door."

Ty grunted helplessly.

"I tried Ronnie, but her room's fully occupied, too."

That gave Ty an idea—a highly unoriginal one, by the sound of things—but before he could mention it, the sprite continued her recital. "Actually, Ronnie was supposed to be in with Megan—only Bryce is there, taking the top bunk.

"The other kids' rooms are full, too. Dru's sprawled on the living room sofa—and snoring so loud, a dead person couldn't sleep there. I started to try the chaise lounges on the patio, but they're taken, too.''

"By who? Er, whom?" *Forget the grammar, moron. Forget the loungers, too. Bless Nadja's curse, be grateful for your great good luck and hustle this woman into this bed immediately.*

Absently, Ty began fluffing the pillows and smoothing the crumpled covers of the king-sized bed.

"Lisette and her musician."

Surprise stilled his housekeeping. "What the heck are they doing out there?"

Marisa laughed softly. "They're talking," she said. "Telling each other their life histories—and hanging on every word. Since they're only up to about second grade, I figured they'd be there awhile longer.

"That's why I came looking for your keys. If you don't mind me borrowing your car, I can sleep at the apartment.''

"NO!" Ty shouted.

"I mean, no," he repeated softly, hoping he hadn't awakened any interfering busybodies. *Not now. Not this close to paradise.* "It's too far away. It's too late to drive through Phoenix alone. There may not be enough gas in the tank. I think one of the tires has a leak. The steering linkage might break. The oil needs changing." Ty ran out of breath and weak excuses.

"If you don't want to loan me your car, just say so." She snapped her fingers. "I'll try the dining roo—"

Ty leaped to his feet. Broadjumped the space between them. Grabbed her by the shoulders. "Dammit, Marisa—you're exhausted. I can't let you drive across town by yourself. And I'm not letting you sleep in the damned dining room."

"Then wher—"

He didn't let her finish *that* sentence either. This masterful macho stuff was kind of fun, he thought, with the right person. A soft-shouldered, feminine person whose head tucked perfectly under his chin and whose curves fit more-than-perfectly against his, uh, non-curves.

"You're sleeping here. With me."

In the silence that followed, Ty could only excoriate himself. *Smooth, Harding. Real smooth.*

Well, he wasn't prepared for romance. Hell, he wasn't supposed to even think about women for six more years.

And he *wasn't* thinking about women.

He *wanted.* One woman. *This* woman. "Marisa?" he said quietly. His hands dropped from her shoulders. They stood only inches apart. "Please?"

With the tiniest of sighs, she stepped through those inches of moonlit darkness into his arms.

Ty didn't waste any more time. With a soft growl, he tangled his fingers in her silky hair, tilted her head, and brought their mouths together.

The usual galaxies exploded around them. His hands stroked down the satin covering her back, then slid around and up her sides. He touched her breasts with his thumbs, his palms. He felt her response through the satin, her nipples beading at his touch.

With a primitive masculine growl, he scooped her up in his arms. Carried her to the bed. Laid her down, then came down after her. Over her. Letting her feel the full extent of his desire against the smooth taut skin of her belly as her nightshirt obligingly rode up to her waist.

He wanted to bury himself in her right now. Claim her like some medieval warrior-knight taking his victory prize.

Instead, he took a deep, shuddering breath, then slowly lowered his head to kiss her. Gently, deeply, thoroughly. Mouth, jawline, neck, lower...

Rolling to his side, he cupped her head with one

hand and kissed her while the other fumbled with buttons, then pushed aside fabric to expose the *real* satin of her skin. His lips began a nibbling path of exquisite, sensual torture along her warm—

"Whatcha doing, Unca Ty? Wrestling?" A small figure thudded on the bed beside them, jolting Ty's hand off Marisa's delectable body. "C'n I play, too?"

Trey. Diane's five-year-old. Formerly cute kid— now, evil incarnate.

"N-no," Ty said, trying to sound normal while his heart pounded and his— Well, need throbbed through him like a bass-freaking-drum. "Wh-what are you doing here?" he asked, untangling his legs from Marisa's, moving backward to give her room as she surreptitiously rebuttoned her nightshirt.

"I hadda go baffroom," the child announced matter-of-factly. "Only I forgotted where it was." He gave an experimental bounce on the bed. "I hafta go pretty bad, Unca Ty," he confessed.

Ty stood, silently thanked God for darkness and drawstring pants, then held out his hand. "Come on, tiger. I'll take you."

Marisa bit her lip as her again-almost-lover escorted his nephew into the master bathroom.

No doubt, Corelli. Pachenko rules. What could be worse luck than being taken to the brink of heaven, then dropped back to earth for the most mundane of reasons?

Turning on her side to face their direction, she listened to high-pitched child murmurs alternating with deep rumbling.

But wasn't Ty being magnificent about the whole thing? Setting aside his personal drives and desires for the needs of a child who wasn't even his own.

No wonder she loved him. Marisa sighed, admitting the truth, savoring the hope it generated. She loved Ty. Wasn't that magic enough to make miracles happen?

"Night-night, M'isa," Ty's pint-sized companion waved to her as he and his uncle exited the master bath and headed for the bedroom door. "Unca Ty's gonna take me back in the bed so's no monsters get me."

"I'm sure you'll be safe with him," Marisa said as she pulled the comforter up. Without Ty's heat, the A/C was chilling. "Sleep tight, Trey."

ENGAGED IN THOROUGHLY satisfying fantasies of a future filled with loving Ty, she'd nearly drifted off to sleep when the covers shifted and the mattress dipped.

Ty's heat warmed her back as he spooned her and his hand slid around her waist. "Now where were we?" he growled in her ear.

As he rolled her to her back, he kept on muttering. "Why in hell do people have kids? They're nothing but pains in the butt."

"You don't mean that," Marisa protested languidly as he applied his lips to an incredibly sensitive spot below her ear.

"Oh, yes. I do," Ty insisted. His voice low but...well, *insistent.*

With his body pressed against hers, his hands and his mouth busy evoking a response—not to mention that hard-muscled leg sneaking between hers... *His brain's disconnected, Corelli.*

So what just came out, came from his heart.

Her interest in making love faded instantaneously. Well, almost instantaneously. "You really don't like kids," she ventured, stilling his hands by wrapping hers around his wrists. "Singly *or* in groups."

"What's to like?" he grated, extracting his hands from her grip, propping his head on one so he could look at her.

Marisa scooted backward. "Oooh, you are unbelievable."

"Why?" Ty asked sharply, pushing himself up to

sit there looming over her. Like large made right. "Because I don't like private, intimate moments destroyed by some little twirp who can't find the restroom by himself?"

Okay, he told himself in the ensuing silence, maybe that was a tad harsh. But dammit, they were in the middle of something awesome here. Why talk about somebody else's kids at a time like this?

"Well, who would?" Marisa responded, but she was still moving in the wrong direction. Putting more damned empty space between them instead of less. "But...you can't expect children to—"

Aw, shoot. He could hear the tears in her voice. Knew they came from her own past.

But, dammit, Marisa wasn't the only one still carrying scars from childhood. After a lifetime of feeling lost in the crowd, Ty needed to know he was number one in *somebody's* heart.

"That's right," he snapped. "Kids and expectations don't mix. Even my dad says the only good kid is one who's already grown up. Which is why I intend to shortcircuit the whole process by skipping it."

"You're...you're not ever going to want a family?"

"No," he said, giving her the worst case scenario. He couldn't promise her a baby, not yet—even if he did find visions of a little ebony-haired sprite alluring. Dammit, he wanted to be wanted for himself.

She rolled onto her side. Facing the wrong direction. *See? She just wants a sperm donor.* A bitter sense of loss overwhelmed him. "Never."

The silence almost deafened him, so after a few minutes, he said, "Come on, Marisa. Be reasonable."

Not with that rigid back.

"This weekend hasn't changed your mind about anything!" the sprite exclaimed from her position at the far side of the mattress.

"Mine?" Ty shot back. "It was supposed to change

yours!'' Angrily, he jerked the covers to his armpits. ''When are you going to see—you have to stand on your own two feet. You can't make anyone else responsible for your happiness, Marisa.

''Not your family. Not a gypsy curse or an evil eye. And especially not some little kid. It's not fair to you or to the ki—''

A yawn interrupted his tirade. His flare of temper fizzled as the last aroused adrenaline ebbed and a rivulet of cold desolation sluiced through him. ''Aw, sprite, let's not—''

''It's late,'' Marisa said tonelessly. ''We're both tired. Let's finish this discussion in the morning.''

Ty waited, but the curvy lump two yards away said no more. Just tugged the comforter up to her hair.

Still… He shifted around, determined to stay awake, to wait, just in case she changed her mind….

THIS TIME, TY KNEW he wasn't asleep. He could pass a damned *polygraph* he was awake!

Only…somebody pounded on the door, then Dru walked in, shoved a mug of coffee in his hand and told him to motor if he wanted to say goodbye to Diane and her family, who were heading back to Tucson.

And when he looked over, there was no spritely bump in the bed.

''Where's Marisa?'' he growled, jerking the coffee from Dru's hand.

''Still sleeping, I guess. She's bunkin' with one of the girls, isn't she?''

''No, moron.'' Ty fought his way out of the covers. Slugged back some of the caffeine juice, then slammed the mug down on the rental nightstand. ''She's not,'' he snarled.

''My, my, we're in another charming mood. Has the course of love hit another little road bump?''

Ty hauled himself to his feet. Yanked open a dresser

drawer and snatched up jeans, underwear, polo shirt. "Love!" He snorted, then issued a semi-synonymous epithet as he stalked off to the bathroom, pausing in the doorway to explain the situation to his dear brother. "And by the way, Dru—shut the hell up!"

"GO AWAY!" NADJA shouted. "I tell you Gypsies are no—" Peering at the visitor on her doorstep, the older woman abandoned her rebel-leader-rallying-the-troops pose. "Come inside, little one," she said gently. "You look as if you have seen *mulé*. Come—we will banish."

Marisa allowed herself to be pulled into Nadja's apartment and pushed onto the worn velvet sofa. "That's a good idea," she said hollowly. Yeah, banishment. Exile the entire male race to some gender-appropriate location—like a black hole at the farthest end of the universe.

The Gypsy Queen sat beside her. Awkwardly patted her hand. "Tchah—it cannot be so bad as you look," she insisted, then tossed her head in her familiar, imperial way. "You must have strong drink to revive fighting spirit."

"It's seven o'clock in the morning," Marisa protested. She'd walked through the predawn darkness until she caught a bus. Sat on the very last seat, watching the stars fade and sunrise bronze Camelback and the other rocky hills that jutted up through the city's sprawl.

"Heartache knows no clock," Nadja replied, shoving a juice glass half-full of brown liquid into her hand. "It marks only the loss of hope."

Marisa choked back a sob. *For a crazy old lady, Nadja Costeceaseu saw too clearly.*

But that was why she'd finally disembarked after three and a half circuits. Then hiked to this tiny, overstuffed apartment.

Because wounded animals hide. And she was bleeding… All hope of a happy ending torn from her by two words. *"No. Never."*

Marisa eyed the liquid suspiciously, then decided it didn't matter if it was poison. "Thanks, Nadja. I knew I could count on you."

She also knew, thanks to her years in foster care, that she'd survive.

That, meaningless as it might be without Ty, life would go on.

And that she'd have to go on with it.

Tilting her head, she let the brown fluid flow down her throat.

Strong drink? The liquid cauterized her tonsils before burning its way down her esophagus. "GLA-ZIVVERPHHTT!"

Nadja pounded her back. "Iz good!" the old lady shouted. "Expel *mulé*. Love will return."

Marisa shook her head. "No," she said when she could breathe and form words again. "There's no—"

"Do not say," Nadja ordered, her gnarled hand moving to the glass globe on the table, her palm covering the orb. "You listen—Nico iz gone. For months now, I do not see. But I still hope. And no matter what his fate or mine…even if hope iz lost, I love.

"Iz whole point, little one," she added softly. "Love iz only point."

Light seemed to spill from the globe as the old lady lifted it. "Today iz not end of journey," she insisted. "Iz merely…" The Gypsy Queen stared into the clear ball, muttering in Romany a moment, then smiled at Marisa. "…detour. Now tell," she commanded, "why you are here and plants are not."

Reluctantly, Marisa related a highly edited version of Ty's party—and his final, antifamily declaration.

"And you believe?" Nadja cackled. "No wonder Mrs. Pachenko can pull wool above your eyes!"

With a start, Marisa realized that Mrs. P. and her pronouncements no longer worried her. Not after facing Ty Harding's flat-out refusal to have children.

Mrs. Pachenko hadn't created Ty's attitude; her evil eye hadn't caused Marisa to fall in love with the one man who refused to share her dream of a family.

And what worse luck was there?

Still— "'Believe, no believe,'" she quoted Nadja back at herself. "Makes no difference, remember?"

With a Romany-accented snort, Nadja handed her young friend the globe. "So—now what?"

Good question, Corelli.

"Look there." The Gypsy Queen crooked a finger at the glass ball. "Seek guidance."

Marisa pretended to obey. Being disillusioned about magic and hope and wonder didn't mean she had to give up politeness, too.

"Do not look at surface," Nadja advised. "Look past—look inside."

With a shrug, Marisa studied the swirl of colors as the curved glass distorted the surroundings it reflected. *The way your childhood distorted your image of a family,* said something deep in her heart. Or her brain.

Or from within the crystal ball?

And your desire for one. Do you truly think you have no value as an individual?

Marisa handed the globe back to Nadja and shut her eyes, but the voice continued. *Do you not know that Ty was right: a child cannot give you a sense of self-worth? That's something the parent gives the child. And you've got to have it, Corelli, before you can give it away.*

"Have you found your answer, child?" the old woman asked softly as she reverently placed the ball in its holder.

"I think so," Marisa replied slowly. *Even if I don't like it.*

"And plants?" Nadja asked suspiciously.

"I'll take them to the flower shop," she said, making a quick decision. "I'm sure Mr. Abelard won't mind."

Marisa jumped to her feet. She needed action. To stay busy while her broken heart healed. To keep the thoughts, the memories, the searing pain at bay. To fill the decades until she stopped loving Ty Harding.

An idea filtered through the numbness she'd felt since leaving his bedroom the second he fell asleep. "I think I'll use them to start a plant rental business," she said. "I'll call it…Green Piece." At least as her own boss she couldn't be fired.

"And then I'm going to start dating." Someone without brown hair or blue eyes. Someone who liked children. Someone whose kisses didn't haunt her, like Nadja's *mulé.*

"Iz good plan," Nadja declared, then, muttering in Romany, marched to the door. "Will not work," she added as she let Marisa out, "but keeps busy until Fate turns Wheel."

"WAVE," DRU INSTRUCTED.

Ty raised his arm. Moved the segment beyond the wrist bone between horizontal and vertical. Reversed the movement. Repeated. "Bye-bye," he recited as Bryce and Megan, the last out-of-town Hardings, headed down the jetway to their damned plane. "Yeah. We'll get together again real soon. Yeah. Great to see you, too. Yeah—"

"Okay, bro." Dru clamped a hand on Ty's forearm. "They're gone now. Quit muttering like some trash-TV audience member."

Ty shut up. Stood there in the Phoenix airport until his brother tugged him down the concourse and out to the parking lot.

Yanking open the passenger door, Dru pointed. "Get in."

As Ty obeyed and snapped on his seat belt, his brother propped a hand on the vehicle's roof and leaned down. "Are you ready to tell me what the hell happened between you and Marisa?"

Ty shook his head. What could he say, except— "She didn't want me."

Dru pushed himself off the car frame, then slammed the door. Practically on Ty's foot. "That's what I thought you'd say," he confided a moment later as he slid behind the steering wheel. "And if I thought that was okay with you, I'd drop the subject."

He gazed at his older brother, who stared broodingly at the glove-compartment latch. "But since it's obviously not…" He cranked the engine. "We're gonna go have a few drinks."

"A few?" Ty needed certainty. Unless given finite, clearly defined tasks to complete, he noticed, he tended to slip into a mild vegetative state. "How many? Be specific."

Dru popped the parking brake and put the car in gear. "We're drinking enough to make you spill your guts," he promised as he backed out of the parking space. "One way or the other."

TY ENDED UP spilling his guts both ways. But it changed nothing. He wanted Marisa. She wanted babies. She wouldn't take him without kids. And he wouldn't have kids just to have her.

"Issa impasse, shee?" Ty said, squinting at his brother as they waved off the cabby and staggered up to his apartment. They'd left the car…somewhere. "Just proves how 'portant is ta make a Plan 'n schtick to it."

"I'll tell ya where you can stick your Plan, bro," Dru said as they helped each other fumble the key into the lock. "The same place your life's gonna be without that woman."

"Wherezat?" Ty asked cleverly, weaving through the living room to stare morosely at the sprite's vacant room. Her stuff was still there, but she wasn't. Never would be again. He *knew* it. He hadda *feeling*.

Even her scent seemed to have faded already. *Place smells like cheap martoonis,* he thought blearily, *'stead o' moonlight.*

"Where the sun don't shine," Dru expounded triumphantly before sliding to the floor.

Ty peered at his sibling's prone position between the sofa and the breakfast bar. Huh. Unconscious.

Just as well. No way Ty boo-hooed in front of anyone. He hadn't cried since he was ten. He didn't now, either. Was humidity or somethin' dampened the pillow on Marisa's bed.

Where he slept until the expletive-expletive phone shattered his eardrum and woke him so Krako could ream him royally out about getting his blankety-blank, sorry-blank self down to the office in time for another stupid meeting with Turrell "The Fleet" Foote.

9

"THIS IS IMPORTANT, Harding!" Krako sonic-boomed through the phone and Ty's cranium. "Now get down here—pronto!"

"Whatever." Ty shuttled the handset to its base. Sat there, elbows on knees, hands holding his throbbing head while his stomach churned and roiled and threatened to send its contents on a field trip to his tonsils.

And that was the good part.

Marisa was gone. *That* was the bad part.

Probably off looking for some other jackass to give her babies.

That was the worst part. Because not only the testosterone-guided components, but every cell of his body still wanted her. Remembered how she looked, how she smiled, how she felt and tasted. How she moved against him.

The way she'd move against somebody else.

Ty found himself on his feet. Snarling. His fingers twitching. "He'd better appreciate her. *And* he'd better know what he's getting into, dammit!" he growled as he staggered out of the sprite's room. "'Cuz if he screws up…if he ruins those kids, I'll, I'll—"

Still mulling nonspecific mayhem, Ty stomped to the bathroom, wrenched the control-thingy and climbed into the shower.

As jets of chilly water stabbed him, Ty thought about his parents and all the mischief they'd had to handle—

the bloody noses, the skateboard accidents, his sisters' date dramas.

"Being a parent's the hardest job in the world," he informed the spray from the showerhead as he soaped and rinsed. "You're on call twenty-four hours a day. You have to know what to do—even when you don't. And trying to preplan is *useless,* 'cuz with kids, you never know what's going to happen until it does."

Shampoo dripped from Ty's hand. The shower beat his motionless body. "Okay, so forget it," he told himself, gingerly applying the shampoo to his head. Lord, even his hair hurt.

Forget her.

He shut off the shower. What idiot sits around pining for a woman who doesn't want *him?*

"Not me," Ty muttered, reaching for a towel. So he'd cared for Marisa. Thought he needed her. It wasn't as if he loved her more than life itself. He had a Plan. He'd just get back to it. Work hard. Forget the scent of moonlight. Amber eyes filled with concern and understanding. Forget warm, spritely smiles. Curls of midnight silk…

Feeling worse than ever, Ty dried off. Shaved. Dressed.

Nudged Dru with his foot until he rolled over and quit snoring. Scrawled *"at work—why aren't you?"* on a charge slip from someplace called Likkered Up, topped it with the car keys, and took the truck. Why the hell not? The cat-loving car dealer *gave* it to him, he might as well *drive* it.

Or park it. He sat—head throbbing, stomach roiling, heart aching—bumper-to-bumper, motionless, on the expressway for almost an hour.

"ABOUT TIME YOU got here!" Krako shouted, dragging Ty straight to the conference room when he finally hauled his tail into the office. "Mr. Foote's got a great new idea."

"Uh-huh," Ty managed, listlessly shaking hands with the mountain in the custom-made suit. "Let's hear it." Sinking into the nearest seat, he commandeered a notepad and pen.

"Go ahead, Mr. Foote!" Krako's jovial encouragement shattered a few more already-fragile neurons. "Tell Harding what you want."

Sheesh—this time, Turrell wanted to replicate Versailles.

With a groan, Ty planted his cheek on the polished cherrywood tabletop. Closed his eyes.

"Mr. Harding?" Turrell asked, genuine concern in his reedy voice. "Somethin' wrong?"

Wrong? Yeah, *everything* was wrong. And nothing could make it right.

The only woman he'd ever wanted was the sprite.

And he'd lost her. And all the luck in the world couldn't change the facts.

Marisa Corelli had enchanted him with amber eyes and soft curves and warm, understanding smiles—while Nadja Costeceaseu and her "estoopid" curse had shredded his Perfect Life Plan.

Leaving him to spend the rest of his life alone, twiddling with the confetti. "No!" Ty protested. "I mean—there's a law against it," he claimed recklessly, ignoring Krako's grunt of disbelief. "No Louis XIV allowed in Phoenix."

"Well, it has to be somethin' special, Mr. Harding," the football player insisted, his high, thin voice at odds with his huge frame.

"I'll get right on it," Ty promised wearily, climbing to his feet. Yeah, that was a plan. Work on Turrell Foote's "special" house. Get on with his life. Get over the sprite—

Once I know she's safe, that she and Baby have a place to stay...

He went to see Nadja.

THE OLD LADY BARRED the door. "She iz not here. I cannot tell where. I make promise."

Ty started to rub his jaw, then shoved his hand in his pocket. "All right." He accepted the stonewall without argument. "Just tell me—is she okay?"

"Why ask?" Nadja peered at him suspiciously.

"She...I—I'm worried about the evil eye—"

"Ha. You still lie to self," Nadja proclaimed, stepping back, starting to close the door.

Desperately, Ty searched his benumbed brain. "B-but we didn't stay together until..." Aargh! What was that silly—? "Until the blue moon."

"Ha. Means only second full moon in same month," the Gypsy Queen reminded him and chortled. "Was Saturday."

Nadja's pronouncement sent his last hope crashing. "Then—"

"Curse is over. No more good luck. Go away." She shut the door in his face. Opened it again. Stared at him, black eyes narrowed. "Marisa iz okay," she conceded. "But you—"

With a bronchial mutter, the old lady grabbed a fistful of shirt and pulled him into her tiny, overstuffed apartment. Full of fringe and color.

But no plants. No sprite. Ty suddenly believed Nadja: no more good luck. He felt as if someone had cut off his legs. Or ripped his heart from his chest.

"Sit," Nadja ordered, then muttering again, she shuffled into the kitchenette. Returned a moment later to place a tall, green glass on the table beside the sofa.

Nadja pointed to the tumbler. "Half-full or half-empty?"

Ty shrugged. "What difference does it make? It's just a glass of water."

"No. Iz luck. Iz life." She smiled sadly. "Iz love without the beloved. Like me without Nico."

"What was I supposed to do?" he protested weakly. "I asked her to stay. I told her I cared for her."

Nadja shrugged, unimpressed. Pointed again at the tumbler. "Iz caring," she asked sternly, "to give half glass?"

After leaving the apartment, he sat in the truck awhile. Seeing again the look on Marisa's face as she held Chet's baby.

Somehow, Nadja had known. Everything. And he couldn't disagree with her assessment, but...

A passing patrol car slowed. Ty glanced up—at the No Parking This Side sign next to his front bumper. As if swimming through old paint, he roused himself enough to start the truck.

He paused, hand on the gearshift, thinking about the old woman inside that little apartment. Waiting for her grandson. He understood her loneliness now. Too well— and that being the Queen of *England* wouldn't ease it.

As the patrol car stopped and the police officer emerged, Ty pulled out his cell phone and called the PI. Rehired him to locate Nico Costeceaseu.

After accepting the parking ticket, Ty drove away. Went by the flower shop, but the sprite wasn't there and Abelard was about as cooperative as an insurance company processing a claim.

Ty kept driving. Somewhere on the eastern outskirts of Phoenix, he ran out of gas. Tried to pay the guy who loaned him a gas can to take back to the truck with an expired credit card. Had written his last check.

Finally got Dru—smirking like a personal-injury lawyer who'd just negotiated a huge settlement on a frivolous lawsuit—to bring him some cash.

"Looks like your luck's run out," the moron said when they got back to Ty's apartment to find all Marisa's things gone.

"Who needs luck when they have you," Ty retorted

automatically, then frowned. It was true. *Just like the sprite said.*

Without his brother, where *would* he be? Still arguing with that gas-pump jockey? In jail for illegal possession of five gallons of super unleaded?

Still sitting in that lavender house missing a woman who didn't love him enough— "Say, Dru, you doing anything tonight?"

"Yeah," his brother replied, hogging the couch. "Baby-sitting you."

Ty winced at Dru's word choice. Then sat on hold for twenty minutes ordering a pizza that never arrived.

In the days following Ty's party, Marisa stayed too busy to think, too tired to feel—putting in her hours at Mr. Abelard's flower shop and getting her business off the ground. All part of her plan.

"Because I will get over Ty Harding," Marisa vowed as she prepared the get-well bouquets Mr. Abelard supplied to a hospital gift shop. "It'll just take a little time. A little effort. A little lu— Nuts!" She absolutely rejected the ridiculous idea of some unseen power affecting a person's life.

Mrs. Pachenko's evil eye had "worked" because she'd believed in it—and interpreted everything that happened to fit it.

Well, she'd left behind that foolish belief—and the last hope he'd change his mind about kids—the minute she'd left Ty's bed.

Even so, Green Piece seemed almost charmed from the beginning. Mr. Abelard and his delivery van had picked up her plants, brought them to the flower shop. They were still unloading them when a floral customer signed up to rent a greenery grouping for her husband's new dental office.

Thus encouraged, Marisa spent an evening—and most of the dentist's deposit—at one of those twenty-four-hour copy places, designing a business card and a price flyer with the help of one of the on-site computer geeks.

When the geek invited her for coffee afterward, she accepted. Through sheer willpower, she managed to sit there for an hour and even make conversation about…something.

She also accepted a lunch invitation from Mr. Abelard's accountant, who volunteered to set up her bookkeeping.

Both nice guys, she supposed, but… She turned down second dates.

She just needed to stay busy. And have kid contact.

So far, she'd resisted the urge to go back and throw herself at Ty, taking whatever "serious long-term caring" he remained willing to give her.

Forget it, Corelli. Even heartbroken women, she told herself, have their pride—and ought to hold on to it as long as possible.

But she could feel herself wanting to crumble like bad concrete.

"I found an apartment," she told Nadja as they made soup from food-pantry selections a week after leaving Ty's…party. Bed. Life. "Near the flower shop. They're discounting the rent in return for me maintaining the interior plants."

"Iz lucky," Nadja commented. "But no hurry. Stay as long as you like."

Marisa stopped stirring. Gaped at her elderly friend.

"Iz lonely without Nico," the Queen of the Gypsies confessed.

Hugging the old woman and promising to visit frequently, Marisa said, "Thanks, but I've got to learn to live on my own."

"You think that iz your Fate?" the Gypsy Queen asked, then shouted a Romany curse as the soup bubbled over. "You see?" she said. "Watched pot boils. What else you believe true iz lies?"

Marisa shook her head. She'd wised to Nadja Coste-ceaseu's trick of pretending to find hidden meaning and significance in the most ordinary events.

She refused to fall for it again. Believing only led to wishing. Which only led to disappointment and disillusionment. And heartache.

"Mrs. Pachenko's *mal ojo*," Marisa said firmly, "was a lie."

"Ha, ha!" Nadja threw back her head. Waved the soup ladle in the air. "You think—because cure works, was no curse. How my Nico would laugh at your foolishness."

Nadja's wistful tone as she mentioned her still-missing grandson refueled Marisa's sympathy—and her regret that Ty's nephew had interrupted their lovemaking.

One marvelous memory to fill the empty years ahead. Was that too much to ask?

"Shall we let the soup simmer awhile?" she asked. Trying to stick to practical realities.

Nadja nodded. "Gets better with time. When are you moving?" she asked, fingering the necklace with the big red stone.

"Tomorrow," Marisa said, lowering the heat. "Mr. Abelard's daughter is away at college, so he's lending me some of her furniture. Lucky, isn't it?" she added wryly.

Nadja merely snorted. Spent the rest of the evening playing with that darned glass ball.

Marisa worked up one-, five-, and ten-year business plans until her eyes crossed. Well, she had to do something besides cry herself to sleep. Tears changed nothing.

She had a right to hold on to her dream, she reminded herself fiercely. Even if the man she wanted to share it with refused.

"I'LL CERTAINLY DO MY best. And thank you very much." Marisa hung up the phone, made a notation, then turned to Mr. Abelard. "Can you believe it? Another big order out of the blue."

"You are one lucky gal," the flower shop owner concurred.

Marisa sighed. Too bad she didn't *feel* lucky. Just tired—from lying awake remembering Ty Harding's addictive, intoxicating kisses, his bone-melting smiles, his quiet steady nature....

Bah. She told herself to get over Ty a thousand times a day. Double that at night. As if saying it equaled doing it.

"That's fantastic!"

Marisa tried to pick up the thread of the conversation. "Uh…oh yeah. There's just one problem," she added. "I've run out of plants."

Mr. Abelard's eyes twinkled under his bushy eyebrows. "That's no problem," he declared, spinning his Rolodex directory. Selecting a card, he handed it to Marisa. "Call Dave. Order what you need. Put it on my account, then pay me back."

"With interest," she managed before her eyes started leaking. Spilling tears down her cheeks over how sweet her boss was.

And how perfectly miserable she felt despite how wonderfully her life was working out.

"Th-thanks, Mr. Abelard." Wiping away tears, she reached for the phone, but before calling the wholesale nursery the florist recommended, Marisa dialed the Big Brothers and Big Sisters' local number. Requested an application.

She'd already volunteered to mentor at the elementary school in her neighborhood. It wasn't enough—even though it looked as if it might have to be....

No. She'd given up the man she loved. She'd darned well find a way to have the rest of the dream she'd yearned for all her life.

BY THE MIDDLE OF THE second week without Marisa, Ty had discouraged Turrell from rebuilding the Alamo, the White House, Tara, a Babylonian ziggurat, the onion domes of the Kremlin and the Guggenheim's spiral.

"Thing is," Turrell said at their umpteenth meeting, "my Mama's comin' out for the next preseason game 'n' I was hopin' to have somethin' to show her. You got any drawings done yet?"

Well, no. All he did at work, apparently, was sit in his office until they sent him home. Where he sat on the sofa until Dru told him to catch some rack-time, then got him up in the morning and sent him to work again.

"I've, uh, got a good start on the layout," Ty lied. Right. Floors. Walls. Windows. Different rooms. "But let's go out tomorrow and look at some houses." Actual, normal houses. "Maybe we'll run across an elevation you like."

"I don't know if Mama wants to live on a hill," Turrell piped.

Ty would have laughed if he felt like it. He didn't. He felt like...*hell. Like he'd been truly, finally cursed.*

THE NEXT MORNING, they drove through several exclusive, expensive parts of the Phoenix Metropolitan Statistical Area without getting much of a read on what kind of house Turrell really wanted.

Finally, after changing *another* flat tire, Ty headed for Paradise Valley. He'd show Foote the locale of choice for several of Phoenix's sports-famous citizens. And he could check on his house.

Well, it *was* his, he admitted tiredly, whether or not he designed, built, bought or lived in it. With a sigh, he turned left, then took the second right.

Suddenly, The Fleet jerked to attention. Pointed a finger the size of a lodgepole pine. "That's it!" he crowed. "That's the house!"

Ty followed the line of Turrell's index finger. "The l-lavender one?" he croaked.

"Yessir! I'd rather have something two-story myself, with more curlicues and dohickeys on it, but that's what I want. It's perfect."

"It's mine," Ty said, disbelievingly.

"How much you want for it?" the mammoth athlete demanded.

"Are you serious?"

"Serious as sudden death." A ham, er, hand motioned to the curb.

Obediently, Ty pulled over and cut the engine. Looked at the behemoth in the Italian-tailored slacks and French-designer polo shirt. "Go ahead," he prompted. This ought to be good. "Tell me why it's perfect."

Turrell flashed a row of white teeth the size of Stonehenge monuments. "Because purple's my Mama's favorite color," he declared. "And I promised I'd buy her a house when I made the pros.

"That's why it's gotta be special—because she's special."

The Fleet's thin voice strengthened as he went on, "See, Mama raised me and my brothers and sisters by herself in a one-bedroom apartment in the poorest part of Philadelphia. All she ever wanted was to get us out of there—and to have a house of her own, 'stead of worryin' 'bout makin' the rent every month."

Turrell puffed out his already gargantuan chest. "I'm gonna give her that house," he said with quiet pride. "Because if you love a woman—don't matter if it's your mama, your wife, whoever—you want her to be happy."

For a minute, Ty actually thought his heart stopped.

Assuring Turrell they'd work a deal on the house, Ty dropped the man off, then headed for the nearest multi-screen theater.

He missed most of the good parts of *Motorcycle Maniacs Muscle In*. Like when the terrorist gang crashed their space-going motorcycles into the fuel tanks stored in the women's prison yard.

All Ty heard was Turrell's voice. *"If you love a woman, you want her to be happy."*

All he saw was Marisa—radiant—holding Chet's little girl.

Happiness for Marisa meant babies. Which meant that if he loved Marisa...

That was the zillion-dollar question, of course. Did he love her? Enough to try to make her happy?

Ty sat through the movie again. 'Cuz the mere thought of being totally responsible for a tiny, helpless human being scared him spitless.

But so did a lifetime without the sprite....

GROWING IMPATIENT, FATE decided to crank the volume. Well, it had a million things to do and back-to-school was just around the corner.

That evening, banned from the theater for life, Ty was arguing—again? still?—with his brother, who seemed to be underfoot all the time these days, when the doorbell rang.

"I'm not going home until you snap out of it," Dru claimed.

"I swear, if you don't get the hell out of my face—" Ty strode through the discarded clothes and take-out containers strewn across the living room, "I'm going to—"

He jerked open the door. "What?" he demanded. "Oh, it's you."

Lisette shook back her golden mane. "Hi yourself. May I come in?"

Ty lifted and dropped a shoulder. Stepped back. "Why not? I'm about to knock my brother's block off. You can be a witness."

A tiny furrow appeared between Ms. Intriguing's brows. "I can't stay long." She glided hip-first into the apartment. "Alonzo's in the car. We just got back from Santa Fe."

The furrow disappeared, replaced by a dreamy expression. Dru rose from the sofa, moved closer, as if he found the whole scene fascinating.

"We've been married eight days, eleven hours and nine minutes," she announced. "I wanted to come by and thank you, since you're the one who brought us together."

"*I* got you together? I don't even know anyone named Alonzo!" Ty protested while Dru sidled around the supermodel.

"The mariachi guy, right?" Dru leaped through the doorway. "See ya!" He dove out of sight.

"That's right. We met at your parents' anniversary party," Lisette confirmed. "It was just like a movie. Like the world had shifted on its equator or something."

Not that it mattered to him, but— "Have you lost your mind?" Ty demanded. "He's a small-time local musician. You're an international supermodel. How can you just…up and marry him?"

Raking back her long hair, Lisette gave Ty a pitying smile. "Because I love him," she said quietly. "And only love lasts."

She waggled her nails in that drying-polish motion. "Not many people are lucky enough to find the one person who completes their life. I'm no genius, Tyler, but I'm smart enough to not turn my back on it just because it doesn't come packaged in Ralph Lauren."

Wishing Lisette and her mariachero the best, Ty gently pushed her backward until she was out of the apartment, then slammed the door. Still heard her quiet claim. *Only love lasts.*

The Fleet's words whispered in Ty's head, as they had since he'd uttered them. *"If you love a woman, you want to make her happy."*

Ty sank onto the sofa. Turned on the TV. Laced his fingers behind his head. Stared at the screen.

He had a decision to make. A simple decision between two simple choices.

Both of which scared him to death.

THERE WAS NO WAY—*no WAY*—he could have fallen asleep in the middle of making the most important decision of his life.

"No way," he mumbled as the pounding on his door repeated. But his mouth was bone dry from hanging open and that sleep stuff had glued one eye closed.

He'd fallen asleep, he realized as he stumbled toward the knocking, because there *was* no decision to make. He loved Marisa. *Loved her!*

That's why he'd been so worried about being a lousy father. *Because* he wanted her happy. Couldn't bear the thought of disappointing her...

Ty grinned. Life was simple again. Needed only a simple Plan. He loved Marisa, so he was going to marry her and—gulp—give her some kids. It was, after all, the Harding way.

The first thing he had to do was— *Stop whoever kept pounding on the door.*

"I'm coming!" Staggering to the door, he jerked it open. Since when had this place become Grand Central Sta— "Nadja?" Ty blinked. "W-what are you doing here?"

The Queen of the Gypsies reached up, clutched his face, and kissed him. "I dance at your wedding!" she exclaimed, giving him a dazzling smile. "I cast spell on all your enemies! I—"

"Just tell me what this is about," Ty suggested.

"Iz Nico! Your detective finds. He calls me." The elderly woman did an exultant little dance step as tears streamed down her lined cheeks. "He iz okay. I thought he left because… Tiny apartment iz no place to raise boy to man.''

She grabbed Ty, kissed him again. ''But no—he goes to school. To be accountant,'' she crowed. ''He keeps secret because iz not Gypsy way. He iz afraid I will be shamed, will disown. Tchah! If makes him happy, makes me happy.''

Ty shook his head. *Okay, okay,* he told Whoever silently, *I get the message.*

''Glad I could help. You need a ride home?''

''No, he brings.'' Another dazzling smile. ''He iz between sessions,'' she said, the last two words imbued with pride.

After fending off another gypsy embrace, Ty said good-night and shut the door. Began kicking the clothes strewn all over the living room into a pile.

He needed to clean this joint up so he could think. Plan.

After what he'd said that last night with her… Only a moron would try to win Marisa back by showing up with a dozen roses and a lame ''let's make babies'' line and expect the sprite to buy it.

Grinning, Ty dropkicked his favorite khakis onto the growing heap. Aw, hell—maybe he'd just rely on luck. Go by impulse.

And if all else failed… He *did* have two wonderful parents, six pretty-darned-supportive siblings and forty million dollars to work with.

10

THE DAY AFTER his wake-up call from Turrell—*and* Lisette *and* Nadja—it looked as if Ty might need all the resources he could tap.

He woke from his first real night's sleep since the sprite's departure good to go.

Unfortunately, his car wasn't: dead battery. The truck had a flat. Again. The laundry lost his dress shirts. The IRS informed him they'd audited his tax return from two years ago, he owed them $701.83 and they were still looking at last year.

None of which bothered him one bit. If the gypsy's curse no longer guaranteed him good luck, he'd live with it. As long as he didn't have to live without his sprite...

The sweat started trickling down Ty's back as he spoke to the receptionist, eyed Krako huddling with Iverson (Delaporte a no-show as usual) and ducked into his office.

'Cuz Ty didn't have a Plan. Only a vague, broad outline. And something to prove.

Taking a deep breath, he dialed the first number on his list.

"Hi, Chet. It's me," he said when his brother answered. "Can I ask you something?"

"I liked her," Chet said immediately.

Ty grinned in spite of his pounding heart, tight chest, clenched gut. "That's great, man," he replied. "But I can pick my own woman. What I want to know is..." He rubbed his jaw, but there was no other way. He couldn't risk damaging some innocent child; he had to know. And this was the best preview he could devise. "Can I borrow Dex?"

"What for?" Chet demanded.

When Ty told him, Chet chuckled. Then he laughed. Then he guffawed. Ty's heart sank.

Reluctantly, he considered alternatives. If he just gave her the babies and stayed out of the way, would that be enough to make the sprite happy? Would it be enough for him? Ty frowned. He didn't think so. If he was going to be a dad, he wanted to *be one*.

He realized his brother had quit laughing, started talking. "...always thought you were the best suited of all of us. You won't get distracted by the mayhem and madness—or ruffled by the whining and begging."

Ty's console buzzed.

"Can you hold a minute, Chet?" Ty punched buttons. "Yes?"

"Turrell Foote's on three," the receptionist said. "Shall I tell the travel agent to run the tickets?"

"Not yet. And tell Turrell I'll call him back," Ty answered, then punched back to Chet. "So you're sure you're okay with lending me your firstborn?"

Ty's brother laughed. "You'll do great. Responsibility's your middle name—and Dex idolizes you. Just don't let him hang around Dru too much," Chet cautioned.

After working out the details of borrowing Dex for a trial parenting run the following weekend, Ty called Bryce and Diane and made similar arrangements, received similar votes of confidence.

Amazed, Ty hung up and sat back to ponder his siblings' apparent faith in his abilities.

He wished he felt so confident. But some things, he realized, can only be learned through experience. *So you show up and hope for the best.*

After informing the receptionist to "book 'em,

please," he set up appointments with his banker, a lawyer the firm used and Turrell, who jumped on Ty's prop-
osition with both size seventeen feet and offered the services of the football team's player-community relations
liaison.

Then—muttering something about an early lunch, Ty
slipped out. Drove past the flower shop. Called Nadja
and cajoled. Even dropped by Bert's "hoibal" shop.

No sprite.

He called the PI, told him to put out an APB asap.

Then, ready to buy another vowel or spin, Ty returned
to the office. Actually did some architecting for a
change—working up ideas for the second part of his
nonplan.

"Working on Mr. Foote's house?" Krako boomed
from the doorway.

Ty jerked his feet off his desk. "Uh, not exactly."
Might as well break it to him. "I think you'd better come
in and sit down."

The news that The Fleet was buying the purple house
earned a moan from Krako—followed, after a few
minutes, by a philosophical shrug.

"So what are ya workin' on?" The older man torqued
his head to study Ty's rough layouts. "Shopping center?
Office park?"

Krako blanched like white asparagus when Ty described his new project. "Low-cost housing?" he whispered.

"A model neighborhood of small, well-designed, af-
fordable homes," Ty corrected. *Designed to show the
sprite the depth of my commitment to families.*

"I'm endowing a foundation with most of my lottery
winnings to purchase the land and offer practically no-
interest loans to working people who can't qualify to
own a home otherwise."

Not all of it; he was saving a few million for Marisa

and a few spritely offspring with midnight curls and big, warm eyes.

When Krako's frown deepened, Ty went into sales mode. "It's good PR. Turrell thinks the football team will be interested in supporting it, too. And he's pledged to equip a playground for the residents.

"It's actually a huge market niche," Ty went on. "The firm could gain an international reputation off it."

"But small houses?" Krako pushed his lips out. Sucked them in. Pushed them out again. Ty recognized this as an indication the man was thinking. He waited.

Suddenly, Ralph beamed. "Feng shui," he proclaimed. "Baby boomers downsizing. Excellent! Work out the design problems on this project, then upgrade the materials and sell to empty nesters looking to cut back on square footage without sacrificing affluent lifestyle."

Jumping up, the man pumped Ty's hand. "Genius, Harding. Pure genius." He headed for the door. "Gotta tell Iverson. He was asking just this morning about your value-add to the partnership."

Shaking his head, but pleased that Krako had found a spin he could live with, Ty met with Turrell.

Picked the man's brain about housing needs of low-income families. "You've got a good point about the cost of watering a lawn and buying equipment to keep it mowed," Ty said.

"'Specially in the desert." Turrell folded his arms across the Mississippi-wide expanse of his chest. "But that's why having a park right in the neighborhood's so important. Lotta folks living from paycheck to paycheck can't afford much entertainment, but everybody needs to spend time with their family."

Hmm. Good point. *I should office at home.* Be available.

"I'm gonna get the team to sponsor youth teams, too," the mountainous football player promised. "So the kids and parents have somethin' to do together."

Ty remembered his parents attending every game, play and recital.

"Thanks, Turrell," he said as the conversation ended. Humble at last and filled with the gratitude Marisa had urged for the fortunate childhood he'd never appreciated before.

Ty spent the rest of the day on preliminary designs.

The rest of the week on appointments.

Then it was time for his child-care lessons. He stayed totally stressed from the moment the airline rep relinquished Dex into his care until Diane and her husband returned from their weekend in Palm Springs.

But he survived.

More importantly, so did the kids. He doubted he'd ever master ponytail-making and he might never love children the way Marisa did, but he now knew he could manage basic parenting.

Which meant he was ready. Unwilling to wait any longer.

He missed his sprite the way flowers miss Spring. Rain. Sun. You get the idea.

"How soon can we make the announcement?" he asked his panel of advisors on the Tuesday after his long weekend with Diane's three children.

"Announcement?" That was the lawyer hesitating.

The banker backed him up. "Shouldn't we wait until we acquire the land? Deal with the zoning people, work up the loan guidelines, plat—?"

Ty groaned. Too much planning. Not enough action. He needed his sprite!

So he applied a technique learned from Alison, Diane's two-year-old: he pitched a fit.

And it worked. "Why don't we stage a big gala?" Turrell suggested. "Invite all the local political bigwigs, let 'em give speeches?"

The others swooned with approval. "It'll cut the red tape in half," one swore in his enthusiasm.

Ty didn't care. He just couldn't wait any longer to confront Marisa. Offer her his heart, his devotion and his ah, conceptual assistance for a lifetime. Starting with fuel-injected, nitro-burning, spine-tingling kisses.

IF he could find her. Even the PI was drawing a blank.

And Nadja's gratitude only went so far. She refused to tell him the sprite's whereabouts. "A promise iz promise," she'd said with a shrug. "Let Fate do own work."

Sheesh—Fate let the sprite walk away from him once. Why trust such an inexplicable force again?

Ty hired six more detectives, then holed up at the tiny office-suite they'd rented to headquarter the project. Feverishly finishing a scale model of the project. Completing the first set of house plans. And trying to come up with a fallback Plan to win his sprite. Something, *anything* that might stand a snowball's chance in Phoenix in August.

He kept his fingers crossed all the time now.

HOW STUPID ARE YOU, Corelli? Marisa asked herself as she declined a concert date from a photographer who'd rushed into the flower shop last week desperate for help with a bridal portrait.

And how long are you going to stay stupid?

He looked enough like Tyler Harding to be a cousin: tall, fit, brown hair, blue eyes. And when she brought up the subject of children—in a general, ever-heard-of-them? way—he gushed, "I want six. At least."

Marisa took a step backward.

The pix-clicker rushed on, "I want to coach Little League and take 'em camping. Be a Cub Scout leader!"

Perfect. The guy was perfect.

Only she wasn't interested. At all. For one simple, glaring reason, she admitted after she'd rented Baby and half a dozen other plants to him for an obscene one-day fee.

She wasn't getting over Ty Harding. Something magical had happened the day he'd saved Nadja from that bus. And right there, right then, she'd fallen for the hottest, sexiest, nicest guy in the world.

She loved Ty. For the way he kissed her. For his patience teaching her to drive. For his crooked smile when he woke from one of his "watching-baseball" naps.

For getting out of bed, without a word of censure, to take his little nephew back to his room... Tears dripped onto a stalk of statice.

But she had to face the truth: she'd never love anyone else the way she loved Ty. Which meant no kids for her.

You should have taken his offer then, Corelli.

Because if she couldn't have children, she might as well not have them with Ty as without him, right?

"Another call for Green Piece," Mr. Abelard yodeled from the customer desk.

"Coming," Marisa said and trudged in that direction. Her business was booming. Going better than she dared dream. And who cared?

Without Ty, nothing mattered.

THREE DAYS BEFORE THE announcement and no sprite. Ty woke in the middle of the night in an ice-cold sweat. Convinced she'd simply packed up and left town.

He went babbling to Dru for comfort. And, being a loving brother, the moron actually supplied it.

Grinning like a madman, Dru retrieved the Sunday paper. Flipped through it, then held out the bridal section, pointing to some society chick's wedding picture. "Don't we know that philodendron?" he asked.

Sure enough—there was Baby in the background.

One of the PI's traced the photographer. Turrell secured Green Piece's services. The Cardinals' community relations flak pulled strings, alerted the media, invited the politicos and booked booze and munchies.

Ty had no plan, no idea how it was going to work, but— He went to see the Queen of the Gypsies, then buzzed *K-I-D*'s receptionist. "More plane tickets, Valerie."

FINALLY, THE FATEFUL evening arrived.

Ty's brain had gone to Majorca, apparently. It took all three brothers—and his mother, embarrassingly enough—to get him dressed and to project headquarters.

It took Nadja to bring the sprite.

"Why didn't you tell me it was formal?" Marisa asked her companion, nervously smoothing down her multihued T-shirt dress.

Although the room was fully coed, her gaze sought out the large male forms wearing tuxedoes. Seeing them reminded her of— *Don't go there, Corelli.*

"And I don't understand what we're doing here, Nadja," she added as she deliberately studied everything but the crowd.

A quickly finished task: aside from a portable bar, the only furnishings were a miked podium, a banner proclaiming The Homecoming Project Kickoff and a display of a tiny toy village.

And some very familiar plants. More déjà vu. Marisa's nerves jumped.

"I am getting first house," Nadja proclaimed. "Nico comes later." Gnarled fingers lifted to her throat, then dropped away as she added proudly, "Now he iz study."

"What happened to your red stone?" Marisa asked, trying to settle her own odd nervousness—and suddenly appreciating the significance of the gypsy's gesture.

"I use to pay Nico's school," Nadja replied with quiet satisfaction. "Was saving for old age, but who needs when can give another lifetime of happiness?"

Marisa blinked at her friend. Started to ask her...*something*.

Before she could utter a word, a man stepped into view. A grinning, lankier version of his brother. "D-ru?"

"The same."

"B-but...? W-what?" Marisa gave up. Let her jaw sag.

"Evening, Mrs. Costeceaseu," Ty's younger brother greeted the older woman. She nodded back.

"What are you doing here?" Marisa demanded, her eyes narrowing.

Dru grinned. "I'm entertaining your friend until it's time to step up to the podium. And I'm kicking off the testimonials."

Marisa closed her eyes, trying to hide her...*disgust, not disappointment*. The man must be drunk. And his brother—*isn't here, Corelli. Give it up*. But she knew her heart never would.

"Ty never cared about playing sports when we were growing up," Dru said, his voice so suddenly serious that Marisa's eyes flew open. "But he spent hours hitting me grounders and throwing batting practice. To help me reach for my dream of playing professional baseball. And he's the one who helped me put the pieces back together when that dream ended on a bad slide into second."

Offering Nadja his arm, he turned toward the bar. As they headed for the liquor dispensary, he spoke over his shoulder, "The other references are around, if you need them. If not, well... Just give the guy a break, will ya? He's a wreck."

Break? Wreck? Other references?

She stood there, dumbfounded, until Nadja came back and hissed in her ear, "Detour iz over. Go!" A bony finger indicated a door on the far side of the room.

Like a zombie, Marisa turned, took a step in that direction.

Another tuxedo intercepted her. Another not-Ty— older, shorter… "Chet?" Marisa choked out.

"Harding solidarity. Better get used to it." Chet was grinning, too. "If you're interested, I'll tell you about the time Sandi had her appendix out. Ty played cards with her for days when the rest of us just wanted to see the scar and split."

She must be hallucinating…

Diane came over. Offered another anecdote starring Ty rescuing a baby squirrel.

Like I don't already know he's the most wonderful man in the world? Marisa thought with a frown. *Why the heck else would I fall in love with him?*

"That's enough," Bryce decided as he, Sandi and Ronnie appeared, followed by Ty's parents. Gwen brushed away a tear and hugged her.

Beyond the Hardings, the crowd mingled and mixed. Drank and perused the little model of the project that somebody was putting together to provide homes for people like Nadja and Nico.

"I understand you supplied the motivation as well as the plants for this shindig," Ty's dad said.

Totally confused, Marisa just stared at him until he pointed to the same door Nadja had. "He's in there. Go ask him."

He's here? She fought the urge to sprint to said door. She did thrust a football-player-sized joker out of her way before reaching, grasping, turning, opening.

Oh God. Her knees threatened to give way as she ogled the hunk twiddling with Baby's leaves. His thick,

brown hair needed cutting but that broad, tapering
back, those long legs were as magnificent as she remembered.

She must have made some sound because he turned
around, one side of his mouth crooking upward, his
blue eyes gleaming.

"Hi, sprite," he greeted her in a husky voice.

"Ty." She curled her fingers into her palms to keep
from reaching for him. "Wh-what's all that—" her
curls twitched to indicate the other room "—about?"

He opened his mouth, but no words came out. Dammit, he should have written and memorized a speech,
but he'd recklessly decided to wing it.

Reaching into his pocket, Ty pulled out the yellow-
diamond ring. Clutched it for courage. "You said
once—" A wry smile flickered like distant lightning
on his mouth. "More than once, actually, that I'm fortunate to have a family that loves and appreciates me."

Her amber eyes glowed but she didn't come closer.
Didn't unfist her hands.

His eyebrows scrunched together. "They did tell you
how much they appreciate me, didn't they?" he asked.
"They were supposed to."

"They did," she assured him, her lips quirking.
"I'm just not sure why. Or what I and my philodendron
are doing here."

"Well, I— It's—" Ty cleared his throat and tried
again. "See, I wanted to show... That is—"

"Cut to the chase, moron!" Dru shouted.

Marisa turned to see the whole Harding clan in the
doorway, the Queen of the Gypsies elbowing her way
to the front.

"I'm beginning to see what you mean about the dis-
advantages of big families," Marisa whispered, turning
back to Ty. "But take Dru's advice—cut to the chase."

As he gazed at the woman who'd taught him the
true meaning of luck, Ty's last lingering concern van-

ished. How could he not love any child who was a part of Marisa?

Opening his hand, Ty held up the yellow-diamond ring. Light hit it, refracted. Filling the air around them with sparkles.

"I love you, sprite," he said with deep, quiet, complete conviction. "Please make me the luckiest man on earth and say you'll marry me and be the mother of my children."

Marisa reached for him as he closed the distance between them. Love and desire and commitment, honor and steadfastness and longing filled his eyes as he lowered his mouth to take hers in a passionate kiss.

To the applause of his siblings and parents, Turrell and Krako, Nadja and Nico, and a hundred people in the other room who had no idea why they were applauding.

"Oh, Ty, you're all the family I need!" Marisa claimed when he let her up for air.

"Ha!" Nadja cackled. "You have—"

"Don't say a word!" Ty and Marisa cried together, their opposing luck transformed into a loving mutual fate they planned to share forever.

Epilogue

MARISA DOWNSHIFTED the Porsche Boxster convertible, then accelerated as she took the last corner. The meeting had run longer than expected, but she'd signed her one-hundredth client—the entire Phoenix campus of a major corporation—to a two-year contract.

Nico will be happy, she thought with a grin. As Green Piece's financial officer, Nadja's grandson thrilled to every addition to the company's healthy bottom line.

Ty, on the other hand… Marisa laughed as she drove slowly down the street. "He'll only ask if I'm satisfied, then make some lewd remark about seeing to *that* himself!"

After almost three years—three incredibly wonderful years, she knew her husband fairly well.

That's why she started chewing her lip even before she pulled into their driveway. *Hope springs eternal,* she thought, but every day demonstrated the uselessness of expecting Ty to change.

Cutting the engine, she climbed out of the vehicle, skirted the dozen or so bikes scattered haphazardly on the cement, and went into the house Ty'd built for her right after their honeymoon at DisneyWorld.

The boys in the living room, two brothers they were adopting to keep together, and a cluster of their neighborhood friends, greeted her arrival without looking up from their videogames.

"Tim got his cast off and Dad said we could have

pizza if everybody wanted to stay,'' Brad called. "They do.''

Nodding helplessly and making a mental note to order salad, too, Marisa asked, "Where is he?"

"Where else?" Brad said with a fatalistic shrug.

Gritting her teeth, Marisa proceeded through the house. Knowing what she'd find when she got there.

Dammit, he'd promised!

Grimly, she stalked down the hallway. Paused in the doorway. Sure enough— "Ty Harding," she exclaimed, "you cannot keep doing that!"

Ty lifted his gaze from the tiny, pink-blanketed bundle he cradled in his arms. One foot kept the rocking chair moving. "But she likes it," he explained earnestly, his tender smile melting away—as usual—her objections to him spoiling their daughter.

Honestly! The man had turned into the baby-lovingest guy in Phoenix.

Not that she minded, Marisa admitted as she crossed the room to kiss husband and child. The way she and Ty loved each other, there was plenty of love to share. And they'd need it, if he had his way.

His goal, he said (always with a delicious, promising leer) was a child to match every gem in her engagement ring.

**3 Stories of Holiday Romance from three
bestselling Harlequin® authors**

*Valentine
Babies*

by

ANNE STUART

TARA TAYLOR QUINN

JULE McBRIDE

Goddess in Waiting by Anne Stuart
Edward walks into Marika's funky maternity shop to pick
up some things for his sister. He doesn't expect to assist
in the delivery of a baby and fall for outrageous Marika.

Gabe's Special Delivery by Tara Taylor Quinn
On February 14, Gabe Stone finds a living, breathing
valentine on his doorstep—his daughter. Her mother
has given Gabe four hours to adjust to fatherhood,
resolve custody and win back his ex-wife?

My Man Valentine by Jule McBride
Everyone knows Eloise Hunter and C. D. Valentine
are in love. Except Eloise and C. D. Then, one of
Eloise's baby-sitting clients leaves her with a baby to
mind, and C. D. swings into protector mode.

VALENTINE BABIES

On sale January 2000 at your favorite retail outlet.

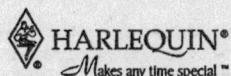

HARLEQUIN®
Makes any time special ™

Visit us at www.romance.net

PHVALB

If you enjoyed what you just read,
then we've got an offer you can't resist!

Take 2 bestselling
love stories FREE!
Plus get a FREE surprise gift!

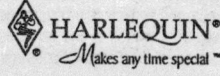

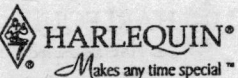

Come escape with Harlequin's new

Series Sampler

Four great full-length Harlequin novels bound together in one fabulous volume and at an unbelievable price.

Be transported back in time with a Harlequin Historical® novel, get caught up in a mystery with Intrigue®, be tempted by a hot, sizzling romance with Harlequin Temptation®, or just enjoy a down-home all-American read with American Romance®.

You won't be able to put this collection down!

On sale February 2000 at your favorite retail outlet.

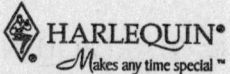

HARLEQUIN®
Makes any time special ™

Visit us at www.romance.net PHESC